SILENT TORMENT

by

Tarn Young

Book One of a Trilogy

Grosvenor House
Publishing Limited

All rights reserved
Copyright © Tarn Young, 2011

Tarn Young is hereby identified as author of this
work in accordance with Section 77 of the Copyright, Designs
and Patents Act 1988

The book cover picture is copyright to Tarn Young

This book is published by
Grosvenor House Publishing Ltd
28-30 High Street, Guildford, Surrey, GU1 3EL.
www.grosvenorhousepublishing.co.uk

This book is sold subject to the conditions that it shall not, by way of
trade or otherwise, be lent, resold, hired out or otherwise circulated
without the author's or publisher's prior consent in any form of binding or
cover other than that in which it is published and
without a similar condition including this condition being imposed
on the subsequent purchaser.

A CIP record for this book
is available from the British Library

ISBN 978-1-908596-75-8

Back Cover:

Old Bridlesmith Gate – A Drawing by Mrs Enfield

*This book is dedicated to
my mum, Joyce and my late dad,
Charles Henry Hill
With much love and grateful thanks for
the wonderful childhood that shaped the future
for my brother, Garry and myself*

Personal Acknowledgements

Prue Phillipson, Author, *'Jeanie's Destiny'* and
'Vengeance Thwarted'
For her sound advice and encouragement
on all aspects of writing a novel!

My 'guinea pig' readers for
their enthusiasm and encouragement:
mum, Joyce Hill
daughter, Joanne Lee
daughter-in-law, Cathryn Young
late mother-in-law, Muriel
friends, Audrey Knight and Louise Pegg

My husband Alan for his editing skills,
patience and encouragement during
the writing of this novel

My son, Stephen and nephew, Christopher
for suggestions and production of the
book cover and web site

My love and grateful thanks to you all

Acknowledgements

Nottinghamshire Archives for allowing the reproduction
of the Ordnance Survey Map featured in:
*Part Two, Nottingham, England, 1841,
Hannah Merchant, Chapter Five*

Nottingham History for allowing the
reproduction of 'Old Bridlesmith Gate',
from a drawing by Mrs W. M. Enfield (1854),
featured on the back cover

'Google' search engine, a huge time-saver! for
the extensive research required
to give this book authenticity and credibility.
Main web sites:
Nottingham History - nottshistory.org.uk
Wikipedia - en.wikipedia.org.uk
The Ships List - theshipslist.com
gregormacgregor.com
Victorian London - victorianlondon.org
Middleton Guardian - menmedia.co.uk/middletonguardian
Salford Hundred - Ancestors, annals and history
BBC - bbc.co.uk
Jstor - archives
On line Parish Clerks - lan-opc.org.uk
'A Brief History of Hosiery Manufacture
and Lacemaking in Nottingham' - williams.gen.nz

Books
'The Writer's Guide to Everyday Life in Regency
and Victorian England from 1811-1901' -
Author - Kristine Hughes
'Nottingham - As it is Spoke' - Volume Four,
Author - John Beeton

Author's Notes

To ensure a credible and authentic story, all locations including, The Highlands, Glasgow and Nottingham were thoroughly researched.

The novel's time frame of 1823-1847 coincides with the emergence of the Industrial Revolution.

Communication and long distance travel was difficult and most journeys' were made by Royal Mail Coach (Penny Post 1840) or on wagons pulled by horses, or on foot. Train travel was in its infancy, with only a few miles of track in use; indeed land and sea travel still relied on the astute use of a humble compass.

Suffice it to say, if it hadn't been invented, it hasn't been included, e.g. baby carriages (prams).

Information with respect to dates, times, specifications and descriptions are accurate. Actual historical events affect the lives of some of the fictional characters, both rich and poor, on land and sea, e.g. sinking of the 'William Brown' off Newfoundland.

In some chapters, the dialogue has been conducted in the local Nottingham dialect, synonymous with the area, 'Narrow Marsh' (map included), where everyday living was a struggle for the unfortunate, but remarkably stoical and optimistic inhabitants.

My fervent hope is that the reader will engage with the characters and events and let their own imagination complete, what I believe to be, a fascinating period in nineteenth century Britain.

'...And fare thee weel, my only luve,
And fare thee weel awhile
And I will come again, my luve
Though it were ten thousand mile...'

"My Love is Like a Red, Red Rose" (1794)
Robert Burns (1759-1796)

PART ONE

*The Highlands of Scotland
Strathy, 1823*

Lizzie Cameron

Chapter One

Out Of The Darkness...

On the evening of Saturday 10th May 1823, Lizzie Cameron lay fast asleep in her bed, until a strange sound, like a wolf howling at the moon made her sit bolt upright. She became fully awake, realising it was her mother's agonising screams, growing ever louder, as she struggled to give birth; the nightmare almost engulfing her as she strove to survive in the battle for life.

Lizzie was terrified and unable to believe such sounds were coming from her own mother, so she clamped her hands to her ears, in an attempt to stifle the awful noise. She buried her head deep into her pillow and prayed for it to stop, but the sounds continued on and on, echoing along the passageway, until ultimately there was silence. The screams ended abruptly, as her mother, Agnes, took the last breath in her fight for life. Only the lusty cries of the newborn, Robert William Cameron, pierced through the silence like the sound of a victim of the night owl, which had swooped down to earth to gather up its prey—

Summer came early in 1823 and the day started much the same as any other during the lambing season in the Highlands. It was a hot Saturday morning in May and Lizzie's father, William had postponed his usual trip to the market in order to make sure there were no casualties with his small herd of expectant ewes. He thought they would be his greatest priority today.

Agnes waved her husband goodbye, then called to Lizzie who was disappearing out of the gate after her father, in the hope he would take her with him. 'Come on lassie, you canna go with your faither this morning. He will be too busy to keep an eye on you as well as the ewes.'

Lizzie's bottom lip trembled, as she had been looking forward to this day for ages. 'Aw mither, I wanted to see the new born lambs. I promise to be good and just sit down and watch.'

Agnes shook her head. 'Not this time lassie, your faither's got his hands full with every ewe ready to give birth.'

Lizzie, her face clouded in disappointment, turned to look at her mother. Agnes almost relented, but the importance of the lambing season left her with no option, so she quickly suggested that they go together to fetch her best friend, Mairi, to play in the yard. 'What say you have Mairi over and she can stay for tea?'

Lizzie wavered for a moment, in case the decision still hung in the balance, but after scanning her mother's face, she realised the battle was lost. Then a compensatory thought popped into her head as she remembered she had acquired four new marbles she could show off to Mairi, so with a huge grin she capitulated, anxious to fetch her friend straight away. She turned towards the croft and followed her mother back into the kitchen. 'All right mither, I'll have Mairi over. Can we go now though, right away?'

'Yes, of course, go ahead Lizzie, and I'll catch you up,' smiled Agnes as she pulled on her well-worn boots.

Lizzie was halfway up the small hill when she stopped to wait for her mother. Agnes had been walking quickly to catch up with her daughter, but slowed as the pain, which had bothered her earlier, got more severe with every step. Thinking it was stitch from hurrying, she dismissed it and carried on walking, until they reached the little croft and found Bridget Mackenzie hanging out a full line of washing. Mairi was helping by handing her mother the wooden pegs as she went along the line.

Bridget looked up as Agnes and Lizzie appeared. 'Why hello Agnes...Lizzie, I was just going to have a brew. Come ben the hoose and I'll get the kettle on.'

Agnes sat down on the settle, leaving the girls to play outside. Bridget handed her the cup of tea, before remarking on her physical condition. 'Why Agnes, you look a bit pale, are you all right?'

'I will be, as soon as I have rested a minute,' answered Agnes, gratefully drinking the hot sweet liquid.

Bridget was unconvinced. 'The bairn's not due yet is it?' she asked.

Agnes determined not to accept fuss, was dismissive of her friend's concern. 'Why no, it is another month. It's just that we were hurrying and I got the stitch that's all. In fact, the pain has already subsided.'

Bridget shook her head in exasperation, knowing her friend's propensity to be stubborn. 'Nevertheless, Agnes, you should start to take things easier you know. Doesn't do to tempt providence. You don't want to go into labour early.'

'I'll be all right Bridget. I had Lizzie easy enough. You can't afford to take it easy when you've a young lassie, a husband and a hame to take care of can you?' stated Agnes with conviction.

Bridget had to agree, but peered with concern at the pale face of her friend, convinced that she was not as well as she purported.

Agnes emptied her cup and reluctantly got up to leave. 'We'll awa now Bridget, blethering won't get the bairn bathed so to speak. Thanks for the tea. I'll ask William to bring Mairi hame about 7 o'clock, if that's all right with you. She may as well stay for some supper. I've a broth in the pot and it will easily stretch to four.'

'Okay, Agnes, thanks,' accepted Bridget with resignation. 'Don't forget though, if I can help you out, you've only to say the word. Promise me you will have a rest while the girls are playing in the yard. Mairi's got some new 'snobs' and I saw Lizzie showing off her marbles, so they'll be busy for hours.

※

Back home, the girls were quickly engrossed in their play so Agnes took the opportunity to lie down on the settle for a rest. She had been dozing for a short while, when an intense pain awakened her and this time, there was no mistaking it for the stitch. It was late afternoon, William was still out in the fields and wasn't due back for another few hours.

Agnes realised that the baby was definitely on the way and she cried out to Lizzie, who came scampering into the kitchen. Her mother was lying on the settle with her hands over her stomach, which frightened her and she anxiously asked if she was all right. 'Oh mither, what's wrong? Have you got a tummy ache?' Lizzie went over to her mother and placed her hand on her mother's abdomen.

'I'll be all right Lizzie, but I need you to be a very big girl and go with Mairi to her hoose and ask her mither to fetch Martha. Tell her I think the bairn is on the way.'

'All right mither, is my little sister coming then?'

Agnes smiled at Lizzie, who had been adamant ever since she discovered she was to have a sibling, that it would be a girl. 'Well I think so, she might be here by tonight if we're lucky. Now go straight there and don't dawdle.'

'We're awa mither. Come on Mairi, I'll race you and last one there's a moose.' Lizzie was out the door and through the gate without looking back.

When they arrived, Mairi's mother was in the kitchen folding up freshly laundered sheets. She was surprised that the two girls appeared to be alone and anxiously asked if William was with them. 'Where's your faither Lizzie? Is he out the back?'

Lizzie shook her head. 'No Mrs Mackenzie, we've come on our own. My mither says to tell you that the bairn's coming and faither's not back yet. She asked if you would fetch Martha and to be quick, because she's got the tummy ache.'

Bridget set out immediately and after dropping the two girls off at Lizzie's gate, quickly covered the two miles to Martha's cottage to request her attendance. The school that Martha owned and ran was closed, as it was Saturday, so without hesitation Martha left her half finished chores and they set out across the fields together.

They arrived just over an hour later to find Agnes in the middle stages of labour. The girls were banished to the parlour with bowls of hot broth, before Bridget helped Martha by fetching clean towels and boiling water.

The labour gained momentum into the evening when William returned from the fields to find his wife in bed, in much pain. 'You can't suffer like this lass. Will I fetch the doctor Agnes?' he asked in a worried voice.

Agnes smiled. 'Don't whittle hain, Martha can see to me. She brought Lizzie into the world didn't she? Where is Lizzie by the way?'

'She is safe and sound in her bed. Bridget and Mairi left after supper. I had to bring a wee lamb back and I've placed him in the barn. Both girls were trying to get him to take some milk and their persistence paid off. He's improved enough to be reunited with his mother first thing tomorrow. The pair of them were so excited, but I reckon Lizzie will have fallen asleep as soon as her head touched the pillow.'

Agnes smiled up at William as the two sat together for a while holding hands, recounting their good fortune in finding each other and being blessed with a healthy little girl. Soon they hoped to welcome another, whom they would equally love and nurture.

William had been stroking Agnes's back and soothing her brow as she stoically endured every painful episode. The unmistakable contractions built up to a crescendo, before gradually subsiding.

When the contractions really began in earnest, just before midnight, Agnes could not disguise the agony any longer and cried out, gripping William's arm. William clung to his wife, terrified that she would be unable to cope with the final stages. He looked determinedly into the eyes of the woman he loved from the moment he first saw her and decided enough was enough. 'That's it; I'll not stand by and watch this any longer. I'm awa to fetch Dr Armstrong.' Then he bent down and kissed his wife, promising to be back as soon as he could.

A frightened Agnes clung to her husband. 'William, William don't leave me. Please stay, I need you. It will be all right. Martha will deliver the baby safely. The doctor cannot help me. There is nothing he can do that Martha can not.'

William had tears in his eyes as he tore himself away from his wife. 'Don't worry my love. I will be back before you know it and the doctor will be able to give you something to help with the pain...I cannot bear to see you like this. I love you Agnes.' He turned to Martha and pleaded for her to do her utmost until the doctor arrived. 'Look after her Martha. I'm counting on you to see her through until we're back.'

William called to his wife as he turned and walked out through the back door. 'Goodbye my love. Don't worry, we'll be with you within the hour. Hold on.'

Determination was etched on Agnes's face, as she watched her husband disappear from sight. Then with tears in her eyes and encouragement from Martha she battled bravely on.

The larger settlement of Bettyhill was ten miles away from Strathy and twelve miles from their croft, over some rough terrain. Despite his exhaustion from a full day lambing, William rode his horse hard, pushing him to the limit. He had no money, but intended to bluff his way into convincing the doctor that he had an amount put by to cover his services.

He arrived at the large house on the outskirts of the town and furiously rang the bell. The house was in darkness and he had an anxious moment or two to wait before lights flickered on in the main hall and the door opened. The elderly maid, who answered in her night attire, was none too pleased to be woken up at this time. 'All right, all right, you can stop ringing the bell for all it's worth; I'm here aren't I. I should think everyone for miles around is up and about. Is there a fire somewhere? There must be an almighty emergency to be ringing like someone demented. Now what is it? This had better be good?'

William answered in an anxious but firm voice. 'Look, I'm sorry, but my wife is in labour and it looks like the baby, or my wife, God forbid, might not survive, so can you get a move on and fetch Dr Armstrong?'

When the maid heard there was a woman in trouble, she immediately showed William through to the library, but her continual banter did not abate. 'Aw, I am sorry to hear that, but she'll be in good hands when Dr Armstrong can take charge of matters. He is a good doctor, one of the best. When my sister Gertie went into labour—'

William was not listening to the maid's chatter and still very distressed, addressed her more sharply than he had intended. 'Yes, yes, stop your blethering and fetch him quickly.'

A few minutes later, Dr Armstrong appeared and after William explained the nature of his call, he quickly collected his bag and set off for Strathy in his trap.

William rode ahead, but it was still a good hour before he reached home.

He dismounted his horse and not bothering to tether him, raced swiftly through the yard into the croft, shouting his wife's name. 'Agnes, he's here. It's okay, it's okay now my love.' But there was no reply. Martha appeared in the doorway with a grave look on her face.

Agnes's pains had been become steadily worse within half an hour of William leaving. The contractions had merged into one intensely painful episode, with Martha unable to do anything to help her plight. Her inability to 'turn' the baby meant both mother and baby may not survive.

Martha was helpless and could not assist Agnes to bring the child safely into the world and, inevitably, Agnes lost her fight for life. She died fifteen minutes before William and the doctor arrived.

William looked at Martha's face and knew instantly that his wife had not survived. 'No, nooooo.' William wailed and covered his face with his hands. 'She's not dead, she can't be. She's my life. I cannot live without her. Why? Why? What's she ever done to anyone?'

William was distraught and did not even ask about his newborn son. His beloved wife was gone forever, along with his hopes and dreams. In that instant, William felt his life was over.

Lizzie, unbeknown to her father, was actually wide-awake and sitting up in bed, transfixed by the nightmare events that were unfolding around her. The howling, which came from her mother, was now coming just as loudly from her father. It was too much for the little girl. She clamped her hands to her ears and sobbed loudly into her pillow, as she realised that she would never see her mother again. What she was unable to comprehend was that life would change dramatically for her father and herself.

Dr Armstrong attended to Agnes and made arrangements for her funeral. She would be buried in the churchyard at Farr, the nearest parish church to Strathy. After checking the baby and making him comfortable, he left the croft without asking for payment.

Two days later, William remained alone in the room he had shared with his wife and where she now lay in a coffin awaiting burial. After saying his final goodbye, he slowly closed the lid shut before striding out into the yard and mounting his horse. He rode at a furious pace over the meadows and scrubland, blinded by tears and totally bereft. He felt he had died with her, but knew he had a responsibility to look after his daughter and so must endure a living death — until the day he could be with his beloved wife once again.

Martha Stewart went through the motions of seeing to Lizzie and the bairn's needs, but she too was distraught and went about her duties in a trance. She felt totally wretched but did all she could to make sure the bairn had everything he needed. She closed the school and stayed over, sleeping on the settle in the small sitting room.

Robert William Cameron's struggle to be born made him strong and he soon began to thrive under the expert care of Martha.

Unfortunately, William continued to have nothing to do with his son who was, ironically, the image of his wife with golden hair and violet blue eyes. Two weeks went by and after much soul searching, he made an impassioned plea to Martha to take the boy and raise him as her own.

He waited for the right moment and broached the subject with Martha. The question tumbled out and there was no going back. 'Martha, I have something to ask you. I am hoping that you will not think badly of me and will understand my dilemma.'

Martha had a feeling that William was psyching himself up to ask her something and she had guessed what it would be. Nevertheless, she felt awkward, which was compounded by a terrible sense of guilt. This may have been partly due to the fact that she and Donald had not been blessed with children of their own so she knew the temptation would be too great to turn him down.

William continued anxiously. 'I want you to take the bairn back to your cottage and bring him up as your own. I just canna cope with the two of them. The farm work would suffer and we'd be banished to the poor house. I can't do that to Lizzie. Will you help me Martha?'

Tentatively she agreed, subject of course, to approval from Donald. 'Maybe I could do that for you William, even though I am not sure that it is the right thing. It's my personal opinion that the bairn should be with his faither, but I understand how difficult it would be for you to manage.'

William's hopes were raised. 'I realise that you will have to talk to Donald to see how he feels, but I would be very grateful Martha because I cannot see any other solution. My situation really is impossible.'

Immediately after the funeral, Lizzie was collected by her father's brother, Drew, to spend some time at his cottage in Caithness. She had enjoyed being with her two cousins, Morag and Annabella, on the few occasions that they had been able to visit them and William reasoned that it would benefit Lizzie to go away for a while: have a kind of holiday to help her come to terms with the tragedy. Now she was back home, sat on her bed, and although William thought she was out of earshot, the muffled voices of Martha and her father carried through the kitchen door that had been inadvertently left ajar.

Lizzie lay quietly, trying to catch the gist of the conversation. She cupped her hand to her ears, straining as her father spoke in hushed tones to Martha. Although she could not hear every word and was too young to understand the implications of such a decision, she could hear that her father was begging Martha to take her brother away.

She held her hand over her mouth to suppress a gasp and prayed that Martha would refuse and try harder to persuade her father to change his mind, but to her horror, she heard Martha finally agreeing to his request. Then everything went quiet and she waited to see what would happen next. She sat still, expecting her father to come and tell her he couldn't go through with it, that he wanted them all to stay together as a family.

However, the decision had been made. William put on his coat and boots and hung his head in shame as the sense of disloyalty he felt to his wife became almost unbearable. He was unable to face Lizzie and marched past her room out into the yard, where he saddled up his horse and rode out to the fields like someone possessed, to seek complete solitude.

Lizzie heard the door slam and with hot tears streaming down her face, buried her head in the counterpane and beat her fists hard into the pillow.

Baby Robert somehow knew that he was about to leave the bosom of his family and began to cry. With a heavy heart, Martha promised herself that never again would she attend another delivery.

CHAPTER TWO

Compromises

Lizzie gained more of an understanding about her parents' lives, as she grew older. She realised how much in love they had been and how her father tried to make life easier for her mother, but it had always been an impossible task with so little money to spare.

William struggled to bring up his young daughter alone, even though she was at school most of the day, he needed to carry out the household chores and work the land. He never appeared to recover from the death of his beloved wife and rose wearily each morning at four thirty to see to the needs of Lizzie, before Bridget collected her for school.

The sun was already peeping out one Monday morning as the dawn chorus forced both William and Lizzie out of their beds earlier than usual. This particular day would be a small step on William's road to recovery, but an unconcerned Lizzie was already rummaging around the coup in her nightwear to find the fresh newly laid eggs their chickens provided on a daily basis. She wandered back into the kitchen humming to herself and placed four large eggs in a basket on the table. Her father busied himself stoking up the fire after vigorously stirring a pan of porridge on the hob. Lizzie knew he laboured hard every day in an effort to put his painful memories behind him, but his life had changed dramatically and he had changed with it. He had become morose and disinterested in all things, except for her.

In a cheerful mood, she crept behind him and put her arms about his waist, as he stood at the sink, scrubbing potatoes for their evening meal. 'Look faither, the hens' have laid some extra large eggs today, so I will cook breakfast for you. I can manage it you know. Bridget left us two rashers of bacon and some fresh bread when she called round yesterday afternoon and I know you love crispy bacon.'

William looked fondly at his daughter, without whom he would not have survived. 'Okay Lizzie, you can have a go, but be careful lassie, that pan gets very hot and I don't want you burning your fingers.'

Lizzie made a good job of the breakfast and William felt cheered. He realised that his permanent low mood was having an unfair negative effect on his daughter, so vowed to be more cheerful and keep his dark moments to himself. He whistled a tune as he helped Lizzie prepare for school, making sure he indulged in some light hearted banter as he placed her books into a canvas bag. 'Now Lizzie, enjoy your day and I'll have your supper ready when you return. We will sit and have it together, as I will be coming hame a little earlier this evening. I can't promise it will be as good as yer mither used to make, but I'll give it a go. Stew and dumplings suit you?'

'Oooh yes faither, that'll be a real treat, it's my absolute favourite,' she said and laughingly chided him on her way out, 'Watch the pan faither, it gets hot you know and I don't want you burning your fingers!'

Her father smiled and felt uplifted by his daughter's infectious laughter. 'Be away with you lassie and I'll see you tonight.'

She was pleased that her father's mood was lifting and her own heart felt lighter as she slid her hand in Mairi's. They ran all the way to school, escorted by Bridget, laughing and singing loudly as they went —

A woman's wark will ne'er be dune.
Although the day were ne'er sae lang;
Sae meikle but, sae meikle ben, -
But for her care a' wad gae wrang...

Lizzie was the brightest pupil in the class. Even though Martha's rule was to treat all the pupils the same, she still favoured Lizzie and gave her extra tuition when she had the time.

At thirteen, Lizzie could have attended the senior Free Church School in Farr and Martha knew that with her natural ability, she could obtain a bursary when she reached eighteen, to complete her education at University.

However, on her thirteenth birthday, Lizzie confided to Martha that her father's stamina had deteriorated and he needed her to help with more of the household chores. 'Martha can I talk to you for a moment, it's about faither?'

Martha was concerned and lead Lizzie to the small office where she conducted all the school's business. 'What is it lass? Your faither's not ill is he?'

'No, no Martha, he isn't ill exactly, but he works so hard and he is not looking too well these days,' she paused, 'I must help him, so I have decided that I can no longer continue with my education. I have to look after the croft now, so that my faither has a chance of keeping our heads above water by concentrating on the farm. He is a proud man Martha and would never ask me to give up my schooling, so I must make that decision. I'm sorry Martha, I know you have helped me greatly and that you were hoping I would go on to University, but my faither has given me the best years of his life and it is now time for me to give him something back.'

Martha looked sad, but understood her dilemma. Then a thought occurred to her, a kind of compromise. 'Well Lizzie, you're a good lassie and I understand your position, but I have a proposition to put to you. What if, after you have finished your chores, you do some schoolwork at home? I could ask Bridget if she would drop off an exercise book with some prepared work for you to complete. She could bring it back the next day for me to mark. I think that would work very well and I am sure, with you being so gifted, that we could also continue with your higher educational needs. What do you say?'

'Oh Martha would you do that for me? I will work really hard, even if I have to stay up until midnight.'

'All right Lizzie, but you mustn't over do it, as you would not be any help to yourself or your faither if you are permanently exhausted.'

So it was, that in the summer of 1832, some nine years after her mother's cruel and untimely death and although still a child herself, Lizzie took on her mother's role.

She woke at first light to stoke the fire and cook her father his breakfast, before he went out to tend the sheep and work the fields. She completed her other household chores, before settling down to her schoolwork, but despite Martha's warning, she would often burn the midnight oil, sometimes not going to bed until well after 12 o'clock, when she fell asleep exhausted.

―――

The years passed swiftly and soon it was Christmas 1835. That year, there was enough food to give them a decent festive meal, but insufficient money for presents. An apple, an orange and three new pennies filled Lizzie's stocking, but all other gifts were handmade. There was, however, one present by the hearth bearing her name, which was too large to fit into her stocking. Lizzie was excited and couldn't wait to reveal its contents. 'Oh thank you faither, you shouldn't have bought anything, we don't have money to spare.'

William grinned. 'Don't worry Lizzie, I didn't actually buy it, I made it, so I hope you like it.'

She undid the pretty blue velvet ribbon tied up in a bow and tore eagerly at the brown paper. Her eyes moistened as she looked down at the large wooden 'keeper' box, which her father had made. She knew he must have spent hours carefully carving her full name on the top and fashioning the small escutcheon and lock. 'Oh, faither it's just about the most beautiful thing I have ever seen. I shall treasure it always.'

'I'm glad you like it Lizzie. It has a false bottom as well for storing special things inside. Bring it to me lassie and I'll show you how it works.'

Lizzie was mesmerised as her father turned the key once to open the lid, revealing a useful space; then he turned the key again, which allowed the bottom of the box to open up, exposing a secret compartment underneath. He handed the box back to Lizzie and threw back his head in laughter at the look of pride and amazement on his daughter's face.

'Oh my, faither, that's so clever of you. Mither always said that you were good with your hands. She would be very proud of you today. You've worked so hard to make my Christmas special.' She went over to him, put her arms around his neck and kissed him on the cheek. 'I shall keep the scripted recordings of mine and Robert's birth inside, the two little embroidered handkerchiefs that mither gave me and the three new pennies from you, to remind me of this special day. Now wait there, as I also have something for you.' Lizzie rushed off to her room to retrieve the parcel from under her bed to give to her father. She had been busy all year making a quilted eiderdown from scraps of material she found or begged from Bridget and Martha. She had cut the fabric into little squares and sewn them together to form a patchwork, filling the pockets with wool from the black-faced sheep, collected at shearing time in July; the coarse springy fibres being ideal for making eiderdowns warm and cosy. 'Here you are faither, made with lots of love for you. I hope you like it.'

The eiderdown began to appear as William tore off the packaging, causing his eyes to fill with tears, which resurrected mixed emotions. He was sad that Agnes could not be with him and he felt guilty that he had shunned his son, but mostly he was happy that he had been blessed with a daughter such as Lizzie.

He smiled as she looked at him expectantly. 'Come here lassie, come and sit with me. Unless, of course, you are now too old to sit on your faither's lap.'

Without hesitation, Lizzie went over to her father and plonked herself down on his knee. 'Faither, I will never be too old to sit with you. I feel so lucky that you are here to look after me. You are the best faither ever.'

William tried to hold himself together and thanked Lizzie before retreating into the kitchen with the excuse that the chicken needed basting.

Lizzie followed him and put the kettle on the hob to boil. 'I'll mash us a cup of tea faither. Then I'll give you a hand with lunch.'

'You're all right lassie, I've everything in hand. It's my turn to cook for you today Lizzie. You have already contributed by baking the cake and boiling the pudding. Now let's have that cuppa, then after lunch, we'll take a walk down by the river and see if we can catch some brown trout for supper tonight.'

It was the best Christmas they had had since Agnes's death. However, they were blissfully unaware that this would be the last one they would spend together in the Highlands of Scotland and that soon their lives would once again take a different path.

CHAPTER THREE

Leaving Strathy

In November 1836, when Lizzie was seventeen, William made the decision to move from the Highlands down to the Lowlands to find alternative employment. He felt confident that his ability to speak the English language, after renouncing Gaelic, coupled with his experience of cattle and sheep, would give him a good chance of securing a position on a farm, as a herdsman, or some kind of manager. Lizzie could turn her hand to several things, including teaching, or perhaps working as a seamstress.

When the dreaded day arrived for Lizzie and her father to leave Strathy, both shed tears. William had risen earlier than usual and had ridden his horse over to Farr where he spent some time at the graveside of his beloved wife, Agnes.

Lizzie understood her father's need to be alone and went for a walk through the meadows, eventually resting on a small outcrop of rocks overlooking the copse. She knew that this was where her father had first seen her mother and their life together had begun. She sat there for a while contemplating their new life in Glasgow. She had heard that the streets were grimy, the skies grey and that the air was filled with smoke and unfamiliar smells. Their only real motivation in leaving was to have the opportunity of finding work.

She felt that never again would she enjoy the freedom of this beautiful part of Scotland, where the air was fresh and clean and her memories were filled with happier times. In Strathy, she felt close to her mother and she promised herself that one day she would return to once again run in the meadow and breathe in the clean fresh air.

Much later, Lizzie stopped by Mairi's house to say goodbye to her best friend. Bridget wasn't surprised, as William had been to see them the previous day to thank her for all the help she had given him over the years. She had forewarned Mairi, explaining to her that the Cameron's had no choice but to make the move to Glasgow. Mairi had been very upset and angry that her friend was going to move away, but understood the choice of a move or the poor house. Her mother had said that if it was the poor house, it was likely they would never see her again. At least they could visit if they moved to Glasgow.

Lizzie walked up the path, as she had done so many times before and as she observed Mairi sitting on a chair under the covered porch she wondered if she would, in fact, ever see her again. Determined to be cheerful, she gave Mairi a wave. 'Hi there Mairi, what yer up to?'

Mairi looked up as her friend approached and returned the wave. 'Nothing much Lizzie, just sitting here waiting for mither to finish washing the scullery floor. I'm glad you came, as I was beginning to think that you would be leaving without saying goodbye.'

Lizzie grinned. 'Never! I would never do that. I am going to miss you so much.'

'Me too. There isn't anyone else who lives as close with whom I can share my thoughts with.'

Lizzie's smile faded. 'You're right. I don't want to go, but my faither says we don't have any choice. It's that or the poor house and I'll not go there. Some say once there, you never get out.'

Mairi gave a wry smile as she stood up and preceded Lizzie into the scullery. 'Mither says your faither has promised to come and visit us when you are settled, so we will look forward to that day.'

They sat at the table discussing the times they had spent together; the hardships, the laughter, the sadness and the close bond they shared. They realised their memories would stay with them forever and whatever the future brought, they would cherish them always.

When Lizzie was about to leave, they hugged each other and promised that come what may, they would meet up again. Then Mairi watched Lizzie until she disappeared over the horizon. She too questioned whether, despite their promise, they would actually ever see each other again.

It was Lizzie's final opportunity to spend some precious time with her brother, albeit she had seen him almost daily over the last couple of weeks. She had been hoping that her father would be reunited with him before they left, but although William had visited Martha and Donald, he had made sure that Robert was not around and had left without making his peace.

Lizzie walked into the kitchen as Martha was cleaning mud off Robert's shoes. When he saw Lizzie, his face lit up and he rushed over to greet his sister. 'Aw Lizzie, have you come to take us down to the beck? Faither Donald has fixed a big rope for me to swing across to Barnes's field. I've come back hame because I slipped on the muddy bank and mither says I can't go agen unless you's with me.'

'All right Robert I'll go with you...if that's okay with you Martha?'

'Why of course, Lizzie, it's always good for you two to spend time together. We'll see you later.'

'See you later Martha. Come on Robert, I'll race you.' Lizzie ran ahead with Robert fast on her heels. 'Last one there's a moose!' she shouted teasingly, using her favourite taunt.

When they arrived, Robert pushed Lizzie across the water towards the other side of the river on the strong rope, which Donald had tied to the large willow tree overhanging the bank. On the inward swing, he leaped in the air and joined her as she hung precariously close to the water.

Lizzie was hanging on for dear life, but laughing as she slipped further down the rope. 'Oh goodness Robert, what did you do that for, the rope won't hold us both. Look the branch is already bending.'

Robert was laughing in unison so much he couldn't get off and they both dropped down into the icy water, coughing and spluttering. Lizzie eventually climbed back on to the riverbank, followed by a bedraggled Robert. 'Oh Lizzie you should have seen your face, it was a right funny picture.'

'Yes well I couldn't believe you thought we could both swing on the rope together.' This seemed the opportune time to tell Robert her news, so she continued, 'I don't know what you will do when I'm gone, you'll not get Mairi to swing across with you.'

There was a long silence before Robert said anything. He looked down and threw a stone into the water before responding dejectedly. 'So you're going then. Mither said there was the chance that you might have to go. I'm going to miss you so much Lizzie and I wish, in some ways, I was going with you, but I know that I can't.'

Lizzie was saddened by their plight and invited Robert to sit beside her on the bank, determined to sound optimistic about the future. 'Listen Robert, when we are settled in Glasgow, I am sure I will be able to persuade faither to send for you. Last Christmas I got the feeling that he knew he had done wrong, but it's difficult for him to admit it. In time, I know he will change his mind. I just hope that you can forgive him when he does.'

'Lizzie I dunna bear a grudge. He had to do it I suppose. I know that and I can't complain about anything really. Faither and mither Campbell treat me like a son and I couldna wish for more. Course I would forgive him, but I am not sure that I would want to leave Strathy. I love it here. After a lot of years, I might want to go, but at the minit, I want to be here. I just wish you didn't have to go.'

'I wish that too Robert, but we have to face the fact that I *am* going. This will be our last day together, but I promise you that one day we will be together again. Now let's get back before we catch our deaths.'

Martha was surprised to see the two young people enter her kitchen, dripping water all over the floor. However, she knew that it would be the last time for the foreseeable future that they would get the chance to spend time together and couldn't be cross, so chuckled at the sight that greeted her. 'Well now you two, you'd better take off those wet clothes and change into some dry ones, you do look a sorry pair.'

Robert grinned at Martha as he pulled some clean trousers off the clotheshorse. 'Thanks mither. It was my fault, we tried hanging on the rope together and Lizzie lost hold, so we both fell into the water. It was quite funny though wasn't it Lizzie?'

Lizzie pretended to be less than pleased and pulled a face. 'If you say so Robert. Personally I could have done without the soaking, but we must look a funny sight hey Martha.'

Martha grinned after handing her some dry clothes. 'Well Lizzie, I thought you were past swinging on ropes, but so long as you enjoyed yourselves. I must say though, you do look rather comical. Come here lassie and dry your hair in front of the fire. I'll put your boots in the oven to dry out while I make you both a mug of hot milk and honey.'

They dried out and felt warmer, but the time came to say goodbye. Lizzie spoke to Martha hugging her close. 'Faither is sorry that he couldn't make it today, but he is really busy packing and loading the wagon. He mentioned that he had already spoken to you about us leaving.'

'Aye lassie, he called over the other night and said his goodbyes. It's a sad day Lizzie and I can't say I am happy about it, but once again it looks as if fate has dealt a bitter blow to your faither and he's not been given a choice. Give him our love and don't forget us Lizzie. Let's hope that one day we will all meet up again.'

Lizzie's eyes filled with tears as she hugged Donald and then Robert, giving him an extra squeeze. 'I promise that one day I will return. Until then, I will think about you all every day and pray that we will be together again soon.'

Before she left, Martha gave Lizzie a little package tied up with string, then turned away to hide her sorrow.

'What's this Martha? You shouldn't be buying presents for me,' Lizzie smiled sadly.

'It's not much lassie, just something to remind you not to forget us until you return. Take the greatest care of yourself and your faither. We will pray that you have a safe journey. Now go lassie before you start me blubbering.'

Lizzie turned to leave the cottage, fighting the tears that were bubbling up in her eyes. She smiled bravely as she closed the door and, without looking back, headed for home.

She walked along the lanes, which were framed on either side by low gorse hedges and allowed the tears to fall, before stopping at a farm gate. An image of her mother's face formed vividly in her mind, as she gazed at the fields in the distance. Agnes was smiling and looking straight into her eyes. In that instant, Lizzie knew that her mother wanted her to be strong and help her father come to terms with the new life that awaited them. Then with renewed purpose and determination, she continued on her way.

※

When Lizzie arrived back at the croft, her father was already piling the last few items of furniture onto the covered wagon. His horse, Barney, was still strong and William thought him capable of completing the long journey, given sufficient rest.

Lizzie had packed a few things of her own, including antimacassars and a couple of pegged rugs, made by her mother, plus the little package given to her by Martha and, most importantly, her 'keeper box', which she had locked. The key was placed securely around her neck with a piece of blue velvet ribbon.

William estimated that the journey would take between eight and ten days, as he did not want to push Barney too hard and risk him becoming lame. After he finished loading the wagon, they took a last look around, before starting on their long journey. Within a week, they would be hundreds of miles away and sadly, Strathy would be a distant memory.

∼⁂∽

They had been travelling eight days when they reached Cumbernauld. The weather had for many days been kind to them, but the last forty-eight hours had brought snow, high winds and a considerable drop in temperature.

Despite William's insistence on resting Barney as often as possible, his horse had tired over the long journey. Most of their food was gone and they relied on snaring rabbits.

It was late evening when disaster struck. They were heading towards a small clump of trees to bed down for the night, when Barney damaged his fetlock as he stumbled on a deep ruck in the road. The horse fell to his knees and William heard a cracking sound, signifying that he had broken a leg. In an instant, he was by his side, cradling his head in his arms. 'It's all right boy...it's all right.' He spoke soothingly to Barney as he released the harness to stop the wagon from falling over, but he knew that things were far from all right.

Without the rigid harness, Barney fell over on to his side and lay there panting. William stroked his head and saw the pained look in his eyes. He moved his hand expertly over his leg, which confirmed the unmistakable break. The bone was jutting out at an angle. William whispered softly and gently to his horse. 'Barney...oh Barney boy, it's no good, I can't help you. I'm afraid it's the end of the road old friend.' The horse looked at his master, his eyes dimming as William continued comforting him. 'I can't see you in pain like this, especially as there isn't any hope of a recovery...You know what I must do don't you...I have no choice...You do...' William swallowed hard. 'You do understand old friend. If there was any other way.'

Lizzie walked slowly over towards Barney and with tears in her eyes, asked her father if there was any hope. 'He won't die will he faither? Please don't let him die. Perhaps if he rests tonight, he will be all right by tomorrow.'

'I'm sorry Lizzie, but Barney is lame, he has broken his leg. I don't have any choice but to put him out of his misery. You know if there was anything, anything at all I could do, I would do it.'

With a faltering voice, William begged Lizzie to return to the wagon while he attended to the unenviable task of shooting his horse.

'No faither, I cannot let him die alone, please let me stroke his head so that he feels safe.'

'Lizzie, you know I cannot let you do that, it's too dangerous. You have to go back into the wagon.'

Sobbing loudly, Lizzie did as she was bade and with a heavy heart, William aimed his gun sure and true to save his horse further suffering.

William wiped away a tear and covered Barney with a blanket, before climbing into the back of the wagon to comfort Lizzie. Later, they sat with a warm drink on the seat at the entrance to the wagon. William observed the look of sadness in Lizzie's eyes and hoping to cheer her up a little, pointed to a little group of stars in the dark blue cloudless sky. 'Listen, Lizzie, see up there in the sky, that little cluster of stars all in a huddle? They call them the 'Seven Sisters' and they are in the Constellation of Taurus. Your mither was born in April, which means her birth sign was Taurus. She used to tell me that we were the perfect match, me being a Capricorn. I like to think that your mither is there among those stars Lizzie and one of the brightest ones is called Miai, which means mother. Father Murdoch was interested in the stars and talked about them at length after your mither died. I would often sit in my chair on the veranda and look up at the 'Seven Sisters', which gave me great comfort. The best thing of all is that the little cluster means 'coping with sorrow', just like we are doing now Lizzie. If we sit a while and think of all the things we have to be grateful for, we will feel comforted.'

'Oh faither, that's a lovely story and I'll remember it whenever I feel sad,' smiled Lizzie as she held her father's hand.

She was cheered by his story, but still felt sadness that Barney had had to be put down. He had been a good horse...a friend who had served them well.

William had lain awake most of the night, knowing they would have to complete the remaining eight-mile journey on foot and he wondered whether they would make it. There had been no let up with the weather and the night was colder than any he could remember.

The following morning before breakfast, they managed, with a huge effort, to pull the wagon down under the shelter of some large trees. They hid it from view and covered it over with rushes and branches, so that they could retrieve it later.

They used the last of the food at breakfast and drank some hot sweet tea, before putting on as much warm clothing as they could; a couple of jumpers and two pairs of woollen socks each, as well as their old long black wool coats. The snow was coming down thickly and the wind had picked up again over night. Both knew it was important that they reach their destination before dark, so they left all their belongings in the wagon, except for two rucksacks. William's contained some documents and a water bottle and Lizzie's her precious box and the small package given to her by Martha.

With heavy hearts they set off mid-morning on the last lap of their journey into Glasgow.

By two o'clock, they were on the outskirts of the city, but both were very cold, tired and thirsty. Their clothing was wet with snow, as were their feet. Water had seeped through their boots, despite two pairs of socks each and both felt the misery of blisters. A short while later, they were, at last, at journey's end. The city of Glasgow stretched out before them.

William and Lizzie were shocked as the city came into view. They stood on top of a small hill and were dismayed by the tall smoking chimneys, the lack of greenery and the drabness of the buildings. They drew closer and they could see many people rushing around the grey streets, seeking shelter from the swirling snow and the wind that crept in under bonnets and mufflers, making them hurry through the cobbled streets to the warmth of their firesides.

William stared in bewilderment at Lizzie, at her cold face and at her wet and bedraggled clothes. 'What have I done Lizzie, we cannot live here in this cold, grey, forbidding place.'

Lizzie was fighting the urge to run and run and never look back, but instead she rallied, as she saw the look of total desolation on her father's face. She spoke with as much conviction as she could muster, her mouth voicing words that she did not feel in her heart. 'Don't worry faither, it won't be as bad as it looks. The day is cold and grey, it will look very different when the sun shines, you'll see.'

William was very proud of his daughter whose gritty determination he had admired through the tough times in Strathy, when their situation looked very bleak. Indeed, she never complains, she's always cheerful, always seeing hope and light, even in the darkest moments. Pride swelled within him as he pulled Lizzie closer to his chest and stroked her hair. 'Lizzie, I think you are right you know, we have survived worse than this and we must be positive. I have enough money to pay for some lodgings for tonight and tomorrow we will look for something more permanent. We may even be able to persuade someone to ride out and collect our wagon, so that we will at least have some familiar possessions around us. We must make our way into the centre of the town, where we will have more chance of finding shelter for the night.' That said, William and Lizzie entered the city of Glasgow.

Chapter Four

Changing Fortunes

Josiah Monks made it his business to visit his parishioners regularly and was on first name terms with a great many of his regular worshippers and even those who he referred to as his 'BMDs' — Those who attended on three, mostly unavoidable, occasions, namely, birth, marriage and death. In the case of 'death' he was referring to the serial mourners who attended any funeral to partake of the food supplied for the wake of the deceased. He still felt these people were worth 'saving' and did his best to coerce them into attending church at least twice a year.

Josiah was a man of around fifty-five years, five foot six inches with a girth to match. His middle had expanded over many years of tea, chat and homemade cakes, consumed at regular home visits with those requiring his sound knowledge and judgement, even if it was not always heeded. He had a kindly face with pale blue eyes topped by big bushy eyebrows. His hair was long and white and stuck out uncontrollably from under his wide brimmed hat, which he wore everywhere.

For Josiah Monks, this night was like most others, except it was bitterly cold and the snow had not stopped for over two days. He still walked the streets in the miserable weather, giving out bread to the needy and advice to those who were up to no good.

William and Lizzie had been looking for lodgings for several hours, without success. They were told that there weren't any vacancies and they should move on, although William had assured them that they had money to pay for a room for the night.

The streets became less busy as dusk fell, but the snow was still falling, descending thickly through the black night sky. William and Lizzie huddled together in the doorway of a store that had long since closed its doors for the night. 'Maybe we should look further out of town faither,' Lizzie suggested, but William's mood had sunk again and he was beginning to think they would be spending the night exactly where they stood.

It was now nine o'clock and the streets were practically deserted. Any folk with a warm dwelling to go to had been long gone. It seemed that a different kind of person was now loitering along the same streets, which had previously been filled with shoppers and early evening revellers, partaking of a drink or two before heading home. This new unsavoury breed of people were poorly dressed and looked to William like beggars and vagabonds. He kept his head down and pulled Lizzie close to him, as far into the corner of the doorway as he could, in case one should approach them for money or worse. He was beginning to think Lizzie was right, that they should move away from the centre and take their chances in the suburbs.

Just as they turned to go, a mysterious plump man wearing a wide brimmed domed top hat stopped at the doorway. He smiled encouragingly at Lizzie and addressed William. 'Well now, what are you two doing out in the city at this time of night. It's not really safe for folk like you to be wandering the streets of Glasgow after dark.' Josiah Monks had quickly appraised the pair in their long black coats and well worn boots, satisfying himself that they were decent folks and guessing they were not from these parts. He looked at William and in a questioning, but friendly voice, asked them their business. 'You are strangers here by the looks of you. Where are you from and why are you here?'

William looked at the man with the big white bushy eyebrows and decided that he was someone they could trust. 'We have travelled down from Strathy in the Highlands to look for work and were hoping to find lodgings for the night, but we have had no luck so far.'

Lizzie interrupted by adding that they had money to pay for the lodgings, but could not find anywhere with vacancies. 'No-one seems to have rooms available and we were going to look further afield sir.'

'Aye well, it's not that folk don't have vacancies, rather that they are wary of strangers and fearful of being robbed or worse, especially after dark. You'll not get lodgings now, so best come with me and you can have a good night's rest and some supper. It's about time I went back home anyway, I have done all I can around here for one night. Tomorrow we will see what can be sorted out.'

William looked gratefully at this man, as if he had been heaven sent. 'Why thank you sir, we are most grateful and are in your debt. What name do you go by?'

William could have been forgiven for not realising that Josiah was a man of the cloth, as his collar was hidden underneath his long black cloak.

'Josiah Monks, at your service. I am the local priest. So what is your name young miss?'

'I am Lizzie Cameron and this is my faither, William,' offered Lizzie.

'Right Lizzie, I've a roaring fire and some good wholesome broth and forgive me, but you look like you could do with a hot bath.'

Lizzie thought she was truly in heaven on entering the vicarage and unable to believe that such rooms existed, stared around in wonderment.

'Come through to the sitting room and sit down for a while in front of the fire. I will find you some dry clothes and you can have the hot meal I promised. I am afraid my housekeeper left last week and I am fending for myself for a while, so supper will not be up to Mrs Carmichael's standards, but it will be hot and there's fresh bread and butter and a mug of hot cocoa to help it down.'

Lizzie and William sat toasting their feet in front of the fire, before hungrily devouring the bread and broth.

A little later, Josiah returned and smiled kindly at Lizzie. 'I have filled up the bath with some hot water for you. Help yourself to the fresh towels in the linen cupboard on the landing my dear.'

Lizzie located the towels and gratefully lowered herself into the water, all her doubts about moving to Glasgow melting away. She lay back, luxuriating in the steamy atmosphere and stayed submerged up to her neck until the water cooled.

Before Lizzie retired for the night, she sat on the small single bed and carefully unwrapped the package given to her by Martha. She was absolutely delighted to find a book of poems by Robert Burns. A hand-written message inside the front cover read:

'With much love to Lizzie Cameron - Take care till we meet again - Martha'

Followed by a quote from the poem, 'Ae Fond Kiss and Then We Sever':

Fare thee weel, thou first and fairest!
Fare thee weel, thou best and dearest!
Thine be ilka joy and treasure,
Peace, enjoyment, love, and pleasure!

Lizzie held the book to her breast and smiled. She pulled the blankets up to her neck and began to read from her favourite poem, *'A Red, Red Rose'*, which likened the words to her love of the Highlands and her promise to return there one day —

'And fare thee weel, my only love,
And fare thee weel awhile!
And I will come again, my love...

By now Lizzie was exhausted and her eyes began to slowly close. The little book slipped from her fingers, as she repeated the last line —

'Tho' it were ten thousand mile...'

Then Lizzie drifted off into a peaceful sleep and a deep feeling of warm contentment.

Chapter Five

Low Wood Hall

Seventeen years after her mother's death, on Tuesday the 12th May, 1840, Lizzie Cameron was enjoying her half day off, sitting on the grassy bank fronting Low Wood Hall. She felt a sudden rush of nostalgia and remembered back to the time when she was small, maybe around four years old: the skies were the same, but the scenery was very different.

She remembered the rugged and wild beauty of Strathy in the Highlands of Scotland. The crofter's cottage perched on top of the hill and the deliberately small plot of land worked by her father to pay the annual rent to the landowner. Money was tight, with only sufficient left to feed and clothe his family.

She recollected the glorious lazy Sunday afternoons spent playing with her best friend, Mairi, on the green grasses of the meadow; a time full of happy memories, before the day in which her life changed forever, when her mother, Agnes, died giving birth to her brother.

Life was cruel, good people died before their time —

Lizzie awoke suddenly from her reverie. The distant sound of the servants' bell, near the main doors echoed along the vestibule entrance wall and into her consciousness. Thoughts of her childhood in Strathy and her journey here had been interrupted by the reality of her new life as senior maid in the Hemingway household of Low Wood Hall.

Lizzie had worked hard, gaining favour with her employers, Howard and Georgina Hemingway, by constantly striving to please this revered family with her loyalty and devotion to duty.

She sat gathering her thoughts and remembered that from this Tuesday, she had been granted an extra monthly half day off, which reflected her new position in the household.

Dottie, the parlour maid, with a 'Dilly Daydream' personality, would carry out Lizzie's duties at these times, but she was often slow to answer the call of the bell. However, when Lizzie heard her scurrying down the hall, she settled down again to her thoughts.

She remembered Josiah arranging for William's wagon to be collected the day after they arrived in Glasgow. Unfortunately, the furniture was damp and had to be dried out, although the soft furnishings were dry and still in good condition.

Fortunately, her father had found work shortly after they arrived in Glasgow, as a senior herdsman, for the owner of a small farm in the north of Glasgow. Josiah Monks being instrumental in securing the position for him, which came with a small cottage adjacent to the farm.

For her part, Lizzie went over to the vicarage every day to help Josiah with the housekeeping and cooking. This arrangement worked well for them as Josiah encouraged Lizzie when she had finished her chores, to make use of the vast amount of books he had acquired over the years, which lined the study walls.

In addition, Josiah paid Lizzie a sum of money from the church funds. This was an allowance given to him to employ a housekeeper and he was quite happy for Lizzie to fulfil this role until arrangements could be made for a permanent keeper. Quite often, he sent her home with left over cakes and bread and the occasional piece of meat for their evening meal. Overall, life was looking better for them both, although they sorely missed Agnes and Lizzie her brother.

William, however, still never spoke about the boy.

Josiah acknowledged Lizzie to be a very accomplished seamstress with excellent cooking and cleaning abilities. Although he was happy to continue her employment, he realised that the church preferred to employ older, more mature women for such a post, to allay any talk of impropriety. Lizzie did not stay overnight, but people still made remarks, so Josiah reluctantly accepted that she could not become his permanent housekeeper.

A few weeks after Josiah had asked around for a suitable position, Georgina Hemingway, owner of Low Wood Hall, approached him on the subject of recommending someone to fill the vacant position of first parlour maid at the Hall. Josiah did not hesitate to recommend Lizzie and advised Georgina that she had much to offer and was worthy of a higher position, but understood she needed to prove her worth.

Lizzie graciously accepted the post and Georgina realised immediately that the girl was very capable. If she stepped up to the mark, she would promote her to senior maid if and when, the position became vacant.

William knew this could be the opportunity for his daughter to make something of her life and after persuading Lizzie that he would manage perfectly well without her, she moved into Low Wood with her father's blessing.

Lizzie enjoyed her work at the large Regency House and was very much valued by the Hemingway family. She had only been there a year when she was promoted to the position of senior maid. The previous post holder had left under a cloud and in dubious circumstances.

A lot had happened in that year, not least of which was the development of her friendship with Katherine Hemingway, the only daughter of Howard and Georgina.

The Hemingway's had three children, David, now nearly twenty-one, Katherine (Kate), seventeen and the youngest Alexander, thirteen.

David had enjoyed a significant allowance from his parents on reaching eighteen and all three children had a large inheritance to look forward to from their grandparents' estate. In addition, their Aunt Jayne had been very generous to her niece and nephews after she was welcomed back into the family, following an earlier indiscretion.

This money, presently in a Trust Fund, with Aunt Jayne acting as Trustee, did allow the children to obtain small amounts from time to time. The whole amount would become available to them on reaching the age of twenty-one.

The three children were very different in personality and, in the case of David and Kate, very different in looks. Kate was attractive with waist length dark hair and blue eyes. She was flirtatious with a very generous nature and in Lizzie's mind, she overshadowed her brother in all areas. Alexander was a charming young boy who shared the same dark hair and blue eyes as Kate.

David was very good looking with light blonde hair and hazel eyes, the complete antithesis of his sister. Unfortunately, he was broody, with an air of arrogance that belied his years, but also tall, and athletic, with many female admirers. His prowess as a horseman meant that the Hall was always full of guests, both male and female, who attended gymkhanas in the extensive grounds and never missed an opportunity to ingratiate themselves with the Hemingway family.

Like Kate, David was flirtatious and very popular, despite his arrogant and sometimes broody nature. In fact, these rather dubious assets appeared to endear him even more to the often shallow young ladies who sought his company.

Lizzie did not enjoy any relationship with David, due not only to her position as a servant, but also to his irrational dislike of her. He was often curt and dismissive, particularly in front of guests. Despite this, Lizzie tried hard to gain David's approval and, occasionally, when she had been especially helpful, David seemed to soften towards her.

SILENT TORMENT

However, this never lasted more than a day, as he would soon revert to his usual obnoxious self.

By complete contrast, Kate had taken to Lizzie from the moment she arrived and looked upon her as an elder sister and confidant, rather than someone employed as a servant. They shared similar looks, both had dark brown hair and they were the same height. The only real difference was in the colour of the eyes, but to the uninitiated they could indeed have passed as sisters.

The girls shared their inner most thoughts and secrets, but Kate was more open and explicit than Lizzie, who sometimes felt a little embarrassed, particularly when Kate enjoyed discussing matters of the heart.

Kate's parents' didn't really approve of such a close relationship, but they turned a blind eye for the most part, particularly as Georgina did not relish discussing 'life' events with her daughter, seeing Lizzie as a sort of mentor. However, both Howard and Georgina Hemingway insisted on a formal relationship between the two girls when visitors and guests were in residence at the Hall.

Overall, Lizzie remained happy and content with her new life, which was, of course, very different to the harsh years spent in Strathy. Lizzie was pleased that, despite her position and without anyone else to confide in, she and Kate shared a special relationship.

Lizzie's thirst for books continued and she spent every spare moment during the week reading avidly, when she wasn't attending to her duties. She listened intently to Mr Lawrence's delivery of lessons to Alexander, or sat quietly in the library reading the many books, which were packed tightly on the shelves. She found maths and English particularly absorbing, but her favourite pastime was to read poetry, which she loved and, of course, Robert Burns especially. His poems, 'A Red, Red Rose', and 'A Bank of Flowers', always reminded her of the love shared between her mother and father and of her home in Strathy, which by now was becoming a distant memory.

༺༻

Lizzie was paid quite well by the Hemingways' and managed to save a little money each week, which she kept with other precious items in the 'keeper' box, underneath a chest of drawers in her bedroom.

The servants' quarters were in the attic of the East wing, where Lizzie's room overlooked the vegetable garden.

The room, though small, was nicely furnished with a single bed, a wardrobe, dressing table and chest of drawers. Pretty blue curtains adorned the window.

William had insisted Lizzie take the pegged rug, counterpane and two antimacassars made by her mother. The embroidered sampler made by Agnes, depicting the little croft in Strathy, the date of her wedding and Lizzie's birth date, hung above the table. Lizzie had added her brother's birth date to the sampler herself.

At the back of the wardrobe and unable to part with them, were the two little dresses, her mother had made, all those years ago in Strathy, when Lizzie was nearly four years old.

Alongside the dresses hung her maid's uniform, which consisted of a blue dress and white apron and three dresses made by herself, with material given to her on her birthday by Kate, plus a coat and bonnet. Lizzie had bought the latter two with her savings from a second hand shop in Glasgow.

It was unusual for servants to be allowed such small luxuries, but the Hemingway's had high expectations in respect of staff morality and standards and were, therefore, generous with those who played by their rules.

Lizzie got on very well with the other servants — Clara Meredith, the cook, who always put aside extra rations for Lizzie to take to her father, on her monthly visits; Dorothy, known as Dottie, the parlour maid; Alice, the between maid and young Jimmy who helped Clara's husband George with the gardening and stabling. The butler and the housekeeper occupied their own separate quarters.

※

On a Tuesday, Lorimer's Farm Produce made a delivery of fresh fish and meat to the Hall. The owner's son, Daniel Lorimer was sweet on Lizzie and she found him very attractive. He was six months older than her and considered to be quite a catch among the local middle class girls, whose families owned small farms around the area. Lizzie, below his class, was a servant without means, so Daniel wasn't under any illusion that his father wouldn't frown on their relationship.

Daniel had dark blonde hair and blue eyes, which lit up whenever Lizzie was around. He knew there would be very strong objections to him marrying her, but she had captivated his heart from the first time their eyes met.

Sometimes, while cook was busy putting the fish and meat into store, Lizzie and Daniel would walk around the grounds and down to the brook. They talked, laughed and ran together, paddling in the cool water before drying their feet off by lying in the meadow. Understandably, these occasions were brief, as Daniel had to continue with his deliveries and Lizzie to her chores. Nevertheless, during these snatched moments, a special relationship began to flourish between them. Once a month after his deliveries were completed, they spent the afternoon together, on Lizzie's extra half day off.

Their relationship only fully developed after a year of walking out together. Before that moment, Daniel had only kissed Lizzie briefly on five or six occasions.

The first time they made love was after he had chased her through the copse of trees and caught her up in the meadow. He had laughingly, but gently, pushed her to the ground before placing his lips on hers and kissing her softly. This had aroused the exciting and breathtaking feelings felt by two young people sharing their first passionate kiss together.

Neither expected the kiss to instigate anything more, but they soon frantically sought out each other's bodies, carried away on a sea of emotion. Daniel eagerly kissed Lizzie's neck and shoulders, as he deliberately pulled her dress down to her waist, which exposed her breasts, before he lightly kissed her nipples. His hands moved sensuously over her thighs and Lizzie knew that she did not have any power to resist him, nor did she want to. He moved his hand further up between her legs and began slowly stroking her most intimate part, arousing her until she was desperate for him to enter her fully. When the moment came for their union to be consummated, they were as eager as each other. Their bodies became one, heightened by feelings that neither had experienced before.

Afterwards, Lizzie felt exhilarated, but deeply ashamed. Giving herself to a man before marriage, was, she had been told, very wrong. 'Soiled goods' was the phrase used deprecatingly, so she considered Daniel's new opinion of her would mean he would not wish to see her again.

Daniel, however, reassured her that this was not so and that, conversely, it would not be the end of their relationship, but the beginning of something special between them.

She wondered how deep their feelings were for each other and whether they were truly in love. After all, he had not mentioned marriage, although Lizzie had hoped he would, but deep down, she knew his family would not consider her a suitable wife and he would be forced to marry someone from his own class.

The sound of laughter brought her back to the present. Turning her head, she spotted Kate and David as their horses trotted toward her. They dismounted and handed them to Jimmy for a rub down before settling them in their stable. A smiling Kate sauntered over to talk to Lizzie. 'Hello Lizzie, have you enjoyed your day?' Kate enquired, whilst David ignored her, striding off purposefully to the main hall.

Lizzie felt sad that David disliked her so much, but replied cheerily. 'Yes Kate, I have been idling my time soaking up the sun and reminiscing. Sounds like you had a good ride. It's a beautiful day.'

'We did actually. David was in a good mood and we rode over to Eastwood, tethered the horses up in Lorimer's field and took a walk into the City. Have you ever been into the City Lizzie? It's so gloriously busy, with people dashing about and others browsing in the shop windows and Hansom cabs with their horses clopping on the cobblestones down the High street. A very exciting place, in fact, where we must go together soon. We could have coffee in Smart's coffee room near the Exchange in Trongate and have a look in the jewellers in King Street.'

Kate's enthusiasm rubbed off quickly on to Lizzie. Not for one moment could she believe it could be possible for her to walk around the town and drink coffee in a public place. It seemed totally outrageous, but maybe something she could do if she were to go with Kate: Kate who was always looking for excitement, especially if there was an element of danger attached. She quickly decided that it was an opportunity not to be missed and questioned her on its feasibility. 'Could we really go together Kate, that would be so much fun? We could wander around the market and peer into those grand shop windows along the High Street and buy some ribbons from Martin's Haberdashery shop.'

Realization quickly dawned as she looked down at her shabby boots and her excitement all but disappeared. 'We would look rather odd together, you in your lovely new blue cloak and me in my old brown one and old black boots. Wouldn't you feel embarrassed?' Lizzie didn't wait for a reply. Common sense told her the idea wouldn't work, but she didn't really want to let it go entirely, so, dismissingly, she repeated the question. 'We couldn't really go together, it's just not possible...is it?'

Kate looked back at her with a glint in her eye that told Lizzie she had something up her sleeve. She grinned and motioned Lizzie to follow her into the summerhouse, where they could not be heard. 'Listen Lizzie, I have been thinking what to do with my older green cloak. You know mother usually sends all our old clothes to the church to sell to make money for the poor box, but the cloak really is hardly worn at all. The only reason I bought a new one is because I don't really like green and blue is so much more me. It would, however, look well on you and we are about the same size,' mused Kate.

'Oh no Kate, your mother would not agree to that. She turns a blind eye to our friendship, but she would draw the line at one of her servants walking out in her daughter's cloak, especially if we were seen by one of her friends. I couldn't possibly accept it,' sighed Lizzie.

'Well I've thought about that too and I have a plan which, if we are clever enough, means she will never know. I will ride Sparks and leave him tethered in Lorimer's field just outside the city boundary. I can take my coat and boots and change in the little disused cottage beyond the old field gate, then walk the rest of the way into the centre, or take a cab ride. I can make sure I have an errand for George on Wednesday, so he will take the trap and you can ask him to drop you off. Isn't that just perfect. What do you think Lizzie?'

Lizzie thought for a moment, 'I don't know Kate, you and David always go riding together on a Tuesday and Wednesday afternoon, what will you tell him?'

Kate smiled knowingly as she continued with her plan. 'I will feign a headache or something after we have ridden over to Bella's and return to Low Wood. He will be delighted to spend some time alone with her. Later I will make a recovery and go riding to clear my head. It will work Lizzie, if we stick to the plan.'

Kate's enthusiasm was such that Lizzie found herself readily agreeing. 'What about my boots, we are not the same size so I couldn't borrow any of yours.'

'That's true, but my green cloak is very long and your boots will hardly show below the hem. You could give them an extra polish and no one will notice. Oh Lizzie it will be lovely to have a friend to go to town with instead of my brother. Boys just aren't interested in shopping,' enthused Kate.

Lizzie smiled and hugged her. 'You are such a good friend to me, are you sure you would not rather go with Bella, she is so sophisticated and would know all the right shops to browse?'

'No Lizzie, Bella is so boring and I can't share secrets with her as I do with you. Despite our different backgrounds, I trust you and you are my dearest friend,' Kate spoke with sincerity.

'All right Kate we'll do it. How will you give me your cloak?' questioned Lizzie.

Kate beamed triumphantly as she informed Lizzie of the final part of her plan. 'Tonight after supper I will talk with mother and explain that I will keep the green cloak to wear on less formal occasions, then I will bring it over to your room when everyone has retired. You can hide it at the back of your wardrobe and on our excursions, you can bundle it inside a bag. Easy!' grinned Kate.

Around midnight, Lizzie heard a gentle tap on her door. 'Lizzie, it's me, Kate, open the door.'

Lizzie unlatched the door and Kate entered. Her eyes quickly scanned the room before she remarked on its lack of space. 'Oh Lizzie this room is so small, how do you cope. I have never been in the servants' quarters before. I didn't realise they were as poky as this.'

Lizzie felt affronted and immediately went on the offensive. 'Well it's twice the size of my room in the croft and the furniture is quite nice. My window looks over the vegetable garden, just like in Strathy, so I quite like it,' Lizzie said meaningfully.

Kate realised that she may have upset Lizzie and quickly made amends. 'Actually, I love your bedspread and that little sampler over the dressing table. Did you make those Lizzie?' Kate questioned.

'No, although I am quite good with a needle. My mother made them for me and they give me comfort whenever I feel sad.'

Lizzie's eyes glazed for a second, but she quickly recovered and smiled at Kate, who continued to be sympathetic. 'It must be so difficult for you, not having your mother around. I cannot imagine how that must feel. I'm so sorry Lizzie,' murmured Kate.

'Don't be, my mother died seventeen years ago and I have learned to cope alone.' Lizzie bit her lip as she gazed down at the floor.

Kate felt guilty, as the last thing she wanted, was to upset her friend. She tried desperately to raise her mood. 'Which you do very well Lizzie, far better than I could ever do. You always manage to make the best of everything.'

Lizzie felt cheered at the compliment and was eager for Kate to stay a while. 'Have you got time to sit and chat Kate? I could fetch some cocoa.'

Kate nodded. 'Well I'll have to skip the cocoa, but I could stay for a while. I have brought the cloak, but I bumped into the housekeeper in the corridor and she gave me a questioning look, but...' she grinned, 'I managed to give her the brush off.'

Lizzie examined the cloak as Kate laid it across the bed. 'Oh it's really lovely. Are you sure you want to give it away?' Lizzie spoke hesitantly, but secretly hoped for a positive reply.

Kate replied enthusiastically and smiled at Lizzie. 'Yes, of course, Lizzie. You help me in so many ways, it really isn't anything much, but it will ensure a successful day out in town.'

Lizzie was relieved that Kate wasn't about to take it away again and joined in her excitement. 'Okay, I will put it to the back of my wardrobe. I can't wait to go. My day off is on Wednesday next week. I will explain to my father tomorrow that I will not be able to see him that day. I do feel quite guilty, as he does look forward to my visits. However, he will not be alone, as Alice Rutherford, his companion, is very good company for him.'

⁂

The girls had been chatting away without realising the time, despite Kate's intention to only stay a short while, when Kate interrupted Lizzie mid sentence because she heard a sudden creaking sound in the corridor outside her room. 'Shh Lizzie,' Kate whispered, 'I think I can hear footsteps outside your room. I don't want anyone knowing I am here.'

Lizzie giggled. 'Don't worry, it will probably be Clara, she is always up and down visiting the toilet during the night. She is slightly deaf, so she won't have heard us.'

'I'd better go now though Lizzie. I will see you tomorrow and we can talk again about the arrangements.'

They bade each other good night and Kate slipped quietly out of the room and back to her own quarters.

Lizzie settled down in her bed, but sleep eluded her, her mind buzzing with thoughts of the little escapade they had planned and whether they could pull it off without anyone finding out. She hoped so, as Kate was a lot of fun, although sometimes she took too many risks. Perhaps it was time though, she said to herself, that I lived a little and went out into the big wide world. After all, I will soon be twenty-one!

⁂

Robert Cameron had followed his father and sister to the lowlands late in 1839, after Martha Stewart's sudden death from consumption in July 1837, followed by Donald one year later, just before his 61st birthday.

Robert inherited Donald's farm, but the happy memories could no longer hold him, so he sold up, using the money to purchase a small farm on the outskirts of Glasgow, where it was easier to employ labourers.

It hadn't taken long to find Lizzie and his father, as the first person he spoke to directed him to the parish priest, Josiah Monks, who readily reunited the family. Lizzie had been delighted to meet up with her brother again and now he lived near Glasgow, she could see him more often.

William's relationship with his son was strained at first, but gradually he mellowed, after realising the wrong he had precipitated seventeen years earlier. They found they had a lot in common with William able to give Robert good advice on farming techniques.

Robert's own cottage was close to his farm so it wasn't practical for him to live with his father, but he insisted on engaging a companion/housekeeper to look after William. He knew that he had struggled with the household chores and cooking after Lizzie left.

Once again, Josiah came to the rescue and introduced Alice Rutherford to William. Alice had just lost her husband and was finding life hard to cope alone. Companionship was what they both needed and suitable arrangements were made for her to live with William as his housekeeper.

Bright and early on Wednesday morning, Kate and Lizzie met in the summerhouse, hardly able to contain their excitement.

'I can't stay long Lizzie, as I have promised to sit with mother and finish embroidering the sampler which she thinks will somehow enhance my skills and make me a better prospect for marriage. She doesn't understand that most men would rather their wives be good in the bedroom than sewing their socks,' laughed Kate.

'Really Kate, you sometimes make me blush. How do you know all these things?'

'Well, instead of reading Charles Darwin's book on 'The Origin Of The Species', which father gave me last Christmas, I read Henry Fielding's novel, 'Tom Jones', which Aunt Jayne lent to me. I saw her reading it on her last visit. I could lend it to you, but you would have to keep it safe. Mother would kill me if she knew I had read it and, more importantly, who had given it to me.'

'Okay, it sounds rather racy, but why not,' mused Lizzie.

'Now Lizzie, about next Wednesday. You need to travel into town and arrive about ten thirty. Meet me outside the new Buchanon Hotel on Buchanon Street, off the High Street. George will know it, as he took mother and father there. They had an invitation for its opening earlier this year. Don't forget to put your green cloak into a bag and polish up your black boots. You could wear that lovely cream bonnet you keep for Sundays and you can take one of my parasols from the hallstand. Ask George to bring the trap round to the back so that you don't attract attention. My parents are travelling to Edinburgh on Monday and won't be back until Thursday morning, as you know. I will keep David busy by suggesting we ride over to Bella's early on Wednesday morning, about eight thirty. Then I will feign a headache and ride down to the disused cottage in Lorimer's field and meet you in town at ten thirty. David will probably stay at Bella's until early evening. After we meet, we can go into the hotel and you can change into your green cloak - then we can have some fun!'

'Gosh Kate, I am really nervous. Supposing someone sees me and asks what I have in the bag. It isn't something I can easily hide.'

Kate thought for a moment and then came up with an idea. 'You can say they are clothes that mother has asked you to take to the church for the poor sale.'

'Mmm, that sounds plausible, but I will try and keep the bag out of sight. Dottie and Alice will be busy helping cook with the baking and Jimmy will be helping George in mucking out the stables, so I should be able to get away unseen.'

※

Georgina Hemingway rang the servants' bell to ascertain the whereabouts of her daughter. She felt it was particularly important for Kate to be an accomplished seamstress, because her daughter was not academically minded. This could prove difficult when running a household of her own after she married. She would probably be better at overseeing the running of the staff, than becoming involved in book keeping. Georgina herself had private tuition. Howard, who was quite happy for his wife to look after any financial business, encouraged her. Howard's passion was hunting, fishing and shooting, in that order and he had little, if anything, to do with running the household.

'That's the servants' bell Lizzie; it will be mother wanting to know where I am. I'd better go now, I'll see you later.'

Kate loved secrets and relished being part of a plan, which involved subterfuge. It gave an air of mystery to her life and she was always looking for a scheme which would give her a rush of adrenalin, just like the times she rode her horse, Sparks, too fast over the moor land. She loved the speed and total abandonment as the horse galloped to her command. The feel of the wind racing through her hair and the sun on her back made her feel alive.

Kate disliked learning and was an inattentive pupil. She preferred to spend her time riding and meeting boys rather than studying. All she really wanted in life was to marry a man who would love her and allow her freedom to ride and shop! She loved shopping and buying new clothes, not just for herself, because she had a generous nature and enjoyed spoiling her family and friends with little gifts. Kate Hemingway was a girl who lived life on the edge, but, inevitably, there would be a cost.

CHAPTER SIX

Executing the Plan

Lizzie looked at her watch, it was eight thirty on Wednesday morning, a week since she and Kate had hatched their plan to meet up in Glasgow town centre. She looked out of the kitchen window and watched Kate and David mount their horses for the journey over to Bella's. When they disappeared from view, she returned to her room in preparation for her visit to town with George.

She carefully polished her black boots and brushed her hair into a chignon on top of her head, allowing some stray dark curls to fall down around the side of her face and the nape of her neck.

She took out her best dress, which she had made herself, with fabric given to her by Kate. It was a pale green and white cotton pin stripe with a white Peter Pan collar and a row of decorative mother of pearl buttons down the bodice and a straight cut pleated skirt. She twirled around in front of the mirror contemplating the effect, which was rather fetching. She thought she would pass muster walking alongside Kate.

She waited until Kate returned, before carefully folding the green cloak, which she placed into a bag, together with her cream bonnet. Then donned her old brown coat, before making her way down through the servants' quarters and out of the back door. George was waiting with the trap and they were soon passing through the large main gates on their way into the city.

Lizzie was a little nervous as she waited outside the Buchanon Hotel for Kate to arrive. The centre was quite busy with people shopping and browsing the delights of the window displays. Excitement began to bubble up inside her as she sighted Kate walking towards her, giving a cheery wave and a smile.

Kate motioned to Lizzie to precede her up the steps and into the main foyer. 'You can change in the powder room. I know the porter quite well, so he won't mind keeping the bag in the little room at the back where guests store their cases.'

The pair proceeded to the main reception desk and the young girl recognised Kate, as she had seen her on previous occasions with her parents, when they took afternoon tea after visiting the galleries. 'Hello Miss Hemingway, will you be taking lunch today?' she asked.

'No, but we may take tea later this afternoon. We would, however, like to use the powder room, as we have some shopping to do.'

The young receptionist glanced at Lizzie. She was surprised at the shabbiness of the coat, but made no comment, as she had learned over the years not to ask questions. When a person was accompanied by someone of high social standing such as Miss Hemmingway, it was really none of her business what kind of company that person chose to keep.

She smiled at both girls, but addressed Kate and gestured for them to follow her. 'Here you are Miss, take your time.'

The receptionist bobbed a curtsy after Kate slipped her a tuppenny tip, then returned to the desk.

Lizzie felt a little humiliated, but soon cheered up when the green cloak slipped easily over her shoulders and after putting on the cream bonnet, she felt transformed.

Kate couldn't help but admire how wonderful Lizzie appeared. 'Why Lizzie you look absolutely stunning, the dress complements the cloak perfectly and your hair looks very sophisticated.'

Lizzie blushed and pushed her old brown coat into the bag, before following Kate back to reception. Kate gave the porter one of her most dazzling smiles and asked him to keep the bag for her.

'Why yes, that isn't a problem Miss, it will be waiting for you when you return.'

With that, the girls disappeared through the doors and out into the throng of people.

'Well Lizzie, what shall we do first? I would like to buy some fabric from that shop in the High Street. I've heard they have had a delivery of some very fashionable cotton fabrics and silks.'

Lizzie did not mind what they did, as she was happy to be walking around in her expensive cloak, feeling like royalty. 'That's sounds nice Kate, I'll just follow you.'

The little bell tinkled as they opened the door of Frobisher's Fabrics. They walked up to the counter and a neatly dressed assistant offered her help.

She addressed Kate in a rather exaggerated upper class voice. 'What can I show you today modam? We have just had a delivery of some wonderful silk and some very modern cottons.'

Lizzie's eyes stared in wonderment at the array of fabrics on offer, all piled high in large rolls on shelves around the store. Kate asked to see some blue silk that had caught her eye near the entrance to the shop. 'Do you like this Lizzie? I thought I would have a dress made for mother's dinner party next month and I also need some lace and pearl buttons. I rather think the latest off the shoulder neckline, leg-o-mutton sleeves and a full hooped skirt, would be pleasing.'

The assistant interceded, ignoring Lizzie, 'If I can offer an opinion modam, the blue silk would really enhance the colour of your eyes. It is just perfect for you.'

'Mmm, you may offer an opinion, but I would really value my friend's opinion, actually. Elizabeth, do you think it is suitable?'

Lizzie looked admiringly at the beautiful fabric draped across the counter. 'Yes, I think the colour is gorgeous. I think you will command many admiring glances. James Renwick had better keep a close eye on you, or he will be in danger of losing out to some other suitor.'

'Oh Elizabeth, you always say the nicest things. Right, I would like sufficient quantity to make up a dress as

I described and please deliver to Low Wood Hall. The address will be in your book.'

The assistant sucked in her cheeks as she felt the dismissal of this prestigious customer, but continued to act professionally. 'Yes, modam. Is there anything else you would like today?'

Kate glanced around the shop and speculated as to whether Lizzie might also be making a purchase, before turning to the assistant. 'Well that depends on Elizabeth. She may have seen something she absolutely cannot be without. Have you seen anything you like Elizabeth?'

Lizzie could not believe that Kate had put her in such an awkward position. She knew that she would never be able to buy more than half a yard of fabric from this expensive shop, but before she could decline, Kate confirmed that anything they bought today should be billed to her mother's account. 'Well Elizabeth, would you like that pastel green cotton chambray I saw you admiring in the window? You will need a couple more dresses if we are to come to town on a regular basis.'

Lizzie was at a loss for words and mumbled a reply. 'Well err, yes that would be lovely and thank you Kate.'

'That's my pleasure, or rather my mother's,' laughed Kate. 'We will take sufficient fabric for a day dress for my friend and five yards of that heavy cotton fabric in bright emerald green as well.'

'Very well, modam. Will that be all?'

'I think so, thank you. Good-day.'

Kate vacated the shop and exploded into fits of giggles, once the door had closed behind them. She mimicked the assistant mercilessly. 'Very well modom, will that be all?'

'You are awful Kate, the assistant was only doing her job.'

'I know Lizzie, but they sometimes sound so pompous. It's all so put on, it makes me laugh. Shall we go to Smarts and have that coffee now?'

Lizzie followed Kate down the High Street into Trongate, where Smart's coffee house stood in front of the Exchange.

'Now Lizzie we need to wait outside until we see a single gentleman entering, as we cannot go into the shop unaccompanied.'

They waited a few minutes, until a middle-aged gentleman, who could have passed for Kate's father, entered the shop and followed him in quickly.

Kate struck up a conversation with the gentleman, who responded immediately by asking if they would like a coffee and slice of cake each.

'Why thank you sir, we will be seated over near the window.'

The assistant did not pass comment on the effrontery of the two ladies, who knew very well that they should be accompanied by a male when entering a coffee house, but as the gentleman had paid for the drinks, he let it pass.

Kate giggled as she seated herself at the table. 'Well that went to plan. It's a silly idea anyway, ladies not being allowed into certain establishments without being accompanied - it's complete tosh!'

'Sometimes Kate, I think you will land us in a lot of trouble. What would that gentleman have thought, following him up to the counter like that?'

'Thought? I shouldn't think he <u>thought</u> anything. He could see we were respectable and, anyway, he enjoyed the flattery.'

Lizzie nodded her head sagely, but secretly thought that Kate would do well to be a little more reserved on occasion and not take quite so many risks. She felt that Kate lived her life 'on the edge' and worried about possible consequences. Then again, she had certainly added some spice to her own life. Kate was very confident in everything she did and certainly knew how to look after herself. Inadvertently, Lizzie spoke her thoughts out loud. 'Maybe, I shouldn't worry so much and just enjoy the freedom.'

'Well Lizzie, good for you, that's the attitude. If we didn't take a few risks now and again, life would be pretty boring don't you think?'

Lizzie nodded in agreement. 'You are probably right. I'll try and relax more. This cake is delicious and the coffee is a real treat.'

※

Later, several young men observed the girls from outside Smart's window as they passed on their way to the bar at the Exchange. Lizzie immediately recognised Daniel Lorimer and her brother, Robert. She quickly looked away, but not before Daniel had seen her face. He was quite surprised at seeing Lizzie in the city centre and turned to Robert for confirmation that he wasn't seeing things. 'Isn't that your sister in there Rob? I didn't know she came into town.'

Robert peered into the window of the coffee house in amazement. 'You are right, it is Lizzie, but who is that sitting with her?'

'Don't you know Kate Hemingway? She is the daughter of the Hemingway's up at Low Wood Hall.'

'Oh, I think Lizzie has mentioned her, but I can't imagine what she is doing sitting having coffee with her.'

The other three young men were also admiring the two beautiful girls sitting in the window.

Finlay McEwan, Andrew Laing and Derek Ramsay gesticulated for the girls to join them outside. They hoped to persuade them to accompany their group to the Exchange and take a drink in the little courtyard.

'Those young men are flirting with us Lizzie. Do you know them?'

'Well yes, I do. It's my brother Robert and Daniel Lorimer, but I do not know any of the others.'

Kate eyed Finlay, speculatively and became interested in talking to them. 'The one with the red neckerchief is rather handsome. Shall we go out and join them Lizzie?'

Lizzie ignored the boys and quietly gave her opinion. 'I don't think we should Kate. We might be seen by someone known to your parents and then our visits will surely be curtailed.'

'There you go again Lizzie. What harm can it do? They all look perfectly well mannered young men. I mean, you even know two of them and I am sure their friends will be equally respectable. Come on, finish your drink and we will go outside.'

Lizzie was not at all sure that this was one of Kate's better ideas and was hesitant in going along with her plan. 'What if we <u>are</u> spotted by someone?'

'Well, what if we are? I doubt it will be any of my parents' friends, as this area is not somewhere they will frequent. Well, I am going, are you coming?'

Lizzie was engulfed by a feeling of fait accompli and meekly followed Kate outside, where the young men were gathered. They were in high spirits and their mood was infectious. Kate was in her element and talking and flirting freely with the boys. Lizzie on the other hand had become withdrawn and stood quietly to one side, until Daniel Lorimer came over to her and struck up a conversation. 'It is lovely to see you Lizzie. I can't believe our luck at meeting up like this. I never realised you came into town, you've never said.'

'No, well I've only ever been once before, when I purchased a bonnet...though it is nice to see you too.'

Now that the ice had been broken, she continued talking to Daniel and visibly relaxed, as she felt more comfortable with the situation.

They soon moved round to the Exchange and sat outside in the warm sunshine and Lizzie even began to enjoy herself. Kate was talking avidly to the other four boys, which meant Lizzie had Daniel's sole attention for the next hour.

Kate suggested that they meet up again the following week and a couple of the group asked if anyone would mind if they brought their girlfriends along, to which nobody objected.

By the end of the afternoon, Lizzie was sorry that they had to leave, but was happy that these visits would give Daniel and herself more time to spend together. Seeing her brother was also enjoyable, as they had never had the chance to rekindle their sibling relationship on a social level.

Throughout the long hot summer, Lizzie and Kate went into town as often as they could.

Lizzie spent as much time as possible with Daniel, without ignoring the others and Kate divided her time equally between the boys, except when they had girlfriends in tow. A new girlfriend would be introduced to the group by the boys every so often, with the exception of Daniel; but everyone accepted these comings and goings, just happy to be enjoying the freedom of being in the city at a time when young ladies were normally chaperoned.

A change to this arrangement came in early autumn, when Kate started going into town on other days, when Lizzie was working. She met up with whomsoever of the boys were around at the time. These visits were also secret and she enrolled the help of her brother to cover the fact that she was going into town alone.

Her brother, David was as anxious as Kate for an alibi, which would enable him to spend time alone with Bella. Under normal circumstances, he could only meet Bella if Kate went over with him to see her, or if Bella visited them at Low Wood. This plan worked well for the three of them. Kate and David would go over to ride with Bella and her parents were happy to allow them to ride through the meadows adjacent to Low Wood Hall. Unbeknown to them, Kate would leave the couple alone and ride off to her own assignation. She would tether her horse in Lorimer's field and leave her riding gear in the disused cottage.

It was on one of these occasions, when she was having a drink with some of the young men, that she realised her strong feelings towards one of them was more difficult to hide. He did bring a girlfriend along from time to time, but there was no one to whom he was committed. For some time now, they had recognised the chemistry building up between them. Just a look, or a brushing of hands, would send a spark of electricity surging through her body.

Kate compared these feelings with those she held for James Renwick, but she knew that the emotions she felt when she was with him did not match her feelings now. So far, James and she had not had the opportunity to take their relationship further and she wasn't sure that she wanted to anyway. She did know that the feelings she had for this particular young man were unlike any she had experienced before. It seemed something special was happening between them, so when the opportunity arose, they made arrangements to meet each other alone.

The meeting place was to be the disused cottage at the far end of Lorimer's field, quite close to the Low Wood estate. Kate reasoned that, she had never seen anyone around when she left her riding clothes in the cottage, so it was unlikely they would be discovered.

The first time they met, they felt a little awkward. Neither had previously had the opportunity to be alone with a member of the opposite sex, without a risk of being disturbed and Kate was always chaperoned when there were young men present. For his part, the young man had taken a few girls out and indulged in some heavy petting on a couple of occasions, but had not yet had the opportunity to be intimate with any one of them.

At the cottage, they talked for a while but both knew that this was only the beginning and they would be powerless to stop the inevitable, as the emotions engulfing them were far too intense.

To give them courage, Kate produced a hip flask, borrowed from her brother, which he used whilst riding on cold days. It contained brandy from her father's drinks cabinet. The spirit fortified them as they sat together on the old worn couch that occupied a corner of the small living room. They felt exhilarated and were further aroused, as the brandy slipped smoothly and easily down their throats.

Now totally relaxed, the pair embraced and their mouths caressed each other's lips and neck, their bodies pressed together passionately and it wasn't long before they were both lying naked on the rug.

Their arousal was complete, enhanced by the sensual smell of Kate's perfume and neither could hold back. Their quest to quench their desires were heightened by the feelings and emotions rushing through their bodies and their lovemaking was frantic. Both were eager to experience the sensual heights of a first sexual encounter.

Long afterward, Kate worried that he might think of her as cheap and easy and she wondered whether he would want to meet with her again. However, her fears were allayed, as he told her that he was just as keen as she and that she had been occupying his mind for ages. He never dreamed she would want to be with him and pointed out the difference in their class status. Kate assured him that she didn't care a fig for class differences and so they both agreed to meet, when possible, once a fortnight at the cottage.

After their frequent trysts, they realised they had fallen deeply in love and promised each other they would be together always; despite the inevitable difficulties of their differing social backgrounds. They vowed to resolve problems, no matter how difficult they became. However, neither could have foreseen in those first gloriously heady days, the problems that would present themselves. These, sadly, would be insurmountable.

Kate's mind was constantly filled with delicious memories of their times together, but she was still happy to go into town with Lizzie whenever they could. The lovers agreed to keep their relationship secret and, although it was really difficult, they worked hard at ensuring that suspicions of their love for each other were hidden from the group.

They continued to meet, even when the onset of winter meant the cottage was cold and unwelcoming. Each brought several luxury items to make their meetings more comfortable. They could not risk building a fire, but still made love by candlelight on dark winter afternoons. Warmth was generated by their lovemaking and drinking Kate's father's brandy, which had become a ritual from the first time they met.

Kate always arrived early to place a lighted candle in the window, as a signal that she was present and ready waiting for him, so that her lover would not have to walk the half mile from the old gate unnecessarily.

The flickering flame could only be seen from the gate, which they had padlocked, each keeping a key. The overgrown bridle path, lead from the gate and dipped down to the cottage. This meant that anyone wanting to reach the cottage could only do so on foot. They would have to leave their horses tethered in the adjoining field. Luckily, during the four months since they had begun meeting, not once did any members of the Lorimer family venture down to the cottage. Consequently, their meetings remained a secret.

In December 1840, Lizzie received the worse news possible. Her beloved father, William, had become seriously ill. He had been suffering for weeks with a really bad bout of bronchitis and was having daily visits by the doctor, paid for by Robert.

Lizzie and Robert were really worried. They realised their father had become morose again, especially so during the dark nights and cold days of winter. Moreover, he had had to give up his job after the autumn, due to his failing health, which didn't help, so Robert struck a bargain with the farmer, who had grown very fond of his father. He would allow William to remain in the cottage, until he was well again. William got his wish, as he was adamant that he did not want to move in with Robert. He stated he was comfortable where he was and was being well looked after by Alice.

During the day, he could be found sitting in his chair, staring out of the window, over towards the meadows and lost in his own thoughts. Sometimes, in the early evenings and despite the cold, he wrapped up warmly and sat out on the veranda looking up at the stars. Often he would smile to himself and at other times he would have a tear in his eye, as his memories of Strathy and Agnes came flooding back, as if it were yesterday.

Both knew that William had never got over the loss of their mother and feared he was giving up on life, even though he was not really old, only forty-six.

Sadly, he continued to deteriorate, despite everyone's best efforts, including the devoted Alice, who had, for a time, lifted his spirits.

The end came early one morning in late December. Dawn broke to reveal a bright blue sky, but there was a chill in the air and Alice had left it a little later than usual to take William his early morning cup of tea. She had pulled back the curtains and walked towards the bed. Usually, William was sitting up ready to face the day, but this morning, unlike other mornings, he had not woken and had slipped away peacefully in his sleep to be with Agnes, his one true love.

Chapter Seven

Destinies

At dawn on a crisp April morning, daffodils nodded their heads in the light breeze under a clear blue sky. Lizzie could hear the bleating of newborn lambs far in the distance, quite clearly, which turned her thoughts to Strathy, where she had sat in the meadows gazing in wonderment at all the beautiful sights nature had to offer.

It was four months since William died, but she thought about him frequently. She consoled herself that her parents were together again, this time forever. There were bad days and better days, but Kate, Daniel and Robert helped her through the bad ones.

Her relationship with Daniel was good, and her brother's farm was continuing to thrive. Life was slowly getting back to normal and the warm spring sunshine cheered her mood, but, unbeknown to Lizzie, it would not last; certain revelations would significantly change her life again.

She fetched a book from the library to read on the grassy bank in front of Low Wood Hall, but as she passed the summerhouse, she heard heart rendering sobbing coming from the open doors. She glanced inside and saw Kate sitting on the floor with her head in her hands. 'Whatever is wrong Kate? What are you doing here sitting on the floor?'

Kate's anguished, tear stained face peered at Lizzie as she stepped inside. 'Oh, Lizzie, it is the worst thing ever. I just don't know what I am going to do. I can't tell anyone, it is just too dreadful.'

'Well Kate, just about everyone will know you are distressed if they hear you sobbing, as if the world is about to end. Do you want to tell me what is wrong?'

After a long silence, Kate sighed resignedly. 'All right Lizzie, I will and I must gather myself together. Let's go up to your room. Are the other servants about, do you know?'

'No they're not, actually, cook has been sent for by your mother, something to do with arrangements for the soiree on Saturday afternoon and Dottie and Alice are preparing bedrooms.'

Kate followed Lizzie to her room through the servants' quarters, still quietly sobbing and obviously distressed.

'Sit here on the bed Kate and I will fetch us a pot of tea from the kitchen.'

Kate became panicky. 'Please do not let anyone see you, because they will wonder why you are taking two cups up to your room.'

'Don't worry Kate, I will be careful. I'll be back in a jiffy.'

Lizzie poured out two cups of the freshly brewed liquid and put two extra spoonfuls of sugar in Kate's. She observed her anxiously as she handed her the cup.

Kate sipped slowly at the sweet beverage and sat back on the bed. She managed, between sobs, to reveal the reason for her distress. 'Lizzie, you are going to be very ashamed of me...I feel so scared for the future...You see, I think I am having a baby,' she wailed.

With shocked disbelief, Lizzie tried to absorb the information that had just been imparted to her, before bombarding Kate with questions. 'Oh Kate, I'm so sorry. Are you sure? Why are you so certain? Does James know?...It is James' isn't it?...Oh my God Kate, I'm sorry, I should not have even asked you that.'

Kate hesitated for a moment, quickly trying to decide the amount of information that could be revealed to Lizzie. She trusted her implicitly, but wasn't sure that Lizzie was ready to hear the truth. At this stage, she decided to go along with Lizzie's assumptions that James was the father. That way, she didn't have to tell her friend a direct lie. 'Oh Lizzie, James doesn't know and I cannot tell him. I must be pregnant, as I haven't had my menses for four months now and I feel nauseous most mornings. I understand that is another sign. Oh…oh…what will I do? What will mother say? Oh Lizzie, Lizzie, I am so scared.'

Lizzie placed her arm around her friend's shoulders and muttered soothing words, while she wildly cast around for more words of comfort that would settle Kate down. To her mind though, the situation seemed pretty desperate. 'Look Kate, why can't you tell James? I am sure he will stand by you. He absolutely adores you as far as I can see.'

'No Lizzie, I cannot tell him…well not yet anyway and maybe never. I need to talk to Aunt Jayne. She will know what to do. Meanwhile, no one else must know. Promise me Lizzie you won't tell another living soul?'

'No, no, of course not Kate. Your secret is safe with me and I think it is a very good idea to contact Aunt Jayne. Why don't you write a letter now and get George to post it for you? Meanwhile, no one will guess you are pregnant, as you are not showing yet and it may not be at all obvious for a couple more months.'

Kate stopped sobbing and felt calmer, having shared her secret with Lizzie and whose advice to write to Aunt Jayne straight away seemed a good idea. 'Thank goodness for the penny post. I will pen a letter to her now. Thank you for listening to me Lizzie, you are a true friend.'

'It's all right Kate. Now try not to worry. I am sure Aunt Jayne will know what to do.'

Kate went off to her room and started to write to Aunt Jayne. She would ask if she could possibly come up and stay for a while to help her sort things out, especially with her mother. She would not reveal the name of the father, but hoped Aunt Jayne would understand her predicament.

She sealed the envelope and lay back on her bed thinking about the dozen or more times they had made love. They had been so careful, quite sure that such a thing couldn't happen; especially because a pregnancy would mean an end to their relationship.

One thing was clear, she did not regret making love with the man she adored, even if it resulted in an unwanted pregnancy. However, that fact would definitely change her future, which was something she couldn't bear to contemplate.

CHAPTER EIGHT

Confessions

Lizzie had just completed her chores and was seated in the library browsing over some backdated weekly periodicals'. One written by Charles Dickens, entitled 'Master Humphrey's Clock', contained a serialisation of the novel, 'The Old Curiosity Shop'. She was losing herself in the story and did not hear Kate approach, but jumped as she suddenly appeared at her shoulder. 'Hi Kate, you startled me, I was really engrossed in this serialisation by Charles Dickens, have you read it?'

'No, no I haven't. Not really my kind of thing,' she replied absently. She did not mean to sound dismissive, but felt her news could not wait. 'Lizzie, I have some really good news. Aunt Jayne is coming to stay with us for a couple of months. She wrote to me and suggested a visit, as she has not been up for a while, due to her business commitments. Aubrey has returned from South America after three months away and feels that Aunt Jayne deserves a break. She has been running the business almost single-handed in his absence. Reading between the lines, she understands my problem and says she will have a long talk with me after she arrives.'

Lizzie put down her paper and turned to give Kate her undivided attention. 'Well, Kate that's excellent news. Perhaps if she also has a talk with your mother, they could work something out...adoption may be?'

Kate thought about this prospect and decided that it might be a good alternative, in the absence of any other suggestion. 'I am not sure Lizzie, but what I do know is that Aunt Jayne will give me sound advice.'

Kate's parents referred to Jayne Munroe as the 'black sheep' of the family. She had a child born out of wedlock when she was seventeen and, although she was not disinherited, her parents threw her out. Her sister, Georgina, Kate's mother, never really forgave her for inflicting such pain on the family, as it had a terrible impact on their parents, especially their mother, who practically became a recluse for years' after.

According to Georgina, Jayne then married a most unsuitable man, named Aubrey Munroe. He gambled and drank a fair bit, but had a huge stroke of luck, when he won a large amount of money, following a dubious 'tip-off' on the horses.

He ploughed his winnings into importing cotton from the American South, eventually building a large cotton-spinning factory in London. He became more successful in 1837, when he capitalised on falling cotton prices. He stockpiled his cloths and sold them on at inflated prices when cotton prices rose again. These successes lead to the opening of a clothing factory in the suburbs of Glasgow.

The sisters were reunited again, following the death of their parents. Jayne gave half of her inheritance to be put in Trust for Georgina's children, in an attempt to show how sorry she was for all the hurt she had caused. In turn, Georgina asked that Jayne be a godmother to her three children.

Jayne was making this particular visit to the family, on the pretext of taking a well-earned rest, but, of course, her real reason was to help her niece out of a sticky situation. She did, however, see this as an opportunity to re-establish good relations with the family.

David was also anticipating Aunt Jayne's visit with relish, as he knew it would liven up the house and bring about some interesting debates. David in particular loved a good debate and Aunt Jayne was always controversial. Besides which, he had noticed recently that his sister had lost some of her joie de vivre. Significantly, she no longer wished to participate in their mutual subterfuge, which had resulted in his liaisons with Bella being severely curtailed.

Lizzie resumed her reading of the Dickens serialisation, but Kate persisted in interrupting her, by proffering information on Aunt Jayne's visit. Inevitably, Lizzie capitulated and resignedly put away the papers before focusing her attention back on Kate, who was glowing with excited anticipation. 'She will be coming over on Sunday, after visiting the Glasgow factory on the Saturday. Mother asked me to organise the airing of the blue room on the first floor in the West wing for her. Could you ask Dottie to see to that and make up the bed for her please Lizzie?'

'Yes, of course...I will look forward to meeting her again,' she smiled.

Kate's thoughts were jumping ahead as she made her next ill thought out suggestion. 'I was thinking Lizzie that we might make a visit to Glasgow next week, as I have missed meeting our friends. It's been over three months since we were last there and I am feeling much better now the nauseous feelings have subsided.'

The real reason was that Kate desperately wanted to see her lover again. Just to be close to him one last time. She knew that they could not continue with their relationship and that they would never again be able to meet in secret. She still loved him so very much but he would never know the reason she failed to meet him at the cottage. He would only be aware that when he arrived at the gate, the light wouldn't be shining in the cottage window.

It was cold inside and the rain had seeped under the door, wetting the floor and rug of the living room and there was no sign of Kate. He could not believe she hadn't turned up without a good reason, so consequently looked around for a message from her. Sadly, there was nothing, no clue at all as to why she had not come to meet him.

He waited for several hours, but left with a heavy heart, believing that she no longer loved him. Because he could not contact her he would have to suffer his pain in silence. In desperation, he visited the cottage on two more occasions, but still she stayed away.

He discovered from the other farmers that the girls had not turned up for the last two weeks either, although Daniel had informed them that Lizzie said Kate was feeling off colour so they would be curtailing their visits for a while.

He knew that if Kate and Lizzie ever met up with the group again, it would be agony for him to bear, if he wasn't to alert the others to his desolation. He had to keep up the pretence that he was happy to meet with them all, but secretly he hoped that she would not join them again — ever, so that he could bear his grief at losing her in isolation.

Kate continued to press Lizzie into going into town once more.

Lizzie obviously valued the outings with Kate very much, as it gave her another opportunity to meet with Daniel, but she wasn't sure, given the present circumstances, that it would be wise for Kate to meet the others. They would certainly enquire as to the reason for their absence. Moreover, although she had told Daniel that Kate had been unwell, it was rather a long time for a young girl to suffer with a malaise. Significantly, she had never been entirely sure that Daniel had believed her because she had been less than convincing, hence her cautious reply. 'I'm not sure whether that is such a good idea Kate, as I'm sure that Finlay has feelings for you. He does not flirt openly, but I sometimes catch him looking at you with a longing look in his eyes, which shouldn't be encouraged now that you are pregnant. James wouldn't be too pleased if he found out and let's face it Kate, the young farmers are below your class,' Lizzie admonished jokingly.

Lizzie was not prepared for the annoyance in Kate's voice as she responded to the jibe. 'You're not my father Lizzie. So what if Finlay finds me attractive, it's harmless fun and anyway I quite like him. I've told you before, the class thing really doesn't bother me. Some of those young farmers can hold really interesting conversations, unlike some of the upper class gentlemen who can only talk stocks, shares and hunting. I get so bored listening to them droning on and anyway, I didn't notice you being in a hurry to take leave of their company on the last occasion. You and Daniel seem closer than ever these days. He seems quite keen on you, rather good-looking too,' mused Kate.

Lizzie didn't wish to dampen Kate's sudden new found zest for life, but anxious that her relationship with Daniel should be played down, she manoeuvred tactfully. 'Well yes, but you shouldn't encourage them so much, as nothing can come of any of it. I would never be considered marriage material by Daniel's family and you are definitely a class above all of them.'

Lizzie felt awkward in divulging information about Daniel to Kate, but she knew she didn't really stand a chance of any future with him and didn't want Kate to think her foolish that she was holding out any hope of a long-term relationship with Daniel.

Unfortunately for Lizzie, Kate continued on this topic, which she found fascinating. 'Sometimes I don't understand you Lizzie, if I am okay with passing the time of day with some very personable young men, why should you be worried about it?'

'I'm not really worried, but as I've said before, it's just that if we were ever caught in their company by any of your mother's friends, we would be in deep water and I would probably lose my job,' countered Lizzie.

'Let's not think about that because, as I have also said before, I can't see any of mother's friends frequenting that particular part of the town. Anyway, it's of no consequence, I would take all the blame myself and say I forced you to go with me. Don't worry Lizzie, nothing will be known of our secret outings.'

CHAPTER NINE

Aunt Jayne's Visit

The front door of Low Wood had been left open, cooling the air in the downstairs rooms, which were unusually warm for the end of May. Jayne Munroe arrived earlier than expected on Sunday morning and breezed into the dining room where breakfast was being cleared away.

She addressed the maid in a cheery voice. 'Hello there, Dorothy isn't it? The butler doesn't appear to be around, so can you let my sister know I have arrived? It's rather warm outside and I could do with a nice cool drink.'

Dottie looked up from loading a tray of dirty dishes, which she was preparing to take to the kitchen. 'Hello madam, yes I will let Mrs Hemingway know immediately. She will probably be a few minutes, as she is over in the West wing, making last minute arrangements for your visit. In the meantime, shall I bring a jug of fresh lemonade for you madam?'

'Yes Dorothy, that would be lovely. Tell Geor...Mrs Hemingway that I will be in the library. I have left my trunk by the hat stand in the hall. Would you be a darling and arrange for it to be taken to my room?'

'Yes madam.'

Dottie hurried away in search of Mrs Hemingway and Jayne Munroe walked along the hall to the library.

Lizzie was returning to the kitchen via the hall, after giving the blue room a last dust over and throwing open the windows to let in some air, when she encountered Jayne Munroe standing at the library door.

Aunt Jayne addressed Lizzie formally, as she knew Georgina did not wish to encourage familiarity with any of the servants. 'Hello Elizabeth, how are you? I can see that you are busy, but I wonder if you could spare me a moment after you have put those things away. Dorothy is informing Mrs Hemingway of my arrival and is to return with some lemonade. Do you think you could bring it instead and we can have a quick chat?'

Lizzie replied apprehensively. 'er...Yes, certainly madam, I will just be a few minutes.'

Jayne watched Lizzie disappear down the corridor and thought what a good friend this girl had been to Kate, who had written all about her in her letter. She was relieved that her niece had someone to talk to, other than her mother.

Lizzie was thoughtful as she laid out the jug and glasses on the silver tray. She had relieved Dottie of this duty, suggesting she go immediately to seek out Mrs Hemingway, because she did not really want to be involved in a long conversation with Jayne Munroe, who might ask some awkward questions. She made her way back to the library, tapped lightly on the door and waited for the invitation to enter.

'Do come in my dear and put the tray down on that table over there. It is nice to see you again, now come and seat yourself next to me on the settee.'

Lizzie bobbed a curtsy and sat nervously next to Jayne Munroe.

'Now Lizzie...May I call you that while we are alone?' Without waiting for a reply, Jayne continued. 'I know I can be quite frank with you, as Kate has appraised me on the details of the predicament in which she finds herself. It is, I admit, a difficult situation, but one in which...and I know you are aware of this...I am not unfamiliar with myself. Now Lizzie, you need to tell me all you know about the father of this baby, as without all the information, I cannot look for a solution.'

Lizzie was quite shocked at Jayne Munroe's forthright manner and she wondered how much Kate had revealed to Jayne in her letter.

Feeling very uncomfortable, Lizzie addressed Jayne with as much confidence as she could muster. 'With respect,

Mrs Munroe, I am not sure that it is my place to discuss Kate's situation with you. After all, I am a servant of the Hemingway's and I do not think that Mrs Hemingway would appreciate tittle tattle from someone in my position.'

Wondering if she had been too abrupt and spoken out of turn, she smiled weakly at Jayne, who took hold of her hand in a friendly gesture. 'Now my dear, I do understand your position, but I am talking to you on this subject as a friend of Kate's, rather than a servant. I know how much Kate values you as a friend and confidant, so please do not worry about any indiscretions you feel you might be making.'

An awkward silence prevailed until the door opened and further conversation was impossible. Georgina Hemingway entered the room, went straight over to her sister and kissed her on the cheek. 'It is nice to see you Jayne. Have you had a good journey?'

'Yes, very good Georgina. It is nice to see you again too.'

Lizzie quickly stood up from the settee to pour the lemonade into two glasses.

Georgina smiled at Lizzie. 'Thank you Elizabeth, you may go now.'

Lizzie bobbed a curtsy and hurriedly left the room, before closing the door behind her and breathing a big sigh of relief.

It was two days into Aunt Jayne's visit before Lizzie could have a proper conversation with Kate, who she managed to catch up with in the summerhouse. 'I am so glad I have managed to speak with you Kate. Aunt Jayne collared me when she first arrived and was asking me questions about the baby's father. I didn't let you down, as I did not reveal anything. Did I do the right thing Kate?'

Kate smiled at her friend. 'You mustn't worry Lizzie, even if you had told her about James, it would not have mattered, as I would have told her eventually anyway. I am going into Glasgow with Aunt Jayne later today for afternoon tea, as mother is busy with her women's sewing group. They meet once a month at Low Wood, but Aunt Jayne politely declined and informed mother that she would like to spend some time getting to know me, now that I had grown into a...in her words...lovely young woman.'

'Well, good luck Kate. I am sure Aunt Jayne won't let you down. I'll see you later...bye.'

⁂

An hour later, Kate was seated in the restaurant of the Buchanon Hotel, pouring her heart out to Aunt Jayne. '...So you see Aunt Jayne, I really do not know what I shall do.' Kate was looking decidedly pale and tearful as she looked to her aunt to lift her spirits by somehow making everything right again.

'The first thing we must do Kate is to make sure you and the baby are well and that everything is progressing normally. I will arrange for you to see a private doctor, who will give you an examination and confirm the pregnancy.' She smiled benignly as she glanced down at Kate's slightly rounded belly. 'Then we need to talk about the baby's future; whether you wish to be married or whether you prefer a different solution.'

'Oh no Aunt Jayne, I am not going to marry the father, definitely not, that is one thing I do know. However, I would not want an abortion and anyway, if my calculations are right, it is too late already. Lizzie thought I might be able to have it adopted. Is that possible without anyone knowing?'

'Oh Kate, are you sure you have considered the other options carefully. Adoption is very final and you may live to regret it. I kept my baby and I do not have any regrets whatsoever. It was a struggle at first, but after I met Aubrey, who, as you know, was not the father, everything fell into place. Are you in love with the father? If so, your position is relatively simple. If he wants to marry you, your mother and I could arrange that very quickly, as you are not showing too much yet. It would not come as a complete surprise to anyone, especially as you have been seeing him for some time. Then you could both go away for a year, say and live somewhere else, returning, if you wish, after a suitable lapse of time. The story would be that you conceived the child on honeymoon and then it was born a couple of months early - perfect you see.'

Kate mulled over this scenario, but knew in her heart that she did not love the man whom everyone had assumed to be the father and they had never slept together. Even supposing she could arrange to meet him soon and seduce him, passing the baby off as his, she could not marry someone she did not love. 'No, Aunt Jayne, I do not love James enough to marry him, so I cannot do that, even if it got me out of my present situation, it would store up trouble for the future.'

'Well, I cannot judge you Kate. When I found myself in the same situation, I did not love the father and foolishly became pregnant because I thought I was being very sophisticated and a bit daring. I do regret losing my virginity to someone with whom there wasn't ever going to be a future, but keeping my daughter was the best decision I ever made. You cannot have any idea of the joy and unconditional love you feel when you first hold your baby in your arms.'

For a moment she considered Aunt Jayne's words. After all, the baby she was carrying was the result of a loving union between herself and the baby's father and to give it up for adoption, would deny their love for each other. On the other hand, it would be impossible for the baby's father and her to be together. Ultimately, Kate could not envisage marrying James just to resolve her predicament. No, she thought, there is only one possible solution. She looked down at the table and came to a decision. 'I have considered everything you say, but I have made the decision to adopt.'

Aunt Jayne could see that, at this moment, there was nothing she could do to change Kate's mind, so resignedly agreed to help her. 'All right Kate, I will help you all I can with the arrangements, but we do have to tell your mother and the sooner the better. I suggest that later this afternoon would be a good time. The ladies from the sewing circle will have left and your father will be at his club, having a drink after today's hunt.'

Kate's heart began to beat faster as she considered the prospect of telling her mother and although her father would not be present, the thought of that meeting filled her with absolute dread.

When they arrived back at Low Wood, George helped Kate and Aunt Jayne down from the trap. Kate looked at her mother's smiling face as she stood in the entrance hall waving off the ladies from the sewing circle. The dreaded moment had arrived and she had an uncontrollable urge to run and keep on running. Fortunately, Aunt Jayne whispered a few words of encouragement in her ear as they stepped inside the hallway. 'Don't worry about a thing Kate, I assure you it will all be all right. Now come along and let us face the music together.'

Aunt Jayne followed Georgina down the hall and called after her, before she started ascending the stairs. 'Georgina, have you a moment, I need a word with you in the library?'

Georgina turned round to see Jayne and Kate looking particularly solemn. Jayne looked directly at her and Kate stared down at the floor, thus avoiding her mother's anxious look. 'Is anything the matter? You both look as if there has been a death?'

Jayne tried to lighten the conversation until they were safely ensconced in the library. 'No dear, it is just something we need to talk about. Shall we go through?'

Georgina looked puzzled but reluctantly agreed.

Once in the library, she closed the door firmly and seated herself in the chair by the window, while Jayne sat next to Kate on the settee, discreetly holding on to her hand.

Georgina looked from one to the other and a sudden fear stabbed at her heart. She was unable to imagine what was about to be revealed, so pointedly asked for an explanation. 'Well, is anyone going to say something, or have I to guess what this is about?'

Aunt Jayne looked directly at Georgina and with a huge sigh, began to break the news gently to her sister. 'Now Georgina,

I want you to try and remain calm, as I am sure we will get through this together.'

Georgina looked over at her daughter and saw the panic in her eyes. She felt even more anxious and looked back at Jayne, knowing that what she was about to hear would not be good. 'Get through what? Just tell me, you are making me very nervous Jayne. I am imagining all sorts of dreadful things.'

Jayne spoke with sympathy. 'There is no easy way to say this...' and looking over at her niece's fearful face, she quietly delivered the news — 'It's Kate, she is pregnant.'

Georgina swayed and looked towards the ceiling where the chandelier seemed to swing above her, until she fell forward from the chair to the floor.

Jayne's response was immediate. She rang the servants' bell for some tea and then helped a recovering Georgina back into her chair, before turning to her niece for assistance. 'Quickly Kate, get the smelling salts from the mantelpiece and give them to me.'

There was a knock on the door and Lizzie came with a tea tray, which she placed on the small table. She looked around at each of the room's occupants and knew instantly the cause of her mistress's fainting episode. She quickly exited back to the kitchen.

Jayne's voice was encouraging as the smelling salts quickly revived her sister. 'Now Georgina, you are not to worry. Everything will be all right.'

A bemused Georgina stared at her daughter in disbelief, as the enormity of the revelation hit her. 'How...how did this happen? I cannot believe you have been so utterly foolish.'

Put on the spot and floundering for an answer, Kate tried to adopt a patronising attitude as a form of defence and with an air of bravado, attempted to lighten up the proceedings. 'Well mother, you know how it happens.'

Georgina eyed her daughter disdainfully. 'Don't be flippant Katherine. This is very serious and I feel you have let us down very badly. What I meant was, that you never really have any time alone with James. You only see each other when he visits you at Low Wood.'

For the second time that day, Kate had to tell a lie, but reconciled herself that it was in everyone's best interest. However, she was pleased that her mother did not ask who the father was, but assumed it could only be James.

Kate sombrely offered an explanation. 'There was one occasion when you and father were away, just before Christmas and James came over unexpectedly. We found ourselves alone; the servants were busy decorating the main rooms downstairs and we were carried away with the moment.'

She looked at her mother, but did not see any sympathy in her eyes, so she quickly followed the explanation with a look of shame and sorrow and, pleading forgiveness, allowed a few tears to roll down her cheeks. She did, in fact, feel genuinely very sorry for her mother, as she faced her worst fears.

In a complete role reversal, Kate went over and placed her arms around her mother's shoulders. 'I am so sorry, mother, really I am. We never meant for this to happen and it was very foolish of us both. Can you forgive me - I am so frightened. I don't know whether to keep the baby or give it up.'

Georgina began to soften towards her daughter, although the enormity of the situation meant that she was not yet ready to offer forgiveness. The thought of Kate keeping the baby almost gave her apoplexy. Angrily, she turned to Jayne and suggested that keeping the baby had been her idea. 'Was this your influence Jayne? I cannot believe you would encourage such nonsense, but I probably shouldn't be surprised.'

Jayne bit her tongue to prevent giving an equally caustic reply, because she knew that this would not help Kate's plight. Instead of inflaming the situation, she remained calm and tried to win her sister over, without revealing the only real reason for her visit was to help ease Kate through this difficult time.

To allow both Georgina and Kate to move forward, in the least painful way, she would use all her effort and powers to persuade her to keep her baby, or failing that option make arrangements for an adoption. 'No actually, it wasn't my influence. I hadn't seen or heard from Kate for a while, until she asked if I would come up to see her, because she was in a spot of trouble. She did not reveal what kind of trouble, so I assumed it would be something she was worrying about unnecessarily. You know how young girls exaggerate. I was, however, delighted to be asked, because I wanted the opportunity to see you all again and we have not had much contact since I was last here at the beginning of the year.

'Now the dilemma is in the open, I will help you all I can to resolve the situation and keep Kate's reputation intact. Consequently, I have been giving it some thought and, with your approval Georgina, I will arrange for Kate to be looked after at a private nursing home, until the birth. The place we should consider accepts unmarried mothers from seven months until confinement. The adoption, if that is what you want, takes place at the home, so Kate can return to Low Wood, without anyone being any the wiser. We can tell friends, acquaintances and others that Kate has taken a holiday with relatives before her marriage.'

Kate cast a quick glance at Aunt Jayne, as she was surprised at the latter part of the suggestion, but thought it would be unwise to 'rock the boat' at this stage.

Georgina became more relaxed as she considered what appeared to be a good solution. It would mean that Kate could still marry James, as she had hoped. Until this situation had arisen, she thought James to be a most suitable future husband for her daughter, although her opinion had now wavered somewhat. 'Very well...thank you Jayne, I do appreciate what you are trying to achieve.' Then, just as she had calmed down, the thought of telling her husband popped into her head and she again became loud and slightly hysterical. 'Oh Good Lord, what on earth am I going to tell your father? He will be devastated. I think he was hoping, as was I, that James would shortly be asking for your hand in marriage and we would be celebrating a wedding in the near future.' Then, looking disdainfully at her daughter, she added. 'Not taking part in some unseemly plot to rescue our daughter's reputation.'

Georgina was still slightly hysterical, as Howard Hemingway strode unnoticed down the hallway. He had intended to spend the afternoon in his study, quietly contemplating the day's events, in his favourite armchair, but as his hand reached the study door handle, he heared a raised voice and turned suddenly. It sounded like his wife's and emanated from the library. Curious as to why she was talking loudly, he approached the library and opened the door. He was surprised to find the small gathering of women huddled together, so he looked to his wife for an explanation. 'Good afternoon ladies, you all look a trifle guilty, what are you plotting my dear?'

Georgina, taken aback at her husband's sudden appearance, stared blankly back at him with an open mouth, unable to come up with an explanation.

Kate looked from one to the other, hoping the floor would swallow her up.

Fortunately, Jayne had the foresight to breeze over to him, plant a kiss on his cheek and ask what kind of a day her favourite brother-in-law had achieved.

Howard, dumfounded at his sister-in-law's sudden unusual display of affection, but flattered none-the-less, was happy to reflect on how well the hunting had gone and how much he had enjoyed the convivial atmosphere of his club.

Jayne continued to flatter him, which allowed her sister time to decide whether to tell him the news now, later or never. Never! was probably the best idea, she thought. 'Oh that's lovely Howard. I must say the fresh air gives your cheeks a wonderful glow. You captured a very handsome man there Georgina!'

Howard smiled coyly at Jayne, who felt at this point, she should offer some kind of explanation herself. 'You must have heard us laughing and getting rather hysterical from the hallway. I do apologize if we disturbed you. We were discussing what a good idea it would be for Kate to holiday with the Grant's in Berkshire...before...and here's the exciting bit, Kate marries James Renwick in the Autumn! There, you can see why there was such excitement.'

Howard, relieved that the news was really rather good, gave a beaming smile all round. 'Oh well, that is good news Kate. I am so very pleased. James is an excellent choice my dear.'

Shocked at Jayne's ability to tell such a bare faced lie and be totally convincing, Georgina didn't know whether she wanted to kiss her sister or kill her. She was not in the habit of lying to her husband over something as serious as this and felt she owed him the truth.

However, when she saw the pride and joy on his face, she knew at that moment, he could never be told the truth. She felt the only choice open to her was to embrace the idea wholeheartedly, in the hope that, with help from Jayne, they could pull it off, without Howard being any the wiser.

Thanks to Jayne's little distraction, Georgina had regained complete composure, as she explained to her husband in detail, the holiday she had planned for her daughter. 'Yes Howard, I am sure you will agree that a holiday will do Kate good. It will broaden her horizons, while giving her time to think about her future. I always think it a good idea for couples to spend a little time apart, before embarking on married life, to be absolutely sure it is what they want.'

Kate sat bemused, totally surprised by her mother's sudden change in attitude. One minute being completely shocked and hardly able to take in the news of her daughter's pregnancy and in the next breath colluding with her sister and telling her husband a blatant lie.

Jayne was also completely taken aback at Georgina's convincing display, but continued to play her own part with conviction. 'Georgina asked me for my opinion and, with your approval, I've offered to accompany Kate on her journey, when I return to London.'

Kate, still silent, watched this charade unfold before her, but felt obliged to say something to her father, who looked a little put out at the arrangements that had been made without his knowledge. She went over to him, put her arms around his neck and found herself taking part in the drama that had been unfolding before her eyes. 'Listen, father, I didn't tell you, because I wasn't sure whether Aunt Jayne would agree to accompany me. James was planning to ask you for my hand, when he comes over next month. He is presently on holiday in South America with his family, where I presume he will inform them of his intentions.'

Kate surprised herself as the invented story rolled off her tongue so easily.

Howard was always happy to give in to his daughter's demands and became less aggrieved, as he gave his approval. 'It's all right Kate, I understand your reason for keeping it under wraps. I had hoped James would come to see me soon. However, I hope you will both be very happy and, of course, I will give my consent. I also agree with your mother that the holiday is a good idea. Can't do any harm to spend some time apart. Your mother and I did just that and it confirms it is something you have not entered into lightly; a mistake many young people make these days.'

Kate felt slightly guilty at keeping her father totally in the dark, but said no more, she was also anxious as to what plausible excuse would keep James from visiting Low Wood, until everything was settled — one way or another.

Kate did a lot of thinking over the next few weeks. Her mind mulled over the various options that had been suggested to her, but none fitted in with what she really wanted...to keep her baby and marry the father. That was impossible, but she found herself uplifted by a quite challenging option that had entered her head...'Maybe it would work,' she muttered to herself.

Aunt Jayne's visit had achieved the desired effect, but before too long, if Kate had her way, Jayne would be making another visit, unbeknown to Georgina. Kate was generally happy with the way everything had panned out, so settled down to write a very difficult letter to James Renwick—

Chapter Ten

The Conspiracy

Kate continued developing the plan she had devised earlier. She had to go through with it; there wasn't any other way. I'd trust her with my life, she thought to herself. It has to work and one day I will see my precious baby girl again.

※

A tap at the door interrupted her thoughts and Lizzie entered the small ward, in The Chestnuts private nursing home.

Kate smiled warmly at her friend. 'Oh Lizzie, it's so good to see you, pull up that chair and come and sit by the bed.' Kate had been eagerly awaiting a visit from her dearest friend, following the birth of her daughter two weeks previously.

Lizzie bent down to kiss Kate's cheek. 'You look well Kate. Where is the baby?' Lizzie asked excitedly.

'We aren't allowed to keep our babies with us, she is in the nursery down the corridor,' Kate explained

'Will I be able to see her?' Lizzie asked.

'Oh yes Lizzie. If I have visitors, they bring her down to me and put her in the cot at the bottom of my bed.'

'Will you ask for her now?' Lizzie could hardly contain her excitement.

'In a minute, but first I have something I want to ask you,' said Kate tentatively.

Lizzie frowned. 'You sound very mysterious Kate, what are you plotting now?'

'Oh Lizzie, you know me too well, but this time I am not sure that you will want to be a part of my plan. I don't have much time to explain things to you and I am scared you will turn me down.' Kate looked searchingly into Lizzie's eyes.

'Well you had better tell me then, but you know I always agree to your plans in the end, no matter how wild they are...and they usually are,' laughed Lizzie.

'Mmm, this time, it's serious I'm afraid. You know I would trust you with my life Lizzie...well...it's not my life I am wanting to trust you with, it's my baby's.'

'What do you mean? Have you changed your mind? Are you going to marry James? Do you want me to take her back to Low Wood until you come home again?' The questions tumbled out following the confusion of Kate's statement.

'No Lizzie...no it's not that. You know that I agreed to have her adopted before she was born? Well, at the time, it seemed the best solution, considering mother would never let me keep her, but now that she is here, I cannot go through with it. It is just as Aunt Jayne described, once you have held your baby in your arms, you can never let them go. The feeling is amazing and they become your first priority.'

Kate looked appealingly at Lizzie. 'You see Lizzie, I cannot give her away to strangers and never see her again,' Kate sobbed.

'What will you do then? Do you have a different solution?' asked a perplexed Lizzie.

Kate looked at Lizzie and in a faltering voice she answered. 'Yes Lizzie, I do, but I cannot do it alone. I have to ask for your help, but it is such a big ask. If you feel it is impossible for you to do, then I will go ahead with the adoption.'

Lizzie looked bemused. 'What is it you want me to do Kate? I don't understand.'

'I...I want you to take my baby far away from here...to...London...to Aunt Jayne's house in fact. She will look after you and the baby, until I can get away. I intend to wait until I am twenty-one, then I will be able to leave Low Wood and join you both. Can you do that Lizzie?' Kate pleaded.

Lizzie was astounded. 'Go to London! How on earth would I get there? It's a million miles away from here, I couldn't do that Kate.'

Kate continued in earnest. 'Please Lizzie, please, you are my only hope of ever seeing her again.'

Lizzie shook her head. 'But it's not possible, I am not capable of travelling so far, I would not know what to do. What about Robert and Daniel? I cannot just leave them without an explanation?' Lizzie was panicking now and turned to Kate for some reassurance.

'I know Lizzie.' Kate felt ashamed because she shouldn't have placed her friend in such a difficult position. 'I have no right to ask you, but I am desperate, I don't know what else to do.'

Lizzie observed Kate's angst and her heart went out to her. 'Please don't cry Kate, I am sure that if you explained your feelings to your mother, she would let you keep her. You could marry James and everything would be okay,' encouraged Lizzie.

'No Lizzie, you don't understand, that's just it, I cannot marry James. He doesn't even know about the baby.'

'But surely you should tell him...he might even be pleased. I'm sure he loves you very much. I've always thought you and he were made for each other and your parents think very highly of him.'

There was a long silence until Kate finally spoke. 'There is something else I have to tell you Lizzie. I don't love James, I never have. My heart belongs to someone else, but I cannot tell you who it is. He is a farmer and my parents would be horrified if they knew.'

Lizzie stared wide-eyed at Kate. 'It's not one of the young farmers we meet in town is it? They are all a nice bunch, but not for you Kate, that's just a bit of fun.'

Kate looked out of the window, hating herself for the lie she was about to tell her friend. 'No, of course not. It's nobody you know. I promised I would never tell anyone of our liaison. I tried to end it just before I became pregnant Lizzie, but I couldn't, I love him so very much and he loves me, so we continued to see each other. Then I realised I was pregnant and I knew we wouldn't be able to see each other again, after the truth came out. Both of us would be in so much trouble.

My parents would disown me and throw me out of Low Wood and he would be ostracised by the people who buy his produce. Most of them are wealthy landowners, known to my father and he would ensure word got around that he disapproved of such a union. Without an outlet for the beef and lamb he sells from the farm, he would lose money and be unable to support us. I will always love him Lizzie, but I have to forget him for the sake of everyone.'

'Oh God, Kate, it really is such a mess. I thought you and James planned to marry in the autumn. I thought that was all agreed.'

'That won't happen Lizzie. Shortly after the episode at Low Wood when we told mother about the baby and Aunt Jayne concocted the story about me marrying James, I wrote to him. I asked him not to come to Low Wood until I contacted him again, as I needed time away to consider my feelings. I told him that I was going to visit relatives in Berkshire for a couple of months to decide my future. Mother still thinks I will marry James and everyone will be happy...well everyone would be, that is, except me. I cannot do it Lizzie. I cannot marry someone I don't love. So you see, the only alternative was to ask you to take her, before mother realises Aunt Jayne made a visit to the nursing home and signed papers to reverse the adoption, which will be finalised next weekend.'

Lizzie looked sadly at Kate and held her hand. 'I have never let you down before Kate, but I just don't think I can do it. You know I am in love with Daniel Lorimer and, although I've never said, I had hopes that he might ask me to marry him one day, despite the class difference.'

Kate placed her arms around Lizzie and with compassion and understanding she gently explained to Lizzie her thoughts on where Lizzie stood in respect of Daniel. 'Lizzie, I do know how you feel. I am sure your love is reciprocated, but he is, unfortunately, in a similar position to me...his father would object strongly to him marrying a girl who is not from his social class. You know my opinion on this 'class' thing, but

I have to concede that until society accepts everyone for who they are and not the amount of money, land and power they possess, we have no choice, but to accept it.'

'I know you are right Kate, but like you, I do love him and cannot imagine loving anyone else...'

They sat there in silence contemplating an uncertain future, when the door opened and one of the nurses breezed into the ward, bringing with her a small bundle wrapped in a cosy pink blanket. She placed the baby in the cot at the foot of the bed and after enthusing over how beautiful she was, left them alone and closed the door. Lizzie peeked into the cot and in that instant she understood her friend's desperation. 'Oh Kate, she is so lovely, so perfectly formed.'

Although surprised at the child's hair colour, which was golden, she commented on her beautiful blue eyes, which were just like Kate's. She stared in wonderment at the tiny bundle then bent down to plant a kiss on the child's forehead and traced her fingers around the tiny face. 'Her skin is so soft and she is so small, like a little doll.' Lizzie's face lit up as she admired the baby, lying peacefully asleep, unaware of the chaos her entry into the world had created.

Kate got out of bed and lifted her baby into her arms before sobbing uncontrollably. I can't give her up Lizzie... I just can't. What am I to do?' she wailed.

Lizzie wondered if there could be another solution, but did not feel confident. 'Let me think about it Kate. I am not going to promise anything, but I will think about it,' Lizzie said thoughtfully.

'Will you Lizzie?' Kate paused as the two girls fell silent, then pleaded. 'I will be forever in your debt if you can do this. It won't be for very long, I promise that in February next year, that's only five months away! I will join you in London to give us security and repay you for undertaking this daunting task.'

There was a moment's silence before Lizzie looked thoughtfully at Kate and saw the anxiety and look of desperation in her eyes. She began to weaken, almost accepting defeat. 'If I do this and, I am not promising, how will I get to London and what will I do there, if by some miracle I manage it?'

'Well, it sounds complicated, but I know it will all work perfectly. You won't regret it if you take the chance Lizzie.'

Lizzie looked at her friend clutching her baby to her breast. When she saw the sad, pleading look in her eyes, she knew with a sinking feeling in her heart and a sigh of resignation on her breath, she was caught in Kate's emotional web.

'All right Kate, let me hear your plan. Why do I get the feeling that you are going to persuade me your scheme is an opportunity that I should grasp with both hands, even though I would be doing this for you and not for me?'

'I know, I know Lizzie, but it might be the best path for you too. We could have such a wonderful time in London and,' Kate hesitated, 'since your father died and your brother is now grown up and managing his own life extremely well, there isn't anything stopping you making a new start in a different city. We could go out as friends on an equal footing and you could embark on a new career. I know you enjoy working at Low Wood, but this will give you your independence and the possibility of a career, perhaps in teaching...when I join you that is! In the meantime, Aunt Jayne will take you under her wing and help out with the baby. I know Aubrey won't mind doing some babysitting while Aunt Jayne shows you the sights of London. You'll soon find your way around the city and there's the social life, of course. Maybe you'll meet the man of your dreams; someone who you will love even more than Daniel Lorimer. You could meet my cousin, Emily, who is great fun and I am sure you will get along with her famously. She will take you to the theatre and introduce you to some of her friends. You could enrol on a training course, which will give you the opportunity to pursue a teaching career. The possibilities are endless and London is the place to be, a place of many opportunities.

'Aunt Jayne has promised that until I arrive, she will give you a job in the office of their factory, three days a week, as she is aware of your excellent English and maths skills. The business is flourishing, so she could do with some help and we can employ a nanny to help you on those days you are working and then you will feel more independent. Aunt Jayne's happy to teach us the business side of the cotton industry, as my cousin doesn't have aspirations to follow in her parents' footsteps. She is looking at a career in journalism, much to her step-father's annoyance, as I think he hoped she would take over the business at some point in the future.'

Lizzie looked aghast. 'My God Kate, you must have been planning this for ages. How did you know where to start?' asked Lizzie.

'I couldn't have done it without help from Aunt Jayne. She visited me in secret last Tuesday and helped to finalise everything. She wanted to travel with you, but she had to get back to the factory by Saturday for an important business meeting. She advised me on the travel arrangements and gave me directions for the best place to hire a carriage from Manchester to Dunstable, where she will meet and escort you on the final leg of your journey.

'Aunt Jayne really favours you Lizzie and will want to repay you for being such a good friend to me. Anyway, now for the nitty gritty of the plan. Firstly, you would not be able to tell anyone, this must be our secret. Your journey will take almost a week, but everything has been arranged and you should consider it an adventure. There is nothing for you to arrange, as Aunt Jayne has pre-planned everything. You would need to arrive here on Monday, which necessitates changing your day off. You shouldn't have a problem though, as the house is always pretty quiet following the weekend. I have already organised some clothes for you; two or three really nice dresses. They have been carefully rolled and placed in a large leather valise, with some underwear, nightwear, toiletries and my special umbrella. Aunt Jayne bought me that from James Smith and Sons, on New Oxford Street. In fact, everything you could possibly need for yourself and the baby. Any personal items can be packed in your own trunk and please take my lovely large blue chamois leather handbag which is in my room at Low Wood. I will give you the key so that you can gain access. You will find it in the bottom drawer of my wardrobe.

'Arrangements have been made for you to stay at the Buchanon Hotel on Monday night, which you are familiar with and I will organise a carriage in the morning to take you the short distance to the paddle steamer, the 'Royal George'. She leaves Broomielaw on the 8 o'clock sailing on Tuesday the 28th. It will take nearly sixteen hours to reach Liverpool docks, which means you should arrive early on Wednesday the 29th. You have been booked into the Adelphi Hotel on Hanover Street for that day and night. If you are not too tired, you could spend the day browsing the Liverpool shops. You will love it Lizzie, such luxury.

'At 8 a.m. on Thursday when you go to the station, there will be a ticket waiting for you at the ticket office for your journey from Edgehill, Liverpool to the Liverpool Road Station in Manchester. Aunt Jayne has arranged a tidy sum of money from my Trust Fund to cover the hotels and the carriage journey from Manchester to Dunstable. With your passage on the ship and the train fare already taken care of, there will be plenty of money left for other expenses that you might incur whilst travelling.

'The coachman will stop overnight at the George Inn in Irongate, Derby, which will take about seven hours from Manchester. On Friday evening you will travel down to Great Brington in Northampton and stay at the Fox and Hounds, before travelling on Saturday evening, eventually arriving on Sunday morning to meet Aunt Jayne. She will be waiting for you in the Old King's Arms, which is a coaching inn in Dunstable. The coachman will make an overnight stop on

Sunday night, before continuing on to Aunt Jayne's house in Carlton House Terrace overlooking St James' Park.

'You can stay with her until you are ready to move into your own accommodation in the city, when she will organise an allowance to be paid into a private account, opened for you. I will contribute to the account so you will be financially sound for the five months until I join you.'

Kate had hardly stopped for breath whilst she outlined the complex itinerary and there was a moment's silence before Lizzie felt able to speak. 'Well Kate, I have to hand it to you, you have planned everything meticulously and I'm overawed, if not totally confused. You have even convinced me that I will be better off moving to London, even though I hadn't any aspirations in that direction at all before today. I am still uncertain about leaving Robert and Daniel without a word...just disappearing overnight. They will be worried about me I'm sure,' sighed Lizzie.

Kate looked earnestly at her friend and tried to allay her fears. 'Lizzie, when you are settled in London, I promise to seek out Robert and Daniel and explain the situation and I will even give them your new address. They could visit you and I will pay for them to do just that. They will understand that you have done this for purely altruistic reasons and it might give Daniel the impetus to ask you to marry him. Things could work out in your favour and Daniel's family would probably accept a bride of independent means.'

Lizzie was swayed by Kate's last argument and made her decision, although she had some concerns. 'I would feel a lot happier if you would do that for me Kate and yes, I will do it. I've probably taken leave of my senses and I am not looking forward to the journey, especially caring for a baby as well...Oh, what if she gets sick, I wouldn't know what to do to help her.'

'Don't worry, there will be sufficient money to pay for a doctor for both of you, in the event, but you both seem very healthy to me. She is feeding well, sleeping and gaining weight and definitely has a great pair of lungs on her!'

grinned Kate. Her mood had changed considerably now the outcome of her plan was nearing fruition.

Lizzie, now totally resigned to helping her friend, began to think about the prospect of leaving Scotland to make a new life in England. She would be sad, of course, as all her life had so far been spent in Scotland. Her memories were here and she was still in trepidation of the journey that lay ahead, particularly with respect to paying for hotels and the like from the large sum of money she was to be given. She was more than scared of the monetary responsibility.

Kate picked up on her friend's uncertainty and reassured her that everything would be all right. 'Lizzie, I know you are thinking that everything you have ever known and loved is right here, but memories travel with you in your head, no matter where you are. No one will ever forget you and you need not worry about money either. I am sure you will soon get the hang of using it!'

Lizzie inclined her head and frowned. 'Yes ...maybe, but I need time to come to terms with such a big undertaking. I will be okay, once I have compartmentalised all aspects of what lies ahead. Funnily, I am coming round to agreeing it might be just what I need, especially as Daniel has not even hinted at marriage. I have probably been keeping a dream alive that will never materialise, so I will need a distraction to enable me to forget him...not that I think you ever forget your first love. I'm sure you will agree with that? How will you come to terms with losing the love of your life? It will be easier said than done, especially if you see him around.'

Kate became sad again, as the enormity of what was to happen engulfed her, but as she looked at her baby she knew this was the only path open that would allow her to see her daughter again. 'You are right Lizzie, it will take a huge effort, but one that I will have to embrace very soon. I will break off all contact with him and he can never know the reason why. He will probably assume I have decided to choose James instead of him and forget me.'

The girls sat quietly for a few minutes, each engaged with their own thoughts for the future, until Kate broke the silence by rummaging around in the bedside cabinet. She left a small envelope inside, but pulled out a drawstring bag and a large packet addressed to Lizzie. She placed them on the bed and explained the contents. 'I haven't opened the package, but Aunt Jayne informed me that it contains the details of the journey and includes the tickets for the steam ship, the Royal George, which are made out in your name, plus the train details from Liverpool to Manchester. Aunt Jayne has written directions on how to find the Royal Mail coach and horse bays in Manchester, which take you to Dunstable. You will need to keep these safe from prying eyes at the Hall and bring them with you when you come on Monday. More importantly, there is a substantial sum of money in the drawstring bag.'

Lizzie hesitatingly took the package and bag from Kate. 'Mmm, you and Aunt Jayne have presumed quite alot, taking the tickets out in my name. How did you know I'd accept?'

Kate smiled compassionately and took hold of Lizzie's hand. 'Because only occasionally in one's lifetime will you encounter a friend who will always remain loyal no matter what difficulties arise and in whom you can trust implicitly.'

'Thank you Kate, that means a great deal to me. I will read Aunt Jayne's instructions thoroughly and, don't worry, I have somewhere very safe that I can hide them. Anyway, I should go and let you get some sleep, because you look as worn out as I feel, now that I know your plans. I will come back on Monday, much better prepared to embark on a new life. By the way Kate, what are you going to call your baby, or haven't you thought of a name yet?'

'Oh yes Lizzie, I have decided that, as she has golden hair and fair skin, I will name her Rosalie, which means fair as a Rose. Do you like it?'

'Yes, Kate, it's a lovely name and suits her - the Rose of England, which is where her new life will begin.'

Chapter Eleven

Daniel Lorimer

Andrew, Daniel, Derek, Finlay and Robert continued to meet outside the Inn at the back of the Exchange in town on a Wednesday, but, disappointingly, Kate and Lizzie had not joined them for over three months. Lizzie told Daniel that Kate had not been well and would probably be going to stay with relatives for a few months. This meant she could only see him on her day off and sometimes on a Tuesday. Nevertheless, they all hoped that both girls would be able to meet them again before Kate went away. Daniel was particularly disappointed, because he had only seen Lizzie briefly last Tuesday afternoon.

Daniel had thought a lot about Lizzie recently and decided, against his father's wishes, to ask her to marry him. He knew it would be difficult and they would face hardship, especially as his father would consider the union an ill-conceived match. However, he didn't care; if he could not share his life with her, he didn't want to share it with anyone else.

Of the four other young farmers who met at the Inn, Daniel's best friend was Finlay, who he confided in. Daniel knew Finlay liked Kate, but doubted he would ever ask her out, being from the Hall. He told him he wouldn't stand a chance, as Kate already had a very keen suitor, James Renwick, who spent a lot of time at Low Wood.

Nevertheless, on occasion, Daniel caught Finlay flashing Kate a look, which spoke volumes about his feelings for her, although Finlay appeared confident his attentiveness had gone unnoticed by others in the group. Daniel also noticed that Andrew, the shy, fair-haired, quiet one among them, had fallen silent on several occasions when witnessing the obvious chemistry between Kate and Finlay. Indicatively, Andrew was unable to disguise his obvious jealousy and questioned Daniel on whether Finlay had asked Kate out. Daniel, however, was unsure, but thereafter, Andrew had given Finlay short shrift on several occasions, which proved his interest in Kate.

Derek, on the other hand, always sat back and remained non-committal, listening to everything that went on around him. He never failed to be amused when observing the differing reactions of each of the men to the wanton flirting that went on. This inevitably lead to a fundamental change in the dynamics of the group, although Robert was as laid back as ever, happy to go along with whatever transpired.

Rightly or wrongly, Daniel decided to confide in Finlay about the idea of asking Lizzie to marry him. He looked around the packed bar and immediately spotted Finlay's head above a cubicle. His shock of blonde curly hair was unmistakeable and the butt of many jokes among the group. They all teased him mercilessly that he should have been a girl.

Finlay acknowledged Daniel as he carried a pint of bitter to the table. Daniel looked hesitantly at his friend, who was enjoying his first drink of the day and noted that Andrew, Derek and Robert were engrossed in a game of darts on the other side of the bar.

With as much bravado as he could muster he delivered his bombshell. 'Hey Finlay, I am thinking of asking Lizzie to marry me, what do you think?'

Finlay didn't answer immediately and Daniel waited patiently for him to finish drinking his pint. Finlay was surprised at Daniel's statement, but tried to respond without appearing too shocked. With an unusually serious face he expressed an opinion. 'There's no denying she is a looker Daniel, but your father will go mad, as she is just a servant, not really what he would want I suspect. Sorry my friend, but I cannot see him allowing that to happen. Not that I agree with all that nonsense, as you know. Take Kate Hemingway, she is just the kind of girl I would marry, nice looking, plenty of money and really good fun. She also has a wonderful sense of humour and is up for anything, if you get my meaning,' winked Finlay.

'Yes, I get your meaning,' laughed Daniel, 'but I reckon you'd get the mitten if you asked Kate to marry you, she is definitely out of your league. Lizzie though is a different kettle of fish. I don't think of her as below my class. After all, her brother is a farm owner. She is not like most servants, who may be a bit slow and naive and she is very well read, a good cook and speaks pleasantly. She also has the loveliest green eyes and a wonderfully neat figure. In fact she is just the most beautiful woman I have ever seen. No, despite the problems we will be up against, I still want to make her my wife and I have decided to ask her next Tuesday when I see her at the Hall.'

'Well, if that is your decision good friend, who am I to dissuade you?' He smiled to himself, confident that he would, at some point, actually change Daniel's mind. After all, he enjoyed his company and didn't want to lose his drinking buddy to some girl he might be keen on. With that thought in mind, he ordered two more pints at the bar, before resuming their conversation. 'How do you know if you will be compatible Daniel? You haven't deflowered her yet, as far as I know?' Finlay joked.

Wishing to preserve Lizzie's reputation, Daniel carefully worded his reply. 'Don't talk like that about her. You can go with many girls Finlay, including those who offer themselves to everyone and who are just out for a good time, but when I make love to Lizzie, I know it will be special.' Daniel looked down into his pint of beer, rather embarrassed at sharing such intimate thoughts with his friend.

Finlay decided not to embarrass Daniel any further, so changed to another tack. 'I know what you mean Daniel, but you should play the field a bit first before settling down, you are still young you know.'

Daniel was affronted at his friend's insinuation that he did not know his own mind, so spoke again with conviction. 'On the contrary, I am nearly twenty-four and feel ready to raise a family and start my own business. Incidentally, I have been thinking a lot lately that my future may not necessarily lie in farming. I quite like the idea of a change. For instance, they reckon there is a lot of money to be had in the textile industry. I have been speaking to an employee of the Houldsworth's factory and he reckons in another decade, spinning will have really taken off. Those investing now could see huge profits in another ten years, especially with the introduction of faster more streamlined machinery. At least I wouldn't be up with the dawn and asleep in a chair by nine in the evening. No, I need to be applying my thoughts to the future and settling down sooner, rather than later. Father is thinking of taking more of a back seat in the running of the farm and I am hoping to persuade him to give consideration to selling up, particularly with respect to the land near the river, as the fishing rights will fetch quite a considerable sum. If he agrees, we could raise enough money to set up a factory. I want to be able to support my wife and children and give them a comfortable life. Anyway, as I have already met the girl I love, why wait?' Daniel looked expectantly at Finlay for an answer.

Finlay conceded that he would not be able to dissuade his friend, so not wishing to spoil their lunchtime meeting completely, he did a quick 'turn about' and agreed with him. 'No you are right, of course. I am just jealous.' Turning the conversation back to himself he admitted his senseless desire to be with Kate. 'It is unlikely that I will ever be with the girl I really want to be with...Kate, the lovely Kate. Just thinking about her makes me weak at the knees. Do you think I stand a chance with her?'

Daniel shrugged. 'I don't really know, she is a naturally friendly person and flirts with all of us. She seems interested

SILENT TORMENT

in you, but who knows what she is really thinking and, as I said, James is already homing in on her and I shouldn't be surprised if a proposal was forthcoming. You will have to be quick, if you are serious. Why don't you ask her the next time the girls come into town? Although, it is over three months, since we all last met up. Lizzie tells me that Kate hasn't been well for some time, but she has been quite vague as to what is actually wrong with her. Hopefully their visits will resume before too long, although it's funny, because they barely missed a week in the previous six months.'

'Mmm,' Finlay mused. 'It was December when I last spoke to her in the group, when you and Lizzie were talking behind the Exchange.' Finlay did admit that he had actually seen Kate in January, but as he did not want to reveal certain aspects of his relationship with her, he continued guardedly. 'I did speak to her alone one day in January. We bumped into one another in town as she was going into the jewellers on King Street to have her watch fixed, so I took the opportunity of inviting her for a coffee in Smart's, where she mentioned some of her male admirer's. Apparently, most bored her to death, with their prattle about stocks and shares, but before we parted, she gave me a quick kiss on the cheek. It was nothing more than that of course, but I felt heartened that we had reached an understanding. She mumbled something about seeing us the next day and I told her I would look forward to it, so I was surprised when they didn't turn up. Apart from Lizzie's information about Kate's mystery malaise, the whole situation is somewhat bewildering.'

Finlay remained thoughtful and considered whether he should question Daniel further about their absence, so in a deliberately disinterested voice, asked him. 'Er, I don't suppose you have heard anything more?'

Perplexed, Daniel looked closely at Finlay's face, which was strangely at odds with his friend's tone of voice, before responding. 'No, no I haven't heard anything.'

Finlay felt he had misled Daniel sufficiently for him to believe his chances of any real relationship developing with Kate were nil. It seemed everyone had secrets and Finlay was no exception.

Daniel was lost in his thoughts, but still found words of encouragement for his friend. 'I expect you will get your chance again.' Significantly, he hoped he would have a better chance with Lizzie, when he saw her on Tuesday, as his intention to ask her to be his wife was now stronger than ever. 'Drink up and we will find the others. I think they wandered off towards the Feathers.'

CHAPTER TWELVE

Goodbye to Low Wood

Saturday's dinner party had been arranged two months earlier in July, but the guest of honour, Jayne Munroe was conspicuous by her absence. Georgina had gone to a lot of trouble to ensure its success and the staff had worked particularly hard, but her sister was unable to make the journey north. Her excuse was she had some very urgent business to attend to in London. This resulted in an empty place at the table and Georgina felt somewhat let down by her sister. However, the guests appeared to enjoy themselves; particularly when Georgina's close friends, Emily and Richard, invited the whole party to join them in Edinburgh on Sunday morning for a special two-day festival that was taking place.

Georgina claimed the dinner party a great success, despite her initial disappointment, so she praised the staff for all their hard work, promising them an extra half-day off that coming week.

Lizzie cleverly chose Tuesday morning for her half day, to cover her abrupt departure. This would follow her day off which had been changed to Monday. Consequently, her absence would not be noticed until Tuesday afternoon at the earliest.

Lizzie had not seen Daniel since the previous Tuesday and on the following Wednesday, her destiny had been decided.

When Daniel made his usual delivery on Tuesday, Lizzie would be boarding the 'Royal George' and sailing on the first leg of her journey.

She had been desperate to meet with Daniel, not only because she missed him, but also because she wanted to find out what she meant to him and whether there was any chance of marriage. Perhaps she would never know. He certainly would not understand her sudden departure, or be aware of her whereabouts, at least until she was settled in London.

Lizzie, preoccupied since she visited The Chestnuts last week was full of trepidation as Monday approached. Her unusual demeanour was noticed by Dottie and Clara, who commented on her sadness. Lizzie tried to sound cheerful, but she had difficulty hiding the anxious wobble in her voice when she tried to keep the tears at bay. She had made a supreme effort at the dinner party on Saturday, because this would probably be the last time she would ever work with the rest of the staff.

A distinct chill heralded in Monday morning, but the sky was bright and clear and Lizzie rose at first light, unable to sleep. She washed and dressed and went down to the kitchen for breakfast, then chatted with cook, Dottie and Alice as usual, before announcing that she would be going to town after lunch, getting a lift with George. George was the only member of the staff beside Lizzie who knew that Kate was pregnant and had gone away to have the baby. The rest of the household were told she was holidaying with relatives in Berkshire. George was sworn to absolute secrecy and was advised not even to share the secret with his wife.

Clara was happy that Lizzie's mood appeared to be brighter. She kept the conversation light and spoke cheerfully. 'Right you are Lizzie. Will we see you later for supper?'

Lizzie smiled. 'I may be back this evening, if not I will probably stay overnight at my brother's, as I am not due back on duty until Tuesday afternoon. I have things to do in my room now, so I will see you all at lunch.'

Lizzie went up to her room to prepare the items she intended to pack. She located her 'keeper' box and checked the contents carefully. Her brother's birth recording had already been given to him, when he moved down to Glasgow. This left her own recording, plus the three pennies given by her father and the book of poems from Martha. She placed the box on the bed and put the important travel information from Aunt Jayne, plus the sovereigns and paper bills into the handbag acquired from Kate, intending to transfer most of the money into the valise later.

She looked around the room to see what else she should take with her and her eyes alighted on the sampler. She took it down from the wall and removed it from the frame for ease of carriage, reminding herself to ask Kate to bring the frame later. She also packed the antimacassars, before adding some undergarments and thick stockings to the pile. Lastly, she carefully folded her green cloak to change into at the hotel.

The rest of the morning was spent in the library, reading poetry and thinking about the journey that lay ahead. Was she doing the right thing?...she could not honestly answer that. Only time would tell.

Later, in her room, she pondered on the fact that her brother would be unaware she was leaving and would not see her for a while. She hoped he would understand, but did not feel comfortable, as she was depriving him of saying goodbye.

Her mind wandered to Daniel. What would he make of her sudden departure? She spoke her thoughts out loud and with passion. 'Daniel, oh Daniel, I love you so much, my heart is breaking. I know that you love me, but now there doesn't seem to be a future for us.'

A big tear rolled down her cheek and she felt empty and alone. Her thoughts of Daniel were overwhelming. Might she never see him again? She stared at her image in the mirror and asked searching questions of her own reflection. 'When we made love, was I just a distraction, or was it because you wanted me to be yours forever? Is your love strong enough Daniel Lorimer? Will you come and find me?'

With her mind in turmoil she admonished her image. 'I know you care for me, but that's where it ends...and that is the truth isn't it Lizzie, you silly, silly girl. You could have your pick of many suitable girls, couldn't you Daniel? The kind that would get approval from your father.'

She sat in silence for a few minutes, before she realised she had finally acknowledged what she believed to be the truth, resigning herself to the seemingly inevitable. 'Yes Lizzie, the best thing you can do is to go away and forget him...there, you have your answer.'

Lizzie wiped away her tears, but the thought of leaving without saying goodbye seemed rather cowardly so she decided to write each a letter, which she would post when she arrived in London. By that time, she reasoned, Kate will have explained the reason for her sudden departure and the letters would not come as such a shock.

She settled down at the dressing table and took out two sheets of notepaper and two envelopes. On the first envelope she wrote Daniel's name and address, then thoughtfully compiled a letter to him.

My Dearest, Dearest Daniel,

It is with great sadness that I write this letter to you. When you receive it, I will be hundreds of miles away and we may not see each other for some time, if ever.

I know you will be shocked to hear of my departure from Low Wood and more so that I left without saying goodbye to anyone, especially to you - the person I love and care about most.

When father and I left Strathy to make a new life in Glasgow, I believed that I would settle there and eventually marry and have children. Scotland is my first love and I could not see anything that would change my desire to be there forever. However, something of great importance came up to change all that, which meant leaving Low Wood to begin another life in London.

Kate will by now have told you the reason for my sudden departure, which will have surprised you.

For a while, I believed we could be together, but, quite rightly, you were never in a position to offer me a future as your wife. I had to be completely honest with myself, which made me realise that it would be all but impossible - me a servant and your family, farm owners. Your parents would not have approved of me and you would have lost everything you had if you went against their wishes. I could not have allowed that to happen, so my decision to move away became easier to make.

If you ever feel the need to seek me out, Kate will give you my address in London, although I cannot think of any good reason why you would want to at this particular time.

Until we meet again, my heart will remain truly broken, but I will always be yours forever.

All my love, Lizzie

When she had finished, she read it thoroughly, before sealing it in an envelope. Next she wrote to Robert and found it even harder to find the right words. She began:

Dearest Robert

It seems but a short time since we found each other again. The last few months have been the happiest of my life. It was so wonderful that father managed to put aside his differences and that before he died you and he shared some happy times together. I know he loved you dearly and deeply regretted the time you spent apart. He told me how wrong he had been to send you away, but it seemed the only option at the time. I know you found it in your heart to forgive him and I am hoping that you will find it in your heart to forgive me for leaving you again.

I never thought I would ever leave Scotland - my home and where my heart is, but something of the greatest importance has forced me to re-consider my future and has presented me with an opportunity to help a very dear friend.

I have not taken this decision lightly and hope you will seek me out so that we will be re-united again.

Kate will explain why I left without saying goodbye, but after I reach my destination and I am settled, she will give you my address so that you will be able to visit me.

Please look after yourself until we meet again. I hope it will be soon.

My love and best wishes, to you always.
Your sister Lizzie.

She placed both letters into the false bottom of the 'keeper' box and securing the trunk, sat on the bed to digest the travel information for her journey to Dunstable. Lizzie thought that the time spent on the ship and the train would prove exciting, as she had never contemplated using either form of transport before. She read the information avidly. The last leg of her journey was on the mail coach to Dunstable, with two stops on the way, one at somewhere called Derby and a second at Great Brington, before finally reaching Dunstable. Lizzie was slightly more anxious about this part of the journey, because she would have to negotiate payment herself. Aunt Jayne couldn't pre-arrange this, as delays with the ship or train were beyond her control and the mail coaches kept to a strict timetable.

Fortunately, she mentioned that several mail coaches left Manchester daily, albeit at around the same time. If there was a severe delay, Lizzie could stay overnight and catch a coach the following day. Aunt Jayne was booked in at Dunstable for a week and would wait until Lizzie arrived.

Satisfied that she understood her task, she went down to the kitchen to eat lunch with Clara, Dottie and Alice. This was a daily ritual, unless she met with Daniel, visited her brother, or went into town with Kate on her day off.

Clara noticed the sadness in Lizzie's eyes as she entered the room. 'Are you all right lass, you seem distracted and a little upset?'

Lizzie took a deep breath but avoided direct eye contact with Clara before she answered the question. 'No, no Clara, I am fine, just thinking something through that's all. It's nothing important really, just a nostalgic moment, which made me feel a little sad.'

Clara looked intently at Lizzie and in a voice that belied her innermost thoughts, cheerfully invited Lizzie to sit down. 'Come and sit here lassie and I will get you some soup. Everyone has moments of doubt and indecision sometimes, it's just natural. You'll laugh at yourself later when you wonder what on earth you were worrying about.'

'Yes Clara, I am sure you are right, it's completely silly…that soup smells delicious and I think I will have a hunk of your home made bread, which always cheers me up,' said Lizzie putting on a brave face.

Lizzie's mood was lifted by the cheerful banter of the women, then she helped Clara wash the dishes staying until they had all left to finish cleaning the larder to make room for more provisions, quite a task in itself.

The time came for Lizzie to leave Low Wood. George had already loaded her trunk onto the trap, which he took around to the back of the Hall. No one would observe their departure in that part of the house and grounds. All the servants were busy attending to duties in the West wing.

She took one last look around her room before making a mental note to ask Kate to bring the rest of her things when she joined her in London, then silently closed her door.

CHAPTER THIRTEEN

New Beginnings

George waited outside in the trap as Lizzie walked to the large oak door of The Chestnuts and pulled the bell. A young nurse in a crisp blue uniform answered the door.

Lizzie adjusted her bonnet and in her best Scots accent formally asked admittance to the Home. 'I am visiting my friend Miss Katherine Hemingway. Would you please show me to her room? My name is Elizabeth Cameron and she is expecting me.'

The nurse bobbed a curtsy, which Lizzie found amusing, as she followed her along the white tiled corridors to Kate's room on the front, which overlooked the gardens.

Kate was excited at the prospect of seeing her friend again and observed Lizzie's approach to the front access door. When she entered the room Kate smiled and kissed her lightly on the cheek. 'How are you Lizzie? I wondered whether you might have had a change of heart and decided not to come.'

'No Kate, I have not changed my mind, but are we doing the right thing? I am still not entirely sure, but I will not let you down. What does concern me is how I am going to smuggle Rosalie out without anyone seeing me - we never discussed that?'

Kate grinned. 'You don't have to smuggle her out Lizzie, it has already been agreed with the Matron. The envelope you saw last week contained a deposition from Aunt Jayne, masquerading as my mother, who, as you know, has never actually visited me here. The matron didn't have any reason to doubt the writer's identity and Aunt Jayne had already introduced herself as my mother when I arrived here. The letter explained that the family had changed their minds about the adoption and arranged for the senior maid to take the baby back to Low Wood, a few days prior to my own return, so that she could be settled into the nursery.'

Lizzie was astonished at the lengths Aunt Jayne had gone to, to help Kate, but when Kate explained the reasons, she completely understood. 'Unlike mother, Aunt Jayne feels very strongly about me keeping my baby, in preference to an adoption. You know she kept her own child, despite huge opposition from the family. She recognised that if I expressed my wish to keep her, I would probably suffer the same fate as Aunt Jayne and be thrown out. Mother would be mortified and father would be devastated, as he is unaware of the pregnancy and it would destroy him to learn of it now. Aunt Jayne struggled on her own for a time before she married Aubrey and doesn't want me to suffer a similar fate, hence her involvement with Rosalie's future.'

Lizzie pondered on the implications for Aunt Jayne and wondered what the consequences would be when Kate's parents found out. 'Won't your mother be furious when she finds out and cut ties with your Aunt Jayne again?'

'She may...that is indeed a possibility, but we are hoping that when she realises it is Aunt Jayne who will be looking after us, she may be more gracious, especially as I will not be at Low Wood, darkening their doors.'

Matron brought Rosalie to Kate, dressed and ready for her journey. She placed her into the small cot at the end of the bed and gave Kate the papers to sign for her release from their care. She smiled at Kate and praised her decision. 'I am so pleased you decided to keep the baby Miss Hemingway. I am sure you and your family will not regret the decision. I only require your signature on the final release papers, as we already have your mother's signature, then your maid will be at liberty to take her back tonight, if that is what you wish?'

'Yes, it is, thank you.' With a flourish, Kate added her own signature to that of the signature of her 'mother's', before returning the document with a smile to the Matron. 'Thank you so much for all your help. I will be staying here another few days, as arranged and then I will return to Low Wood myself.'

Matron took the document and with her good wishes for Lizzie's safe journey back, she left the room.

Kate picked up Rosalie and held her close to her breast, knowing that it would be some time before she would be able to hold her close again. She knew she must be strong so summoned all her courage, before addressing Lizzie. 'Now Lizzie, if you look in the side cupboard near my bed you will find a sling which Aunt Jayne commissioned especially to carry Rosalie whilst travelling. It is made out of calico and slips securely around your neck, to hold the baby across your breast.

'I finished packing the large valise with the items required on the journey, so you will not need to keep opening the trunk. All births have to be formally registered now before they issue an official certificate, so here are the important ones. Promise me that you will only open the envelope containing Rosalie's certificate in an emergency. I have my reasons, which I will reveal to you when we meet up again. There is also a letter from our solicitor, which states my agreement for you to be Rosalie's guardian, until I can join you in London. It is merely a formality, in case anyone asks any questions on the journey, although that will be extremely unlikely.'

Kate pressed Rosalie to her breast one last time and kissed her head. She breathed in the baby scent and retained it in her senses, before passing her reluctantly to Lizzie. 'Well Lizzie this is it, the start of your journey to London. I will miss you both so very much, but I know you will take great care of Rosalie and in a few short months, we will be together again.'

Lizzie placed Rosalie securely into the sling and kissed Kate on the cheek. She reassured her that Rosalie would be safe in her care. 'Oh Kate, I will miss you too, but you are right, it is the only way. I will love Rosalie as my own and take the greatest care of her for you.' With that, Kate pushed the button to summon the porter who duly arrived to take the valise out to George, waiting patiently at the front of the Home.

❦

It was nine o'clock when Lizzie arrived at the Buchanon Hotel. George carried the smaller luggage to the front desk and asked for a porter to transport the large trunk. Then he said goodbye to Lizzie. He squeezed her arm tightly and asked her to take great care of herself and promised that their secret would remain with him alone.

Safe in her hotel room, Lizzie gave Rosalie a bottle of milk and settled her down in the small cot. She changed into her nightwear and sat for a while at the window, which overlooked the City of Glasgow. She gazed at the night sky and saw the 'Seven Sisters', twinkling as brightly as ever. The full moon cast shadows on the dark streets, which gave her mixed feelings. She felt strangely elated and free, but there was also sadness in her heart, as she thought of everyone she was leaving behind. How long would it be before they were reunited? Would she ever make the journey back to the Highlands to see Mairi, just as she had promised?

She shook her head, wiped her eyes and promised herself that from this moment, she would only look to the future. That was the only way she could rid herself of the doubts that played around inside her head.

Before she went to bed, she transferred a large sum of money from her bag into the valise and took out the envelope containing Rosalie's birth certificate. For a brief moment she held it in her hands and wondered who the father could be, but she kept her promise and left it sealed. Eventually, she locked it safely in the false bottom of her 'keeper' box, along with her own birth recording.

The only items she kept in her bag were her travel tickets, which she would need tomorrow when she sailed, the solicitor's letter concerning her guardianship and the money for incidentals. She also decided to place the book of poems in her handbag, so that she had something to read on her journey.

Dawn broke all too soon to reveal a misty grey day, which did nothing to lift Lizzie's mood. She was trying hard to remain positive, but seeing the rain beating down on the pavements below dampened her spirits.

Rosalie cried out to be fed and changed, so Lizzie responded quickly, threw off the bedclothes and attended to her needs, before taking a bath herself. Now she was ready to embark on this, her greatest and most adventurous journey so far.

After a rather hurried breakfast, Lizzie placed Rosalie in the sling and went to reception where the porter had stacked her luggage. The receptionist requisitioned a cab and a short while later she stood on the dockside, waiting to board the 'Royal George.'

The quayside was busy with people rushing about. Fishermen were already putting their catch into baskets to sell at market and flower sellers called out to passers by, hoping to sell their posies before the blooms faded and drooped on the wet and dreary quayside.

Other passengers were in high spirits and chatted excitedly to their partners and children, despite the rain.

Lizzie felt slightly lost so concentrated on Rosalie for comfort. She was pressed close to her breast and she could feel her warm body through her cloak. She felt a sudden rush of love for the baby that had been placed in her care only a few short hours ago. Lizzie smiled and murmured encouraging words, even though they would not be understood. 'Well Rosalie, this is it, the start of a new life for both of us.'

Lizzie boarded the Royal George at 6 o'clock, two hours before sailing. At the same time, the loved ones she had left behind were beginning their day.

Kate Hemingway looked sadly out of the window with tear filled eyes. She surveyed the room, which only yesterday seemed bright and full of love, but now seemed cold and hostile.

At around the same time other seemingly normal events were happening. Daniel Lorimer was cheerily loading up his cart with meat and fish, ready to deliver to Low Wood Hall, whilst rehearsing the speech he would make to Lizzie when he asked her to be his wife.

Robert Cameron was already out in the fields tending to his flock and whistling a tune as he went about his work, totally unaware of his sister's departure.

Clara, Dottie and Alice were busy in the kitchen preparing for another normal day at Low Wood and Georgina and Howard were starting their journey back from Edinburgh.

<u>At present, everyone was unaware of the circumstances of Lizzie's departure, but all would in some way be affected by the devastating sequence of events about to unfold.</u>

Chapter Fourteen

The Journey

The opulence of the ship surprised Lizzie, as she walked to her cabin through the saloon, which was furnished in Rosewood and crimson. She slowed momentarily and marvelled at its grandeur and wondered about the people who would be travelling on the ship with her.

The Royal George was one of the first ships to have a hull built of iron and was relatively new, having been commissioned only two years previously. This particular iron clad was one of two ships built by the Glasgow & Liverpool Royal Steam Packet Company. Lizzie's cabin was in first class, which meant she would have a porthole to look out to sea. On reaching the door numbered 12, a sense of excitement and adventure overwhelmed her, as it was the first time she had been aboard a ship...any ship, let alone such a leviathan as the Royal George. Disappointingly, however, the cabin was smaller than she imagined. There was only a bunk, a small wardrobe, a cupboard with an inset basin for washing and a bucket for transporting water, which left very little room for movement. Consequently, she was grateful for the porthole, which made the room seem less claustrophobic. Her trunk had been stored below with the other passengers' luggage but she retained her bag and the valise. Before exploring further, she decided to feed Rosalie her milk before going up on deck to see the ship leave port.

The rain had eased and the skies were less grey, although there still seemed a threat of bad weather. She wondered if they would set sail on time and whether the passage would be rough.

Lizzie leaned against the guardrail with the other passengers who were waving to loved ones standing on the dockside. She was surprised at how the ship dwarfed the throng of people lining the shore. Many waved scarves and handkerchiefs, as the 'Royal George' slowly left the harbour behind and headed for the open sea.

A half hour into the voyage the sea became calmer, as the rain stopped and the dark clouds rolled away into the distance.

The journey to Liverpool on board the ship did not turn out to be as exciting as Lizzie had anticipated. They had been underway for several hours, when the skies blackened again and the wind grew stronger. The sea whipped up huge waves and the vessel began rolling and pitching. An inexperienced Lizzie thought they might capsize, so she made Rosalie as comfortable as possible. She tried lying down on the bunk to avoid being seasick and to get some sleep, but this made the experience worse until the water bucket justified its existence. 'Will it ever end?' she said out loud, vowing never to board another ship in her life.

Several hours later, the sea state improved, so she decided to risk going up on deck to calm her nausea. It was two in the morning and she had not had any sleep, but strangely felt quite peckish. She wondered if there was a chance to obtain some food, because she had already missed lunch and dinner, so with Rosalie in the sling, made her way up the companion way to the main deck. Surprisingly, several hardy passengers had gathered there discussing a delay of several hours due to the tides. The ship would have to anchor off until there was sufficient water on the flood tide to take her over the bar and see her safely docked. At least the ship had stopped its evil motions and Lizzie, although quite exhausted, was feeling much better. Several passengers had seated themselves around the deck and were ordering hot drinks from the stewards, when she noticed a young couple talking animatedly with a small boy. They were seated next to the accommodation bulkhead, away from the ship's side. Moments later, the boy ran to the rails in pursuit of a seagull, before his mother realised the danger. In that instant, the ship rolled suddenly and threw several of the passengers off balance, including the boy who lost his footing. He was about to go overboard, when quick as a flash Lizzie grabbed his arm and pulled him to safety, with Rosalie still secured in the sling.

His mother ran over, gripped him by the shoulders and berated him unmercifully. 'Douglas, I've told you to stay close to your father and me whenever we are up on deck. What on earth made you run off like that?'

The boy was quite shaken by his ordeal and began to cry, which was made worse by his mother's anguish. 'I'm sorry mother,' he stuttered, 'I just got excited and chased the seagull.'

His sad little face prompted his mother to pick him up and cuddle him. She held him close and all her anger disappeared when the reality of the situation hit her. She turned to Lizzie and smiled broadly, holding out her hand in thanks. 'Thank you so much. I dread to think what could have happened if you hadn't acted so quickly. My name is Amy Brandreth by the way and this is my son, Douglas. We are travelling home to Manchester with my husband, Charles, who is seated over there. Would you like to join us? I am sure Charles would like to thank you for saving Douglas from a certain accident.'

Lizzie held out her hand and smiled back at Amy. 'Yes please, that would be lovely. Is Douglas okay now? I pulled him back rather sharply and hope I didn't hurt him.'

'Yes, he is fine thanks to you. We were just about to go below for something to eat, even though it is early in the morning. Do you feel like eating anything yet? We have been quite sick up until now, but are feeling much better and really quite hungry. Douglas thought it was quite an adventure staying up all night, as none of us could sleep. We thought if we came up for some fresh air and had a bite to eat, we could then relax a little until the ship docks later.'

Lizzie gratefully accepted and was cheered by the friendly banter between husband and wife and their little boy. She introduced herself and offered a fabrication of her actual circumstances, which enabled her to answer any questions about the epic journey she was making alone. 'My name is Elizabeth Cameron and I am travelling with my baby, Rosalie. I am going on to London to meet up with my husband Daniel, who is staying temporarily with my aunt. We are starting a new life there where my husband will manage a cotton factory.'

The couple seemed impressed with her story, which gave Lizzie confidence to embellish it further. She realised she may have to repeat her imagined circumstances on several more occasions, before reaching her destination. This couple were eager to listen, so she was anxious to try out her story. 'My husband travelled down to London two weeks ago to find us somewhere to live and prepare for our arrival.'

Amy looked suitably impressed and was full of admiration for Lizzie's courage in travelling alone. 'Oh gosh, I don't think I could travel all that way without Charles. We live in Manchester and Charles moves around quite a lot in his business. Occasionally, Douglas and I go with him, but I never travel far alone. It must be quite an undertaking for you, especially with a newborn baby. Aren't you a little nervous that your arrangements might not go to plan?'

Lizzie looked confidently at Amy and found herself explaining that she was a seasoned traveller and not afraid of making the journey alone. 'No...no, I travelled quite a lot on my own before I met Daniel, although this is my first time aboard a ship.' Lizzie knew this last statement wasn't a total lie, as she had travelled down from Strathy to Glasgow, an undertaking in itself, although, of course, she wasn't alone. Nevertheless, the lie was justified, given the circumstances.

Any further conversation was curtailed by an announcement from the captain who confirmed a delay of several hours before the ship could dock. He apologised for the inconvenience and hoped everyone was feeling better now that the sea state was calmer and that food would be available in the dining hall.

Amy, Charles, Douglas and Lizzie enjoyed a pleasant meal together with the conversation focussed on Douglas and Rosalie, until Lizzie retired to her cabin. Both she and Rosalie slept until the shipped docked at 9.15.

Lizzie disembarked amidst a throng of other passengers. She felt a little lost, so was very grateful when Amy and Charles came over to wish her well with the rest of her journey. Charles helpfully arranged for a cab to take her to the hotel.

Lizzie's cab swayed leisurely into Liverpool, a town with a population comparable with Glasgow. She was amazed how alike the two places were. The docks seemed just as busy in this, the third largest port in England. The window of the cab was open slightly and Lizzie listened intently to the unfamiliar dialect of the voices in the street. When eventually they arrived at the Adelphi Hotel on Hanover Street her money management skills were tested when she paid a porter to take her luggage up to the first floor.

Lizzie was in awe at the splendour of room 32, which overlooked the front of the hotel. The large high windows gave her a lovely view of the street below, where cabs, drawn by black horses with red plumage, pulled up outside the entrance. Their passengers looked very grand, as they alighted from their coaches. Kate had told her that the hotel's reputation extended throughout Europe and she wondered if the people she observed had travelled from abroad. At this point, Lizzie felt extremely happy and danced around the room with Rosalie, laughing as she sat down on the bed with its lovely blue counterpane. 'Oh Rosalie, I think we have gone to heaven,' she said, smiling as she picked her up and cuddled her to her breast.

Once Rosalie had been bathed and fed, she placed her in the small cot at the side of her bed, where she immediately fell asleep. Lizzie looked in wonder at the tiny form and traced her fingers around the soft skin of her face. She whispered to the sleeping child in complete contentment. 'Rosalie, sweet Rosalie, what destinies await us both?'

Chapter Fifteen

Marcus Van Der Duim

Lizzie unpacked a few items from the valise, including the lovely dresses Kate had rolled up for her to avoid creasing and sat for a while on the seat by the window reflecting on her journey so far.

Things hadn't exactly gone to plan, but she had managed fairly well, given the circumstances. She wondered how the people she had left behind viewed her sudden departure, especially Daniel - was he disappointed or angry, or was he even upset that she had gone. She reluctantly remembered her promise to herself to only look forward to the future from the moment her journey began and to try and put the people she cared about to the back of her mind, at least until she had completed her journey.

Just as she was about to move away from the window, a tall gentleman alighting from a cab caught her eye. He was well dressed, fairly young, devastatingly handsome and he appeared to be alone. She sat fascinated as he made his way towards the hotel foyer and wondered if he had just arrived or was returning to the hotel. Were a wife and family waiting for him perhaps? Not many men made her heart skip a beat, but this one was an exception, so she carried on daydreaming until a glance at the clock indicated it was almost lunchtime. Should she go down to the restaurant, or order room service? She chose the restaurant, but was a little dubious about dining alone. It was bad enough that Kate and herself were unaccompanied when they went into Smart's café in Glasgow and she still remembered the embarrassment of following an elderly gentleman inside. Moreover, this establishment was much more splendid and one just couldn't attach oneself to someone else here.

Kate informed her she would be able to arrange for a sitter to look after Rosalie while she ate in the restaurant, but Lizzie still had misgivings, until fortuitously, there was a light tap on the door. Lizzie rose to open it and to her amusement she was greeted by a maid who curtsied and enquired if Lizzie required anything. She gathered herself together and decided to go down to lunch, after ascertaining that a sitter was available. The maid smiled deferentially and responded in a broad Liverpool accent. 'Yes ma'am, I will arrange one for you. Will there be anything else?'

Lizzie remembered the same phrase used by the assistant in Frobisher's and suppressed a giggle. This hotel was renowned for its cuisine and splendour, even in Europe, but it was nice that the staff were friendly and pretty much down to earth…no 'modom' this and 'modom' that here. Lizzie beamed at the young maid and thanked her by giving three pennies as a tip.

Lizzie changed into a lovely pale green cotton dress that Kate had had made for her with the fabric bought from Frobisher's in Glasgow. She piled her hair on top of her head and secured it with a slide, before admiring herself in the mirror. Now she was confident that she could carry off her deception in the restaurant of being a 'well to do' lady. 'Yes Elizabeth Cameron, you have come a long way from your days in Strathy. You'll do, I think.'

In the restaurant, the maitre de showed her to a table for two in the window. She perused the menu and decided on an assortment of sandwiches, cakes and a pot of coffee. While she was waiting for the food to arrive, she noticed the tall, good-looking gentleman, whom she had seen earlier arriving at the hotel. He was talking earnestly to the maitre de and gesticulating in the direction of the table at which she was seated. In fact, he appeared to look straight at

Lizzie, who glanced away, blushing furiously, to gaze out of the window.

Out of the corner of her eye, she could see the stranger walking purposefully in her direction. He couldn't possibly be joining her she reasoned and quickly checked the other tables to see if there was another lone diner, but there wasn't. Not surprisingly, her heart began to beat faster and she found herself hoping, rather irrationally, that he would sit with her. In the next moment he stood directly in front of her, introducing himself. 'Good afternoon, my name is Marcus Van Der Duim and I am visiting Liverpool on business from my home town of Ghent in Belgium. I think this may be presumptuous of me, but I wonder if I could join you at your table?'

Completely at a loss as to what would be the most seemly thing to do and surprised that this handsome stranger would want to seek out her company, Lizzie found herself staring blankly at the young gentleman.

He returned her gaze and informed her that he had observed her from the moment she entered the restaurant. He had ascertained she was dining alone and, although it wasn't the 'done thing', he would risk asking if he could join her. Lizzie, unsure of how she felt about this stranger taking lunch with her, was excited at the prospect nevertheless. Kate would have told her to 'live a little and have a good time.' So with her heart going ten to the dozen, she looked directly at Mr Van Der Duim and as confidently as possible, agreed to his request. 'Yes, please do er...Mr Van Der Duim.' Hoping the pronunciation was correct, she looked into his deep blue eyes, shaded by long curling lashes, which surprisingly reflected a certain sadness. In an instant she realised that here was a man in whom she could trust. She smiled agreeably and introduced herself. 'I am Elizabeth Cameron and I am very pleased to make your acquaintance.'

Mr Van Der Duim seated himself opposite Lizzie, who thought what a lovely warm smile he had. However, this was momentarily overshadowed by a deep sadness, which flickered across his face, although this quickly disappeared. 'Well Elizabeth Cameron, may I be so bold as to ask why such a beautiful woman as yourself is travelling alone?'

Lizzie's thoughts were running wild at this stage. Should she tell the truth or deceive him with the story she had concocted for herself back in Glasgow? She felt she should probably stick with that, as it was much simpler than the truth.

She hesitated for a moment, feeling less confident about keeping up such pretence, without her face betraying her. She studied his face carefully and decided his eyes belied the confidence of his persona. What tragedy had he suffered in life? she wondered. She wished she could tell him the truth, that she was single and without a child, but then immediately felt guilty about denying Rosalie's existence.

Lizzie realised that she had not replied as Mr Van Der Duim was looking intently and expectantly at her. She felt herself blushing again as she stammered her reply. 'I...I'm...travelling alone...I mean I am not exactly alone, but I am going down to London to be with...to be with—'

Her sentence went unfinished as Mr Van Der Duim, looking puzzled at her inability to answer a straightforward question, but feeling sorry that he had placed her in an obviously difficult position, came to her rescue. 'I am so sorry Mrs Cameron, I should not have put you on the spot like that, do forgive me.'

Lizzie looked again at Mr Van Der Duim and decided that she really wanted to get to know him. Why had she had the notion that a good-looking gentleman could possibly have suffered any kind of tragedy? Right now the sadness had receded and was replaced by a sincere interest in her reply, despite the apology for putting her 'on the spot.'

Lizzie smiled inwardly and decided to tell him the truth, even if it meant he would get up and leave when he heard the circumstances of her flight, which seemed completely preposterous and unbelievable even to her. Taking a deep breath she started to tell her story. 'I do forgive you for asking, but I fear you will not approve of what I am trying to do. Firstly, I am not married. I am, however, travelling down to London on a mission to help out a very good friend of mine. She found herself in a spot of trouble and had to decide whether to have her baby, who was born out of wedlock, adopted, or to keep it. It transpired her father was not told about the pregnancy and her mother would not allow her to keep it, so adoption seemed the only answer. However, following the birth, she found she could not give the baby away and she had the idea that I could take Rosalie, her baby, down to her aunt's in London. She intends to join us in five months, when she becomes of age...'

Lizzie continued with the story, as Mr Van Der Duim watched her, fascinated by her beauty and surprised at her fortitude. He had never been so captivated by a woman as he was now by Elizabeth Cameron. Even his wife Belle's good looks did not compare with the all round beauty this woman exuded, a woman who had obviously overcome huge personal difficulties to help her friend. He was full of admiration for her, but, more than that, he was strangely drawn to her. He hoped she would be staying another night at the Adelphi, so that he could meet with her again. An hour or so ago, he never knew this woman existed, but now he was completely mesmerised. Fleetingly, he reminded himself that he had acted spontaneously many years before, which ultimately resulted in a terrible tragedy. However, this particular woman appeared to be a completely different 'kettle of fish' to Belle, who had betrayed and finally left him, taking their son with her.

Briefly, his mind wandered back to the time after his son was born. Their relationship had deteriorated because of the long periods they spent apart and so she took a lover. What he didn't expect was that her lover would be his best friend - a double betrayal! But enough of that, what had he promised himself only last week? That if there wasn't any news of his son, excruciatingly painful as that might be, he would have no choice but to accept that he was gone and some how continue with the process of living.

When he looked at Lizzie again and saw the warmth and sincerity in her eyes, his mood lifted and thoughts of the tragedy were shelved, possibly to be relived again during a time of solitude. His wife was already forgotten, his son, despite his promise to himself - never.

Lizzie began to realise Mr Van Der Duim was looking intently at her and she began to feel a trifle uncomfortable. She wondered what he thought of Kate's plan in persuading her to undertake such a journey and of her own decision in agreeing to do it. Eventually, she came to the end of the story. She looked up and he smiled at her whilst reaching over the table to place his hand over her own. A little shocked, but pleased nonetheless, she did not withdraw her hand. He was just about to speak, when a waiter interrupted and asked them to choose from a trolley filled with delicious sandwiches, cakes and pastries.

An embarrassed Lizzie quickly pulled her hand away in the presence of the waiter, but Mr Van Der Duim took charge of the situation, asking him to leave a selection of the fare, accompanied by a pot of coffee.

Soon after the waiter moved away from the table, Mr Van Der Duim spoke to Lizzie. 'Elizabeth...may I call you that?'

Lizzie nodded her head in agreement.

'You could call me Marcus if you like,' he grinned and smiled appealingly.

Again Lizzie nodded her consent.

'Well Elizabeth,' Marcus continued, 'I have listened to your story and what you have told me has been inspiring. This Kate is a very lucky woman to have you as a friend. Friend's such as you are very hard to find and I should know, since I've travelled extensively all around Europe and have encountered many different personalities.'

Blushing to her roots, Lizzie thanked him, but denied Kate was so lucky, as she felt Kate had also been a very good friend to her.

Marcus smiled warmly. 'Elizabeth, you are too modest. I have been most impressed with how you have coped so far. Not many women could travel halfway across the country with a baby in tow, let alone one that wasn't theirs.'

'No, maybe not. But enough about me, tell me about yourself Marcus? You travel a lot...you must have had a very exciting life.'

Marcus looked sheepish as he gave his reply. 'Oh well, I wouldn't exactly say that, but my life has not been without incident.' He left it at that for the time being, unsure of how much of his life he wanted to reveal. 'Tell you what Elizabeth, I will continue this conversation this evening over dinner, if you will agree to dine with me?'

Lizzie found herself wanting to agree with that arrangement, but the reality was that by tomorrow morning she would be on her way to Manchester and out of his life. She even felt sad at the thought of never being with him again. Her face betrayed her feelings, which she was not adept at hiding, being unused to the company of someone so self-assured. She even likened him to a male version of Kate, who would have been in her element had she been in Lizzie's shoes. Nevertheless, she felt obliged to let him know of her position and the fact that it would be pointless continuing their friendship. Reluctantly, she advised him of her decision to curtail any further assignations that might be suggested following their meal. 'Mr Van...' Lizzie started to address him formally.

'Marcus please,' Marcus corrected her.

'Marcus, I have really enjoyed your company, but I think I should explain to you that I still intend to continue my journey on to London, as arranged. I will be catching a train to Manchester early tomorrow morning, so there really isn't much point in us getting to know each other further.'

Marcus's face clouded over, but he wasn't about to give up so easily. 'Well Elizabeth I too have enjoyed spending time with you and am disappointed that you have to leave so soon. I was hoping to spend some more time in your company. You say that you will be catching the 8 a.m. train to Manchester, but that leaves the rest of this afternoon and evening for us to get to know each other better, please agree to see me this afternoon and for dinner this evening. You may feel it is pointless, but it cannot do any harm and you never know, our paths may cross again some time in the future. In the event, we would no longer be strangers.'

Lizzie was unsure if it was a good idea, as she was already becoming attracted to this man, who had suddenly appeared in her life and turned it upside down. She was afraid of being hurt and that any more time spent in his company might leave her feeling confused and more alone than ever after they parted.

Marcus could feel himself losing the battle and quickly put on his most persuasive smile, as he tried to talk Lizzie into seeing him later that day. He again placed his hand over hers and looked directly into her eyes, imagining he could see into her soul. He felt confident that there was something special happening between them. 'Elizabeth, I know that we have only just met and it is not usually the 'done thing' for a lady to keep the company of a gentleman whom she knows nothing about, but I assure you that I am very honourable and will take great care of you during the time we spend together. We could take Rosalie for a walk this afternoon and I could show you around Liverpool. I come over here every six months or so on business, so I know all the best places to visit. What do you say?'

There was a moment of hesitation, when Lizzie felt it would not be sensible to continue their relationship, but she allowed her heart to rule her head as she remembered something Kate had said to her in Smart's coffee house in Glasgow. *'If we didn't take a few risks now and again, life would be pretty boring don't you think?'* With the decision made, Lizzie smiled at Marcus and accepted his invitation.

Later that afternoon, Lizzie waited in the foyer wearing her green cloak over her pale green dress with her favourite bonnet. Rosalie was in the sling and she was waiting anxiously for Marcus to arrive. Two minutes elapsed before she saw him descending the stairs and once again her heart skipped a beat. He instantly came over to her and placed his arm around her waist. Although she was quite stunned by his attention, she quickly gathered her composure.

'You look absolutely lovely Elizabeth, I am so pleased you agreed to allow me to escort you around Liverpool.' Then he turned his attention to the baby and stroked her cheek. 'So this is the famous Rosalie. Well she is almost as lovely as her guardian. I hope you don't mind, but I have ordered a cab to take us to the east of the centre around St George's Plateau.' With a glint in his eye and obvious enthusiasm, he spoke extremely knowledgeably about the area. 'We can look around St George's Hall which was built in 1840. It is, I understand, of European neo-classical architecture and stands between St George's Plateau and the formal terraces of St John's Gardens, which are still vibrant with colour at this time of year. Does that sound suitably impressive?' Observing her bewildered face, he gave a little laugh. 'I am teasing you Elizabeth, I am not so knowledgeable of local history. I found this information on a leaflet at the hotel desk, but I have been there before and it really is worth a visit.'

Grinning, Lizzie allowed Marcus to take hold of Rosalie, while she boarded the coach.

Thankful that Marcus wasn't turning out to be the complete intellectual, Lizzie thought it would be a lovely idea to see the Hall. It was a warm autumn day and the leafs on the trees were the colour of deep golden russet. There were some late roses blooming along the walkways and the deep blue hydrangeas were still at their best. The coach and two cantered along the busy thoroughfare and Lizzie felt warm and happy, in fact happier than she had felt for quite some time. Marcus was very attentive and ensured that Rosalie's needs were also fully met.

By the end of the afternoon, Lizzie felt very confused about her feelings for this relative stranger, particularly as she was supposed to be in love with Daniel Lorimer. For the first time since she left Glasgow, she felt a little guilty that thoughts of those she had left behind had not been to the forefront of her mind. She felt most disturbed and questioned her love for Daniel again. She tried to remember her feelings when she was close to him, warm, exciting and with a desire to be with him forever. Right now, those same feelings were rising up inside her as she sat close to Marcus, with one difference; she felt that these feelings were reciprocated. After all, Marcus had sought her company, despite her background and class. In fact, since being fully aware of her circumstances, he had told her how much he admired her.

He was looking at her now, amused by the wonder on her face as she experienced the sights of Liverpool. 'Are you comfortable Elizabeth, or would you like to walk for a while. We could take afternoon tea and then walk up to the Plateau, before it is time to return to the hotel.'

'I am fine Marcus, but perhaps it would be nice to stretch our legs for a while.'

Marcus ordered the coach driver to pull over to allow them to disembark. He requested his return in a little over two hours, which would allow them time to take tea and have a slow walk up to the Plateau. Unfortunately, the afternoon went all too quickly and soon it was time to return to the hotel.

On reaching the entrance of the Adelphi, Marcus stepped onto the walkway and helped Lizzie and Rosalie down from the coach.

'I will see you to your room and then I will be waiting for you at 8 p.m. in the lobby for dinner.'

Lizzie could no longer deny that she very much wanted to share this evening with Marcus and readily agreed to the arrangements.

Once inside her room she twirled around with Rosalie, a raft of emotions whirling about in her head. She decided that she wanted to meet up with this man again, after this evening, some time in the future, but not too distant. Then reality started to take over.

She spoke out loud and questioned her feelings for Marcus, which were becoming stronger with each passing hour. 'Lizzie, oh Lizzie, what is happening to you? Where have all these emotions come from? You must be quite mad, as you hardly know Marcus at all.'

Know him or not, the fact was that she was powerless to stop herself falling for him, unbelievable though it may seem. 'You must try and keep a lid on what is happening here. You might get hurt again,' she thought, but was unable to stop smiling to herself and whispered to Rosalie who was lying contentedly in her cot. 'You are such a good little baby, for which I am so grateful. I could not have coped with this journey if you had been fractious and unsettled. I am so lucky that things have turned out this way. Kate would be so proud of me, taking such a chance with a complete stranger.' It was then she realised that she no longer looked upon him as a stranger at all. In fact, over the few hours she had spent with him, she felt she had known him forever.

Lizzie made arrangements for a sitter to watch over Rosalie for the evening. She was settled in her cot, following a bath and a bottle of milk and Lizzie felt confident that she would not wake up until the following morning. She felt that Rosalie knew she needed to be the perfect baby, so they could both reach journey's end, without mishap. 'One day,' she said looking fondly at Rosalie, 'I will tell you all about our little adventure.'

Lizzie washed and changed into the dress which Kate had packed for her to wear on a special occasion, perhaps for dinner on the Royal George, or for dinner tonight at the Adelphi. It was quite an exquisite garment, in blue silk, with the latest off the shoulder neckline, leg-o-mutton sleeves and a full skirt. Lizzie remembered Kate purchasing the material in Frobisher's for a summer dinner hosted by her mother. Kate intended wearing it on one other occasion, this August on 'The Glorious 12th' - the start of the red grouse shooting season. Unfortunately, due to her pregnancy, the dress had been too tight and she was very upset. Lizzie, however, was able to put on a couple of underskirts to allow the dress to swish around as she walked.

Marcus was already in the foyer when she came down the stairs. He gasped in astonishment at her loveliness and beauty when he saw her.

He stood up immediately and came over to her, just as she reached the bottom step, then took her arm to lead her towards the restaurant. 'Elizabeth, you look stunning. I feel so honoured to be accompanying you to dinner tonight.'

Lizzie smiled at him and returned the compliment. 'And I am so lucky to be dining with such a considerate and handsome stranger.'

His clear blue eyes scanned her face, pleased with her attractive and warm smile. 'Well, we're no longer strangers are we Elizabeth? I feel I have known you for such a long time already.'

Lizzie was flushed with excitement at the prospect of spending a whole evening with Marcus and took her place at the secluded table by the window that they had occupied earlier in the day.

The waiter took their order and they sat for a moment gazing into each other's eyes and holding hands across the table, laid with a pure white linen cloth and a small vase of freesias, which scented the air with their sweet smell.

Lizzie surprised herself by opening the conversation. 'Marcus, you said at lunch that you would tell me about yourself. I am very interested to learn all there is to know.'

For a moment he hesitated. Should he tell her the awful truth or make up some wonderful life of travel and adventure, unhindered by any form of tragedy or betrayal? He looked again into her eyes, deep pools that one could be lost in forever and never want to emerge - Realisation came to him suddenly, like a bolt of lightning, that this was possibly the woman he wanted to be with forever. He smiled inwardly to himself and vowed that, God willing, he would do everything in his power, never to let her go. His one concession would be to allow her to take Rosalie to London to complete her mission. He made a further vow to always tell her the truth. With that silent promise, he began his story. 'Well Elizabeth, until recently, I lead a very contented life. My parents were happily married and there was much laughter in our household. I was an only child and, sometimes lonely, but it wasn't without its compensations. I was lucky enough to attend a good school and later University, which is where, in a way, my troubles began.

'In the summer of 1836...just after my eighteenth birthday...my best friend, Andries Dubois and I were given the opportunity by my father to travel with him to England on business. We were to stay in Liverpool for a month. We had a great time, even though we struggled initially with the language and met a lot of interesting people. Two people in particular...Belle Campbell and her friend, Caroline Stewart.

'I could tell immediately that Andries was attracted to Belle, but she also flirted outrageously with me and Andries eventually bowed out. This meant we could enjoy our time as a foursome and not favour either girl. We learned that they had left their homes in Scotland and were seeking a more exciting life in England. In fact, Belle's ambition was to eventually emigrate to America; although Caroline was quite happy to settle in Liverpool. Anyway, inevitably, we paired off, me with Belle, surprisingly and Andries with Caroline. By the end of our holiday I was completely smitten. She was older, more experienced, outgoing and a lot of fun and I was fairly naïve, so I invited her back to Ghent. I persuaded my father to allow her to travel with us and, like the good sort he is, he even paid her passage. Andries, however, sailed without Caroline, promising her he would return one day. Of course, I knew that he had no intention of returning, as he was a womaniser and just out for a good time.

'Belle and I were married when I was nineteen and she was twenty. She never spoke of her family, although I knew they lived in Scotland. She never made contact with them, because she wanted to live life to the full and see the world, hence her decision to move to Liverpool. That would be her starting point she said, until she could afford to travel further afield and leave her unambitious family behind.

'We lived with my parents for a while, until I went into business with my father and rented an apartment in the centre of Ghent.

'Unfortunately, Belle didn't really take to life in Belgium. She struggled with the language and often stayed in the apartment for days without venturing out. I tried hard to help her integrate, but she wasn't interested. In fact, she became obsessed with emigrating to America. She said it was the land of opportunity and that Ghent was a dead-end place where nothing happened. Then 'out of the blue' she became pregnant and our son, Jack Benard was born on 21st December 1838.

'Things began to improve, or so I thought. Then when Jack turned one, she became distant and never had any time for us as a couple. She started going out more and leaving Jack with my mother. I was away for months at a time with the business and our relationship deteriorated.

'Earlier this year she suggested that she and Jack accompany me to Liverpool on a business trip. I was somewhat surprised, as she had never shown any previous interest in returning there, but pleased nonetheless. She said the idea had come to her when she had 'bumped' into Andries at the weekly market and he mentioned that he was thinking of taking another trip to Liverpool for old times sake, to seek out Caroline. Apparently he had fond memories and had been thinking about her a lot lately. I was sceptical of his motives. Andries entertained many girlfriends over the years since he returned to Ghent. Never once did he mention Caroline since that initial foray to Liverpool, but maybe he was ready to settle down now.

'Belle told me that Andries had missed my company and hadn't seen much of me lately. He felt we had drifted apart over the last couple of years, probably due to my business commitments, but that we should get together for a catch up. I agreed, as I thought it would give me more time to spend with Jack and maybe bring Belle and me closer together. What an idiotic idea that turned out to be.

'Anyway, we booked a passage to arrive in Liverpool on Saturday the 27th February and planned to stay at the Adelphi for a month. This would enable me to meet with my business associates and also have time to relax and see the sights.

'Andries stayed at a small hotel on Lime Street and I did wonder why he didn't want to stay at the Adelphi, but he said he preferred a smaller, cosier establishment. I thought he meant it would be easier to sneak Caroline into his room, without being seen, as proprietors of small establishments usually turn a 'blind' eye to such shenanigans. In truth, it was easier for Belle and him to have clandestine moments together, without fear of being discovered.

'After a couple of weeks, I had chance to wind down from business meetings and felt more relaxed than I had for years, with more time to spend with Belle and Jack. I did notice that more and more we were joined by Andries, who appeared to have forgotten his quest to find Caroline.

'On occasion, Belle asked if I would look after Jack, while she took the opportunity to go shopping. I agreed as it gave me more time with our son and I got a lot closer to him while Belle was off spending money. She enjoyed the whole shopping experience and Andries didn't seem to mind being dragged along. It must have been during these times that they were planning their passage to America.

'Then on Tuesday the 16th March, she returned from an afternoon shopping and suggested an evening alone together. We arranged to have dinner in our room, which gave her the opportunity to drop the 'bombshell', which shook me rigid. She thought our marriage was a 'sham', that I didn't pay her enough attention and was away for long periods, leaving her to cope with Jack alone. I agreed that the situation wasn't ideal, but assured her that when the business was reasonably established, I would not have the need to go away for such long periods. We would be able to afford to employ someone who could manage the Liverpool side of the business. She said that she wanted someone who would show her a good time and take her out to the theatre and music halls. I reminded her that we had responsibilities and, although my mother would look after Jack, who she loved to have stay over, it wasn't fair to expect her to be at our beck and call every weekend. I said we would be able to go out to the theatre on occasion, but that we should do things together as a family and take Jack out as often as we could. She responded by saying I was boring, never wanting to do what she wanted, but that it was too late anyway. They had not meant it to happen, but Andries and her had fallen in love, and wanted to be together.

'I was extremely shocked and hurt and unable to comprehend how this could have happened in such a short space of time. She told me that they had been seeing each other for several months, on the occasions I had been away on business. Apparently, it was my fault, that I had pushed her into seeing him, as he was the only person in Ghent she knew, initially seeking him out for friendship. I had a barrage of questions to ask her, but in the next breath she advised me that they were going away and taking Jack with them.

'Anger and disbelief rose up inside me and I wanted to strike Andries, in fact, knock him senseless for what he had done. I could not believe that both my best friend and my wife had completely betrayed me. Then the worse news of all, or so I thought, was that they would be sailing on the 'William Brown', on Thursday, bound for Philadelphia. My whole world fell apart as the realisation hit me that I may never see my son again.'

Lizzie looked at Marcus with tears in her eyes, as she tried to imagine the awful reality of losing a child. 'Oh Marcus how could they do that to you? Couldn't you have made her see how cruel that was?' She placed her hand over his and squeezed it lightly. Her whole body outraged by such a callous act.

'No Elizabeth, I tried, oh how I tried, but she was adamant about leaving me and there was nothing left to salvage. I would never, ever, raise my hand to a woman Elizabeth, but at that moment, I wanted to put my hands around her neck and squeeze the life out of her for what she was about to do.

'We argued bitterly as I tried to convince her that Andries would soon tire of her, especially with a young boy tagging along. When another pretty face took his eye, he would be off. One thing I knew about Andries from the moment he reached puberty, was that he was and always would be a womaniser. What I never expected was that he would take my woman and, more importantly, my son away from me.

'We had been such close friends, even though I knew he was a philanderer. All the way through school and University, we had an unwritten rule that we would never move in on each other's girlfriends and he seemed to respect that...until Belle.

'Anyway, I could see that any pleading or reasoned discussion was futile, especially so when she stated she was moving out of the hotel that evening to stay with Andries until the ship sailed. She was adamant our marriage was over and I knew then I had lost. I obviously tried to salvage what I could from the situation, as Belle was no longer important to me and Andries an enemy, no longer my best friend. What I couldn't contemplate was never seeing my son again. I made her promise to keep in contact with me for Jack's sake and let me know their address so that I could visit. I vowed to travel to Philadelphia as soon as they were settled - not to try to win her back, but to spend time with my son, the most important person in my life.

'I think I knew that Belle hadn't loved me for some time. If I had been honest with myself, I would have admitted that I too no longer loved her. Those feelings had died even before we came to Liverpool, but I believed that marriage was forever and that we should try and make it work for Jack's sake. I hoped that, over time, she could be persuaded to allow me to take him back to Ghent for a holiday.

'Finally, the discussions came to an end and she agreed to my request. She packed her case, gathered up Jack's things and left me standing there alone in the hotel room, my little boy asking her why his daddy wasn't going with them. It broke my heart Elizabeth, as he waved his little hand and blew me a kiss goodbye. For the next hour I stood there feeling totally bereft. I thought that was the worst moment of my life...I was wrong. It's funny isn't it that sometimes one feels nothing could get any worse...then it does and you wish you could have been left to cope with the original moment?'

Lizzie nodded in agreement and looked tenderly at Marcus as he relived his experience.

'Anyway on the 18th March, I stood on the dockside and watched the 'William Brown' sail out to the open sea. With tears in my eyes, I waved my son goodbye. Belle held him in her arms...it was to be the last time I saw them.

'I stayed on at the hotel, not wanting to make the journey back to Ghent without Jack. I wandered around for days, doing nothing but thinking dark thoughts of how my future would be without my son. I felt lonely, betrayed and really low.

'Almost a month later on the morning of the 19th April, I awoke with a sense of foreboding, the skies were grey and I could not shake myself from an irrational fear that pervaded my body. I went down to breakfast at 8 a.m. and calculated that the 'William Brown' would be somewhere off Newfoundland, where it would be four thirty in the morning - three and a half hours behind Greenwich. Jack would still be fast asleep as dawn broke...I wasn't to know until ten days later that he would never see the dawn break ever again, not that day nor any other day, as the ship had hit an iceberg at 10 p.m. on the previous night, South East of Cape Race, Newfoundland and my worst nightmare had come true, I would never see my son again.'

Lizzie listened in silence to the awful tale that unfolded; how the news was brought to Liverpool by the captain of the 'Royal William', which had stopped off at St John's, Newfoundland for supplies. The names of Belle Van Der Duim, Jack Benard Van Der Duim and Andries Dubois were among those missing, feared dead.

It appeared that some passengers had survived the initial sinking, but died later after being ousted from the overcrowded lifeboats. Confirmation came several weeks after the fateful day that Andries Dubois had perished in the initial sinking, but no information was available with regard to Belle and Jack. They were not on the list of those passengers that had survived. Hope faded over the next few months that his beloved son would be found alive.

Silent now, a sad Marcus looked up at Lizzie who still comforted him with her hand on his. 'Maybe they did survive,' Lizzie said, hope rising in her voice. 'Maybe they managed to get into a lifeboat and were rescued. Perhaps Belle was confused and couldn't remember who she was,' she paused, 'Marcus that could have happened. Jack may yet be found.'

Marcus gave a wry smile and was grateful for Lizzie's optimism, although he did not believe it could be true. 'No, Elizabeth, I want to believe it, but I have to accept that I may never see Jack again. I promised myself last week, that if there was still no word of them being found alive, I would have to pick up the pieces, go back to Ghent and get on with my life. I will always live in hope of course, that one day I will see him again and for that reason I must go on. Putting my life on hold will not achieve anything. If by some miracle he is alive, I need to be fit and well and waiting to welcome him home.'

Lizzie nodded. 'Yes, you must try, but just how you will cope with such a dark cloud hanging over you, I don't know. I wish I could do something to help, but I am not sure I can ease your pain.'

Lizzie's mood had gone very flat. She looked down into the depths of her coffee cup and a big tear rolled down her face. She had never felt so much sorrow for anyone, even Kate's sadness on the night she left with Rosalie on her journey to London could not compare with this.

Conversely, Marcus felt suddenly uplifted by Lizzie's concern and was gladdened in his heart that he had met such a warm, sincere person to whom he could confide his innermost thoughts. He felt sad, however, that he had burdened her with his own troubles and immediately felt the need to make amends. 'Look Elizabeth, what has happened to me is a tragedy that cannot be undone, but since I have met you, there have been odd moments where my head has not been filled with such sombre thoughts. You have brought some light into my darkness and have given me a reason to move on with my life. I want to suggest something to you,' he paused, as he looked searchingly into her eyes, hoping to find a flicker of the warmth and eagerness he had seen earlier in the evening. Lizzie returned his gaze and could not disguise the overwhelming desire to be with him. Encouraged, Marcus decided to declare his feelings for her. 'We should agree to put our pasts aside and look forward to the future…A future which I can well see us facing together. What do you say?'

Lizzie suddenly found herself lost for words as she gazed back at this man who, despite his devastating loss, seemed to know exactly what he wanted in life and, inconceivably, that appeared to include her. She had never met anyone quite like him and, guiltily, her thoughts turned again to the love she had held for the handsome and caring, Daniel Lorimer. Some how this man was different, he was confident and decisive. She knew instinctively that he would take care of her and love her, no matter what obstacles befell them. She was almost carried away on a wave of hope and a belief that her future lay with this stranger, a man she had met only hours before. But the promise she made to Kate reminded her that she must leave tomorrow morning and continue her journey to London.

She was about to deliver her reply when Marcus grasped both her hands in his own and spoke urgently to her. 'I know what you are thinking Elizabeth. That we have only just met and it could be a mistake. Maybe you cannot believe that I am serious, but I am. I am also prepared to wait until we can be together again. I understand that you must fulfill your promise to Kate and I wouldn't expect any less of you. But after you have completed your mission, you will be a free woman...free to do exactly as you wish...free to return here and be with me. Please don't say no,' he paused, 'Let's take our coffee through to the lounge where we can be more comfortable and less vulnerable to the prying eyes of the other diners.'

Lizzie smiled at Marcus and agreed to his request. They walked through to the cosy and intimate lounge area, Marcus's arm went around Lizzie's waist and those heady exciting feelings washed through her body. He looked intently into her eyes and held her gaze before speaking his thoughts. 'You know Elizabeth, this need not be the end, it could be just the beginning. I have to see you again soon. Please say you agree. Even now I cannot imagine my life without you.'

Happily defeated, Lizzie acquiesced and wished that she could stay here with him, but she knew she would have to complete her journey, before she could see him again. 'Marcus, I feel the same way and you are right, we have to see each other again and I am glad that you understand that I must make the journey to London,' she paused, 'that I must keep my promise to Kate. It will be five months before I can meet with you again. Are you sure you want to wait that long for me?'

Smiling now, Marcus held her close. 'I will wait for as long as it takes. We will make a pact. I will be waiting for you here in the Adelphi at the table in the window, in five months from now. The date will be the 1st March 1842 at 12 noon. Will you promise to be there Elizabeth?'

Lizzie looked into Marcus's eyes and saw that he meant every word. She felt that, despite her feelings for her first love, Daniel, which had inexplicably diminished, this man, without a doubt, would be the one with whom she would wish to spend the rest of her life. 'Marcus, I promise to meet you. Nothing will stop us being together.'

'Elizabeth, I have something else to tell you. I realise this is very sudden and it has been such a short time that we have known each other, but I have fallen in love with you. Is it possible that you feel the same?'

Lizzie was on cloud nine and could barely contain her happiness. 'Can this be happening to me?' she thought. 'Is this just a dream?' She knew she was wide-awake when she looked again at the expectant face of Marcus Van Der Duim, willing her to reciprocate. 'Yes Marcus, yes, I do love you, very much...although I am a little afraid that this has happened so quickly. Are you sure you are in love with me? What about Belle?' Lizzie continued without waiting for Marcus to reply. 'I know I love you and want to be with you, but still can't believe you would want me. After all, I have no material things to bring to you and, until recently, I was just a servant.'

Marcus gave Lizzie a smile that melted her heart as he again confirmed his commitment to her and felt he should take things a step further by proposing that she become his wife. 'Elizabeth, you say you have nothing to bring, but you have everything I would ever need. You are kind, understanding, beautiful and, most importantly, you love me. That is more than enough for any man.'

Marcus clasped her hands and knelt before her and even though a few guests were discreetly looking at the scene unfolding before them, he wanted to propose properly to her. Looking up into her eyes he spoke softly. 'Elizabeth Cameron, will you do me the honour of becoming my wife?'

Lizzie eyes were wide and her love for this man shone out for all to see. 'Oh Marcus, yes, yes, I will. I do love you very much.'

Moving away from the glare of people in the residents lounge, he escorted her to her room. Outside the door he circled his arms around her and kissed her softly.

Lizzie did not want the moment to end, but realised the time was coming for them to part. She decided to give Marcus something as a sign of her intention to meet with him again. 'Listen Marcus, I would like to give you something to keep for me. Will you wait here while I fetch it from my room?'

Lizzie went straight to her bag and took out the little book of poems by Robert Burns. She placed a bookmark on the page containing her favourite poem, 'A Red, Red Rose', and handed it to Marcus, explaining why it was so precious to her and requesting that he keep it with him until they were together once more. 'When you are feeling sad, read this poem to remind yourself that you are no longer alone. That in five short months, we will be together again, never to part. Bring it back with you to the Adelphi on the 1st March at noon, place it on our table by the window, look up and I will be there,' she paused, 'It will be a sign of our commitment to each other.'

He looked down at the words underlined by Lizzie and realised how important this book was to her and that the words captured her intentions perfectly. He spoke them out loud and both knew that nothing would prevent them meeting in five months time.

> *'And fare thee weel, my only luve,*
> *And fare thee weel awhile!*
> *And I will come again, my luve...*
> *Tho' it were ten thousand mile...'*

Wishing to add something of his own to seal his love for her, he felt inside his pocket and pulled out a silver sixpenny piece. 'Elizabeth, I also have something for you to keep. My grandmother placed two silver sixpenny pieces in my hands when I was born to bring me luck. They worked, because they brought us together. Keep this one close to you, it will keep you safe until we can be together again. It has a little hole near the top so you could thread it through with some ribbon and keep it around your neck. Now come over to the window with me, I want to show you something.' Marcus guided her over to the large window at the end of the corridor and stood behind her speaking softly, his arms around her waist. She could feel his breath on her neck and she wanted to stay there forever with him beside her, just looking up at the stars. The moon was bright and cast a romantic glow on the couple standing alone together.

Marcus pointed towards the horizon where the stars were twinkling in the night sky. 'See there, below the W shape, that is 'Cassiopeia' and the group of stars dangling from the left edge of the 'W' is 'Perseus'. It is high up in the sky all winter, so it is not too hard to find. Every evening at 6 p.m. wherever we are, we can both look up and seek out 'Perseus'. Legend says that 'Perseus' and 'Andromeda' were married and lead a long, happy life together. He keeps watch over her. I will watch over you Elizabeth when we are together, but for now, I must leave you.' Then he kissed her before turning and walking away, but looking back he called to her once more. 'Vaarwel maar niet voor eeuwig' my love, goodbye, but not forever, keep safe for me.' Then he was gone.

Back in her room, Lizzie was heady with excitement and quickly undid the ribbon she always wore around her neck, which held the tiny 'keeper' box key. She threaded the silver sixpence and tied it back around her neck. The sensation of Marcus's kiss, which had sealed their future together, still lingered, as she gazed at the stars from her window and thought - never before had they seemed so bright.

CHAPTER SIXTEEN

A Change of Plan

Lizzie awoke suddenly to the sound of voices emanating from the street below and the bright morning sun streaming in through the window of her room. She had overslept and her train had left for Manchester one and a half hours ago. She groaned silently as she looked around the room trying not to panic. 'Keep calm Lizzie, you will just have to catch a later train,' she said out loud. 'It's not the end of the world, you will be able to do that,' she convinced herself and rushed around the room, grabbing items to throw into her valise. She still found time to smile as she recalled the sensuous kiss planted on her lips by Marcus the night before, that even now sent shivers through her body.

She shelved her thoughts, emptied her handbag onto the bed and sorted through her papers. The solicitor's letter, which she no longer needed to keep in her bag, was relocated in the false bottom of the keeper box and that in turn was carefully placed in the trunk. The punched tickets from her journey on the 'Royal George' were slipped into the side pocket of her valise.

There was no sign of Marcus when she entered the foyer at 11.45 a.m. An enquiry at the desk confirmed he had checked out at five a.m. to catch the ship back to Belgium.

The cab took fifteen minutes to arrive at the station and by the time she summoned a porter to transport her luggage to the first class booking hall, it was gone twelve.

Fortunately, the elderly booking clerk understood her dilemma. He took out his ledger, found the booking entry and with the help of a rubber, made an alteration to the time and re-issued her tickets. He handed them over to Lizzie and winked. Unable to resist a pretty face, he smilingly informed her of procedures. 'I'm not supposed to re-issue pre-booked tickets, but I can see you are in a bit of a pickle. You are very brave travelling alone with a baby young lady. I hope you know where you are going, as it is easy to get lost around the stations.'

Lizzie returned his smile as she responded to his advice. 'Oh yes, I know it can be confusing, but I am going down to London to be with my husband. Thankfully, the next stage of my journey will be the last. I'm travelling by Royal Mail Coach to Dunstable to meet my aunt.'

The elderly clerk tipped his hat as she turned to leave. 'Well you will have to hope there aren't any more delays as the Royal Mail Coaches leave promptly at 4 p.m. Good luck my dear and keep safe.'

'Thank you, I will,' smiled Lizzie.

However, when she arrived on the platform, she heard an announcement concerning the 2 o'clock train, which had been delayed, due to a points' failure. It would not be leaving until 3 p.m., which meant Lizzie's arrival in Manchester would now be around 4.20 p.m. The train, yet again delayed, eventually reached its destination at Liverpool Road station at 4.40 p.m.

On arrival, a porter transported her luggage to the Royal Mail coach parks where she found the coaches had left at 4 p.m. sharp, just as the booking clerk had indicated. It was now a quarter to five and she was desperate to find a solution to the dilemma she now faced. Should she find an hotel, or should she try to reach Dunstable at the agreed time to meet Aunt Jayne by other means? The porter was unloading her luggage as she spotted a coach and four close to where the Royal Mail coaches had been waiting. Maybe, she thought, I can persuade the driver to turn out tonight.

It was apparent that he had not been hired, as most passengers would have left already, preferring to travel by Royal Mail coach. They were more comfortable and charged a fixed fee, whereas, independent coach drivers could charge what they liked and depart a good hour or so after the Royal Mail coaches. At this time of year, the nights were beginning to draw in, with dusk falling around 5.30 p.m., consequently, an independent would have to complete the whole journey in darkness.

However, Lizzie desperately wanted to keep to her schedule, so she approached the coach driver, who smiled down at her from the cab. He seemed a 'cocky' sort and rather too sure of himself, standing with one foot on the ground and the other on the coach step. For a moment she was tempted to hail a cab, find an hotel and continue her journey the following morning. However, when he came towards her and stood by the luggage, he appeared more friendly.

Lizzie approached him cautiously. 'I was wondering whether it is too late to travel tonight on such a long journey, especially without the advantage of the daylight hours. I was hoping to reach Dunstable on Sunday morning to meet with my aunt, but if I wait until tomorrow that won't be possible. Would you consider a night run to Derby?' In anticipation of a positive response, Lizzie gave him one of her most persuasive smiles.

The coach driver grinned and nodded his head in a gesture, which meant he was willing, provided the price was right.

'I will pay you six sovereigns for your trouble, which I trust will make up for your loss in taking only one passenger. I will also give you the money now for the whole journey to London,' said Lizzie hopefully, taking the money from her bag.

Jack, the coach driver, quickly calculated she would be paying almost double his usual charge per passenger. Furthermore, the likelihood of any other passengers materialising this evening were negligible, so he was more than happy with the deal. If he could just persuade the young lady to stop off at Nottingham instead of Derby, then he could meet with his lover, Molly Brown. That would be more than worthwhile and an added bonus. 'All right, Miss, I will be happy to take you, provided you don't mind stopping off in Nottingham instead of Derby, where I have some business to conduct. It is only sixty one miles to Nottingham and ninety one miles to Derby, so we should arrive in Nottingham earlier, maybe around 10.30 this evening.'

Lizzie considered her position and after an assurance from Jack that Nottingham had some excellent coaching inns, she agreed.

'Allow me to help you aboard. Considering there are only yourself and the little one, your valise can go inside. The trunk will be safe enough strapped to the rear of the coach. Well miss, the horses will travel quicker with a lighter load, so with a bit of luck, we will make good progress. By the way my name is Jack…Jack Garrett at your service.' Jack extended his hand and helped Lizzie settle Rosalie down, offering a thick blanket to keep her warm and cosy. He placed the valise up against the seat, which transformed it into a small bed, so that Rosalie would not fall out.

Lizzie began to warm towards this young man, who went to great pains to ensure their comfort.

Jack Garrett placed the fare money given to him by Lizzie in a worn leather pouch, which he kept around his waist. When he opened his jacket, Lizzie noticed a small pistol protruding from his pocket, which she assumed he kept in the unlikely event of trouble. Her naivety of travelling with an independent driver clouded her judgement and consequently made her more vulnerable.

There were still instances of coaches being robbed by highwaymen, particularly the independents' as they travelled alone. The Royal Mail Coaches had a guard and a driver up front to safeguard the passengers and the sacks of mail they were transporting.

It was 5.30 p.m. when the coach and four cantered out of the city on the road to Nottingham. The journey was fairly uneventful and they made good time, arriving at their destination a little after 10.30 p.m. Jack dropped Lizzie off at the King's Head in the area of Narrow Marsh. She took the valise and, at the suggestion of Jack, left the trunk strapped to the back of the coach, after an assurance that it would be quite safe. Jack then went in search of Molly Brown, barmaid at the Loggerheads public house. He smiled to himself at the thought of the long night of drinking and passionate lovemaking ahead of him.

PART TWO

Nottingham, England, 1841

Hannah Merchant

Chapter One

Decisions and Consequences

On Friday the 1st October 1841 Clara Milligan's day started the same as any other in the last eight years. Her routine of rising at 5 a.m. Monday through Sunday never altered. She cooked the men in her life a hearty breakfast, maybe one egg, if they were lucky, a rasher of bacon, some tomatoes, a slice of fried bread and a large mug of tea. The youngest members, Tillie and Alice rose at 6 a.m. and the whole process began again.

Clara's husband, Arthur, had a day off and her son, David, although presently unemployed, was looking forward to being at home with the family at the weekend.

The Milligans' were a close family, Clara was 38 years old, Arthur 40, David 22, Matilda, known as Tillie, 10 and little Alice, 8.

Clara was a jolly, easy-going woman, with brown hair, that protruded from under a dolly cap. She wore the cap when attending to the various domestic duties around the house, along with a blue apron tied over a brown dress, which only just covered her ample bosom. Black boots which had seen better days, completed the spectacle.

Clara married Arthur when she was fifteen and a half, having become pregnant at fifteen with her first born, David. They were in love and there was no doubt in Arthur's mind, after Clara gave him the news, that he would wed her as soon as her parents gave their consent.

Her parents were disappointed when she told them, but her father reasoned that it wasn't unusual for girls of their class to find themselves in such a predicament and immediately gave his blessing. He knew his Clara was a good girl with a kind heart and if she loved Arthur that was good enough for him.

Clara and Arthur lived with his parents in Foundry Yard, until they managed to rent a dwelling in Knotted Alley; both places were located in Narrow Marsh, one of the poorest areas in Nottingham. Their dwelling had a back yard, accessed via an alley. This ran behind the other houses in the terrace, eventually leading to the area behind the pub. The landlord allowed Clara to keep her cart there in exchange for a supply of the Milligans' fresh milk.

Most of the terraced houses in the Marsh were 'back to back' - joined together in the middle, with only one door at the front of the house. Number fourteen Knotted Alley was the exception; it had two entrances and the use of the side entrance by the pub, which lead directly on to Leenside.

Arthur worked in a 'drift' mine to the south of Nottingham before they married. Clara had also worked at the mine, sorting coal on the surface, but Arthur made Clara give up this hard, dirty work the day she announced she was pregnant. He said no wife of his would work at a mine. He too, came out of the trade when he was lucky enough to be given two cows by an old farmer at the Marsh Farm in Kirke's Yard. Arthur had dragged the man's son to safety during an accident at the mine and he was extremely grateful to him.

The Milligans' kept the two cows in the backyard and sold milk from there, until Arthur obtained his cart. This gave him the wherewithal to deliver the milk to the local area.

Unlike most milk producers thereabouts, Arthur kept his cows and his yard meticulously clean and avoided any close proximity to pigs, which spread brucellosis, an infectious bacterial disease. Clara helped with the milking and prepared the milk for sale. More often than not, the product was of passable quality and not infected with the disease.

To supplement their coffers, Arthur worked as a boatman on the canal, loading and unloading goods onto barges.

This job provided him with an opportunity to increase distribution of his milk, butter and cheese. Clara also turned her hand to the making of the bi-products in her own small scullery. They were reasonably off compared to most other folks in the Marsh, as most only managed to survive week to week, using their own ingenuity. They were often reduced to stealing, bartering or begging for food. Any legally earned money paid the rent and kept many from being thrown into the workhouse - something to be avoided at all costs.

Tillie was employed as a maid of all works at one of the large houses on St James' Street. She had one Friday off in four. David was seeking work, something other than drift mining or working on the river; although some said he had aspirations beyond his station. Alice would probably follow her sister into service when she became nine, because her family were well respected in the neighbourhood and known for their honesty and hard work.

Today, as a special treat, Arthur took the girls down to the annual Goose Fair. They were delighted when their dad won twice on the 'coconut shy'. They couldn't wait to get home so that he could drill holes in the top of the nuts to extract the sweet milk inside.

On their return, Clara, who had been preoccupied all day, patiently waited for the coconut ritual to end, so that she could have a quiet word with Arthur about their son. When the girls were ensconced in the parlour with a pile of coconut and a large glass of milk each, Clara took Arthur to one side. 'Lissen Arthur me duck, I want yer ter teck our David aht later and have a word we 'im abaht finding a job. A know he's looking ter find summat berra than mining or barging, but a don't think we can carry on mecking ends meet wi'out another wage. Cause, a want 'im ter berra hissen, but am afraid, needs must me duck.'

Arthur looked kindly at his wife and had to agree with her reasoning. 'Aye, yer right Clara me duck. We'll ga fer a walk along the cliffs later and I'll 'ave a word we 'im.'

Clara, feeling relieved, finished peeling the potatoes for their evening meal of crusty bread and broth.

Lizzie Cameron was breakfasting at the King's Head on Friday 1st October and looking forward to visiting the Nottingham Goose Fair after lunch, as suggested by the landlord's wife. She would not be travelling on the next leg of her journey until later that evening, as the coach driver had some business to attend to in the town. He had informed her that he preferred to travel overnight anyway. She was to meet him at the Loggerheads on the west side of town at eight o'clock that evening. After lunch, Lizzie wrapped Rosalie up warm, strapped her into the sling and then, following directions given to her by the landlord, set off excitedly towards the centre of the town.

She walked through the narrow streets and made a mental note of landmarks along the way to guide her return later. It was less than half a mile on foot, so she soon entered the Market Square where the main fair was in full swing.

Lizzie's eyes were out on stalks as she surveyed the scene unfolding before her. It was as if she had walked into a winter wonderland. All around the Square were gaslights, linked to the stalls, which shone brightly and glinted like hundreds of tiny stars.

Everything imaginable was being sold. There were livestock stalls with geese, hens, cattle and wild animals. Entertainment booths included a Madame Tussaud waxworks, amateur theatricals with dwarfs, numerous fat ladies and several gypsy singers. There was an abundance of refreshment stalls, which complemented those selling local lace, hosiery and willow baskets. Sweet stalls sold 'whipcords' and 'liquorice lights' and the surrounding streets were lined with other vendors selling their wares, all vying for trade in a cacophony of light and sound.

Lizzie wandered around, stopping now and again to buy some lace and other small items she could carry back to the inn to pack into her valise.

The wonderful aromas invading her nostrils convinced her to gravitate towards the stalls selling teas, cocoa and delicious looking cakes and pastries.

One of the stallholders' noticed Lizzie as she carried Rosalie through the crowd of jovial revellers, who were pushing and shoving to make sure that they weren't missing anything. The stallholder leaned forward and spoke to Lizzie, as she struggled to get her purse out, whilst keeping Rosalie pressed close to her breast. 'Hello love, you look a bit weary, how about a nice cup of char?'

Lizzie stopped and looked at the woman who was selling tea and pastries from a stall, which looked clean and respectable. 'That would be lovely, thank you and I will have one of those delicious looking scones.'

Daisy looked hard at Lizzie as she spoke and realised instantly that she was not from the local area. 'You're not from around here are you?'

'No, no I am not. I've travelled down from Glasgow with my baby, on my way to London.'

Claiming Rosalie as her own gave her a strange feeling of unreality, but she already loved her little charge. Indeed, she would be looking after her as her own for quite a while. She had immediately realised since embarking on the journey, that she needed to embrace the whole idea of motherhood pretty quickly and was slowly engaging with Rosalie's needs, but she still had a long way to go.

'She is beautiful, what's her name?'

'Rosalie...her name is Rosalie, which means fair as a Rose.'

'Can I hold her for a few moments while you drink your tea?'

Lizzie hesitated at first, but the woman was very friendly and she couldn't see the harm. Her arms were getting quite tired supporting the sling and it was a relief to hand Rosalie over for a little while.

The stallholder gazed down at the tiny bundle. 'Hello little one, oh you are lovely and not very old either.'

Lizzie drank the hot tea gratefully and the two women were soon conversing freely.

The stallholder did not wish to pry, but was curious as to why this young woman was alone, so gave her own name to boost Lizzie's confidence. 'My name is Daisy and my husband, Archie, is selling some lovely hand made crafts just over there. Are you here on your own?'

This wasn't the first time that Lizzie found herself explaining her situation but it didn't get any easier. She decided to revert back to her original story, only changing her surname to Lorimer. She decided taking Daniel's name would be preferable to revealing her own name to a relative stranger. To introduce Marcus, would be an added complication, so once again she outlined her imagined position, using Aunt Jayne's address as her intended destination. 'My name is Lizzie Lorimer and I am travelling down to London to be with my husband. We are moving down from Glasgow to Carlton House Terrace off Pall Mall.'

'My, oh my, that is a coincidence.' Daisy called across to her husband, beckoning him to join her. 'Here, Archie, this young lady is Lizzie Lorimer and she is travelling down to London to meet up with her husband. You'll never guess where he is living…close to St James' Park - would you believe it?'

Archie left his stall for a moment and came over to introduce himself. 'Good day to you, Archie's the name, Archie Pickering. My lovely wife's parents live in that neck of the woods. Her mother works in a cotton merchant's shop in St James Street, not far from St James' Park. 'Ain't that right Daisy?'

'Yes, yes, it's true. I haven't seen my mam for three years now, as we travel round a lot. I do miss her though. Listen, I hope you don't think I am taking a liberty, but I don't suppose you would be kind enough to call in on her place of work sometime when you are out and about and give her our love and good wishes? She'd be made up with that.'

Lizzie wondered if she could ever manage such a thing, but, anxious to please, she found herself agreeing to the request.

'Well yes, I probably could. Can you give me her name and address and I, yes...I will definitely do that for you?'

'Wait a minute, have you got a bit of paper Archie?' Daisy eventually wrote down the information on a piece of grubby notepaper produced by Archie.

'I'll just write her Christian name, which is Hannah and to remind you, I will put that she works in a Merchant's shop at 64 St James Street - there how's that?'

Lizzie read the scrawly writing - Hannah - Merchant, 64 St James Street. She carefully folded it and placed it inside the pocket of her dress.

Lizzie was just about to move on when Archie suggested she have a look at a small cart that Daisy's sister had been given to transport her newborn baby. It had been strengthened and modified by their father, who added a little wicker hood to protect the baby from the elements. The cart had been an ideal size for a premature baby, but the child grew quickly, so was abandoned to their parents' cellar. Archie dragged it out years later to sell on his bric-a-brac stall at the fair. It was made of metal, which needed a new coat of paint and it had suffered some damage to the wicker hood. However, it was big enough to carry Rosalie, as she was a small baby and only a few weeks old. Of course, Rosalie would outgrow it in no time at all, but Lizzie didn't care. She was grateful to be relieved of the arduous task of carrying Rosalie back to the King's Head, despite the odd looks she might incur pushing the strange contraption.

'Well, it would be really useful to transport Rosalie back to the inn. How much do you want for it?'

Before Archie could put a price on the item, Daisy spoke up and pointedly looked at her husband, lest he should embarrass her by asking for money, especially from a young woman who had just agreed to take an important message to her mother. 'We don't want anything for it do we Archie? It really won't last very long and after you have been so kind as to agree to call on my mother, you must take it and we wish you well.'

'That really is most kind. Are you sure you don't want anything for it? I am happy to pay you a few shillings.'

Archie put out his hand to accept the coins and began to thank Lizzie for her generosity. 'Err Tha—'

Daisy brushed him aside and shook her head. 'No, really we don't want anything at all. Please accept it as a gift.'

Archie reluctantly agreed and straightened out the bedding inside the carriage. He felt guilty for trying to make a few coins out of it, so he added some sheets and two worn, but warm blankets off the stall, before handing it over to Lizzie, who smiled gratefully. 'Oh, well, all right, thank you very much and I won't forget to look in on your mother, Daisy.'

Lizzie laid Rosalie inside the carriage and tucked her in securely, so that only her golden curly hair peeped out from the blankets Archie had given her. To make it extra secure, she tied one of the sheets around the entire cart so that Rosalie was strapped in and cocooned against the elements. Then it was time to return to the King's Head for tea before proceeding to the Loggerheads Inn to meet the coach for her journey down to Great Brington. It was now dusk and a little foggy, so she pulled her green cloak close around her and wheeled Rosalie off in the direction of Narrow Marsh.

Lizzie was worried she wouldn't remember her way in this unfamiliar city. She walked down the steep and narrow Drury Hill, which she recognised from her outward journey to the fair, but as the fog became thicker, her ability to distinguish the landmarks, became less apparent. Instead of turning left along Narrow Marsh in the direction of the King's Head, she continued on down Turn Calf Alley, away from the Marsh and down Trent Row, which lead directly to the canal. She peered through the fog and eventually came across a small track meandering along the bank above the water, which she walked along for a short while. There was no one around to ask directions and nowhere seemed familiar.

It was getting colder but she stopped and tried to regain her bearings. It was then she heard a thudding noise, which frightened her. The noise became louder, but the fog and the darkness made it difficult to distinguish the direction from which it was coming. She looked around wildly but too late Lizzie recognised the sound of thundering hoofs and turned to see a loose horse bearing down on her. She pushed the cart away from its path, but was knocked to the ground on the grassy verge, as the horse thundered past into the darkness of the low-lying fog.

❦

Albert Green and Michael Drake staggered drunkenly along the towpath. They had also lost their bearings in the fog and taken a wrong turn in their efforts to find their accommodation at the Loggerheads public house. They were, however, feeling pretty pleased with their haul of trinkets, pocketed from unsuspecting revellers at the fair, when they inadvertently stumbled across a dark object blocking their way, as they swayed and teetered along the path.

What they thought was a pile of old rags they nearly tripped over was, in fact, a woman, lying on the grass with a green cloak wrapped around her body.

Albert passed a derogatory comment to his partner in crime. 'Look at 'er, she looks proppa drunk.'

'Are ya sure? She could be dead. Gee 'er a bit of a nudge.'

Albert pressed the end of his toe firmly against Lizzie's torso, but she did not move.

'Hey, Michael, ya could be right, she in't movin.'

Michael considered what to do but didn't think much of taking responsibility for this woman, especially if she was dead. 'Aw, come on Albert let's be off, I'm parched and in need of a stiff drink.'

Albert, who was not opposed to taking items of clothing or boots from the dead, if it would earn him a copper or two, came up with the idea of removing her cloak. 'Let's nick 'er cloak. It in't no good ta 'er now. What da ya say Michael?'

'Come on then, 'urry up. What ya' goin ta' do we it anyrode?'

'We can flog it, numbskull. What d'ya think we goin ta do we it? Wear it? ya daft sod.'

Albert swiftly removed the cloak from Lizzie's body and also took her handbag for good measure, then he pushed her towards the canal, until she was almost in danger of tumbling down the bank.

Neither of the two men had noticed the upturned cart, which lay half hidden under a hedge, or, for that matter, heard the faint cry of a baby.

Michael looked suspiciously at his friend, as he thought he had spotted him removing something from the bag. They always shared any profits, with a consequence that he rather timidly confronted Albert about his actions.

His voice wavered as he asked tentatively. 'Is there oat in the bag Albert?'

Albert glared, but lied straight faced to his friend. 'No there in't and ta prove it, I'll sling it in the river.'

Too afraid to argue, Michael watched the bag float off on the current.

Albert, anxious to leave the scene, pushed Michael along the path, urging him to move on. 'Right, quick, get goan Mike. Ya too slow, ta catch a coad.'

The men ran off towards the Marsh area and disappeared into the persistently thick fog, which obliterated the landscape, cutting down visibility to a few feet.

Lizzie remained partly concealed and semi-conscious on the bank, totally oblivious to the unrelenting nightmare that was about to engulf her.

CHAPTER TWO

Jack Garrett and Molly Brown

At 8.30 p.m. on Friday evening, Jack Garrett was patiently waiting in the bar of the Loggerheads Inn, warming his feet on the blazing log fire. Every now and again he would glance up at the clock above the bar, sigh and feel ever more frustrated with the fact that his passenger, Mrs Cameron, had not turned up for the ongoing journey to Great Brington. He resolved that, if she didn't turn up in the next fifteen minutes, he would encourage Molly to accompany him down to London, where a killing could be made if he returned with a full coach. Mrs Cameron had, after all, paid more than enough for the whole outward journey, on Thursday evening. Her agreement to stop off in Nottingham instead of Derby, so that he could attend to a 'little business' had sealed the deal. That 'business' was for him to spend the evening and an entire morning with his mistress of nine years, Mrs Molly Brown, landlady of the Loggerheads Public House. He spent the early hours of Friday in Molly Brown's bed and the rest of the day propping up the bar. He was, however, careful to stagger his drinking, being drunk in charge of a coach and four, would certainly get him reported. Moreover, if word got round, he could easily lose his livelihood.

Jack always took this route down to Great Brington, in Northampton. Some passengers did not pre-book any of the Derby inns en-route and many were willing to take 'pot luck' on their arrival. Most were not averse to stopping off in Nottingham where a host of comfortable coaching inns were situated. In fact the first week in October made Nottingham a very popular overnight stop, with the visiting 'Goose Fair' continuing all week. This eight-day festival gave Jack the opportunity to spend plenty of free time with Molly Brown.

Initially, Jack met Molly on one of his overnight stops when requesting a room for the night. That room soon became the one in which Jack Garrett frequently bedded down. Molly's husband, Bill, was a sailor and away for long periods, so Molly needed little persuasion in succumbing to the charms of young Jack.

Another five minutes elapsed before the door to the Loggerheads was thrown wide open, allowing the cold swirling fog to enter the room which momentarily reduced the temperature in the warm bar. Two men, barely able to stand and stumbling over themselves, staggered in.

Albert Green left Michael Drake seated in a corner, then trod an uncertain path to the bar to order a couple of pints. He liked the look of the barmaid, so decided to chance his arm by suggesting she might like something more intimate to take place with himself. With not the best of approaches he leaned drunkenly close to Molly's face and, slurring his words, made a clumsy attempt at seducing her. 'Nah then me duck, 'ows abaht you an' me gerrin tagether later fer a bit of comfort this coad night?'

Albert Green fancied himself as a ladies man and in his delusional state, thought she would fall for his dubious charms. Yes, he thought, with a little bit of flattery and the promise of the rather grand cloak he had pilfered from the body of the woman on the towpath, Molly Brown might just be the woman to let him into her bed. His earlier successes at the fair and on the towpath had gone completely to his head and he thought he was in with a good chance. After all, he consoled himself, what were barmaids like her asking for anyway? made up to the 'nines', with breasts straining out of a low cut dress. She was obviously offering herself to anyone eager enough to take up the challenge. Encouraged by his own ego and false perception of her needs, he cupped his hand around the back of Molly's neck, pulled her towards him and whispered in her ear. 'I bet yu'd look a real beauty in an expensive cloak and I've got just the thing in me bag 'ere. What d'ya say we slip off up to ya room to try it on?'

Jack, who was observing the unfolding scene from where he was seated, wasted no time in getting up from his chair and, grabbing Albert by the throat, threw him up against the pillar at one end of the bar. 'What do you think you're on with? That's my girl you're messing with, get goin' before you feel the force of my fist.'

Taken aback by the sudden ferocity of the larger man, Albert immediately sobered up and backed off, making out he had been joking with Molly, only wanting to offer her a good quality cloak, without any other intention in mind.

To prove his point, Albert triumphantly pulled the green cloak out of his bag, like a rabbit out of a hat. 'Look mester, 'ere's the cloak I was telling ya abaht, ya can 'ave it for a few pence fa ya lady friend, though it's woth more.'

With sudden interest, Jack took a closer look at the cloak that Albert held up thinking he'd seen it somewhere before. 'Where did you get it from? You obviously didn't buy it?'

Albert quickly summed up the situation and didn't much like the threatening manner adopted by Jack. He thought it best to come up with a half-truth, to save himself anymore aggravation.

He turned to Michael for back up and launched into his explanation. 'We fount it, din't we Michael? On the bank dahn by the River Leen.'

Michael, trying to disassociate himself from his mate, nodded his head then quickly moved to a seat by the door, where, if he needed to, he could make a quick escape.

Jack looked keenly at Albert and threateningly accused him of stealing it. 'That's a likely story. Now come on where did you get it?'

'It's true we did find it. It did belong to someone. It wah this young woman who we fount lying on the towpath. She were dead and we shouted fer 'elp. There 'appened to be a doctor come by on 'is 'orse and he removed her cloak when he examined her. He arranged fer her to be taken away, burr'ee left her cloak on the bank. I picked it up and ran after him, but he'd disappeared inta the fog,' he paused, 'In't that right Michael?'

Michael, stunned by the cock and bull story conjured up by his friend was now full of admiration and quick to back up his story. 'Yeh, that's exacly wot 'appened, just exacly that. She were dead as a dodo, so 'ad no need forrit. So we din't see the 'arm in it.'

Jack was now very interested in the young woman who had been found 'dead', as he realised the cloak could have belonged to his passenger Mrs Cameron and she may be the 'dead' woman they were referring to.

Jack backed off and released Albert from his stranglehold, then started to quiz him about the woman. 'All right, all right, I'll decide later whether I believe you. Did you get a good look at this woman?'

Albert visibly relaxed as Jack, who seemed much more interested in the 'dead' woman, than beating seven bells out of him for attempting to bed his fancy piece, moved a safe distance away.

'Well it wah difficult gerrin a good look at 'er, as she wah lying on her stomach we 'er face on one side, but it looked like she 'ad long dark brown curly hair. Looked like a rich bitch, din't she Michael?'

'Yeh, that's right, looked well off I'd say.'

'Was she completely alone then?' Jack continued to quiz the two men closely.

'Yeh, she wah definitly alone.'

Jack sat down at the table and tried to reason why Mrs Cameron would be without her baby, but couldn't come up with an answer, although he was sure the cloak belonged to her. Of course, the men might be lying and could have robbed her of her possessions after attacking her, removing the cloak after she was dead. In which case, they would not have admitted she had a baby with her. That would have made them even more evil than he suspected. This scenario seemed to fit with the fact that Mrs Cameron had not met with him at 8 o'clock, as agreed. Significantly, it was now nearer nine and she still hadn't appeared.

Jack was anxious to continue with his journey, so turned his attention once more to Albert. He decided to drop the inquisition because, if she was dead, he concluded, there was little he could do about it. The law would catch up with them soon enough anyway.

'Well, as it happens, I am inclined to believe you, but if I catch you even glancing in Molly's direction while you are here, you will wish you hadn't been born. Now give her the cloak and don't give me any more backchat. Sit in the corner and keep out of my way.'

Albert and Michael didn't need a second invitation to seat themselves as far away from Jack as possible, although Albert summoned up the courage from somewhere to inform Jack he was going to give Molly the cloak anyway. 'Yeh well, she can 'ave it, we've no need forrit. Allus we want is to sit quietly here and sup us pints.'

With that, both walked to the far end of the bar, sat down at a table and took out a box of dominoes. Whispering to Michael, Albert talked up the situation that he had found himself in. 'Who'se 'e think 'e is? If he'd pushed me much further, I'd 'ave given 'im what for. All talk he was.'

Michael gazed into his pint and suppressed a grin before replying sarcastically. 'Oh aye, ya certainly would've given 'im what for. I could see he wah terrified of ya. Pity ya didn't meck oat from the cloak though.'

'Uh, it wah covered in mud anyrode. Probably wun't 'ave got oat forrit. Still we made quite a bit from the fair and there's still four more days ta go.'

The pair lapsed into silence and continued with their game. The only break in the proceedings was when Michael knocked on the table to signify his inability to follow on with the next brick.

Albert grinned. 'Er, I won that, so ya owe me a ha'penny. I'll teck it out of what we've made on terday's little haul.'

⁕

Jack decided that he would not wait any longer for Mrs Cameron to turn up. He surmised that she was probably either dead, if those two scoundrels were to be believed, or had changed her mind about completing her journey. His thoughts returned to persuading Molly to accompany him to London. Using his extensive charms, he placed his arms around Molly's waist and kissed her lightly on the neck. 'Well my lovely, how about you accompanying me to London? It would be a sort of holiday and you could spend a day there before returning to Nottingham. Come on, Molly what do you say?'

Molly considered her position at the Loggerheads. Her husband would not be returning for another few weeks and she rarely went on holiday, or had any time to shop for nice clothes. Each day was the same, opening up the bar to put up with lecherous, drunken layabouts, who thought that a bit of flattery entitled them to get into her bed.

Jack was different, he gave her some respect and always treated her well. She had loved him deeply for years, although hadn't voiced as much. In fact, if things were different, she would consider running away with him for good. Sadly, he had not asked her to do that, but maybe one day he would.

⁕

Sylvie, the barmaid helped out when Bill was away and normally offered to look after the inn when Molly visited her mother in Leicester, or when Molly needed a short holiday. This came with a proviso that she should occupy Molly's room overnight, so she would not have to walk home through the dark streets late in the evening, after the pub closed its doors. Sylvie was thirty-four and not long parted from her cheating husband of fifteen years. Since she now lived alone, she was always anxious about walking through the Marsh area to her small two up, two down terrace.

※

To Jack's delight, Molly agreed to go to London with him, provided Sylvie was in agreement.

Jack went out the back to tether the horses, while Molly sought out Sylvie in the kitchen. She readily agreed to the proposal and told Molly that it was about time she had some fun. Molly quickly threw a few items into a case and was ready and waiting for Jack to help her aboard the coach. She preferred to ride up front with him, rather than inside the carriage. Jack cast a covetous eye on Lizzie's trunk, which was still strapped firmly to the rear of the coach. He would ask Molly at their next stop if there were any items she would like, as Mrs Cameron was probably dead anyway and would not have any further use of its contents.

It was 9.45 p.m. when the coach and four drove out of the yard on its way to Great Brington. The fog was quite thick now and it would take an hour or so longer to reach their destination.

Molly snuggled up to Jack and pulled the dark green cloak close around her body. She felt quite the lady, despite the cloak's origin and convinced herself that it wouldn't be any further use to its owner but every use to her. She had also put on thick woolly under garments and a long thick dress to overcome the cold foggy weather that was to be experienced riding up front with Jack.

Despite the fog, they made good time and arrived in Great Brington at 5.45 a.m. where Jack was afforded his usual room. A weary Molly and exhausted Jack did not surface until two o'clock on Saturday afternoon.

It was a clear moonlit Saturday evening as they set off on the penultimate leg of their journey. Weather permitting; they were hopeful of arriving in Dunstable in less than four hours.

Thankfully, the weather held good and they arrived at their destination in a little over three and three quarter hours. Their evening meal was accompanied by some fine wine and they retired at 10.30 p.m. for another night of passion. It would be the last night they would spend together.

⁕

The weather turned foul as they began the final leg of their journey late the following afternoon. The fog came down thick and yellow, forming a blanket over the countryside, which made the journey arduous and slow. The temperature dropped and they were grateful to have had a substantial lunch and a couple of brandies before they set off.

For several miles, Jack picked his way gingerly over the rough terrain, barely able to see but a few feet in front of him. Very occasionally, the fog was patchy and sometimes it cleared sufficiently to allow the horses to gallop.

They felt warm and comforted by the drink. Despite the weather, Molly was in a playful mood and they laughed and joked with each other, as the four horses, without the restraint of the driver, galloped on at pace. This particular stretch of road was straight and easy under foot, but neither Jack nor Molly had noticed the gathering speed of the horses as they sped onwards over a brow and down the hill. Too late, the distracted Jack spotted the fallen tree, which was lying across the highway. In a gallant effort to halt the horses in their tracks, Jack gave the command to stop. 'Whoaah, there, whoaah...hold up...hold up...'

But the momentum of the gallop was too great and the horses careered into the tree, overturning the coach and throwing Jack and Molly from their seats. They hit the ground with force and for a few moments, except for the shallow panting of one horse, which had somehow survived the fall, no sound broke the eerie silence.

Molly Brown lay on the hard ground and refocused her eyes on the overturned coach, hanging precariously on the edge of the steep bank that dropped down through the forest to the dried riverbed, some fifty feet below. She painfully dragged herself to a sitting position and surveyed the carnage. Her mind took in the still figure of Jack lying under the coach with one leg and foot trapped beneath the wheels. 'Oh God no...no...Jack are you all right? Oh please say you are all right?'

Molly waited for Jack to respond, but his limp body lay lifeless on the ground.

She crawled painfully to a tree and managed to haul herself up. Then opened and shut her eyes several times to steady herself, until the dizzy feeling in her head lessened. Eventually, she staggered over to Jack and knelt down before gently stroking his head. She sobbed and shouted out to him in an effort to make him hear her, but Jack did not respond. Maybe, she thought, he had knocked himself out and if she kept talking to him and smoothing his brow, he would wake up and everything would be all right. But in her heart she knew he was gone, his face told her so. She had seen that look before on her father, just after he died, neither peaceful, nor asleep - just empty.

After sitting with him for what seemed hours, Molly realised that she was there alone in the cold darkness, unable to see more than a few yards in any direction. The wretched fog had descended once again, covering the grisly scene in a hideous yellow mask.

Molly sat forlornly on the damp ground. Sobbing uncontrollably, her hot tears, like molten lava sailed over her cheeks and down her neck. She felt totally wretched and realised that her dream of ever sharing her life with Jack had gone forever.

Molly was hardly able to tear herself away from Jack, but knew she must assess her own position, in order to survive this dreadful ordeal. She looked towards the area around the fallen tree and realised three of the horses were dead. However, by some miracle, the fourth one, which had been at the back of the rig, was on his feet and free from the broken shackles that had linked the horses together. There might be a way out for her, if, of course, the horse was fit to ride.

She gazed over the edge of the steep bank down to the dried riverbed and saw that a trunk and her case had burst open and were lying at the bottom, their contents scattered over the hillside. She peered through the trees, to determine what she could salvage. There were a couple of blankets, some thick stockings tangled around the branches of a bush and a little further down, a woollen garment of some kind.

If she could work her way down the hill, which was fifteen or twenty feet into the trees, she may be able to recover some of the items. She removed her cloak and began slipping and sliding down the rough terrain until she came to rest against a large tree trunk. She managed to disentangle the woollen stockings, retrieve the two blankets and also the woollen garment, which turned out to be a jumper.

She started her climb back up to safety, when she spotted a carved box wedged between two branches. She carefully pushed and pulled until the box became free. She shook it expectantly, to see if it contained any money, but disappointingly, although locked, it appeared to be empty. There wasn't any sign of a key, but Molly decided to take it anyway, as she thought she might be able to open it up then pawn it later, should she ever escape this hellhole and make it back to Nottingham. For that she needed money. She reached the top of the bank and laid the items on the ground then put on the thick woollen stockings, over her own. She intended to use one of the blankets for the horse, the other would be placed over Jack's body.

Molly approached Jack and suddenly remembered he had a moneybag strapped around his waist. It would have to be recovered out of necessity, so she carefully undid the buckle and slipped it off, before placing a kiss on his cold cheek.

Molly apologised for taking his money and covered his shattered body with the blanket.

An examination of the contents of the small leather pouch revealed that there would be more than enough money to pay for her journey to Nottingham, but first she must make the journey back to Dunstable.

A sad battered and bruised Molly was surprised how few injuries she had suffered. Her face, arms and body were covered in blue marks and there was a small cut on her head, but fortunately, none were serious. Her left wrist felt slightly sprained, but that was all and she felt thankful that she had survived, despite Jack's horrible death.

She then examined the horse to see if he was hurt and ran her hand over his thighs and fetlocks. To her immense relief he appeared none the worse for his encounter, so she carefully placed the blanket across his back, whilst stroking his head and whispering soothing words.

She tethered him to a tree and looked around for their water container, which she found intact, together with the supper they had packed but not eaten. She gave the horse a drink and ate two bread buns before taking a few sips of water herself, keeping the rest for the onward journey.

※

Molly was not familiar with riding horses and was not looking forward to another ordeal, but then she had her first stroke of luck that day. A coach and four appeared in the distance and eventually pulled up beside her. All the passengers seemed appalled at the scene of devastation that met their eyes and stared in disbelief.

The driver jumped down from the front of the coach and walked briskly over to Molly to offer his help. 'My God, Miss. What on earth's gone on here?'

Relief washed over Molly as she recounted and relived her experience. She asked if he could give her a lift, but the driver felt obliged to ask his passengers if the young woman could join them on their journey. All the passengers were extremely sympathetic and readily agreed. He smiled at Molly and gave his consent. 'Listen Miss, my other passengers don't object to you joining them for their onward journey. I can take you as far as Derby, which is the stage post nearest to Nottingham. However, I still have to charge you for the privilege. Unfortunately, I have to keep an official account of all passengers and the Royal Mail wouldn't take too kindly to me giving you a free ride.'

Molly was just thankful that the coach had been passing and she obviously had sufficient money to cover the journey to Derby. It was a comparatively easy task to arrange the final leg to Nottingham.

A relieved Molly voiced her acceptance. 'I'd like to take you up on your kind offer sir.' Then holding back tears, she asked the driver about reporting Jack's death. 'I would like to inform the authorities about Jack Garrett's death as soon as possible. Can we do that at our next stop?'

The coachman looked over at the covered body of Jack Garrett and assured Molly he would take care of it. 'Well miss, I can let the authorities know when we stop overnight in Dunstable.'

Molly smiled weakly, suddenly remembering the horse. 'What do you think I should do about the horse? I was going to ride him back to Dunstable.'

'Well now miss, there's not much I can do about that. Best thing would be to let him go. He'll get picked up by someone, that's for sure. Now once me and the guard have moved this tree trunk out of the road, we can continue our journey.'

Twenty minutes later, she was helped aboard and the coach and four got under way. Molly tearfully glanced back at the body of the man she loved and although she felt very sad and guilty to be leaving him there, she still thanked God for a second chance at life.

CHAPTER THREE

64 St James Street

In compliance with his wife's wishes, Arthur Milligan suggested an evening stroll to his son, David. The promise of a pint or two at the Loggerheads was sufficient to lever him out from the comfort of the fireside, after two helpings of his mother's broth and four slices of thickly buttered bread.

The fog hung heavily as they walked along St Mary's Cliff, past Lover's Leap. They noted that the fig trees were heavy with fruit, following the mild spring and were reminded that they would be ripe for picking in another few days. Clara would work her magic with a fig tart and some wonderful jam.

After a couple of pints in the Loggerheads, where David chatted for a while with Sylvie the barmaid, they headed back along Narrow Marsh towards Turn Calf Alley. This was not their usual route, but Arthur was anxious to prolong their return home until he had discussed the all-important subject of David's job prospects and his ambivalence to becoming a boatman, or drift mineworker.

David's argument was that if he could get another six months of study at the Mechanics Institute, he could earn twice as much as a clerk than as a mineworker. However, after Arthur had explained the family's immediate monetary crisis and the worry it was giving to Clara, David agreed, somewhat reluctantly, to find a job to help boost the 'coffers'. He realised that perhaps he had been a little selfish and his dream of getting out of the Marsh, had to remain just that - a dream - at least for the moment.

They continued on, crossing Canal Street and after walking down Trent Row towards the canal, David stopped in his tracks when he sighted what he thought might be a body on the towpath.

'Hey dad, what da ya think that is dahn there. Looks a bit like someone's fell ovver after too much booze.'

Arthur strained his eyes to see through the yellowy fog, which had lifted slightly, but still hung around.

'Yer could be right David, let's ga dahn and 'ave a look.'

Arthur and David made their way towards the river and when they were within a few feet of the huddled figure, they could see it was a young woman with long dark brown curly hair. She was face down on the muddy bank and was barely moving.

'Quick David turn 'er ovver and see if she's a'right,' said a concerned Arthur.

David knelt over Lizzie and gently turned her over on to her back as her dark brown curls slid away from her muddy face. He cupped her head in his hands and spoke to her in a soft voice. 'Now me duck, are ya a'right. Can ya 'ear me?'

Dazed and uncomprehending, Lizzie slowly opened her eyes and found herself looking up into the face of a man about her own age, who was nice looking with longish dark hair, curling up at the ends. He was wearing a dark brown jacket over a white shirt and had a red neckerchief tied around his throat.

Lizzie felt dizzy and disoriented, but muttered a reply. 'Oh dear, I am not sure. I feel very cold and I have no idea where I am.' She was confused and could not understand why she was lying on the ground, looking down towards a canal.

'Well ya on the towpath fronting the canal at the minit, but we'll soon 'ave ya sorted.'

In an authoritative voice, Arthur gave orders to David. 'Lissen son, I think yu'd berra 'urry back 'omm and fetch the cart, as we need ta get this young woman inta a bed. Find ya mam and tell 'er ta stoke up the fire and warm up the rest of the broth. 'Urry up lad, I don't think she's long for this world.'

'Right ya are dad, I'll gerroff!'

David ran as fast as he could go, in the direction of Narrow Marsh, leaving his father to comfort Lizzie. 'Now me duck, what's ya name? And what ya doing aht here in just a frock?'

She gazed at the man leaning over her, but she couldn't help him with either question, as she had no idea herself. 'I...I've no idea...what my name is...or why I'm here, but I don't feel well. I'm so cold,' Lizzie muttered comprehensively.

Arthur removed his jacket and laid it over Lizzie for warmth and protection, because he could feel her cold clammy skin through her cotton dress and petticoat.

It took David five minutes to arrive back home. He called to his mother as he ran upstairs to fetch a blanket. 'Hey mam, we've fount a young girl dahn by the towpath and she's practically frozzen ta death. Dad sez, can yo stoke up the fire and warm up the broth, cause we bringin 'er back on the cart.'

'Oad yer hosses lad, what ya goin on abaht? Who've ya fount and what's she doin dahn there? No one in tha right mind ud be dahn there in this weather.'

'A dunno know mam, allus a know is we bringin 'er back ere.'

'Al'right son, yu'd berra be quick and gerroff back there as fast as ya can. If she's bin aht in this weather fer any amount of time, she'll be 'arf dead be now. I'll get the fire cracking and heat up the broth.'

It took David a full eight minutes with the added weight of the cart to get back to the towpath. He hardly dared ask his dad the question and tentatively braced himself for a negative answer. 'Is she okay dad?'

Arthur shrugged. 'Just abaht, but we need ta ger'er 'omm quick as ya like, or she won't be. 'Elp me lift 'er on ta' cart.'

Arthur and David gently lifted Lizzie onto the cart, laying her on a rug that David had placed there, before covering her with a blanket.

Just as they were about to leave, they heard a small whimpering sound nearby, which seemed to be coming from under the hedge that curved away from the bend. David was the first to ask the question. 'My God, what the 'ell is that?'

'Teck a look lad, it sahnds like it's coming from under the 'edge bottom.'

David walked over to the upturned object, which was half hidden under a large bushy hedge, covered in wild roses and found the small cart. On further investigation and to his amazement, he discovered a small baby tucked inside.

'Oh, God, I'll ga ta the foot of ow stairs, dad, it's a baby. It must be 'ern. Me mam 'ull ga mad if we teck that 'omm as well. What's ta' be done abaht it?'

Arthur chided David with his answer. 'Well we'll leave it 'ere, shall we?' he paused and grinned, 'don't be a daft sod, we 'ave to teck it we us. Nah come on and bring it ovver 'ere.'

'I'm telling ya dad, me mam 'ull ga barmy. It's all very well, teckin a gel back, burra baby as well in't no joke.'

'Look lad, we can't leave 'em 'ere, they'll both be dead in the next 'our, so look lively.'

Clara was waiting at the door as they entered number fourteen Knotted Alley. 'Quickly Arthur, bring 'er through.'

Arthur carried Lizzie through to the parlour, followed by David. He laid her down on an old straw mattress that Clara had dragged down from upstairs. Both men were concerned as her pale, cold face returned their stares.

'Cum outovit, let the dog see the rabbit, ya gormless pair,' said Clara as she rolled up her sleeves and quickly set about ministering to Lizzie's needs. She assertively pushed her husband and son out of the parlour into the kitchen where the baby cart stood just inside by the window.

At that moment, Rosalie let out a loud wail and Clara nearly jumped out of her skin. 'In the Lord's name, what was that?'

David returned to the parlour with Rosalie in his arms and offered an explanation, albeit one he didn't think his mother would be happy to hear. 'It's a baby mam, it's 'ern, but we 'ad ta bring it, otherwise it would've died.'

'I can see that lad. I don't suppose you could've left 'em there. We'll see what's ta be done.' Speaking kindly, she addressed Lizzie. 'Now, me duck, can ya manage a bowl of this nice hot broth and some bread, while I see ta ya baby girl. It is a girl innit?'

Lizzie was completely non-plussed. She couldn't understand what these good people were saying to her. It was as if they were talking a foreign language, but she could only answer their questions with a question of her own. 'I'm so sorry, I am really confused and I cannot think for the moment who I am. Do you think the baby is mine?'

Clara looked at Lizzie aghast, then from Arthur to David for an explanation. 'Don't ask me mam, I've no idea,' said David shrugging his shoulders.

She looked at Lizzie's frightened face and frowned, deciding to forget about who she might be at present. Who wouldn't be confused after lying on a towpath in this weather, for Lord knows how long, with just a frock on, albeit a thick quality cotton. In a kindly, calming voice, she advised Lizzie to get some sleep. 'Look me duck, best get yersen aht o' them damp clothes and I'll dry 'em by the fire. Then ya should get some sleep and don't worry, I'll see ya baby's kept warm and fed.'

Arthur and David continued to be amazed at the events of the evening, which had started out as a simple walk along the cliffs and finished up with them welcoming two more hungry mouths into their small, cramped, two up, two down, little terrace.

Clara found a long fleecy nightie that she had long since grown out of, which would do for Lizzie, until her own dress and petticoat dried. She came bustling back into the room to find Arthur and David still talking animatedly.

"Adn't yo two berra get choppin some more wood. It won't chop itsen ya know and try and scrounge some nutty slack from Mabel in Foundreh Yard. 'Er husband, Sam, allus manages ta gerra bag ovv the stuff from 'is shift at the mine, although, one of these fine days, 'e'll get caught and 'auled off ta' prison...I wun't be at all surprised either. Them coal managers are strict as 'ell when it comes ta nicking oat. Teck 'em some fresh milk and explain what's go-an on 'ere.'

Arthur and David retreated quickly out of the door while Clara helped Lizzie change into the dry nightie, after fetching another blanket to keep her warm. When Lizzie removed her dress and petticoat, her hand fingered the blue velvet ribbon tied around her neck and she mentioned it to Clara. 'I have a small key and a silver sixpence tied around my neck on a ribbon. The key must be for a case or box or something. Did you say that I hadn't anything with me when I was found?'

'Yes, that's right me duck, if ya did 'ave oat, it must 'av bin stolen. I imagine everythin' will become clearer tamorra, so don't yo worry none. Now come and lie down 'ere. Our Arthur has moved the mattress closer ta the fire and put it on the wooden structure that our Tillie used to use fo'rra bed, afore wi gorra berra un. It's not the best, but a think yu'll find it comfy enough.'

Clara continued to talk soothingly to Lizzie, telling her that everything would sort itself out and that she would feel better in no time. 'Now me duck, yo snuggle dahn on that, get some rest and it'll all seem berra...' The sentence did not get finished before Lizzie had fallen into a deep sleep.

Arthur and David entered the scullery in a rather noisy fashion, carrying with them the chopped wood and a small bag of slack from number three.

'Shhh! yo two, she's fast on and dun't need waking up just yet. I've dried 'er frock, so that when she wakes she'll feel more comfortable in 'er own clothes.'

Arthur, still curious as to whom she was, tried debating the question once again, but got short shrift from Clara.

'Look Arthur, does it marra who she is, she can't ga anywhere in 'er state. She needs a few days rest up, then we'll look at it agen.'

Arthur nodded sagely. 'Yes, you're right as allus Clara me duck, but we an't got much room fa two more bodies in this 'ouse. I'm not suggestin she go just yet, but wi should try and find out who she is. She may 'ave 'n 'usband aht looking fo'rra, or family uz mebbee worried sick.'

'Well yes, I agree we ya, but until she knows 'ersen who she is, there in't much we can do abaht it. Anyrode, both of ya sit yersens dahn and 'ave a nice cuppa.'

Lizzie slept on whilst Clara fed the baby and changed her nappy a few times, but, apart from being hungry and wet, Rosalie seemed none the worse for her escapade. It was fortunate that Lizzie had the presence of mind to push the cart away from the oncoming horse and that it landed upside down under the hedge. This action and the warm blankets that she had been wrapped in, acted as a shelter against the elements.

While Lizzie was asleep, Clara heated up her flat iron and began on Lizzie's dress, but when she came to the skirt, she had trouble pressing the iron flat onto the fabric. There was something bunched up in the pocket. She put her hand inside and pulled out a crumpled piece of paper. ''Ere Arthur, 'ave fount a piece of paper that wah in 'er pockit. It's got some scribbly writin on it, but a can't quite meck out what it sez. 'Ave a look our David, a think it's an address or summat.'

She handed David the piece of screwed up paper, after smoothing it out with the iron.

'It's a bit smudged, but a can just meck it aht mam, it's a name...Hannah...Merchant, a think. Then it sez 64 St James Street.'

Triumphantly Clara announced her verdict. 'Oh well, sahnds like it could be 'er name and address. That solves that mystry then. Fancy 'er living on the same street us our Tillie works, wahrra coincidence. She'd not wandered far then, probably aht fer a walk with the baby. A should think that's 'er name. What da ya think Arthur?'

Arthur nodded his head sagely. 'Well me duck, sahnds like it could be, or why would she 'ave it in 'er pocket? She probably wrote it ta give ta someone while she wer aht or summat.'

Clara was quite pleased with herself that she had discovered the all-important piece of paper and agreed with her husband before making another suggestion. 'Yes Arthur, I think yer right! If we call 'er that when she wakes up, mebbee she'll remember who she is.'

'Good idea me duck, then as soon uz she's on the mend, I'll teck 'er back 'omm ta St James Street. Ya might call in there David. Yer cun ga we our Tillie fust thing tamorra.'

'Okay dad, that's fine be me. I'll give our Tillie a treat and wheel 'er in the cart. She loves go-an on the cart, mam.'

'Aw right David, but don't get lingrin abaht, as wi've got a milk delivery later.'

⁂

Clara had been watching the young woman as she slept and tried to piece together a logical story to fit her circumstances. She decided that she was either a nanny or the child's mother, but could not decide which. She was out walking the baby when she had some kind of accident that made her forget who she was. One thing was certain, the baby had been wearing expensive clothes and was tucked up with warm blankets in a kind of baby cart. The mother, despite only wearing a dress and petticoat, looked as if she came from a middle, upper class family. All the items appeared tailor made and of good quality thick cotton.

It was around ten thirty when Lizzie finally began to stir, still dazed and half asleep. She gazed in bewilderment at her surroundings, but nothing made any sense to her.

Clara arose from her chair by the fire and poked the coals in an effort to rekindle the flames, then she dropped the poker, which clattered noisily onto the hearth.

At that point Lizzie became completely awake and sat up in bed, so Clara immediately went over to her with a cup of hot, sweet tea. 'Sorry me duck, did a wake ya? How ya feeling nah? Ya baby's just gone back ta sleep, so we can 'ave a quiet five minutes we a cuppa. It's Hannah innit? A fount ya name on a scrap of paper in the pocket of ya frock, so that's a relief innit?'

Far from being a relief, Lizzie felt even more confused, as the name Hannah meant nothing to her at all. However, because no other name sprang to mind, she felt she ought to settle on that for the moment. 'I am not sure whether that is my name or not, because I still cannot remember anything, only waking up on the towpath and seeing someone bending over me. I want to thank you for saving my life. I suspect I would not have survived, if your husband and son had not found me and the baby and brought us to your home.'

'That's our pleasure me duck, or should a say Hannah. 'Ere's the piece of paper wi ya name and address on it, mebbee the address will set ya mind thinkin. By the way, me name's Clara and this 'ere is me husband Arthur and me son David. It was them who fount ya lying on the path.'

Lizzie looked at the crumpled paper, but neither the name, nor the address seemed familiar. Whoever she was, she owed this family her life and smiled gratefully at the men who were sat at the table with a mug of tea, into which they dunked some home baked biscuits. 'Thank you both very much, I am greatly indebted to you.'

'That's al'right Hannah. As me wife sez, it's our pleasure.'

Lizzie tried to sit up on the bed, but winced in agony as she felt a sharp stabbing pain shoot through her leg. 'Ooo, oh dear, I think I may have hurt my leg, it feels quite painful. My side also feels a bit sore. Do you think you could have a look please Clara?'

Clara gently eased up the nightie to reveal a large bruise on her ankle and another one near her knee.

After asking the men to look away, she lifted the nightie higher to reveal another bruise on Lizzie's thigh. 'Well ya look like y'av bin in a fight we a boxer me duck. There's two big bruises on ya leg and another on ya thigh. I could try rubbing grease on em, or failing that, our David could teck ya ta the General Hospital. It's fer folks like us as can't pay. Let 'em 'ave a quick look at it. What da ya think?'

Lizzie wasn't sure which was best, so decided to go with the grease for the time being, even though it sounded unpleasant. 'Well, perhaps we could put some grease on them and see how they go. Would you mind doing that for me Clara?'

Clara gave a little laugh. 'Sorry me duck, am not laughing at ya, but ya do talk a bit funny. I'd swear ya won't from these parts, but ya perhaps moved 'ere from somewhere else. I will see wahrra can do. Arthur, fetch me some lard from the pantreh and I'll smooth some o' that on. It's norras good as butta, but it'll do the job right enough.'

Arthur did as he was bade and Clara smoothed the lard over the bruises, then wrapped Lizzie's leg up with a clean cloth. 'There, that should fix it. We'll 'ave another look at it tamorra.'

Lizzie wondered whether she ought to go home to the address on the piece of paper, if indeed it was her home and not trouble these good people any longer. 'I could perhaps go home, or at least see if the address on the paper is in fact my home. My family may be worried about me and I have brought a lot of trouble to your door,' she said, turning to David. 'I think I can walk, if you would help me David.'

Clara frowned. 'We won't 'ere of it me duck, will we Arthur? Wouldn't purra dog aht on a night like this. The fog's hardly lifted and it's coad and damp. No we insist ya stay at least 'til tamorra. Now 'ow about some supper? A've some nice bread and jam and a mug a tea.'

Lizzie thought better than to argue, as it might have offended them and they had probably saved her life after all. Before she could make a comment, Rosalie woke up and Clara brought her over to Lizzie. 'There there, little one. We don't know ya name yet, but we're sure ya mam'ull remember it when she sees ya?'

Clara handed Rosalie over to Lizzie, along with a bottle of milk to feed her. Lizzie looked down at the baby and wondered if, in fact, she was hers. Unfortunately, the little face that was smiling up at her did not provide a definitive answer. The baby's hair was curly and golden, unlike her own dark locks and she had violet blue eyes. Were her own eyes blue?

She voiced her thoughts to Clara. 'She is lovely, isn't she, but I don't know if she is mine. I am sorry, but I just can't remember. I will look after her though, until we know the answer, but I don't know what to call her, as I can't remember her name.'

'Tell ya what Hannah, she were fount under a 'edge covered in wild Rose hips down by the River Leen, so why don't ya call 'er Rose or Rosie for the time being. It's as good a name as any.'

Clara would not know how close to the truth she was.

'All right Clara, Rosie it is. Now then Rosie have a drink of this nice warm milk and then we'll get your nappy changed, if I can manage it.'

'Don't ya worry yersen gel, yo just feed 'er an' I'll see ta the mucky bits till yo on ya feet again. Perhaps by tamorra.'

The following morning David took Tillie on the cart to her place of work. He put on a clean shirt and polished his shoes, so that he looked a bit more respectable.

After dropping Tillie off, he walked up to the door of sixty-four St James Street and knocked on the elaborate knocker on the front of the shiny black door.

A few moments elapsed before a maid appeared and requested his business. He removed his cap and explained why he was there, then the young maid left him on the doorstep and closed the door while she went to find her mistress, who was seated in the drawing room. 'Begging your pardon ma'am, but there is a young man at the door asking if a Hannah Merchant resides here. He said that the young woman was found with her baby on the towpath near the River Leen on Friday evening and her name and this address was found in the pocket of her dress.'

Mrs Phillips looked perplexed as she gave her reply. 'Really, well as you know Sara, we do not have anyone of that name residing here, either now, or in the past as I recall. Please inform the gentleman and bid him good-day.'

Sara returned to the door and delivered the message to David, who felt he should ask once again, in case she was mistaken. 'Are ya sure she don't live 'ere. This address was definitely written on the paper. She's got long, dark brown curly hair and was wearing just a frock?'

'Yes, I am sure. I am so sorry, but if you don't leave now, my mistress will not be too pleased. So good-day sir.'

With that, Sara closed the door, leaving David standing on the step, wondering what he should do next. 'Well,' he said to himself out loud, 'there's noat a can do, but ga back and tell me mam the news. That'ull leave us in a fix fer sure.'

Clara was clearing away the breakfast dishes and had just made a fresh pot of tea, when David entered the scullery. 'Come on in lad and sit yersen dahn at the table. 'Ave just brewed.'

'Aye, thanks mam, but I don't bring good news. The owners of sixty-four St James Street are certain that no one of that name lives there and they were none too pleased at me calling either.'

Clara folded her arms in disgust. 'Damn cheek, some ovv these snooty uppa class folk 'an't got no manners at all.

Well, I don't know what ter do next David. We'd better wait 'til ya dad gets 'omm and then decide.'

Lizzie listened to the conversation, to which she had not had any input, but now she would contribute something. 'Thank you for trying your best to find out David, but I think I should go now. I cannot stay here eating your food and taking up your time any longer. I really am so very grateful to you all.'

Clara appraised Lizzie and knew she couldn't just let her wander off. 'Now don't talk daft me duck, where ya go-an ta go, ya don't know who ya are, or where ya from, so what's the point of just wandering off. No, Arthur will agree wi me, yu'll have ta stay 'ere 'til we can sort summat aht. Now drink up ya tea, afore it gets coad.'

In the short time she had known Clara, she appreciated that arguing would not do her any good and consequently accepted defeat and drank the tea.

Arthur arrived home from work, half expecting Lizzie to have returned to her own home. He was, therefore, somewhat surprised to see her sitting in a chair nursing the baby.

Clara realised Arthur would be concerned if Lizzie had to stay in their home for much longer. Their money wouldn't stretch far enough to feed another two mouths and the sleeping arrangements would be doubly difficult. Arthur was a good man, but had to consider his family first, so she quickly reassured him, in the confidence that Lizzie's memory would shortly return and she would return to her own family. 'Lissen Arthur, David 'ad no luck at number sixty-four. They hadn't any knowledge of anyone named Hannah ever livin there. Perhaps we got the number wrong and she lives further on, mebbee eighty-four or summat. The address on the paper was a bit smudged. Allus we know is that it is definitely St James Street.'

Arthur was upset and disheartened, but also at great pains not to let Lizzie feel uncomfortable, so outwardly agreed with Clara. 'Aye, 'appen you're right me duck. She'll probably feel better in the mornin and remember all about what she was doin down on the towpath.' Arthur turned and smiled at Lizzie. 'I expect it'ull all come rushing back, hey Hannah me duck?'

Lizzie didn't feel too hopeful, but played along with Arthur's optimism, although not convinced. 'Yes Arthur, I am feeling somewhat better already and I am sure I will remember something by tomorrow. It is really kind of you all to let me stay here.'

Lizzie didn't think that another day would make any difference, so that night in bed she prayed her memory would return and she would regain her identity. Even though the Milligans' were the kindest people, they needed their lives back. Lizzie realised it must be hard to feed four people, let alone two more. What was her own life like? With more questions than answers milling around in her head, she remained worryingly awake, trying to make sense of it all. Eventually, in the early hours she gave in and lapsed into a troubled sleep.

CHAPTER FOUR

The Fragility of Life

On Tuesday, 28th September, Georgina Hemingway was still awaiting the return of Lizzie after her morning off. She was surprised to discover that she had not reported at noon, to start her duties. It was now two o'clock and there was no sign of her. She asked the cook whom she passed on her way to the kitchen if she knew of Lizzie's whereabouts. 'Clara, did Lizzie say anything to you on Sunday about returning today?'

Clara looked sheepishly at her mistress as she contemplated her reply. She thought it unusual that Lizzie had not come home for supper on Monday night, but assumed she had stayed with her brother and would return today at noon. 'No madam. She did mention that she might be staying with her brother until she returned today, but nothing else, I'm sorry to say.'

Georgina sniffed and went off to the library to write a letter to the bureau about engaging a new senior maid.

A week later, on the afternoon of Tuesday the 5th October, Jayne Munroe was seated in her room in the Old King's Arms, Dunstable, where she had spent the last three nights waiting for Lizzie. She was beside herself with worry because Lizzie had not arrived as planned.

Lizzie was not among the passengers that stepped off the coach on Sunday morning. She had questioned the coachmen and the passengers and gave a description of Lizzie and Rosalie, but none had seen the young woman with the baby. They did suggest that if her train was delayed, she might have missed the coach departures. The coaches would have left within a short time of each other, so if she had missed them, she would have had to wait until early the following morning for the next coach.

Strangely, she did not arrive on Monday either, which caused Aunt Jayne to worry that she had suffered some kind of mishap. She tried to think rationally and decided that the logical explanation was that Lizzie or Rosalie had been taken ill and needed to recover before continuing the journey.

Her hopes began to fade on the afternoon of the third day and she reluctantly decided that she would have to write to Kate to let her know that Lizzie had not yet arrived.

She felt more than a little worried as she put pen to paper, knowing that she was partly responsible for placing Lizzie in a near impossible situation. Maybe, it was all too much for her; after all, the only other journey she had made had been with her father, when she travelled down to Glasgow from Strathy. On that occasion, Lizzie had not been responsible for anyone's welfare because that task had fallen squarely on her father's shoulders. How they expected her to travel hundreds of miles with a baby in tow, without anyone accompanying her...It was too much, she thought and they should not have asked her to do it.

She felt very guilty and wished that she had stayed at Low Wood a little while longer and accompanied Lizzie on her arduous journey, halfway across the country. She wondered what they had been thinking, but reminded herself that the situation was utterly desperate and under any other circumstances, they would not have asked her to undertake such a commitment.

She sighed as she dipped her new metal pen nib into the pot of indigo ink and began writing.

My Dear Kate,
I hope you and the family are all well. I hesitated with respect to writing to you sooner, but felt I needed to inform

you that, disconcertingly, Lizzie failed to meet me, as arranged, on the morning of Sunday 3rd October. I thought she might have missed the train, or that the ship had been delayed, which would, of course, have interrupted her journey to Dunstable. However, she did not arrive the following day either.

I stayed on at the King's Arms, in the event that she or Rosalie wasn't well. They could have stayed at the Adelphi for longer, until they were able to travel, but it is now Tuesday afternoon and they have still not arrived.

I will stay until tomorrow morning and leave on a coach that came in today.

When I arrive back in London, I will do my best to trace Lizzie's journey. Perhaps you could ascertain whether she embarked on the 'Royal George' as planned, if so, she must have reached Liverpool.

I will write to some friends of mine who live in Bootle and ask them to make a few enquiries at the hotel and the station to see if anyone remembers them. It's not an everyday occurrence for a young girl and a small baby to be seen travelling alone.

If she caught the train in Liverpool, she must have reached Manchester, but that's where the trail may, unfortunately, go cold.

Please try not to worry too much at this stage, as it is possible that illness has prevented them completing their journey and Lizzie has been unable to let me know. I have managed to get hold of copies of Liverpool and Manchester newspapers and there aren't any reports of anything untoward happening to them, so we must think positively. I will leave a letter for her here, in case she turns up after my departure.

I am sorry to say I blame myself for agreeing with your suggestion that she undertake such a journey. In hindsight, it was probably too ambitious to expect a young girl to embark on such a demanding journey alone.

I hope you can forgive me Kate, but I too, acted in desperation, although I felt the organisation of the journey was fool proof. However, this may yet prove to be the case and I may be worrying needlessly. I will write to you again when I arrive home. Please write and confirm that she did indeed board the 'Royal George'.

I will close now and pray that Lizzie and Rosalie have not come to any harm.

Take care my dear,
Your loving Aunt Jayne xxx

Kate Hemingway was lying on her day bed looking out of the window. She could see Lorimer's fields on the horizon, but could not see the little cottage, as it was beyond the copse in the next valley. She could picture it in her mind, however and relive the glorious times she had spent there with her lover, just the two of them. How she wished she could turn back the clock, but it was done and there was no going back. It was over a week since Lizzie's departure and she excitedly waited to receive a letter from Aunt Jayne, confirming their safe arrival.

Three days later, Jayne's letter arrived. It had been placed on the silver dish on the hall table. Anxious to read the contents, Kate skipped breakfast and went straight up to her room. She lay on her day bed and unfolded the two sheets of white paper. Her eyes scanned the words down to the signature at the bottom of the second page and she quickly established that Lizzie had not arrived in Dunstable. Her hands were shaking as she started again at the beginning, trying to digest the enormity of such disturbing news. When she reached the end, she felt sick and very scared. What on earth could have happened to them?

The reality of the situation sank in and she began to panic. What should she do? What if they <u>had</u> met with an accident? According to Aunt Jayne, there hadn't been any untoward reports, but there still could be. Supposing it was splashed across the front page of the 'Morning Chronicle'.

Kate was totally convinced something terrible had happened and pictured the headline appeal in her mind: 'Mystery Woman and Child fall in front of the Liverpool to Manchester train - Do you know this woman?' There might even be a picture of Lizzie, which her mother would be sure to recognise. Then questions would be asked, the awful truth would emerge and her mother would never survive the scandal. No, it would be better if she told her the truth sooner, rather than later.

Half-heartedly and nervously she roamed the large house in search of her mother. Her father had gone for an early morning ride, so she was safe on that count and David was holidaying with Belle and her family. Alexander had gone with him as he was on a school break for two weeks.

Kate poked her head furtively around the library door and spotted her mother writing furiously at her desk near the window. She looked up as her daughter entered. 'Hello darling. How are you?'

'All right mother...I think,' then, hesitating slightly, continued, 'well...no actually, I do have something to discuss with you.'

Georgina Hemingway looked quizzically at her daughter and gestured for her to sit down on the comfortable lounge chair next to her desk. 'Oh? are you feeling all right? I mean, no after effects from the birth or anything?' She continued without waiting for a reply, anxious that her daughter wasn't about to deliver more devastating news. Georgina reminded herself that she had only just about recovered from the trauma of keeping the baby a secret from Howard and was physically more relaxed now that that awful situation was behind them.

She smiled warmly and put her hand out to her daughter in a caring gesture. 'I know it is difficult for you at the moment Katherine, but given time, you will come to terms with the adoption. I am sure you have done the right thing. Anyway, I expect you will be hearing from James soon. I understand he is back from his travels and we can all look forward to a spring wedding.' Georgina spoke positively, in the hope that it would somehow negate the possibility of further bad news spewing from her daughter's mouth. She couldn't cope with any more, definitely not.

Kate wished she had the steadying influence of Aunt Jayne to assist her. She knew how to handle her mother with the knack of putting everything right; although this latest dilemma appeared even to be beyond Aunt Jayne. She fixed her eyes at the floor and buried her toes in the deep pile of the Wilton rug, which usually made her feel warm and comfortable, but not this time. She took a deep breath, sighed and addressed her mother in a pitiful voice. 'Mother, it's all gone wrong. I...I didn't have my baby adopted. I gave her to someone to look after until I could look after her myself, but now the pair of them have disappeared.'

Georgina went deathly pale as she struggled once again to comprehend her daughter's latest bombshell. 'What on earth are you talking about dear? I'm afraid you aren't making much sense. Do you mean the couple that adopted her have disappeared? If so, I really don't think that it concerns us. As I said—'

Kate interrupted her mother mid-sentence. 'No mother, that isn't what I mean. I mean she never was adopted. I gave her to Lizzie Cameron to look after until I reached twenty-one and then I was going to join her in London and we were going to bring her up together. But I haven't heard from her. It's as if she has disappeared off the face of the earth.'

Georgina's eyes flashed manically as she glanced around wildly. She pursed her lips as the shock of what she had just heard sunk in. 'Are you completely mad Katherine?' she stuttered almost incoherently, 'what on earth were you thinking of?' She ranted on with the immediacy of an express train, not pausing for either an answer or, indeed, breath. 'You will have to get her back and we will re-instigate the adoption process again with the nursing home. Sometimes Katherine, words fail me. What on earth will James think? You need to start acting like an adult, because if you insist on being irresponsible, you will surely be in danger of losing James altogether. What does he say about all this?'

Kate looked down at the floor and tried to keep her emotions in check as she replied apprehensively. 'He doesn't know.'

Georgina's voice rose two octaves above hysterical, as she struggled with Kate's incomprehensible utterance. 'He doesn't <u>know</u>? <u>What</u> doesn't he know?'

Kate trembled at the outburst, but continued nervously with her explanation. 'He...he doesn't know <u>anything</u>,' she paused, unsure of how her mother would react to her next devastating confession. 'He doesn't even know I was pregnant. He...he's not...he's not the father, so why should he know?'

This last revelation was just too much for Georgina to bear. She stood up from her chair and held Kate's arm in a vice like grip as she manhandled her out of the room. 'Go to your room and stay there until I can join you. I need a very large brandy and time to collect my thoughts. You are such a disappointment to me Katherine. I am sure I do not know what I have done to deserve a daughter who brings about such calamitous behaviour.'

Kate pulled herself away from her mother's clutches and ran up the staircase, hot tears stinging her eyes. She turned around at the top of the first flight and flung a tirade of abuse at her mother who was now standing at the foot of the stairs. 'I hate you...I hate you...you never understand me. You expect me to be perfect like you and I'm not. Are you sure Aunt Jayne isn't my mother?' The words were out without a thought to how her mother would react to this latest suggestion.

Angry and appalled at her daughter's behaviour, Georgina ran up after Kate and shook her by the shoulders, which momentarily put them in danger of overbalancing and falling down the stairs. 'What did you say? Has Aunt Jayne something to do with all this?'

Kate realised her mistake and tried at once to rectify her outburst. 'No, no of course not, it was my decision. Aunt Jayne knows nothing about it.'

Georgina peered closely at her daughter's face and noticed how she had coloured up. 'Are you sure about that Katherine? If she has, you need to tell me now?'

Georgina took a firm hold of Kate's arm, but once again she wriggled free and in doing so, caught her mother acutely off balance.

Unable to stop the forward motion, Georgina toppled and fell down the stairs, hitting the banister as she tumbled from one step to the other. Kate watched in horror, until her mother came to rest between the bottom step and the hallway. 'Oh my God mother. Are you all right?'

The silence was palpable and when she didn't receive a reply, she jumped down the stairs two at a time. In extreme anguish, she lifted her by the shoulders and began to shake her. 'Mother, mother, speak to me?' There was no reply, Georgina's head lolled around and came to rest on her shoulder.

Panic rose in Kate's chest and bile flooded up into her mouth. She shouted out for help as she cradled her mother's head in her arms whilst watching a trickle of blood seep out of the corner of her mouth. 'Hurry someone, hurry, my mother's had an accident.'

Moments later, Clara and George came running across the hall. They stared down at the scene before Clara managed to speak. 'What on earth's happened Kate? Has Mrs Hemmingway fainted or something?'

No sound came from Kate as she stared back open

mouthed at Clara. George tried to take control of the situation and gently laid Georgina on the rug in the hallway, before putting his arms around Kate as she stared blindly at her mother's prostrate figure. He asked Clara to watch Kate, while he checked Georgina for a pulse, but his grim look said it all as he shook his head. Clara's hand went involuntarily to her mouth in shock, but authoritatively she lead Kate away to the sitting room. 'Come with me Kate. You need to sit down. I'll pour you a brandy.'

Kate, her face ashen, sat down on the settee. Clara placed a large glass of brandy into Kate's hand, which shook as she raised it to her lips, but nevertheless, she drank the golden liquid straight down. Then Clara put her arms around Kate's shoulders. 'There, there Kate, don't worry. George will ride over to Dr Brownlow's immediately and request his attendance. I'm sure your mother will be all right.'

Kate turned and in an anxious voice asked the fearful question. 'She's dead isn't she?...Oh my God Clara, I've killed my mother.'

Despite the fact that Clara was pretty sure Mrs Hemingway was indeed dead, she couldn't be definite and spoke in a calming voice. 'No...no, of course not Kate. But I think she may have lost consciousness.'

With more hope than conviction, Kate made a request. 'Please go and see how she is Clara, but come straight back.'

'All right lass, try not to worry.'

Clara closed the door behind her then ran along the hall to where George was still bending over his mistress. 'Is she all right George?' asked Clara in an agitated voice.

George shook his head and confirmed the worse. 'I'm afraid not Clara. She doesn't have a pulse. I think she is dead.'

Clara was just about to say something when the front door opened wide and Howard Hemingway walked in. He removed his hat and cloak and set them down on the hall-stand, before looking towards his study. His wife was lying prostrate on the floor and Clara and George were bending over her, with concern showing on their faces.

He stopped in his tracks and looked to the pair for an explanation. 'Good God, George, Clara, is she all right? Has she fainted?'

George responded in a grave voice. 'I'm afraid not sir. She took a fall down the stairs and...and...I can't feel a pulse.'

Swiftly, Howard Hemingway crossed the hall and knelt by the still body of his wife. He placed his index and middle finger to her neck and the awful truth became clear. 'Oh no, Georgie, no...please...please don't leave me.' Howard bent down and kissed his wife on her forehead, but knew there was nothing he could do. With tears in his eyes he gently carried the limp body of his wife through to his study. He laid her carefully on the couch and picked up her hand, caressing it with his lips. 'I love you Georgie. I always have and I always will. How has this happened? I am so very, very sorry, my darling girl.'

Howard sat for several more minutes with his wife before ringing the bell for attention. George immediately appeared in the doorway. Howard collected himself together and made a request for help. 'George, take the trap over to Dr Brownlow's. He has been our doctor for the last fifteen years and will know how to proceed.'

'Very well sir, I'll go straight away.'

George turned to leave the room when suddenly Howard realised that his daughter was not around. 'George, where is Kate? God knows how this will affect her.'

'Kate is in the sitting room sir. She already knows that Mrs Hemingway is in a bad way. I have not, as yet, informed her of the awful truth.'

'All right George, leave it to me, I will go and see her myself.'

'Right you are sir...Mr Hemingway, I am so very sorry.'

Howard nodded his head. 'Thank you George, I know you are.'

Howard entered the sitting room and could see his daughter standing strangely still, staring out of the window. She did not turn as she felt her father's presence close to her. He placed his hand on her shoulders and gently guided her to the couch. There was an empty liquor glass lying on the floor, which he picked up and placed on the sideboard. He filled two fresh glasses and handed one to Kate, keeping the other for himself. 'Listen, darling. I need you to be very brave. I have something to tell you and you need to stay calm. I am afraid your dear mother has passed away. She—'

Kate interrupted the flow of her father's conversation. 'I know,' she said, in a voice barely audible. 'I know...because I killed her.'

Howard, startled but fearful for his daughter's state of mind, pulled her head down on to his shoulder and began stroking her hair. 'You didn't kill her darling. She fell down the stairs. It was an accident. I suspect she slipped and couldn't stop herself from falling.'

Kate continued 'She didn't slip father, it was my fault she fell. I pulled away from her grip and she overbalanced... I killed her...I killed her. I killed my mother.'

Howard recoiled in shock, as he grasped the significance of the statement, but after a few moments silence, he regained his composure and again placed his arms around her shoulders, before speaking calmly to his hysterical daughter. 'Listen to me Kate. You didn't kill her. What happened? Were you passing each other on the stairs and somehow she overbalanced?'

'No father, you're not listening to me. Nobody listens to me. We were arguing. Mother had gripped my arm and I pulled away from her. In a second she was falling, over and over down the stairs. She hit her head on the banister. I didn't mean it to happen father...but the fact is, it was my fault.'

Oh good Lord...Howard thought, as he looked into the blank face of his daughter. What on earth was so devastating that Georgina felt the urge to physically take hold of their daughter by her arms? Whatever it was, right now, he needed to protect her. 'Kate, listen to me. Whatever this is all about, you didn't kill your mother...It <u>was</u> an accident. Do you hear me? I will get Clara to put you to bed and when Dr Brownlow arrives, I will ask him to give you a sedative.'

※

Several days later Kate Hemingway was sat in a chair in her room when there was a knock at the door. She hadn't left her room since her mother had died and had refused any food offered, only drinking water.

There wasn't any response from his daughter, so Howard Hemingway knocked again. 'Can I come in darling?' said Howard through the closed door. 'It will do you good to talk. Clara has made you some fresh soup. You should try and eat something you know.'

Kate knew she had to tell her father the reason she was arguing with her mother and she was really worried about his reaction. So far he had been really understanding, but that might all change when he heard the truth.

Her father spoke again. 'Kate, open the door please darling.'

Reluctantly, Kate unlocked the door and her father entered. Swiftly he placed the tray on the table and put his arms around her. 'Here we are, try and have some soup Kate. You can't survive on water alone. Will you try and eat some for me?'

Kate turned her nose up at the soup, but saw the pained look on her father's face and felt anxious to please him. 'All right father, I will have some in a minute. First,' she hesitated, 'first I need to tell you the reason mother and I were arguing.'

Howard looked sadly at his daughter, concern etched in his worried face. 'If you are sure you are ready Kate. Remember, whatever it is, we can come through it together. I know it was always your mother that dealt with any crises, but I promise you, I am ready to step up to the mark.'

Kate looked at her father with fresh eyes. He has just lost his wife yet he doesn't blame me for her death and now he is willing to help me through a situation he knows nothing about. She sat down on the bed and smiled weakly. 'I am all right and I will tell you everything, but you aren't going to like it and I am not sure that you will be able to put it right either. In fact, you may even throw me out...It's bad father...really bad.'

Kate told her story without embellishment and her father remained silent throughout. He held her hand as it came to a close, then looked into her eyes and in a surprisingly understanding voice, gave his advice. 'Well Kate, I am not condoning your actions, but rightly or wrongly, you did what you thought was right at the time. It seems to me that you were put in an impossible situation and I honestly don't know what I would have done in your position. However, you need to know that your mother loved you very much and, just like you, she would have sought what she considered to be the best solution. Listen darling, I need to go away and consider what we should do next, so I will leave you to eat your soup. I will come back later to see you.'

After Howard left the room, Kate breathed a sigh of relief, astounded at the attitude her father had adopted. She had not felt this close to him for years, although she had been the apple of his eye when she was small and they did lots of exciting things together.

She remembered the time when Alexander was just a baby, she was five and David nine. Her father bought them a tent and they camped out in the grounds. They had the best time, listening to ghost stories and being frightened by them. They loved it. Her father cooked them a meal on a campfire and they stayed out all night. It had been terribly exciting and now it seemed they had been given the opportunity to rekindle their relationship again, albeit under the direst of circumstances.

She had loved her mother, despite their many differences and she would miss her terribly. Life would never be the same. It would take time for all of them to come to terms with their loss. The guilt, of course, would remain with her forever, until the day she died. She did, however, feel confident that her father would sort out this terrible mess, although the thought that her baby was missing and that she may not see her for some time remained uppermost in her mind.

Howard went to his study to think. What Kate had told him had been quite shocking. Not only was the baby not James's, but there was now little prospect of her marrying him either. She didn't love him and he knew he would not be able to persuade her otherwise. Of course, if James knew what had happened, the likelihood of him wanting to marry his daughter was, he considered, very slim indeed. No, marriage was now out of the question. He had a lot to think about.

He talked himself through that dreadful day. Georgina had been fit and well that morning as he had kissed her goodbye. He had ridden out over the meadow and was feeling particularly at one with himself and life in general. His daughter was to be married and Georgina seemed happy and content of late, rekindling some of their earlier closeness. Yes, he had thought, things were looking up, so much so that he had arranged for them to have dinner together in the evening, just the two of them. But it wasn't to be, by lunchtime, his dearly beloved wife was dead and his daughter believed she was responsible - life was so fragile he thought sadly.

However, out of the tragedy, a glimmer of hope for the future had arisen. Somewhere out there was a baby girl...his granddaughter. Right now though, there was the matter of his own daughter's well being. He had already made up his mind that they would not stay at Low Wood any longer. He would speak to his financier and they would leave the house by the end of the week. They would go away, all of them. He would buy another place, maybe in England...Anywhere, far from here. He could not bear to stay at Low Wood now Georgina had gone. There were too many memories...too many painful memories. They would start afresh. Anyway, David would be getting married himself in the summer, so there would just be the three of them. They would survive and later, he promised himself, when they were settled, he would begin the search for his granddaughter. No matter how long it took, he would bring her back home.

The slums of Narrow Marsh, Nottingham, depicting:

- **O** The Milligan's home in 14 Knotted Alley
- ✸ The Armstrong's home in 3 Foundry Yard
- ◀ The Mitchell's home in 41 Foundry Yard
- ✚ Tommy Bradley's home in 13 Lowe's Place
- ▫ The Loggerheads Public House on Narrow Marsh
- ◆ The King's Head coaching inn

CHAPTER FIVE

The Residents of Narrow Marsh

Despite exhaustive enquiries the length and breadth of St James' Street, David drew a blank with respect to Lizzie's identity. Reluctantly, the decision was made to allow Lizzie and Rosalie to continue living with them.

A week after her ordeal, Lizzie felt able to venture outside, while Rosalie was left in the capable hands of David, who was still looking for a job. It had been suggested by Clara that Lizzie accompany her on her milk delivery round, so she would get to meet some of the neighbours.

'Well me duck, let's be off. Rosie 'ull be al'right we ow David. A often left me girls wi 'im when tha wah little, when a needed ta ga aht.'

'Well Clara, I am ready to face the world again and thank you David for looking after Rosie. I hope she won't be too much trouble.'

David patted Rosalie's back after placing her against his shoulder and looked warmly at Lizzie assuring her she was in good hands. 'Yer a'right Hannah, am used to it. See yer later.'

Clara collected the cart from the pub yard and ambled through the twitchell pushing it with both hands. She had got used to the weight over the years and now found it relatively easy to manoeuvre around the narrow streets. 'Fust people a want yer ta meet are Mabel and Sam Armstrong. They don't pay us oat, because Sam gets us coal in exchange fa the milk. They live at number three, Foundreh Yard, so it's just around the corner.'

They were just about to turn into Foundry Yard from Leengate when a middle-aged woman, wearing ragged clothes and carrying a bottle of some indeterminable brew, came staggering towards them. Clara put down the cart and stood with her hands on her hips. 'Nah then Aggie, wot yer up ta. Looks like yer drunk agen. 'Ave yer 'ad oat to eat?'

Aggie Fisher stood still for a moment, leaning with her back to a wall. 'Ey-up...Clara. It is Clara in't it?' Aggie peered at her and slurred her words as she took another swig from the bottle. 'A 'ed a pasteh yestdee mornin, but noat since. Can yer spare oat fer a poor oad woman?'

'By 'eck Aggie, yer don't 'arf stink woman. Best thing a could gi yo is a bar of soap fer a good wash, but a doubt that's goin ta 'appen...not this year anyrode,' she said, keeping her distance.

Lizzie was shocked to learn that women like Aggie Fisher existed. According to Clara, she roamed the streets, begging for a mouthful of food, which she usually washed down with gin, when she could get money to buy it. She also sold her body for pennies to any desperate man who wished to have his way with her, if he could manage to get past the awful smell, of course. Not that Aggie Fisher was an ugly woman, because in her younger days she would have been considered quite a catch. It went wrong when she became pregnant at fifteen and married the father, who was a merciless bully and beat her black and blue. In desperation one day she retaliated and hit him over the head with a shovel. Fortunately, or unfortunately, depending on one's point of view, he didn't die, but suffered damage to his brain and spent the rest of his short life incarcerated in the asylum. Aggie Fisher was imprisoned for a while, but was later shown leniency because of the circumstances. The judge determined that she had suffered untold abuse and hit her husband as an act of self-defence. She was released aged thirty-five, but to stay clear of the workhouse, pretended she had somewhere to live. This wasn't true, of course and she had roamed the streets ever since. The local police knew her well, but turned a blind eye as long as she didn't cause any trouble. They considered she was harmless and, the victim of unfortunate circumstance.

⁂

Clara was the kind of woman who would help anyone in trouble and Aggie Fisher wasn't an exception. ''Ere Aggie, a can spare yer tuppence and al gi yer a jug o' milk.'

'Aye, thanks me duck. 'Al teck the moneh, burra'l not be wanting the milk. Can't stand the stuff missen.'

Clara shrugged as Aggie took the two penny pieces. 'Please yersen Aggie. We'll be off nah. ''Ave a lot o' milk ta deliver. Tarrar.'

Both women watched as Aggie Fisher stumbled off towards St John the Baptist's church to see if the vicar could spare her any food. The tuppence given to her by Clara would come in handy for her next bottle of gin.

Lizzie watched the retreating figure disappear down a narrow alley and wondered apprehensively what the other residents of Narrow Marsh would be like.

''Ere we are then,' advised Clara as she knocked loudly on Mabel Armstrong's door.

Mabel looked up from washing the breakfast dishes, dried her hands on her apron and went to open the door. 'Ey-up Clara me duck. 'Ave yer brought us some milk. A wah saying this morning ta Sam that yo'd be rahnd this mornin.' She invited Clara in and noticed Lizzie standing to one side. 'Oh, and whose this yer got wi yer?'

Clara introduced Lizzie before they stepped into the scullery. 'This is Hannah Merchant, the young gel Arthur fount on the towpath. Al tell yer all abaht it ovver a cuppa tea. Thanks fer the nutty slack by the way.'

Clara and Lizzie sat down at the scullery table and Clara told Lizzie's story to Mabel. After she had finished, Mabel peered closely at Lizzie, unsure what to make of this well dressed young woman who had turned up in their midst. 'Well...Hannah, let meh welcome yer ta the Marsh. Am not sure yer gonna like it 'ere though me duck. Ad 'ave thought yer belonged somewhere a bit posher than this.'

Lizzie smiled, looked over at Clara and back to Mabel. 'Hello Mabel. May I call you Mabel? or do you prefer Mrs Armstrong?'

Mabel laughed her head off at the thought of anyone who knew her well referring to her as Mrs anybody. 'Well me duck, fust thing yer need ter get straight is, wi don't stand on ceremony 'ere. Wi might not 'ave much money, but we all one 'appy family. Except that is, for one or two of 'em who we don't class as 'family' and you'll get ter know who they are soon enough. In't that right Clara?'

'Aye, me duck that's right enough. Them's the ones wi call Mrs. 'Am not planning on introducing 'er to any o' that lot today mind. Just the usual crowd.'

Lizzie jumped in. 'I'm just pleased to be alive Mabel. If it hadn't been for Arthur and David, I wouldn't be here at all. I have met with nothing but kindness since I arrived here, so I think I will manage very well.'

'Aye well me duck, best advice a can gee yer, is try and dress a bit more plainly like. Some folks round 'ere can get right jealous of someone like yo and yer set yersen up fer abuse. A don't mean any offence ter yer, but Clara knows what a mean.'

Lizzie smiled as she graciously took in the advice offered by Mabel. 'Thank you Mabel. I will bear that in mind for the future.'

Clara nodded in agreement and enquired of Mabel's husband. 'Is Sam on a shift then Mabel?'

'Aye yeh. Sam's allus on a shift, even when it's not his shift, 'e'll try and get someone to gee 'im a shift. A don't see a lot on 'im at the minute. 'E's trying ta bring in extra money fer Christmas.'

They sat with Mabel for twenty minutes, until Clara decided that they had to be away, or she'd be down on her sale of milk for the day. 'Well Mabel, we'll be off nah. Tarrar me duck.'

Clara and Lizzie also visited Ida Mitchell, after first ascertaining that her husband, Bill was out as usual, propping up the bar at the Loggerheads.

Ida Mitchell was a woman who suffered the undeserved abuse of her husband, especially when he came home worse for drink. He was a small insignificant man with thinning dark hair and a moustache and because of his unreliability, often out of work. He became quite a monster if he could not find money for a drink and often left his wife short of housekeeping. In the absence of his wife, he beat his young son Jimmy, who he constantly denied was sired by him, citing the rent man as the guilty party. This conclusion was unfounded, but Ida was made to pay, despite her innocence.

By comparison, Ida was a kindly woman who did her best to protect her son and herself by ensuring the house was kept in good order. When Bill came staggering home, there was always food on the table with his slippers warming by the fire. Unfortunately, he was always ready to pick an argument over the smallest indiscretion, which left Ida with little time to chat. Her job, according to her husband, was to remain in the home all day, cleaning, cooking and mending, hence Clara's habit of checking that Bill was not at home, before spending time with her friend. Clara explained to Lizzie that Ida's neighbours often helped her out by giving her 'left over's', when she was kept short of housekeeping money by Bill. Lizzie warmed to Ida straight away, but felt very sorry for her circumstances.

After visiting similar characters on their rounds, Clara and Lizzie headed home, but on the way, they bumped into Nellie and Tommy Bradley. Clara only passed the time of day with her because she felt sorry for her son. 'Lissen Hannah, yer see them two crossing ovver the road towards us. A don't like geeing 'er the time o' day. If it weren't fer Tommy, I'd never speak ter the woman. Tommy's a special case, but, unfortunately, he's a bit simple in the 'ead.' Clara tapped her temple with her index finger to confirm the meaning and lowered her voice to a whisper. ''E's tuppence ha'penny ta the shilling.'

Lizzie had not heard the saying before, but from the inflection in Clara's voice, she guessed the lad had mental health problems. 'Oh, right then Clara. Will we be speaking to them today?'

'Ooh aye, yes me duck. I allus speak ter Tommy. 'Is dad left 'em when he were two. Can't say a blame 'im either, she's a right 'arraden that one.'

Nellie Bradley drew level with Clara and greeted her in a matter of fact voice. 'Morning Mrs Milligan. Who yer got wi yer?'

Clara looked shrewdly at Nellie Bradley and ignoring her greeting, turned her attention to Tommy, who stood shuffling his boots into the loose dirt on the walkway. 'Ow are yer, Tommy me duck? This 'ere's me friend Hannah.'

Lizzie went to shake his hand, which made him blush, so he looked down at the ground before speaking. 'Ey-up 'annah. Me name's Tommeh, Tommeh Bradleh.'

Lizzie smiled as she addressed Tommy. 'Well Tommy. I'm very pleased to meet you.'

Tommy tipped his cloth cap as he nodded and smiled at Lizzie, because he'd never seen anyone quite so beautiful as this woman who stood before him. So much so, he instantly became ashamed of his own looks and apparel and quickly turned away, pretending to be interested in something further down the street.

Nellie Bradley gave a grimace as she spoke to Lizzie. 'What's up wi yo. What yer talking like that fer? Are yer a foreigner? Wi don't get too many o' them round 'ere.'

Taken aback, Lizzie explained that, although she wasn't local to the area, she didn't consider herself a 'foreigner', whatever that meant to Nellie Bradley.

Affronted by Nellie's attitude, Clara picked up the handles of the cart and turned up the twitchell in disgust, Lizzie followed behind. Before they disappeared from view down the pub yard, Clara remonstrated with Nellie. 'Yo a cheeky bitch Nellie Bradleh. No wonder yer 'usband left yer. A bet 'e cun't gerraway fast enough.'

Not to be outwitted, Nellie made a remark of her own. 'Never mind, abaht my husband. Who da yer think yer are Clara Milligan? And who does that silly trollop think she is, talking all queer like? Yu'll not fit in round 'er miss, wi all yer airs and graces.'

Clara bundled Lizzie away, apologising for her confrontational outburst. 'Am real sorry abaht that Hannah. Some folks round 'ere's got no manners, no manners at all.'

'It's all right Clara, I'm a stranger after all and some people might not take too kindly. It makes them feel insecure and suspicious. I expect I'll get used to it in time.'

'Aye, well me duck we's ter be thankful there in't a lot like 'er.'

Clara was exhausted from the morning's efforts and even though her contribution to the coffers was minimal on this occasion, she was highly satisfied with the day's events, so was quick to take up David's offer of some freshly brewed tea.

CHAPTER SIX

Expectations

The following Saturday, Tillie Milligan came hurrying in through the front door, cheeks aglow and full of excitement. She couldn't wait to impart her news to her mother who was baking bread at the scullery table.

Talking ten to the dozen she explained what had occurred. 'Mam, yu'll nevva guess what's 'appened terday. Mrs Phillips came round ter tea wi me employer, Mrs Askew and when a brought the cake and tea through, a 'eard Mrs Phillips asking madam if she knew of a good seamstress. The one she employed a couple o' weeks ago, just upped and left wi'aht a word. Well a knew Hannah wahrra dab 'and at sewing and thought o' them lovely anticassers that she made fer yo mam. So, a bobbed a curtsy and dared ta say: Beggin' yer pardon madam, but a know a really good person that wah the best seamstress 'ad ever seen. Madam gev me a bit ovv a look, as if ter say remember me place, but then she smiled and asked me who it wah. A said, she's not from rahnd 'ere, 'cos she talks different, but 'er name's Hannah Merchant and a could ask 'er ter come and see Mrs Phillips if she wanted me ter. Then Mrs Phillips said a could ask 'er to bring some samples of 'er wock and if it wah good quality, she'd offer 'er a job and yu'll never guess what mam, she lives at number sixty-four. In't that funny mam, number sixty-four where wi thought Hannah had lived before 'er accident? Did a do the right thing mam?'

Clara listened intently to Tillie, even though she was used to her talking quickly. It seemed to Clara that she had definitely done the right thing, albeit she was concerned at her audacity in interrupting a conversation being held by her employer. 'Aye well Tillie, it's summat of a coincidence fer sure. Am not sure yer should 'ave interrupted Mrs Askew, but it's turned aht a'right, so yer can tell Hannah yersen, she's feeding Rosie in the living room, but don't disturb 'er 'til she's finished.'

Tillie hovered around the door between the scullery and the living room, until Lizzie looked up and saw her standing there. 'Come on in Tillie. Come and sit with me.'

'Well, me mam sez 'av got ter wait 'till yer've finished feeding Rosie,' said Tillie, hesitating.

'Oh it's all right Tillie, you can come in now,' said Lizzie placing Rosalie in her cot.

Tillie sat with Lizzie and told her what Mrs Phillips had suggested. Lizzie was pleased that she might be able to secure some kind of work to help pay towards the upkeep of the Milligans' household bills and agreed to take some samples to Mrs Phillips on Sunday morning when Tillie was next on duty. Consequently, she was busy all Saturday with the needle, intending to impress Mrs Phillips with the diversity of her sewing skills.

On Sunday morning Tillie and Lizzie arrived at St James Street and Tillie pointed out Mrs Phillips' house, which was only three doors further up the road from where she worked at Mrs Askew's.

Lizzie was rather nervous, especially as she had to bring Rosalie with her, because Clara was busy with her milk round. She wondered whether Mrs Phillips would be unhappy with her having a baby in tow. However, Mrs Phillips was delighted with the samples, Lizzie's appearance and the manner in which she conducted herself. The result was that she not only offered her the position, but said she could bring Rosalie too and they would see how it worked out.

Mrs Rachael Phillips had three children, Olivia, Isobel and Laura, aged nine, eleven and six months respectively. The two older girls had a private tutor, referred to only as 'Barnes' or Miss Barnes during lessons. However, in private, they had a less flattering name for the strict, straight laced, upright woman, whom they both secretly disliked. It amused them to call her 'Specky', which alluded to the pince-nez she perched on the end of her very thin straight nose.

Myrtle Barnes was a fifty six year old spinster, with greying hair swept into a tight bun, secured by a large hat pin. She was tall and thin with large bulbous eyes, which appeared larger still when viewed through her silver, oval, rimless, pince-nez. These were attached to a fine gold chain, which folded away into a button-sized eyeglass holder. When not in use they were pinned to the breast pocket of her very plain grey dress.

Without her pince-nez, which she very often forgot to bring with her, Myrtle struggled through entire days, frowning and squinting through fish-like myopic eyes. This really amused the girls and lessons took a back seat in their quest to invent even funnier nicknames for the unfortunate woman.

Barnes took lessons four days a week, tutoring them in Latin, Divinity, English, Maths and History. Despite her unusual appearance, she was very good at her job, but the girls were often bored and inattentive, because she failed to inject even a minimal amount of humour into the lessons. This lead them to inject their own humour by counting the amount of times Miss Barnes pushed her pince-nez back up her long nose. This meant that her vision was foggy or unclear at best and on occasion, the girls could be seen counting silently while she would chastise them for mixing up maths with some other subject, totally oblivious to the real reason for their enthusiasm.

Rachael Phillips also employed a housemaid, Sara and a nanny, Augusta. Despite her severe sounding name, Augusta was a jolly woman of around thirty who looked after Laura and was now quite happy to attend to Rosalie. Rachael's husband, Charles, was a financier who worked long hours at his office in the city. He often arrived home after the girls had gone to bed, so had little, if any, input into their upbringing.

The new arrangement worked very well and Lizzie was happy in Rachael Phillips' employment. She became very fond of all the girls and, on occasion, helped Olivia and Isobel with their homework, especially with English and mathematics, for which she had a flair.

Times were hard in the Marsh and Lizzie noticed that more frequently than not, there wasn't enough food to go round. In addition, the house, which was an overcrowded two up, two down, was cold when coal for the fire was scarce. Lizzie shared the larger upstairs room with the two girls and Rosalie. Whilst Clara and Arthur slept in the second bedroom, David had a bed in an alcove under the stairs in the living room. The scramble to wash in the morning was all but impossible, so Clara arranged for the two girls to wash in the evening. Their father, David and Lizzie were the only members of the household allowed to wash at the scullery sink early in the morning. Arthur and David were always up first and left the house before the girls came down, so at least Lizzie had some privacy when using the facilities. Clara fitted in her ablutions after everyone else had left, before starting her own milk round.

David finally secured a job in a knitting factory, in the spring of 1842. He was initially taken on as an odd job man, but by observing the knitters operating their machines, he quickly learned the trade. Within six months he was given an opportunity to become a framework knitter himself and at night he could be found at the Mechanics Institute, learning maths and English. Lizzie also helped in his tuition when she had the time, because his thirst for knowledge was growing by the day and he was determined to make something of his life. His intention was to prove to Lizzie that, unlikely as it may seem, he might one day become a suitable marriage prospect.

David kept his passion for Lizzie private and didn't give any indication that he looked upon her as anything but family. He never allowed his feelings to surface, although he hoped that one day she would see him in a different light.

Unfortunately for David, Lizzie's feelings for him were not reciprocated. She was hugely fond of him as an adopted brother but not, as he might have hoped, as a future husband. Consequently, he was destined to be a very disappointed man.

By and large, Lizzie and the Milligans' managed to work around the difficulties created by their cramped living conditions, but their quality of life improved greatly following David's promotion in August 1843 and Lizzie's spectacular rise to the post of tutor to Olivia and Isobel in October 1844. Lizzie had been summoned to join Mrs Phillips in her study, where she was given the good news. 'Do come in Hannah and sit here by me. I have asked Sara to bring some coffee and biscuits through.' Then smiling at Lizzie she explained the reason for their little talk. 'You look worried Hannah. I would reassure you, that you have not done anything wrong, quite the contrary. You know how pleased I have been with the way you have embraced your role here. It has not gone unnoticed how unselfishly and ably you assist the girls with their homework and give guidance with any little life problems they may encounter.'

Lizzie relaxed a little as Mrs Phillips heaped on the praise and returned her best smile in gratitude for painting such a glowing picture. 'Thank you Mrs Phillips, I am indeed very fond of the girls and I love my work here.'

Mrs Phillips nodded her head and smiled. 'Good, good Hannah, I am very pleased to hear it. Now though, I have some news which may come as a surprise.'

Lizzie became anxious again as Mrs Phillips' voice took on a rather sombre tone. 'I have to tell you that Myrtle Barnes has given me notice to leave her employ with us. I am afraid it has come as rather a shock, as one doesn't realise how quickly time passes. Myrtle was fifty-nine a couple of weeks ago. I knew her eyesight had been failing her of late and I should have realised her dilemma and been better prepared. She does not really want to leave, but, if I am honest, her eyesight has become progressively worse over the last six months and it would be folly for her to continue teaching the girls in those circumstances. Somewhat significantly, she recommended that you take over the role of tutor.' Rachael Phillips nodded agreeably at Lizzie, causing her to blush, but that didn't prevent a feeling of excitement bubbling up inside her.

Mrs Phillips continued. 'I am, of course, in complete agreement with her suggestion, so would like to offer you the post Hannah. I am totally confident of your ability to educate the girls to a high standard and do not believe I could find anyone more suited to the role. Initially, it will only mean a small rise in pay, but after a period of, shall we say, a month, I am prepared to pay you the full rate of a tutor. Now Hannah what do you say?'

Lizzie could hardly contain her excitement, but inwardly calmed herself, eager to maintain a professional manner in front of her employer. 'Well thank you very much Mrs Phillips, I am very happy to accept.'

Rachael Phillips nodded her head in satisfaction as she appraised Lizzie of the new arrangements.

Over the following weeks, Myrtle Barnes became a real friend to Lizzie. She encouraged her to spend any spare time she had in reading books from the study, which would enhance her literature skills. She introduced Lizzie to a collection of periodicals, which Myrtle had read avidly herself while preparing literature lessons for the girls. They included the weekly 'Clock', which featured serialisations by Charles Dickens. 'Now my dear, I do not know how much you know about Charles Dickens, but he has written a serialisation entitled 'Barnaby Rudge: A tale of the Riots of 'Eighty'. This refers to the 1780 no-popery riots, which I think you will find very interesting. I chose this particular one for this year's literature lessons and we have made good progress. Chapter forty-seven provides the reader with a good insight into how some people suffer with afflictions of the mind, which is of particular interest to me. I did intend this chapter to be included for the girls in the first of next term's literature lessons, beginning in the New Year.'

'Why thank you Myrtle. I will indeed read them with interest. I imagine they will prove very illuminating and it will give me chance to prepare my first literature lesson for them.'

The following day Lizzie immersed herself in the papers. She had not read a great deal on Dickens, but had a strange feeling of de je vue: A strong sense that she had read a serialisation by the great man before, although this seemed a lifetime away. It made her feel strangely detached from the present, so she sat for a while, struggling to remember some far off memory, but the harder she thought, the more distant it became.

Obviously disappointed, but encouraged that a distant memory had fleetingly resurfaced, Lizzie applied herself with renewed vigour to the task in hand.

She had intended to read the entire serialisation, as per Myrtle's suggestion, but as she perused chapter forty-seven, she was intrigued by Barnaby's 'idiocy' and 'lunacy' characteristics. In particular the meeting of Barnaby and his mother with a 'country gentleman' in the 'Commission of the Peace' who tried to horse-whip Barnaby. His mother pleaded that her son was of weak mind, but the 'gentleman' retorted: *'There's nothing like a flogging to cure that disorder. I'd make a difference in him in ten minutes, I'll be bound.'*

The widow then advised him mildly: *'Heaven has made none in more than twice ten years, sir.'*

The gentleman retorted. *'Then why don't you shut him up? We pay enough for county institutions, damn 'em. But thu'd rather drag him about to excite charity - of course.'*

This last verbal blast of dissent, which Lizzie found very disagreeable, made the subject for her first lesson, very easy to make. It would, she decided, be a point for debate: How did Barnaby Rudge cope with the affliction he had been dealt in life and were 'institutions' as ghastly as they were made out to be?

The answer to the latter question was answered, surprisingly, by Myrtle Barnes, when Lizzie solicited the opinion of the tutor on the merits of her first lesson. Myrtle discreetly and confidentially told Lizzie of the experiences of her late brother, who had been incarcerated from the age of twenty-two in such an institution.

Lizzie now understood Myrtle's interest in this aspect of the story. She had had direct experience of institutions through her brother and, therefore, was able to throw some light on the myths surrounding such places.

'You know Hannah, these places are shrouded in mystery, but my brother, Albert, was treated with nothing but kindness by the staff. I believe he was happier living there, although he never recovered, in preference to suffering ridicule from all sorts of ignorant people on the outside.'

Myrtle's perspective gave Lizzie much food for thought and she began to see her in a very different light.

The Dud

People often laugh at me because I'm just a dud
They say I'm very simple - do you think they should?
They never try to help me, to bear my sad complaint
Some say it's all my own fault - others' know it 'aint.
For I was born without the mind, to learn as others' do
So please don't laugh, think instead...
It might easily have been you.

Charles Henry Hill

CHAPTER SEVEN

Misconceptions

Life was indeed improving for the Milligans'. David was bringing home good money on 'piece work', Tillie was now a parlour maid and Alice had joined her sister as a maid of all works at Mrs Askew's.

Lizzie considered finding rented accommodation for her and Rosalie in the New Year, which would ease the crowded conditions at number fourteen. The Milligans' could manage without her financial contribution, but she could not leave before Christmas, as Clara wanted the whole family, including them, who she thought of as her own, to celebrate together.

Early in December a significant event occurred that would cause repercussions for the whole family. The death of their neighbour Nellie Bradley would affect their lives more than they could possibly imagine.

The discovery of Nellie Bradley's body only came to light when someone in Lowe's Place noticed a strange smell emanating from number thirteen. Their suspicions were further aroused when they realised that Nellie Bradley hadn't been out of her house for several days. This was most unusual as her habit of taking a constitutional on a daily basis with her son always attracted attention.

A neighbour had knocked on Nellie's door, which was eventually opened by Tommy in a heightened state of fear. His mother had died four days earlier and he hadn't known what to do. The stench that hit the neighbour was so bad that she did not cross the threshold but instead informed the authorities directly. They immediately sent an undertaker to remove the body. More days passed before Clara heard that Tommy hadn't ventured out since his mother had died almost a week ago. She was concerned that he wasn't feeding himself, so decided to make it her business to ensure that he had at least one good meal a day for the next few weeks. She ladled some left over stew into a bowl and covered it over with a tea towel, then poured a couple of bottles of stout into a jug. Lizzie was included in her plan. 'Lissen me duck, would yer mind tecking this round ter Tommy Bradley. 'E might be cheered up if 'e sees yer sunny smiling face. If I go and 'e sees my ugly mug, 'e'd be even more depressed.'

Lizzie laughed as she listened to Clara's self-deprecation. Clara Milligan was no beauty, but she did have a kindly face and a warm heart. Nevertheless, Lizzie was happy to oblige.

She walked round to Lowe's Place and knocked on the door of number thirteen. It was several minutes before Tommy answered, but Lizzie could see him peering through the scullery curtains to see who was knocking at the door and there was a look of pleasure on his face as he answered it. 'Oh it's yo Hannah. Come in me duck.'

Lizzie hesitantly stepped inside the scullery, shocked at seeing the place in such a mess. She placed the bowl and the jug of stout down on the table, then turned to Tommy. 'Clara was worried about you, as your neighbours said they hadn't seen you since your mother died. I was so sorry to hear about that.' She then asked a question she already knew the answer to. 'How are you coping?'

'Well me duck, it's nice of yer ta ask meh. But as yer can see...not very well. It's difficult keeping the 'ahse clean and missen as well.'

Lizzie felt very sorry for Tommy and suggested she make him a cup of tea, but not before she offered to clean up the scullery a bit. All the surfaces were cluttered with rubbish of one kind and another. 'Look Tommy, you go and sit in the living room and I'll make us both a nice cup of tea.'

'Thanks Hannah. Yer a good sort and a pretty one at that.' Tommy blushed to his roots to think he had made such a comment and quickly made an escape to the living room.

Lizzie spent a good half an hour clearing up the scullery before putting her head around the door. She smiled at Tommy who was poking the dying embers of the fire with a large poker. 'The tea's ready Tommy, come and sit down at the table.'

When Tommy saw the transformation Lizzie had made to the scullery, it brought a tear to his eye and he felt a sense of relief that a woman cared enough to help him in this way. 'My God Hannah, it an't nevva looked like this. Me mam allus had other things ter do and this room was allus full o' stuff, peelings and pots and all the laundry piled up in a heap. A nevva knew it could look like this.' He hoped he could persuade her to stay for longer than it would take to drink her tea, so he pulled out a chair for her. 'Can yer stay fo a bit Hannah?'

Lizzie was anxious to get back home, but didn't want to hurt his feelings, so she stayed another ten minutes before making an excuse to leave. Unfortunately, quite soon, the ramifications of her visit would come back to haunt her.

Two days later, Lizzie left work a little later than usual. It was six o'clock and dusk had fallen a couple of hours earlier.

Usually, Tillie and Alice Milligan accompanied Lizzie on her homeward journey, but the last two days they had both come down with a fever and had been unable to work. Clara was worried sick that it could be something serious, as many of the Marsh children had come down with cholera and, worryingly, some had died.

Lizzie felt nervous as she walked alone. Some of the dark narrow streets on her route did not have lights. She stopped for a moment as she made her way up St James Street, thinking she had heard footsteps behind her, but it was eerily quiet as she looked down towards Beast Market Hill. During the day it was a busy thoroughfare crammed with sheep and cattle pens, but at night it was pretty much deserted. She continued, wrapping her cloak more tightly around her before quickening her step, her breath distinctly visible in the cold early evening air.

She stopped again at the top end of the street to listen for footsteps and quickly turned around. There was no one in sight, but as soon as she resumed her journey, she heard the distinct thud of boots on cobbles. Frightened now, she turned the corner into Walnut Tree Lane and hid down the small alley leading to St Nicholas' Church.

She breathed heavily and flattened herself against the wall, placing her hand over her mouth to stifle any sound. She stood motionless for several minutes, but no one passed the end of the alley. Thinking she had been mistaken or the person wasn't following her at all, she decided it was safe to continue on her way.

However, as she turned back into the lane, she was grabbed around the neck from behind and a gruff voice growled menacingly into her ear. The man had seen Lizzie turn into the alley so ran quickly down Castle Gate to cut through the churchyard. This brought him immediately to the end of the alley, where he waited for his opportunity to strike.

Surprisingly, the man addressed Lizzie by name and spoke in a vaguely familiar voice. 'Nah then, oad up Hannah. I knows yer've bin wanting ta meet up wi me an't yer?' Without waiting for a reply the man continued, his stale breath wafting up Lizzie's nostrils. 'I'm not go-an to 'urt yer. A just want us ta 'ave a little chat. Don't be scared. If yer promise ta keep quiet, I'll teck me 'and off yer mouth, right?'

Lizzie was petrified and just nodded her head in agreement. He released his hand and changed his grip, then dragged her back down the alley, pushing her roughly against a wall. In the struggle, neither noticed that the ribbon around her neck holding the keeper key and silver sixpence had become unfastened and had fallen to the ground.

Lizzie pleaded with him to let her go. 'Please, please don't hurt me. Please let me go, I've a small baby at home and she'll be needing her feed.'

The man pushed himself closer to her and the light from the street lamp shone directly onto his face, which Lizzie instantly recognised. She gave a silent groan, when she realised it was Tommy Bradley. She was shocked at the anger in his voice and the violence he displayed towards her. It appeared even more shocking because the last time they had spoken she had shown him nothing but kindness. Was he intent on doing her harm, or having his way with her? It didn't add up.

She knew he could be unpredictable, but not like this. It was common knowledge that he had never been with a woman, so, thought Lizzie, was he taking his opportunity now - surely not?

In a ploy to give him the chance to release her unharmed, she decided to offer him money, pretending she hadn't recognised him. 'What is it you want? I have some money I can let you have, but I don't have it with me. I promise I won't tell anyone. I have no idea who you are, but if you come home with me and wait at the bottom of the street, I will bring it to you.'

Tommy Bradley grinned in the darkness, the light showing his yellowing teeth and unshaven chin. 'Nah then Hannah, I know yer recognise us, so let's not keep pretending. When yer came ta see me the other day, a could tell yer were beggin fer it. Me mam allus said yer wah a teaser. Ya can't expect a red blooded male not ta notice yer.'

Lizzie was surprised that Tommy continued to taunt her. It seemed totally out of character and she was really alarmed. Supposing he had lost all sense of reality? Supposing the death of his mother had completely tipped him over the edge. What was he capable of? Surely he wouldn't rape her.

Tommy, became more confident by the minute. 'Think yer a cut above the rest on us, but yer not. Me mam said for allus we know, yer wah flung aht by yer 'usband fer putting it abaht. I know your kind. Beggin forrit, but pretending to be innicent as a newborn babby. Well I'm not daft like tha say, I cun see right thru yer and it's not yer money am after.'

Lizzie was really frightened now and thought about shouting out to attract attention, but Tommy Bradley was a big man and although simple minded, would be quick to react. There would be no pleading with him in this mood and even if she managed to scream before his hand came once more across her mouth, it was likely to be ignored by anyone within hearing distance. The church yard was a favourite place for young couples taking advantage of the cover of the thick hedging that grew all around the boundary. No, she thought, I need to keep calm and hope that, initially, if I go along with whatever plan he has, I will be able to persuade him that it's not a good idea, especially as I know his identity.

Lizzie remained silent, waiting to hear his demands. What he said next, however, wasn't what she was expecting to hear. 'Now look 'ere miss 'igh and mighty, as a said, am not go-an to 'urt yer, provided yer do as a say and don't even think abaht shouting aht, cos a might change me mind. You an me are go-an to walk back 'omm ta'gevva, all friendly like. Yo cun walk in front, but if yer try oat, I'll meck yer sorry, and there's no need forrit to be like that. I know yer want to be wi us.'

Lizzie, although confused, decided her chance would come later to wriggle out of his control and get away. 'All right, all right, I'll come with you Tommy, but you are making a terrible mistake, there'll be people wanting to know where I am.'

'Don't meck us laugh. The Milligans' 'ull think yer've boggered off agen, leaving them ta look after yer bastard child. As me mam said, yer 'usband din't come looking fer yer when yer wah fount by the canal did 'e?'

Lizzie was really shaken by Tommy's uncharacteristic attitude, but retaliated saying. 'It's not the same, Clara knows I would never desert my daughter.'

Tommy was lost for words, knowing what she said could be true. He became more agitated. 'Shurrup yo. Nah git moving and don't fergit what a said.'

Lizzie moved slowly down the street, feeling Tommy Bradley's large hands firmly gripping her left arm up around her back. She knew she mustn't risk upsetting him, but needed to outwit him some other way, after all, it shouldn't be that difficult, although Tommy had been a figure of fun in the Marsh all his life and especially since his mother died, so this situation might make him more unstable and unpredictable.

Instead of taking the main route down Chesterfield Street, which risked bumping into someone they knew, Tommy unceremoniously pushed and shoved her down the narrow Castle Alley. When they reached the bottom half of Gilliflower Hill, they couldn't be seen by anyone coming out from Brewhouse Yard and once on the riverbank, they walked briskly along the towpath, eventually arriving at number thirteen Lowe's Place. The house was on the left hand side, at the end of a small terrace, which was blocked off by a wall and an outside lavatory serving the entire terrace. This meant that there was only one way in and one way out. Luckily for Tommy, the yard was deserted and he quickly unlocked the door and pushed Lizzie into the scullery, sliding the top and bottom bolts into their holes and securing the door. Satisfied they had not been seen, he gleefully turned the key in the lock and placed it on the table.

The smell, which met her as she stood in the small room, made her gag. She struggled to control the desire to be sick and placed her hand over her nose and mouth as she surveyed the scene before her. The room that she had cleaned herself only a few days earlier was again in a very bad state, with unwashed pots and pans piled high in the sink. A dirty old lace curtain hung across on a piece of string at the window and an old pegged rug, which Lizzie had taken out and shaken in the yard, covered the floor. The table, which stood at one end, was covered with a dirty oilskin cloth, on which sat an unfinished meal and half a loaf of stale bread. There were dying embers of a fire in the grate and the room smelt damp and musty. Lizzie was mystified, as Tommy stood forlornly in the scullery, unsure of what his next move should be. Something must have triggered Tommy's actions today and no doubt she would soon find out what that was!

※

When Nellie Bradley died, Tommy became a prisoner in his own home and only ventured out after dark. He continued to remain inside his home, even after Lizzie had taken the stew round.

Tommy had been utterly devoted to his mother before her death, but more out of fear than anything else. He was the dutiful son, but she treated him as a general dog's body and reduced him to fetching and carrying. His father left when Tommy was two year's old. He obviously preferred the company of younger women and told people that his wife was a frigid bitch, who denied him his rights in bed. Ever since that time, Nellie Bradley hated men and loathed women even more.

When Tommy reached puberty and got the urge to go courting, Nellie made sure that she put a stop to the one and only likely relationship that might have had the good fortune to succeed. Mary Ellis, the daughter of a neighbour had been scarred down her face when she was ten years old. Tommy had gone to Mary's aid, but had been too late to stop an unprovoked attack on the young girl, when she got in the way of a rampaging gang of youths, escaping through the Marsh. Nellie calculated that if the pair ever married, she would lose her home, so accused the young woman of being a whore. She convinced her son that Mary would leave him as soon as someone else took her fancy.

Nellie kept Tommy well away from the 'conniving bitch', as she called her and made sure he never had any time to himself. He became the laughing stock of his neighbours when word got round that he was still a virgin at twenty-five and they even concocted a rhyming song for their daughters to sing. They would throw up their skirts, point their fingers and chant laughingly every time he came out of his door. Tommy would hang his head in shame as the words echoed through his head: *"Tom, Tom the idiot son, show him yer cunt and away he'll run. Back to Nellie his half wit mum, Tom, Tom the idiot son".* The never-ending name calling and chanting, coupled with the controlling antics of a harridan of a mother had a profound effect on Tommy.

Lizzie knew that Tommy was not altogether of sound mind, but thought him harmless, until now. Clara had told her he was 'tuppence ha'penny to the shilling', but he had never, apparently, been predisposed to violence.

Now, with his mission accomplished, Tommy reminded himself of the reason he had brought Lizzie to his home. He pulled the curtains in the scullery to one side, to ensure that there was no one lurking about in the yard. Satisfied, he manhandled Lizzie through the middle door into the living room, making sure he had the back door key securely in his pocket.

This room was in an equally squalid state, with two old worn chairs facing each other immediately in front of the fire and a further dirty rag rug placed by the hearth. An old dresser, which covered most of one wall, was cluttered from top to bottom with all manner of knick-knacks and household items. In addition, a peculiar smell pervaded the room, a mixture of rotting cabbage and body odour.

Tommy had not spoken since they arrived, but when he did finally speak, his tone of voice had changed completely and his manner had become almost subservient.

Lizzie was taken by surprise, but went along with his request for her to be seated in the old rocking chair, with the worn fabric, by the side of the fire. He spoke in a low soft voice, totally unlike the one he had used earlier, which had been loud and threatening. 'This 'uns me mam's chair, but she's gone, so would yer do me the honour of sitting in it Hannah and I'll meck us a cup a tea. Mam taught me ta meck tea fa 'er. She sez a 'ave ta warm the pot fust, then put the tea in, then pour the water on it and leave it ta mash. Da yer want a biscuit Hannah? 'Ave got some in a tin in the scullery where me mam allus kept 'em. Yu'll like it 'ere, cos I'll look after yer and not let anyone 'urt yer. Am sorry a wer rough when a brought yer 'ere, but a din't think yer'd come if a just asked yer ta.' Then looking ashamed and with a tear in his eye, he apologised for calling her names. 'A din't mean any o' the things a said abaht yer either. It wah me mam who told me yer wah one o' them kind of women. I've never thought oat like that abaht yer Hannah.'

Glancing around the living room, he realised it wasn't up to the standard of a respectable woman, so he sought to clarify his intentions. 'It's a bit of a mess a know, but am go-an ta tidy it tamorra, so yu'll feel more at 'omm. A think, once it's bin cleaned up a bit, we'll be very 'appy 'ere, you an me.'

Lizzie was shocked at this sudden turn of events, but felt relieved that he wasn't about to attack her. She felt relatively safe from immediate harm, having considered his opinion of her. In one way, she knew she had the upper hand. She wasn't sure yet how she would deal with the situation, so she decided to adopt a more friendly attitude and then later, consider her escape.

In this surreal state, Lizzie and Tommy sat in front of the fire. Tommy had politely requested that Lizzie collect a bucketful of coal from the cellar. 'Am sorry Hannah, but until a cun trust yer not ta leave, yu'll 'ave ta fetch the coal yersen. Once yer get ta understand that a don't mean no 'arm and we cun stick ta'gevva agenst the rest of 'em, I'll be fetching the coal missen. Yer do understand, don't yer?'

Lizzie carried on agreeing with Tommy. 'Err, yes, yes Tommy, I...I understand.'

Tommy was much more relaxed now and, happy that Lizzie wasn't making any attempt to escape, he began to think he had been right about her feelings for him when they last met. 'A knew we'd be ta'gevva one day Hannah.' Then blushing furiously he continued. 'A knew it when yer came ta see meh after me mam died and yer was very kind ta meh, bringing meh a stew and a jug o' stout. A was supprised, o' course a wah, you being a bit lah de dah, but a could see it in yer eyes that yer wah after coming 'ere, me being alone and wi'out a woman. Am not sure as we cun manage the baby though. All that crying gives me a 'eadache, but we'll see 'ow we go.'

Oh God, now she understood. She had felt pity for him when she had taken Clara's stew and a jug of stout. No one had seen him for days when Clara sent her round, as an excuse to see if he was managing by himself. After all, he had left Nellie Bradley dead in the house for four days before anyone realised. Lizzie remembered someone saying she had gone in her sleep, sitting in her rocking chair in front of the fire. The very chair she was now sat in. She shivered and tried not to think about it. In her wildest dreams she could not imagine how Tommy Bradley could mistake pity for desire. The idea was completely crazy...

Lizzie wondered what Clara would be thinking and whether, when she realised how late it was, she had asked Arthur and David to go looking for her. Someone would find her, she was confident of that, but she hoped it wouldn't be the police, as Tommy Bradley needed help, not a prison sentence, but for the moment she was stuck in his house, watching and waiting for her opportunity to escape.

Clara Milligan was up and down at the window like a 'Jack in the Box', worried sick about Lizzie. It was now nine o'clock and she was usually home by six, half past at the latest. Tillie and Alice were already in bed and the rest of the family were in the living room, except Arthur, who was standing at the sink in the scullery, pumping water into the kettle for a cup of tea. After setting the kettle down on the hob, he made a suggestion. 'Clara me duck, she'll be all right. She's perhaps called in on one o' the neighbours' fer a chat. But ta set yer mind at rest, David and me ull gerroff aht and trace the steps she would 'ave taken when she left St James Street.'

Clara's shoulders slumped as she considered the alternatives to Lizzie's disappearance. 'Well Arthur, a know fer a fact that she wouldn't be chatting at a neighbour's 'ahse. She allus comes straight 'omm when shiz with the gels and there's no reason for 'er not ta 'ave done that ta night. Supposing summat's 'appened to 'er. Supposing she's bin knocked down or summat worse. Supposing she's bin attacked...Oh Arthur, yes supposing she's bin attacked. A should 'ave sent our David ta meet 'er after she left wock.'

Arthur placed his arms around his wife's shoulders in an effort to comfort her. 'Now me duck, David din't get 'omm until seven o'clock and 'e came from the opposite direction. If it ud bin 'is night fer go-an to Mechanics on St James Street, then mebbee, burr'ee dun't ga there 'til the evening, so 'owd 'e supposed to get 'issen the other side o' town be five thirty. Talk sense Clara me duck. Anyrode, we'll gerroff now, although I expect she'll walk in through that door in the next five minutes, chiding yer fer worrying yersen.'

Arthur put on his overcoat and boots and calling to David, made his way to the scullery door. David passed his mother on the way out and lightly touching her shoulder, offered a few encouraging words himself. 'Lissen mam, Hannah 'ull not put 'erssen in any danger, not after the towpath episode. As me dad sez, she'll walk through that door any minit. Don't worry mam, she won't come ta any 'arm. We'll see yer in a bit.'

'Aye, a'right me duck. See yer later.'

Arthur and David stood at the bottom of Knotted Alley, but before beginning their search, they looked up and down the street to see if anyone was lurking about. To trace Lizzie's steps, they needed to continue along Leenside and follow the road as it merged with Canal Street. After that, they would ascend Finkhill Street into Walnut Tree Lane and turn right on to Hollow Stone, finally turning right again into St James Street. They began their search by turning in the opposite direction to Lowe's Place, where, unbeknown to them, Lizzie was sat in the rocking chair waiting for Tommy to fall asleep.

It was gone ten thirty that evening before Tommy Bradley's eyes began to close. Once or twice in the last five minutes Lizzie thought he was asleep, only for him to wake with a start, open his eyes wide and smile over at her. Her own eyes remained transfixed on her captor. She had now been at number thirteen Lowe's Place for four hours and was barely able to keep awake herself, after the trauma of the preceding hours. She stared at Tommy as his head fell forward on to his chest. She could see the door key slipping out of his hands and prayed it would fall onto the rug and not on to the flagstone floor, which would be sure to wake him immediately. Luck was on her side as it fell silently on to the rug. She waited another five minutes to be sure he was fast asleep, then carefully stood up and tiptoed over to pick up the key. When it was in her hand, she moved silently towards the middle door and out into the scullery. Her heart was beating so loudly that she thought it would leap out of her chest, as she carefully undid the bottom bolt. Unfortunately, the second bolt was at the top of the door so she would need a chair to stand on, in order to reach it. She carefully lifted the chair from beneath the table and carried it across the scullery. She was just climbing on to the seat when the middle door flung wide open and the large frame of Tommy Bradley filled the space. 'Aw Hannah, what yer doing?' Tommy asked in almost a wail. 'Don't meck me have ta get mad at yer. A thought we 'ad an understanding you an' me. Nah look at yer, trying ta leave uz all on uz own, just like me mam did.'

Lizzie quickly thought of a believable reason why she was attempting to go out of the door and smiling at Tommy, offered her explanation. 'No, no Tommy, you've got it all wrong, I wanted to use the lavatory and didn't want to wake you.'

Tommy frowned quizzically at Lizzie, unsure whether she was telling the truth, but he gave her the benefit of the doubt and accepted her explanation. 'Oh right then Hannah. Now I'm awake though, a better wait fer yer outside the lavvy. Yu'd better teck a candle, or yer might trip ovver summat.' He felt along the shelf with his hand, without turning his back on Lizzie and picked up a candle. He lit it in the dying embers of the scullery fire and dripped wax onto a broken saucer, sufficient for him to stand the candle upright. Tommy handed the candle to Lizzie, opened the door then followed her the few steps to the lavatory.

She realised her chances of immediate escape were pretty slim so she resigned herself to spending the entire night in his mother's chair, but hoped that first thing in the morning, she would have another opportunity to get away.

Arthur and David had taken the obvious route to St James' Street, but eventually took a short cut through Melville Street on to Greyfriar's Gate. They constantly kept their eyes peeled for any signs that Lizzie had walked that way. 'Keep looking around David, even on the ground. Yer never know if she dropped summat, it would mean she had got this far at least.'

'Aye, yer right dad. Am a bit worried though, we an't got much further ta go and there's bin no sign of 'er yet.'

'No lad, but we can't give up. Let's ga dahn Walnut Tree Lane. I'm sure that's the way she would come. It guz past the back end of St Nicholas Church. Yer often get courting couples around there. Mebbee if there's anyone abaht, they might 'ave seen 'er.'

David walked a little way in front of Arthur, looking for any clue. He was nearing the alley that went down to the churchyard when something shiny on the pathway caught his eye. He bent down to get a closer look and shouted for

Arthur to come over. 'Dad, dad, a think 'ave fount summat. Look 'ere, in't this Hannah's blue ribbon with the shiny sixpence and key that she allus keeps around 'er neck?'

Arthur inspected the item closely. 'By lad, I think yer right. Looks like it could 'ave been pulled off in a struggle, rather than dropt. It's not good lad...it's not good at all. I think we need look no further. Come on, we can call at the police station off Timber Hill near the Exchange.'

Clara Milligan had not left her scullery window since Arthur and David began looking for Lizzie over an hour ago. She gave a start as both men came up the twitchell and through the back door. They gave Clara the news with grim faces. 'Nah sit dahn and don't panic Clara, our David fount Hannah's ribbon that she allus wears around 'er neck. We went straight ta the peelers and toad 'em shiz missing. The sergeant said they would get straight on it and not ta worry.'

Clara took an intake of breath. 'Not ta worry! Oooh no, I'll not worry missen. Ya wouldn't would yer, when one of yer own's gone missing, at night, in the dark...no, no a won't worry.'

'Calm down me duck. Getting 'et up abaht it in't gonna 'elp Hannah is it? Nah a suggest we all 'ave a cup of cocoa and wait till the morning and look at it afresh.'

'Well, yer right Arthur me duck. But yu'll not stop me worrying all the same. God 'elp 'er if someone's gorra locked up or woss...'

'Nah then, Clara, let's not talk like that. We don't know oat yet. Anyways, I'm go-an up ta me bed, am boggered and 'ave an early shift tamorra. Night me duck.'

'Aye, a'right Arthur and thanks fer looking any rode.'

It was a long night for Lizzie, but eventually she managed to doze off. Now it was early morning and she could hear

Tommy shuffling about in the scullery. She tried to stand up from the uncomfortable chair, when he appeared at the middle door, all smiles and holding a cup of tea. 'Mornin Hannah. 'Ow are yer terday. Rested a 'ope. 'Ave brought yer a nice cup o' tea in me mam's best cup. There's just the one little chip in it, but am afraid a an't gorra saucer. Any rode, that'll warm yer cockles. While yer were asleep a fetched a bucket o' coal from the cellar to bank up the fire. It'll be roaring away in a couple a minutes.'

Damn, Lizzie thought, I might have had the chance to escape while he was down the cellar...until she realised he would still have the key, even if she did manage to unbolt the door. Disappointed, she smiled at Tommy as she accepted the cup of weak tea, some of which had slopped over on to the rug.

Last night she devised a plan, which she thought might work. When she went to the cellar for more coal, she noticed a grille, which let light through from the outside. She wondered how difficult it would be to open it and crawl through the space. However, she needed Tommy out of the way to give her chance to explore the possibility. Fortunately, she didn't have long to wait, as Tommy decided he was going to the toilet.

He was rather embarrassed, as he announced his intention. 'While yo's 'aving yer cup o' tea, I'm off ta the lavvy...sorry, toilet, but am go-an to 'ave to lock yer in Hannah am afraid.'

'Right Tommy. I'll just sit here and wait until you are back.' She wondered how long he would be, but immediately got some idea when he picked up a handful of cut up newspaper squares from off the scullery table. She heard the key turn in the lock and quickly went down the cellar steps. It was surprisingly light and she could instantly see the grille at the far end of the room, above a pile of coal. It would be imperative that she climbed up the pile without getting dirty, as Tommy would be immediately suspicious if she failed to escape and she was covered in coal dust.

Gingerly, she picked her way to the top. Only her hands got dirty as she placed them on the lumps of coal to give her some leverage. She shook the grille to see if it would come loose, but it appeared to be locked shut. Through the bars she could see straight into the yard where there was a good view of the toilet. She had been forced to use this facility the previous night, much to her chagrin. There might have been a chance of attracting someone's attention by calling out, but the yard was empty, apart from a black mangy dog, which was nosing around some rubbish dumped outside the opposite house. Perhaps if she threw a piece of coal in its direction she would cause it to bark and someone might be irritated enough to come out of their door. She bent down to pick up a piece small enough to fit through the grille, but as she was about to hurl it between the bars she saw Tommy, wiping his hands on his trousers and striding purposefully towards the scullery door. She quickly scrambled down to the floor of the cellar and up the stairs and she just had time to wash her hands in the scullery sink. For the rest of the morning, Tommy never ventured outside again and the only time Lizzie spent in the cellar was to fill up the bucket with more coal for the fire.

After a few hours, Lizzie began to feel hungry and it gave her the idea to persuade Tommy to go out and buy some food. This would give her sufficient time to look around for the key to the grille and make her escape. 'I'm a bit hungry Tommy. Do you think you could go out and buy us some food? I have a little money in my purse if it will help you.'

'Aw yer a'right Hannah, I've bin planning this since a saw yer last. 'ave got plenty o' food in the cupboards to meck yer oat yer want. A was just go-an to suggest a nice stew and a thought wi could meck it ta'gevva, but a wasn't sure how ta start.'

Lizzie groaned inwardly then thought of another reason for him to venture outside. 'All right Tommy, I'll help you to prepare it. You will need some meat. Do you have any?'

Tommy's forlorn look spoke volumes as he realised he didn't have any meat. 'A 'aven't got meat, but 'ave got some 'taters and some turnips and carrots. In't that what we want?'

'Yes, yes Tommy we do need those things, but we also need some meat to give the stew some flavour. Shall I come with you to the butcher?'

'Ah Hannah, we in't ready ta step aht ta'gevva yet,' laughed Tommy. He hadn't been outside in daylight for nearly a week, before early yesterday morning when he followed Lizzie to work. There hadn't been anyone around and he had managed to sneak out of the yard before he was seen. Now though, it was the middle of the day and there were young girls playing hopscotch just outside his scullery door. If he ventured outside, he knew what would happen and he just couldn't face it.

Lizzie again encouraged him to go out to the shop. She used her most persuasive voice and tried to instil some confidence in him to make the journey. 'Listen Tommy, we really do need some meat. I know you fear the name calling and chanting from the young girls, but you should just ignore them and walk by with your head held high. They'll soon get fed up if they realise you are not taking the bait. Can you do that for me?'

Tommy thought long and hard. Should he go out and put up with the silly girls shouting at him and please Hannah, or should he refuse to leave the house? He was considering which option would benefit him most, when she went over and patted him on the shoulder. She assured him that he could manage it if he did as she advised. 'Listen Tommy, I really would be very grateful if you could manage to put your fear behind you and walk straight on past them. It will only take a matter of seconds before you reach Leenside and it will be all over. What do you say?'

Tommy made his decision. 'Al'right, I'll do it fer yo. I don't need yer money though, cos 'ave still some left in the tin. Yu'll 'ave ta ga back inta the other room in case anyone sees yer.'

Tommy Bradley opened the door and locked it behind him. Within seconds the chanting started and inside Lizzie made a dash for the cellar, where she could attract the attention of the girls, but by the time she had climbed to the top of the pile of coal, only their backs were visible as they ran to their homes. Their mothers' were now anxious for their daughters' to stay clear of the man they referred to as 'mad as a March Hare'. Tommy had been fair game while ever his mother was alive, but since her recent death, he had become stranger than ever, never venturing out. The neighbours feared he might attack them if he was pushed.

Lizzie went back up to the living room and began her search for the key to the grille. She started in the scullery and methodically emptied each drawer, taking care to ensure everything was back in its place afterwards. In the living room, she looked in every container on the dresser, but to no avail. She wrang her hands together in frustration before venturing up the stairs, which rose up from behind a door in the living room. There was one bedroom on the first floor and the other up a set of stairs, which lead to the top of the house. After discovering the door to the attic room was locked, she was relieved to find the other bedroom door opened without difficulty. Inside, were an unmade single bed, an old wooden chest of drawers, a small single wardrobe and the inevitable rag rug on the floor. She hastily rummaged in the three drawers, but there were only a few pairs of women's drawers, some thick stockings and a jumper. The wardrobe revealed two blouses and an old blue coat, with nothing in the pockets but that was all. Disappointed, she descended the stairs and went back into the scullery. Lizzie realised she hadn't investigated the high cupboard, so she climbed on a chair, only to find it full of cracked cups and mugs and a rusty tin where Tommy kept his money, but no sign of a key.

Time was moving on and she estimated that she only had about five more minutes before Tommy returned. She sat down at the scullery table dejectedly. Think, she said to herself, if this was your house, where would you keep the key to the grille?...Suddenly she had an idea. The cellar would be the most obvious place. She smiled to herself as she rushed from the scullery and back down the cellar steps. This time she searched intently on the floor and on the walls...but there wasn't any sign of a key, only several old tin buckets, a yard brush and some old rags. Then finally she located the key as she climbed back up. It was straight in front of her, hanging on a hook on the cellar side of the door. In her haste to take it down, she almost tripped over the top step, but then she held it safely in her hand. She knew that there would not be enough time now to undo the grille and get away before Tommy returned, so she put the key straight into her pocket. Pleased with her success, she felt inspired to begin preparing the stew, as she would need to keep her energy up, in preparation for an escape.

David Milligan had been searching the streets for Lizzie all morning without success. Around 1 o'clock he decided to return home, intending to resume the search after lunch. When he entered Leenside, Tommy Bradley was coming in the opposite direction. Tommy was about the same age as David, who had always felt sorry for him. He felt that most people misunderstood him and that if his neighbours left him alone, he wouldn't harm anyone. Despite his lack of progress on the Lizzie front, David felt obliged to speak to him and ask of his welfare. 'Ay-up Tommy...yer alright?'

Tommy went bright red. It was as if the words 'I've got Hannah Merchant in my front room' were emblazoned on his forehead. He fidgeted uncomfortably and responded in a trembling voice, which gave out more information than he intended. 'Ay-up yersen David...A 'ant done oat wrong.'

David was surprised at Tommy's unusually guilty manner, but knew he was generally frightened of everything, including his own shadow, so he spoke kindly to reassure Tommy that he was only making polite conversation. 'A never said yer 'ad. Wot yer bin doin wi yersen then? An't seen yer fer ovver a week. A wah sorry ta 'ear abaht yer mam dying Tommy. It must bi difficult fer yer on yer own.'

Tommy felt flustered but thanked David for his concern and tried to explain where he'd been. 'Thanks David. Am al'right...What da yer mean, am on me own? Am norron me own any rode. 'Ave got...' Then realising David was unaware that Lizzie was now living with him, he changed his story. 'A mean, a am on me own. 'Ave got nobbdi nah ta look afta meh.'

This bemused David and he wondered if Tommy had any other family now that his mother had died and whether someone, unbeknown to his neighbours, had moved in with him. Perhaps, he wasn't sure of the question. 'Well, yer either on yer own, or yer not, which is it? And what's in yer bag Tommy?'

Tommy blushed again and confused, didn't answer for a few seconds. 'A mean, a am on me own. A definitely am on me own and thiz noat in me bag.'

David knew Tommy was a bit simple, but was genuinely interested in his welfare, so undeterred by his confusing answers, he pursued the issue of the bag. 'Of cause yer've got summat in yer bag. It's not full o' fresh air is it? What's up wi yer Tommy? Am only interested ta see if yer managing?'

Tommy calmed himself a bit. He had never been afraid of David, who had always treated him with respect and he realised he was making a bit of a joke about the contents of his bag.

'Aw yes, a know it's not fresh air,' he laughed. 'That's funny David, that is. It's just some meat 'ave bought for us stew. 'Ave got to get back to cook it fer 'er, so I'll be off now.'

David became more curious as Tommy alluded to making a stew for more than one person. He considered that there might be more to Tommy's last statement than met the eye, so he decided to ask him if he had seen Lizzie on his travels.

'Da yer know our Hannah is missing Tommy? She din't come 'omm last night. Me mam's worried sick abaht 'er.'

Tommy dug his boot into the dirt of the path and lowered his eyes before replying. 'No...no, I din't know she wah missin.' Then becoming braver he made a suggestion about her disappearance. 'Perhaps she's boggered off. Perhaps she don't want ta come 'omm, 'ave yer thought a that?'

David was surprised at Tommy's attitude. Something was bothering him he thought. He looked uncomfortable when Hannah was mentioned. Surely he...no...it was ridiculous...he wouldn't have the nerve. He laughed to himself at the absurd idea that Tommy had anything to do with Hannah's disappearance. Obviously, he thought, he doesn't know what to say to me and feels awkward answering my questions. He couldn't believe he had thought such a thing. Tommy Bradley might be a bit simple, but he's completely harmless, so David said goodbye and shook his hand. 'Ah well, if yer find oat aht Tommy, yu'll be sure to let us know. Teck care o' yersen. Tarrar.'

Relief washed over Tommy's face, which didn't go unnoticed by David. He was now positively cock-a-hoop, with a spring in his step and completely different to how he appeared moments ago. 'Aw right David. If a see oat of 'er I'll let yer know. Tarrar.' He waved and smiled broadly as he left.

David's eyes followed Tommy as he turned into Lowe's Place. He scratched his head and puzzled at the strange conversation that had taken place, before continuing on home; a disturbing thought still niggling at the back of his mind.

Clara sat at the scullery table, her eyes red from crying. She had not done any work all morning, except to see to Rosalie, Tillie and Alice. There was a pile of washing by the dolly tub, which she brought inside on cold days and the breakfast pots were still in the sink. She looked up as David entered. 'Well? 'Ave yer fount oat aht?'

David pursed his lips together as he gave his reply. 'Not yet mam, but am go-an aht agen this aftow. 'Ave just seen Tommeh Bradleh on Leenside, a think 'e's gerrin woss mam. He can't seem ta ansa a simple question nah.'

'Aye David, 'e's ta be pitied though. 'Is mam was a right sod to 'im. A 'ate ta say it, but 'e's berra off wi'out 'er. Though 'ow 'e'll manage on 'is own, God only knows. 'E's harmless enough though, despite the name calling he puts up with.'

David's mind was still engaged with the conversation he had just had with Tommy and he absently agreed with his mother. 'Aye, yer right there mam. I'll just meck yer a cuppa, wash these pots and then I'll 'ave a wash missen, get some lunch and gerroff agen. Is tha oat yer want from the shop mam?'

'Yer a good lad son. Yer understand why am just not up to oat today. Yer dad 'ull need summat fer 'is tea ta night, so yer can get me a barm loaf and he cun 'av some 'omm made strawberry jam that's in the cupboard. Yer dad's partial ta strawberry jam. Am not 'ungry missen. Teck fourpence from the tin me duck.'

David looked at his mother's sad figure sat at the table and his heart went out to her. They were all worried about Lizzie, he more than any of them would know, but his mam had taken it especially hard. Trying his best to cheer her up, he placed a cup of tea and a biscuit in front of her. ''Ere yer are mam, drink this. There's an extra spoon o' sugar in it. Yer need ta eat summat, or yu'll be neither use na ornament when Hannah gets back, which she will mam, a just know it. 'Ave a good feeling that she'll be fount before ta night.'

Clara looked up at her son, grateful for his kind words of comfort. 'Da'ya think so David...Da'ya think so? I hope yer right son. A just hope yer right.'

※

David called at the shops later on that afternoon and decided to take a look down Lowe's Place, not entirely convinced that Tommy didn't know anything about Lizzie's disappearance. It was 4 o'clock and the light was failing as he entered the top end of the terrace. He had never been in the yard before and was unsure which house Tommy lived in. At present he wanted to remain unseen; after all he didn't have any proof that anything untoward had occurred.

Candles were burning in most of the houses and he looked to the bottom of the yard. He saw that there was only one way in and one way out. The yard came to an abrupt end at the single lavatory and brick wall, which separated it from a waste area and the warehouses to the rear. His eyes were scanning the row of houses, when he suddenly became aware of a hand reaching out of a grille fronting a house at the bottom end next to the wall. The hand was extended through the grille up to the elbow and was waving a handkerchief. Oh my God, David thought, could it be?...He walked rapidly to the end house and stood with his back against the wall. Then he heard a voice calling to him from the grille to the left of where he stood. 'David, David, it's me, Hannah. Don't speak, just listen. I haven't got much time. Tommy Bradley has me prisoner here, but I don't want you to go to the police David. What I want you to do is to knock on Tommy's door and keep him occupied. That will give me chance to open the grille and get out. Come back at nine o'clock when I will be able to come down to the cellar again for some more coal. Can you do that?'

David was clearly shocked at Lizzie's suggestion that they didn't involve the police, but under the circumstances, thought it best he went along with her request, despite several misgivings. 'Oh my God Hannah. Are yer sure ya don't want me ta fetch a peeler? Will yer be able ta gerrout yersen?'

'Yes, yes I have the key and can escape if you can keep him occupied for several minutes. I have to go, he's calling me.'

Tommy Bradley went to the top of the cellar and peered down to where Lizzie was filling up the bucket. 'Are yer a'right Hannah. Da ya want me ta 'elp yer?'

'No, no Tommy. I can manage. I've nearly finished.'

Lizzie came up a few minutes later and Tommy put the coal on the fire.

Lizzie had been genuinely pleased that Tommy had found the courage to go out on his own, but keeping her prisoner was wrong and he needed to understand that.

In his mind, she had become his family and, consequently, thought now that his neighbours would accept him.

Lizzie suspected Tommy would be in trouble with the law if they knew what he had done, but, if she could escape without them finding out, she could get him much needed help.

Tommy told Lizzie that he had met David. 'Oh yes, Hannah, I 'ad a chat wi David Milligan just nah. 'E wanted ta know 'ow a were doing nah me mam's dead.'

Lizzie's ears pricked up at the mention of David and realised that whatever their conversation entailed, it was why he had come looking for her. Lizzie realised that Tommy had unwittingly revealed more than he should and asked more about their meeting. 'Oh...yes. What else did he have to say?'

'Well, 'e toad me yer wah missing, but a pointed aht that yer might not want ta ga back. 'E seemed surprised, but he dun't know about yer coming 'ere. That's all, then a came back wi me shopping.'

※

It was a couple of minutes to nine when Lizzie suggested she fetch some more coal. 'Tommy, I think the fire is getting low. Shall I fetch some more coal? If I get a couple of buckets, it will last the rest of the evening.'

'Aye, that's a good idea Hannah. There's another bucket dahn there.'

Lizzie had just reached the mound of coal when she heard David knocking loudly on the door. She strained her ears to listen for Tommy opening it. Tommy paled on hearing the knock and shouted down to Lizzie from the top of the cellar stairs. 'There's somebody knocking on the door Hannah. Nobody comes visiting us. Shall a answer it?'

Lizzie's heart was beating fast as she replied. 'Don't worry Tommy, I'll stay down here so I won't be seen and you answer it. It might be important. Perhaps it's the funeral parlour bringing your mam's death certificate.'

'Aye, yer could be right. A haven't received it yet.'

Tommy shut both the cellar and middle door, before gingerly opening the back door a few inches. He was surprised to see David Milligan standing outside, smiling and holding out a bag for him. 'Ay-up agen Tommy. Me mam was worried abaht yer and sent me round with some food. Canna come in?'

Tommy trusted David, but eyed him suspiciously. However, he knew Lizzie was safely ensconced in the cellar with the middle door shut, so he stepped aside to let David in to the scullery. In a concerned, but friendly voice, David placed the bag on the table and proceeded to empty out the contents. 'Nah then Tommy, thiz a fresh loaf, some milk, butta, a jar o' jam, some eggs and a couple o' rashers o' bacon. That'ull keep yer go-an fo'rra few days.'

'Aye, well thank yer mam David. It's right good on 'er. Well a berra gerron. A an't had me suppa yet. So tarrar David.'

David wasn't about to leave just yet, as he knew Lizzie would need a good few minutes to get out of the cellar and away down the yard. He continued the conversation and asked Tommy about his mother's funeral which he knew was scheduled for Monday week, as there was a seasonal backlog of burials. 'Me mam sez that if yer want 'er ta meck some samwidges and stuff for yer mam's wake, she'll be 'appy ta do it.'

Tommy was anxious to get rid of David, but felt obliged to stand and talk to him for a bit. After all, he thought to himself, he's no reason to think that Hannah's here. No reason at all. 'Ah well, a might teck 'er up on that. It's next Monday yer know. In fact, da ya want to come David? Me mam din't 'ave many friends and a would like it if yo and yer mam could find the time ta come.'

David was pleased that Tommy's sudden desire to talk meant that Lizzie would have plenty of time to break free. The more time he could give her the better. 'Well Tommy, I'll do me best and am sure me mam 'ull go. 'Ave yer time fer a cuppa nah Tommy? Am fair gasping missen.'

Tommy wasn't sure whether he should give David any more time. After all, Lizzie was down the cold cellar and he didn't think she would be happy having to wait down there. 'Well a can't really David, 'ave things ta do before a ga ta bed.'

David didn't want to push it, so the time he had managed to spend in Tommy's scullery came to an end and he reluctantly turned to go. Glancing out of the window he saw Lizzie running hell for leather out of the yard. He breathed a sigh of relief, as he said goodbye to Tommy. 'Right Tommy, well, perhaps another time eh? I'll gerroff then, tarrar.' David pulled the door to behind him and immediately he could hear Tommy securely bolting it and turning the key in the lock.

David strode purposefully out of the yard and caught up with Lizzie as she was hurrying along Leenside. 'Wait up Hannah.' David took his coat off and placed it around her shoulders, settling his arm around her back as they continued together. He was pleased that she didn't object so he left it there, feeling very close to her at that moment.

'Thanks David, thanks for not fetching the police. I'm okay, Tommy didn't mean any harm, he's just misguided that's all.'

David smiled at Lizzie, glad to have her back. 'Well, a guess yer could be right, but 'e 'ad no business keeping yer prisoner like that. Come on, let's get yer back in the warm. Me mam 'ull be ovver the moon that yer back Hannah. She's bin right choked up and 'asn't eaten since yestdee mornin and...and a cun't be 'appier missen.' Then blushing to his roots he added. 'Yer know yer mean the world ta mi Hannah. There's noat a wouldn't do fer yer.'

Lizzie smiled at David and returned the compliment, putting her arms around him in a sisterly fashion. 'I think the world of you too David. I couldn't wish for a better brother, even if we were blood related.'

David's face dropped as Lizzie uttered those final words, which cut like a dagger through his heart. The realisation that Lizzie's feelings for him were sisterly and not as he had hoped, with someone she would want to share a bed, was the final nail in the coffin. They continued in silence, eventually turning right into Knotted Alley.

They entered the scullery where Clara waited. She was off her chair in seconds, pulling Lizzie to her ample bosom. 'Oh Hannah, 'ave bin aht of us mind wi worry. Where've yer bin me duck and why are yer covered in coal dust?'

'Oh Clara it's a long story. Right now though I'd be glad if we could have the tin bath in the scullery, so that I can get rid of all this dirt.'

Clara looked expectantly at David. 'Don't just stand there ow David; fetch the bath in, while a boil up some water.'

David, utterly devastated, went outside to fetch the bath, which hung on a large hook on the wall. He stood for several minutes, anguish and hurt etched clearly on his face, wondering how he could ever change the strong sexual feelings into similar brotherly feelings held for Tillie and Alice. God, he loved that woman with every fibre of his body. She would never know how he ached to hold her in his arms and make love to her, make her his for ever; look after her and cherish her until the day he died.

He thumped his fist on the wall as he tried to rid himself of the unrelenting pent up feelings, which surged through his body every time he looked upon her. But it was no good, she would never be his - not in the way he wanted. He must move on, find a way through his heartache. It felt worse to him than a bereavement. If she were dead, the pain would lessen over time, but she wasn't dead, she was very much alive! He felt sure he would never love anyone else as much as he loved her. Could he brave it out? Seeing her day after day...seeing the warm 'sisterly' look in her eyes and having to look back at her, not as his lover, but as his sister. He would have to remove himself from the situation and never see her again. No...he reconciled...not that...he couldn't cope with that. He had to do it...the alternative could not be contemplated.

His miserable thoughts were suddenly interrupted by his mother's enquiring voice. 'David, wot on earth are yer doing aht there? Hannah's waiting ta have a soak and the water's gerrin coad. Yer've not got ta melt some metal down and mould it inta a bath, just teck it off the wall and bring it through. Sometimes a wonder where yer 'ead is; not wi the task in 'and that's fer sure...David!'

Trying his best to hide the hurt he felt, he quickly carried the bath inside, set it down on the parlour floor and exited to the living room on the pretext that his shoes required polishing.

An hour later the family sat round the scullery table eagerly listening to the story of Lizzie's dramatic escape from Tommy Bradley's cellar. The girls were in bed, but Clara, Arthur and even David, trying his best to suppress his feelings, were all agog. Eventually, the story came to its conclusion and Clara was the first to speak. 'Well Hannah, it were a brave thing that yer did, but 'ave known Tommeh all his life and ta me knowledge, 'e's never 'urt a fly, so mebbee ya were right not ta get the bobbies involved.' Clara reached over to stroke Lizzie's arm. 'We're that pleased ta 'ave yer back though. What's yer plan abaht Tommeh nah then?'

Lizzie was eager to share her thoughts with them all, as she explained her idea. 'Well, Clara, I had plenty of time to think while I was with Tommy and as I see it, if the police find out, he'll be carted off to gaol. He'll never get a job, so the alternative to that is the workhouse and no one would want to go there, so I think we should consider,' she paused as the little group looked expectantly at her, 'the asylum on Element Hill. I know that sounds awful, but we need to think about his welfare. I have heard that he would be comfortable, have a clean bed to sleep in and all his meals provided. He could even have visitors. I remember Myrtle Barnes once told me about her brother who had been incarcerated in an asylum. We had been discussing the Charles Dickens serialisation, 'Barnaby Rudge', in Mrs Phillips' library. People like Tommy were flogged and chained up, but she told me that treatment of the mentally unstable was changing rapidly and they were no longer treated this way, but cared for and nursed back to health. I thought I might go there myself and see what the situation is before I do anything else.'

Clara looked a little shocked at this suggestion, but was prepared to accept Lizzie's assessment. 'Ah well me duck, it's up ter yo really. As yer say, what's the alternatives: prison if the law gets ter find out abaht it, or the wock 'ahse and God only knows yer wouldn't want ter ga there. Well it's Satdee tamorra and I'll watch Rosie if yer want ta go.'

David interrupted eagerly. He was still coming to terms with Lizzie's unwitting revelation, but realised he was still desperate to keep her friendship, even if that was all it would ever be. 'I'll ga wi yer Hannah. Am not wocking tamorra.'

'Thank you David, we will go first thing in the morning. Let's hope that Tommy stays put, then perhaps we could go round to see him together.'

<hr />

Lizzie and David went to find out what they could about the asylum and were surprised at its location. It stood high on a hill with a lovely view over the valley.

The Matron informed them that they would have to see an 'Overseer' of the poor who was required to inform a Justice of the Peace of all 'lunatics' and 'idiots' within their parish and provide a medical certificate stating whether or not they required admission. She assured them that they had a good number of 'keepers' now at the asylum which meant that personal restraint was no longer required, also that the inmates had their own rooms, just as Lizzie had been told. She allowed Lizzie and David a brief look around and both were impressed with what they saw.

<hr />

Later, Lizzie, David and Clara sat at the scullery table and Lizzie described the building to Clara. 'They have large, well-ventilated apartments, separated into wards and all inmates are given the best medical care. There are even bathrooms and the patients are allowed out in the lovely courts and gardens, which look out over the valley.'

'Aye well, Lizzie, am impressed, we'd all be berra off there by all accounts,' said Clara laughing.

Later, after lunch, Lizzie went in search of the 'Overseer' to plead Tommy's case. Fortunately, he was a kindly man who was anxious to do his best. He promised that Tommy would be examined sensitively, before the Justice rubber-stamped the papers, agreeing to his incarceration.

Lizzie and David went round to see Tommy. It wasn't an easy meeting, but Lizzie was confident she could persuade him that it would be in his best interests. Lizzie stood back as David knocked on the door. It was a couple of minutes before Tommy, unwashed, dressed in a dirty shirt and trousers and barefooted, answered the door.

When he saw Lizzie standing there he started to cry. He spoke directly to her, his voice little more than a whisper. 'Yer din't want ta be wi meh did yer Hannah. Am not good enough fer yer am a?'

Lizzie smiled. 'It's not that Tommy, but I will explain if you let us inside.'

'Right then, yu'd berra come in, but a 'aven't 'ad chance ter tidy up,' said Tommy in shame.

Lizzie spoke encouragingly as she stepped through the door into the scullery. 'Don't worry Tommy, it doesn't matter.'

Lizzie and David went through to the living room and Tommy stood forlornly at the middle door. 'A did wrong din't a? A know a shun't 'ave kept yer 'ere, but a thought yer wanted to come. A suppose the police 'ull come fer me nah and I'll be put in gaol.'

Lizzie reassuringly gave Tommy hope. 'No Tommy, the police don't know what you did. We've come to see if you would like to leave this place and be looked after by nice caring people. You would have a bath, clean clothes and a clean bed. They would give you three meals a day and some nice hot drinks and you will be able to go into the gardens to look out over the valley. What do you think?'

'Well Hannah, it sahnds like 'eaven, but a can't afford ta ga somewhere like that.'

'It's all right Tommy, you won't have to pay, it's free,' explained Lizzie.

'It's free? Well why don't yo and David, Clara and Arthur and the gels live there then?'

Lizzie gave an amused smile as she answered Tommy's question. 'Well Tommy, it's only for special people. People like you who haven't anyone to look after them, who can't find a job and who wouldn't be able to have the money to buy food and coal for the fire.'

Tommy thought for a moment and looked at his surroundings. 'Ave got food Hannah and coal in the cellar, so a can look after missen.'

'Yes David, for the moment you can, but what about next week, next month, where are you going to find the money then?'

'Ad not thought abaht that Hannah. Mebbee yer right. What do a 'ave ta do ta get there?'

'Don't worry about that Tommy. I will take care of everything for you,' Lizzie reassured him.

Tommy's face broke into a grin. 'Would yer Hannah. Would yer do that fer me?'

Lizzie placed her hands on Tommy's shoulders. 'Yes Tommy I would. We have to go now, but I want you to put your belongings into this bag with anything else you want to keep that is special to you and be ready at two o'clock this afternoon. I have explained about your mam's funeral and they have agreed to take you there and bring you back on Monday. Clara, Arthur, David and me will be attending as well and Clara will be organising the wake. Is that all right with you?'

'Oh, aye yes that'ull be grand Hannah. Me mam ud be that pleased ta 'ave some friends there ta see 'er off. Thanks...thanks a lot Hannah.'

⁂

Lizzie was allowed to accompany Tommy to the asylum, where a doctor examined him. She stayed to see him settled in his room and felt quite sad, but knew it was for the best. When it came to goodbye, she kissed him lightly on the cheek. 'Listen Tommy, you haven't got to worry about people calling you names or anything anymore. I will try and visit you from time to time to see how you are getting on, but I am sure you will be happy here.'

With tears in his eyes, Tommy put his hand to the spot where Lizzie had planted a kiss. 'Thanks Hannah. Yer a good gel. I'll not ferget yer and am sorry fer what a did. Ya promise ta come and see me though. 'Ave not got any friends, only yo and David.'

Lizzie held back tears as she pulled away and turned to go. 'Of course we will come and see you Tommy. Take care of yourself. Goodbye.'

Lizzie walked out into the fresh air and stood for a moment looking down over the valley. She could hear the birds singing in the trees, below the bright blue winter's sky and smiled to herself, satisfied that Tommy would be happy here. She observed him standing at the window, waving to her as she made her way down the long drive. With one final wave, she disappeared from his view. The large heavy iron gates closed behind her, as she spoke out loud to herself. 'Hannah Merchant, or whatever your real name is, even though times are hard, you have a lot to be truly thankful for. Unlike Tommy, who treads the path of life alone, you are surrounded by good friends and neighbours and that is worth any amount of riches and one day your memory will return and you will resume your true life.'

Chapter Eight

What Price Coal?

Lizzie had been unable to find any suitable accommodation outside the Marsh area, but despite the cramped conditions, life slowly got back to normal and everybody rubbed along quite nicely. However, in early February 1845, Lizzie's life was again affected by her Marsh neighbours.

At the ungodly hour of 5 a.m. a commotion was building up in Foundry Yard. There was so much loud yelling that Clara Milligan was alerted from around the corner in Knotted Alley. Clara was straining to hear what was happening without success, so she whipped off her apron and threw it down on the scullery table. She joined the other residents, some still in night attire eagerly gathering in the street to watch the spectacle.

A police officer and another man could be seen banging loudly on the door of number three, although the occupants, Mabel and Sam Armstrong had lived in the yard for fifteen years without a hint of any trouble.

It was a few minutes before the door opened a fraction. Mabel Armstrong, in her dressing gown and slippers, peered apprehensively at the officer and the onlookers. Her hair was still in rag curlers, which poked out from under her turban and she looked frightened.

The community policeman was asking after Sam, accompanied by George Rowan, the much hated mine manager. Mr Rowan looked menacing in his long black overcoat and highly polished shoes, with his ruddy face partly concealed by a top hat. 'Are you Mrs Armstrong?'

asked the tall slim officer. 'We understand Samuel Armstrong lives here and we need to talk to him with regard to the possible theft of some coal.'

Mabel looked both men up and down and decided they weren't stepping foot over the threshold without good reason. Standing firm with her hands on her hips, she tried to brazen it out. 'Yes, 'e lives 'ere, what ovv it? 'e 'en't done oat wrong. My Sam's a good man. Wocks 'ard at that pit fa next ta noat. Yo know that Mester Rowan. One of ya best men is Sam. Nevva gives ya no trouble. Wocks like a black.'

Not about to bow down to what he perceived as meaningless 'clap trap', George Rowan interjected with a few words of warning. 'Look Mrs Armstrong, you're not doing him any favours barring us from speaking to him. It could be worse for him if you don't allow us access to discuss this matter. You could be charged with preventing the course of justice and with being an accessory to his crime, so I suggest you move out of the way and let us pass.' George Rowan took a step nearer to Mabel in an effort to intimidate her, but the young officer put his arm across to stop him, intimating that he would be dealing with this matter himself in his own way.

A seriously frightened, but determined Mabel continued to stand her ground and still wouldn't allow the two men past her front step. The officer, although partly sympathetic towards the poorly paid miners, insisted on talking to Sam, as it was his job to uphold the law. His actions belied the fact he thought George Rowan was an obnoxious man, with a bigoted attitude. He wanted to gain access without confrontation, so in a less threatening voice than Rowan's, appealed to Mrs Armstrong's common sense. 'Look Mrs Armstrong, it really would be in Sam's best interest if he spoke to me willingly, I really need to have a word.'

Just as she was about to accept defeat, the jeering and booing directed at George Rowan became louder and some of the crowd picked up stones to hurl at the hated man, which had the effect of empowering Mabel to continue to block entry to her home.

From his bedroom window above, Sam Armstrong observed the situation escalating into a riot, so before the police officer could blow his whistle for reinforcements, he went downstairs and appeared behind his wife then opened the door fully to allow the two men entry. He spoke quietly to her as she meekly followed him inside. 'It's no good Mabel, it's all ovver,' he said, shaking his head.

Mabel's sobbing could be heard above the abusive name calling of the baying mob, as she closed the door behind her.

The inevitability of the outcome of the incident temporarily silenced the growing crowd as Clara Milligan stepped forward as spokeswoman and addressed her neighbours in a firm voice. 'Nah listen all a yo lot. The party's ovver and we not doing the Armstrong's any favours standing aht 'ere gawping. We all know what it's abaht and it could be anyone ovv us in their position. So a suggest we all ga indoors and mind us own business.'

There were half-hearted calls of 'E can't prove oat, rotten bastard' and 'We'll meck Rowan pay fa this', but the majority knew there was nothing they could do, either to help Sam, or make Rowan pay. Gradually, but reluctantly, the crowd dispersed until the terrace was quiet again, although it didn't stop the more persistent residents from peeking behind their nets to see if Samuel Armstrong would be taken away.

Word quickly spread around the neighbours who had missed the spectacle and rumour was rife about Sam's misfortune and the reason for the visit by an officer of the law. Many of the neighbours began to panic in case they too were indicted as accessories. In an effort to get rid of the evidence, they painstakingly loaded the nutty slack from their cellars into scuttles and on to already blazing fires. All were dismayed at having to waste coal, which would have lasted another three or four days at least.

Arthur Milligan stumbled out of bed, after being disturbed by all the shouting. He was having a wash in the tin bowl in the scullery, when Clara came marching in from the street, muttering under her breath something about 'kettle' and 'black'. The rest of the words were barely audible to Arthur, who at that moment was blissfully unaware of the seriousness of the incident. Consequently, he approached the subject of the commotion in a fairly disinterested voice. 'What's up then Clara. What's gone off aht there? summat and noat, as usual I'd say. Is Aggie Fisher drunk agen?...Bit early even fo'rer?'

Clara looked worried. The repercussions from this incident could be far reaching. She had received coal from Sam which could implicate her own husband and many others in the terraces for all that matter, all being potential accessories to the crime. She gravely related the information gleaned so far. 'No Arthur. I'm afraid it's more 'an that. The community 'peeler' and George Rowan 'ave bin ta see Sam abaht the theft of coal and we know wiz all guilty o' that one.'

Arthur suddenly became more interested and temporarily discontinued his ablutions. 'Oh bloody 'ell Clara, what 'appened then?'

'Don't know that yet Arthur. The four of 'em went inside and shut the door on us lot. So we'll 'ave ta see what 'appens. I've said a hundred times, it were a dodgy thing, nicking coal, 'specially off George Rowan. Eyes in the back of 'is 'ead that one. Mean as coal muck itself. 'E'll gerra sentence fa sure. I 'eard the other day from a relative visitin the Jones's in Byron Yard that a friend o' theirn got seven years deportation. Think on that one. 'E's only got to oppen 'is gob and the 'ole of the street ull be forrit. We'll all be goin ta Ostrala if the courts 'ave their way. Well, we's as guilty as Sam, wi knew it wa stolen, but we've all bin like bloody ostriches wi ow 'eads in the blinkin sand. Nah we'll all be paying forrit.'

Clara turned pale at her own summary of the situation and stared wide eyed at Arthur, waiting for his response. She needed something positive to allay her fears, but none was forthcoming, although her eyes bored into the back of his head as he continued his ritual.

Arthur thoughtfully swilled the cold water up his arms to rinse off the soap, before drying them on the threadbare towel that hung on a hook by the sink. He turned to look at his wife and in an effort to calm her, played down the consequences that might befall them all. 'Let's not panic me duck. A can't see Sam splittin on us, 'e in't the sort. 'E's one ovv us and 'e'll teck 'is punishment like a man. 'E knew the risk, but took 'is chances. 'E's same as the rest on us, wock night and day to keep us family aht o' the wock 'ahse. Everybody nicks stuff, but only 'cus they can't meck ends meet. It's not summat we'd do if wi got a decent wage.

'One way or annuva, wi 'ave no choice. It's that or beggin and it's no use beggin round 'ere, yu'd get noat worth 'avin, but a'l admit if ya sat still long enough, someone ud 'ave the shott off ya back and the boots off ya feet. Thu'd not be woth oat, but thiz someone allus woss off than yersen.'

Clara felt somewhat calmer as she listened to Arthur's understanding of the situation, cheerfully accepting that he could have a point. 'Well ya could be right Arthur...and as there's noat wi can do at the minute, I'll mash the tea and get ya breakfast on. Wi've no eggs by the way. Sorry baht that me duck. Yu'll be able to eat in peace though, as the gels not be up yet and 'ave not 'eard Hannah abaht.'

Clara was much calmer now and even hummed as she went about cooking the breakfast.

However, this peaceful scene was short lived, as she pricked up her ears to catch the renewed shouting and booing, which once again floated in through the open scullery window. She came quickly out of her reverie, as if she had been doused with a bucket of ice cold water and slapped Arthur's breakfast on to a plate. The fat made a trail on the floor from the pan to the plate and all the way to the table, then she was gone, out of the door like a whirlwind, hoping she hadn't missed anything.

Arthur shouted after her to stay inside, but she was half way down the alley and his words fell on deaf ears. 'Clara, it's noat ta do wi us, stay in here me duck, we don't want no trouble...Clara!'

Clara shouted back with renewed vigour as she had decided it was everything to do with them, now she had had time to think about it. Her earlier admonishment of her nosey neighbours was long forgotten, so she fully immersed herself in the unfolding drama. She called back to Arthur, as she progressed from the main street into Foundry Yard. 'It is ow business Arthur. We need ta know what's 'appnin...' With that she was first in line, joining in the name calling of the pit manager, as Samuel Armstrong, with fear in his eyes and shaking like a jelly, was marched unceremoniously off down the street.

Clara cupped her hands to her mouth and shouted like a fishwife, after the retreating figures. She was not usually given to making a spectacle of herself in public, but she enthusiastically joined in with the rest of the mob. 'Go on ya yella bellied upstart. Pickin on an innicent man. 'An't ya got anythink berra ta do wi ya day?'

The three men totally ignored all the abuse being hurled at them and disappeared around the corner. The angry mob followed them through the Marsh and along High Pavement towards the gaol and courthouse, where Sam would spend the night.

Sam's wife, Mabel was sobbing uncontrollably on her doorstep in between calling for her husband's release, long after they had vanished from sight. 'Samuel...Sam, A luv ya. Come on back. Let 'im go, 'e's an innicent man. Ya scum yo are Rowan, pure scum...I'll see ya tamorra Sam at the Magistrates. Don't worry me duck, they've got noat on ya...Tha can't do oat, miserable beggars.'

The street was now almost empty, but for a couple of women; Aggie Fisher, who was still enjoying the moment, completely unaware of what was happening around her and

Clara Milligan, who stood shaking her head, muttering obscenities under her breath.

Mabel Armstrong, looking utterly dejected, gave one last howling noise, then went inside and closed the door.

Sadly, Clara made her way back to her own house and entered the scullery. Then with a disturbed look on her face acknowledged her husband.

Arthur gave a weak smile and placed a fresh mug of tea on the table for her, before speaking in a concerned but firm voice as he repeated his thoughts on the matter. 'Clara me duck, there's no use 'arping on abaht it, because there's noat wi can do. So come on, sit dahn 'ere and drink up ya tea.'

'Ta me duck, but a think I'll go ovver later ta see Mabel anyrode. She wah in a right state, shouting an' bellowing long afta they'd took 'im away. I'll drink me tea and have a sit dahn, as a feel totally boggered ta say it's only just gone six o'clock in the mornin! After lunch thiz some washing as needs doing before it mecks its own way ta the dolly tub. I'll start me washing today, so's a 'ave more time ta spend wi Mabel tamorra. If shiz goin dahn Magistrates, she'll want us to ga wi 'er. Right nah she probbly needs a bit ovv time to 'ersen, so I'll teck missen ovver abaht five o'clock ta see wahrra can do...precious little a think. I'll teck 'er some fresh milk, so we can 'ave a cuppa. Although a feel awash wi the stuff today already.'

Arthur wasn't sure that it was a good idea for Clara to become involved, but he knew better than to argue with her when she was adamant about a cause, so he thought it best to agree with her plans. 'All right me duck, do as ya please, ya usually do in the end when yuv gorra bee in ya bonnet.'

At a quarter to five, Clara put on her hat and coat and took a jug of fresh milk, before opening the scullery door and shouting goodbye. 'Tarrar Arthur, I'll see ya in a bit.'

Arthur sat in the living room keeping a low profile, which lessened his chances of any further speculative conversations and misgivings from Clara. He called cheerfully after his wife as she disappeared down the alley. 'Ooh aye, right me duck, see ya.' He was pleased that Clara was in a more positive mood and felt more relaxed as the day had progressed. Consequently, he decided to have a bit of 'shut eye' while there was no one else around.

※

Sam and Mabel lived in a back-to-back house, which was rented by a landlord and not by the mine manager, like so many others in the Marsh terraces. Clara knocked on the door at the front of the property. A short time elapsed before Mabel appeared, red eyed and suspicious of everyone she might find at the door, but Clara smiled greeting her warmly. She came straight to the point without mincing words. "Ey up me duck. Canna come in? 'Ave brought some fresh milk fa us ta meck a cuppa. Ya look boggered.'

Mabel was relieved, as Clara had always been a good friend as long as she could remember. The Milligans' supplied fresh milk and the Armstrong's reciprocated with a bag of 'nutty slack'. 'Come in Clara. Ya right, am worried sick abaht it. It's bin a long day, but a can't rest or oat fa thinking abaht what'ull 'appen to 'im.'

Clara entered the scullery and immediately took charge by seating Mabel in a chair, before making a mug of tea for them both. 'Ere we are me duck, drink that. 'Ave put two spoons of sugar in it. It must 'av bin a right shock fo ya.'

Mabel began crying again, adding further streaks to the already tear stained face.

'Nah then Mabel, yo let it all aht,' said Clara stroking her head and in an effort to soothe her troubles away she spoke in a worldly-wise voice. 'Try not ta worry Mabel, a bet 'e'll be back before ya know it. 'E's a nasty piece of wock that George Rowan, but 'e'll not prove oat, Yu'll see me duck.'

Mabel shook her head. 'Ad like to believe ya Clara, but 'e's already seen the evidence dahn the cella. Sam allus keeps the cella door locked, but the peeler said 'e 'ad ta unlock it and let 'em see inside. So wi din't 'ave no choice.'

'Aw right, but ya cud 'ave said ya bought it legal like from a merchant,' Clara suggested.

'We 'alf tried that one, but the peeler wanted ta see the receipts, an wi din't 'ave 'em, did we? Anyrode, Rowan said 'e 'ad a witness who saw 'im nicking it, who said 'e would testify or summat agenst Sam, so we din't 'ave a leg ta stand on.'

Clara didn't really have an answer to give to Mabel that would make her feel any better, so while she was thinking, she took big gulps of tea from the large mug. Silence reigned until she decided to try and find out exactly what Mabel thought the punishment would be for stealing the coal. 'Even if 'e's fahnd guilty, surely they won't pur'im away?'

'Well Clara, yo 'eard same as I 'eard from Mrs Jones, a friend of theirn got deportation, not even gaol. At least if 'e went ta goal, ad see 'im agen.'

Mabel started afresh with the tears, her body shook and she became inconsolable. Clara, however, was not to be defeated and tried looking at the positives by offering suggestions to help her face up to Sam's predicament. 'Nah lissen ta me Mabel. 'E won't get deported, not fa nicking a measly bit o' nutty slack. But ya might 'ave ta face up ta 'im spending a bit o' time in gaol, but it won't be long. 'E'll be aht in no time at all.'

Mabel began to feel a little calmer. The thought of deportation was something she felt she would be unable to cope with but even time in gaol seemed unbearable. The reality was that Sam would be given some punishment and she knew it would be more than a fine. 'Da ya think 'e'll gerra sentence then and not be deported?'

'Well am not go-an ta lie ta ya and yo wun't want me ta. As I see it, I think 'e'll gerra light gaol sentence, praps, three months and if 'e does Mabel ya can count on us ta see ya through it. An there's others' an all that'ull 'elp aht. Those that yuv given ya coal away ta all these years. Wi've all bin guilty o' tecking it, though I've tried ta help yo an all wi the supply of milk.'

Mabel wasn't so sure that her neighbours would help out. People had short memories and anyway could only spread their own meagre provisions so far. Their own families would come first. 'It's very kind ovv ya Clara, ya a good friend ta meh, but am not sa sure abaht others. Evry penny counts and wi've all got kids ta support.'

'People can allus spare summat, even if the've 'ardly got oat. Aggie don't starve does she, but she 'ent gorra penny ta bless hersen wi.'

'No that's true enuff, but then she guz scavenging in bins, an am not abaht ta start doin that.'

Clara grinned. 'Cause not, but the baker round the corner's allus givin 'er 'is left ovver stale bread and thiz a lot ya can do wi stale bread in't tha?'

Mabel nodded. 'Well ya right Clara. 'Av got ta pull missen together. Am no good in this state. It won't 'elp 'im will it?'

'That's the spirit Mabel. Nah then if ya want, I'll ga wi ya ta Magistrate's tamorra.'

Mabel looked gratefully at her friend. 'Ad like that Clara. Am go-an abaht 8 o'clock, so I'll meet ya at the top o' the Marsh.'

'Right Mabel, I'll be go-an nah. I'll see missen aht. Tarrar me duck.'

A few days later the whole street heard the news that Sam Armstrong had been sentenced to nine months hard labour. It would have been infinitely longer, but for consideration by the magistrate of his previously unblemished record. Fortunately, for the time being, his wife and daughter could not be thrown out of their home, as it was rented from a private landlord, otherwise the family would have been sent straight to the workhouse. Nevertheless, Mabel had no idea how she was ever going to pay the rent, whether to a landlord or mine owner. She had already decided she would finish up in the workhouse anyway. It was just a matter of when.

Like many others, Clara had not thought of anything else for the first few days after the news broke. She was thankful that Sam had kept his mouth shut about the involvement of the rest of his neighbours. On the Sunday, a week after the arrest, she considered how to offer practical help to her friend. Money was obviously tight and probably out of the question, so she could only offer left over's'. In her case, a little fresh milk and a small amount of butter and cheese. However, that night in bed, she came up with an idea that might help Mabel pay the rent. It would need careful handling, so she needed to talk over her plan with Lizzie the next morning.

After a restless night, Clara rose early, dressed and drank a mug of hot tea in the scullery. The plan she had formulated would be of benefit all round. Lizzie came in to give Rosalie her breakfast before settling her down with some toys and was greeted by Clara. 'Mornin Hannah me duck. Did ya 'ave a good night?'

'Yes, thank you Clara, Rosie slept until six a.m., so I feel well rested. I'll make myself a cup of tea and join you, before I set off to Mrs Phillips. Do you want another?' asked Lizzie, taking two clean cups and saucers from the drainer.

'Yes me duck, I'm parched this mornin. Bin tossing and turning all night. In fact, 'ave got summat to ask ya Hannah,' said Clara, tentatively.

Lizzie made a fresh pot of tea and the two women sat down together at the table. Lizzie looked expectantly at Clara, waiting to hear what she had to say.

''Ave bin thinkin abaht Mabel's situation an a think 'ave got a solution, but a need ta run it past ya first.'

'Okay Clara, what is it?'

'Well ya know 'ow Mabel's fixed fa money. She'll not be best placed ta carry on paying the rent much longer and then 'er and little Nora 'ull be off ta the wock ahse. There'll be noat else forrit. I was wondring if wi could suggest fa yo an' Rosie to move in wi 'er fer a while and ya could contribute ta the rent. Mabel could look after Rosie while you're at wock. What da ya think of it? Ya know a love the bones of ya both but, ya need more space yersen and it'ud be selfish of me to try and keep yer wi us any longer.'

Lizzie thought for a moment and realised that it would be a good solution for them all. She had been with the Milligans' for nearly three and a half years now, as they had insisted she stay, but it was difficult for them all, despite the fact that she contributed a good amount to the finances now that she worked as a tutor at Mrs Phillips. She was lucky to be able to take Rosalie with her to St James Street, but realised that as she got older, it wouldn't be practical. This way, Rosalie would get the attention she needed, Mabel's rent would be taken care of and the Milligans' could reclaim their house again. 'Clara, that's a really good idea, but do you think Mabel would want us there? Sometimes Rosie can be a bit boisterous and I wouldn't want her disturbing anyone—'

Mabel interrupted. 'Never me duck, she'd rather lissen ta Rosie all day long, than be dragged off ta the wock 'ahse and little Nora would love a playmate. Now what say we go and see 'er tanight when ya get back?'

'Okay Clara. I'd better get ready for work now, as I don't want to be late, but I'll try and get away early.'

Clara wiped away a tear as Lizzie left the room. The thought of them leaving would break her heart.

※

Mabel was surprised to see Lizzie at her door, but nevertheless invited her in. Lizzie told Clara that she thought it would be better for her to go alone, so she left Rosalie at home and went straight after work. 'Come on in Hannah. Yu'll afta excuse the place, I'm afraid I've let it go this last week. Me minds bin elsewhere, yu'll understand.'

'Don't worry Mabel. You sit down and I'll make us a nice cup of tea. I've bought some biscuits that Mrs Phillips gave me today. She wanted them eating up before they went soft.'

'Well that'ull be luvly, a 'aven't 'ad a biscuit fa months, then only plain broken ones at that. Noat as nice as these ones. The've even got choclat on 'em. A could get used ta this, but chance ud be a fine thing.'

'How's things going for you Mabel? I expect it is very difficult for you to manage now?'

'Aye well, it's impossible me duck. When Sam's money from the pit runs aht in a couple of days, that's me done fa. A can't afford to pay the rent anymore. So we'll be fa the wock 'ahse fa sure.'

'Well Mabel...maybe not. I've got a proposition for you that I'm hoping you will find acceptable. It was Clara who thought of it. How would it be if Rosie and me moved in with you and Nora? I have got a well paid job now and could easily afford to pay your rent and help keep us both; provided you could look after Rosie for me during the day. You could do some lace work at home. There's plenty of factories wanting women for finishing work and between us we should be able to manage quite well.'

Hardly able to believe her ears, Mabel's eyes filled with tears, but this time they were tears of relief, as all her prayers appeared to be answered. 'Well Hannah, I don't know what ta say. God bless ya me duck. Yer've bin 'eaven sent. A couldn't 'ave 'oped fa anything ta save us, but 'ere ya are, offering us a lifeline. I'll be fa ever in ya debt.'

'No Mabel, we will be in your debt and so will Clara. Clara and Arthur took me into their home, despite it being full to the rafters. Now they will be able to get back to normal. Rosie and me will still have a roof over our heads and you can stop worrying about paying the rent.'

CHAPTER NINE

Christmas in the Marsh 1845

On Friday, the 22nd December 1845, Lizzie, Olivia and Isobel spent an entire morning making paper chains, holly wreaths and pretty painted pinecones. They were decorating the halls and living areas of number 64 St James Street and the whole house seemed to embrace the Christmas spirit. Garlands hung from chandeliers; laurel, cedar, spruce, ivy and mistletoe graced the tables, banisters and elegant columns around the large rooms.

All the left over trimmings were placed into a large box for Lizzie to take home, along with her Christmas present - A book by Charles Dickens' entitled 'A Christmas Carol'. It was wrapped in bright red tissue paper tied up with a beautiful white bow. Earlier, Rachael had beckoned Lizzie to the library and placed the gift on the low coffee table with a grateful smile. 'Well Hannah, I am really pleased with the progress you have made with the girls. I must admit that when Myrtle Barnes gave me notice, I was quite horrified and worried that I would not find a suitable replacement, but you have not let me down. In fact, between you and me, the girls have benefitted greatly from having someone...how shall I phrase it without disrespect to Barnes, whose loyalty to this family has been unquestionable over the years...someone,' she inclined her head, 'a little less formidable in their approach...you Hannah! I hope you continue to be happy here,' she said as she raised her eyebrow in inquisitor fashion, to which Lizzie smiled and nodded her assent.

'Good, good...I am so pleased.' She handed the parcel to Lizzie. 'I bought you this little gift as a token of our appreciation Hannah. I do hope you like it. The girls helped me choose and assured me it would be something from which you would derive a lot of pleasure.'

Lizzie felt a trifle uncomfortable as she looked down at the beautifully packaged parcel. She hoped that Mrs Phillips had not spent a lot of money on it. It was a total surprise to receive a gift from her employer and she felt a little awkward, especially as her presents for the family were all hand made.

However, Rachael put her at ease at once. 'Don't be embarrassed dear, it really wasn't too expensive and Charles and I are greatly indebted to you for the exemplary way you are tutoring Olivia and Isobel.'

Before Lizzie could respond, she surprised her again. 'There is something else I want you to have. Sara has packed up a hamper for you. Charles receives too much from his clients' and I am sure you can make good use of the items.'

Lizzie was overwhelmed with Rachael's generosity and graciously accepted both gifts. 'Thank you so much Mrs Phillips and I, too, have gifts for you. I embroidered a cotton handkerchief each for the girls and here is a present for you.' Lizzie produced a small, flat parcel containing a beautiful sampler depicting the 'Tree of Life', with its seven fruits, representing the Spiritual, Mental, Emotional, Physical, Relational, Vocational and Financial aspects of life. She had spent hours on this project. 'I hope you will accept this hand made gift from myself. I am afraid I could not afford to buy anything, but it does come with my grateful thanks for the opportunity to tutor Olivia and Isobel.'

Rachael Phillips took the gift and placed her hand over Lizzie's own. 'Hannah, my dear, you really shouldn't have gone to so much trouble. I will open it on Christmas morning,' she paused, unsure whether the time was right to express the thoughts she had been having since Lizzie had arrived to take up her post. Rachel had become very fond of Lizzie and often mused on how she would feel herself, having to live a life of such uncertainty; not knowing her roots and in a situation, which was probably very unlike the one she would have enjoyed before her accident.

She was full of admiration for this young woman, who was striving to provide a better life for her daughter. She swallowed hard and made the decision to tell Lizzie how much she wished things could be different for her. 'I know we never talk about your background or about the dreadful events on the tow path that day, but I hope with all my heart that one day you will re-discover your past and be reunited once again with your family. They have truly lost a wonderful person. There I have said it.' She looked at Lizzie and hoped that her bold statement had not distressed her.

Lizzie was so touched by her employer's concern that she was unable to continue the conversation momentarily and her eyes misted over in sadness. 'Thank you Mrs Phillips, I hope so too.' A thoughtful Lizzie stood up to leave. 'If it is all right with you, I will join the girls in the sitting room and put the finishing touches to the decorations.'

'Yes, yes Hannah, of course, I do hope I have not upset you?'

'No...no, I am all right. One day I hope to bring you the good news I dream about, but until then, I am unable to express my feelings adequately.'

'Why yes, I understand dear. If there is anything we can ever do to help you in your quest, please do not hesitate to ask.'

Lizzie smiled. 'Thank you, I will.'

She left the room and her mood brightened instantly on hearing the infectious laughter of the girls echoing through the hall and she soon joined in their merriment and determination to hang the mistletoe from the large chandelier in the sitting room.

When Lizzie became the full time tutor to Olivia and Isobel Phillips in October of 1844, she gained a pay rise. This enabled Rosalie and herself to move to Marsden Court. The timing had been opportune, because Sam Armstrong's early release from prison meant his return home in October. Although the Armstrong's were happy to have Lizzie and Rosalie living with them, an extra person in the home made the living arrangements quite difficult. Their house was even smaller than the Milligans', so by mutual agreement, they moved out, giving Sam and Mabel much needed time together to become reacquainted.

Marsden Court, situated off Turn Calf Alley, consisted of two rows of houses with little dormer windows. Each had a lovely back garden and number four had a wonderful flowering fig tree, to which Lizzie had attached a swing for Rosalie. It was definitely a step up from the dreary grey yards just around the corner.

Rosalie had been looking expectantly out of her bedroom window since six o'clock on Saturday morning. It was now seven o'clock and she was still in her dressing gown. The snow had been falling steadily all night and the windows were covered in little starbursts of ice where the frost had covered the small panes and there were long icicles hanging down from the eaves. She contemplated reaching out of the window to break one off and suck the icy cold water, but thought better of it when she opened the window and an icy blast of cold air rushed in to her warm bedroom. She brushed the snowflakes off her nightie, gave a little shiver and quickly closed the window, before wrapping her dressing gown closer around her. For a while longer she traced her fingers along the frosty patterns on the window whilst frequently looking up and down the street for any signs of her best friend, Jimmy Mitchell.

Lizzie arranged with Mabel to take Nora, Tillie, Alice, Jimmy and her new friend in Marsden Court, Annie Leach, down to the River Leen to gather fir cones and berries for the Christmas festivities. They were all to arrive after breakfast.

A large box of paper decorations sat on the parlour table, where Lizzie had divided the paper strips into colours and disentangled the holly and mistletoe. She had placed the items into six piles so that the children could each make their own decorations. Several pots of coloured paint, glue with six brushes and a large jar of water were placed in the centre of the table. She smiled to herself and wondered how long it would be before the children spilt paint and water on to the oilcloth, or worse!

Lizzie turned her attention to her second task of the morning, that of ladling the creamy porridge into a dish for Rosalie's breakfast.

She wondered why her daughter hadn't appeared and called to her from the parlour. 'Rosie, I hope you are dressed, because your breakfast is ready. The others will be here at eight and I've a lot to do before then. We need to get a move on.'

On hearing her mother's voice, Rosalie realised she hadn't had a wash or dressed herself ready for breakfast. Now her porridge was waiting on the kitchen table, so she would not have time to change. Instead, she charged down the stairs two at a time singing her favourite Christmas song, 'The Holly and the Ivy' at the top of her voice.

Lizzie turned around to see her daughter sat at the breakfast table still in her night attire. 'Rosie Merchant, you've been up since six o'clock and you still aren't dressed. As soon as you finish your porridge and milk you must be up those stairs and washed and dressed before I finish washing the dishes.'

Rosalie looked suitably chastised. 'Sorry mam, a lost track of time. I've been looking out at the snow and tracing my fingers on the windows where Jack Frost has left his pretty patterns. Can we build a snowman later mam? What shall a put on today?'

Lizzie could never be cross for very long with Rosalie. She was often a 'Dilly Daydream', but never meant to be disobedient; except, of course, when she was out playing with Jimmy Mitchell. Then she would throw caution to the wind and get herself into all sorts of scrapes.

It was very cold today so Lizzie warmed Rosalie's boots, hat, scarf and gloves in the side oven, in an attempt to keep them warm as long as possible. Lizzie looked fondly at her little girl as she contemplated the intricacies of building a snowman. 'You can put on that new blue jumper I knitted and your long serge skirt, oh and don't forget to put on some warm knickers and a vest. If you are good, I promise, we will build a snowman later. Perhaps all your friends can help too.'

'Okay mam. Good idea!' Rosalie was already climbing the stairs as Lizzie started collecting the breakfast dishes.

At eight o'clock the group of friends were assembled ready for the walk down to the river. Lizzie instructed the children to walk in twos behind herself, with Tillie and Alice, the elder two first, followed by Jimmy and Annie, then Rosalie and Nora, with Mabel bringing up the rear.

By nine o'clock they had collected quite a few bags of cones and berries and had even managed to track down some ivy that was growing wildly over a wall, which separated the towpath from a farm.

While the two adults were busy sorting out the cones, Jimmy Mitchell whispered to the girls and boasted about a rope he had secured to the Weeping Willow tree close to the wooden footbridge. 'Lissen yo lot. If we can meck an excuse ta walk a bit farther around the next bend, we can 'ave some fun swinging on the rope I tied ta the big Willow tree. Who wants ta come wi me?'

Rosalie was the first to agree. 'Oooh Jimmy, I do, it'ull be great fun.' Then taking the lead, added. 'We all do don't we?' she said with relish. The others nodded in agreement, except Annie Leach who was a little unsure and not normally allowed anywhere near the towpath.

Jimmy was pleased with the response. He was eight and third eldest, but he considered that he should be in charge, being the only boy. He put forward the excuse needed for them to get away and excitedly outlined his plan. 'Wi cun say wi've seen some fir trees on the other side of the river an' wi just go-an ovver ta get some more cones,' he explained with satisfaction.

The girls, however, were not at all impressed. Tillie folded her arms, put her head on one side and gave a loud 'Tut', thinking she had a much better idea. 'Mrs Merchant isn't going to let us girls go over that rickety old bridge is she?'

Jimmy sighed, why was it no one ever thought his plans were any good? Why do girls always have to have the last say? Jimmy shrugged his shoulders in defeat as he asked Tillie to propose her idea. 'A'right then clever clogs, what da yo think wi should say?'

Tillie looked smugly at the group. 'Well, we could say we wanted to build a snowman and the best place forrit is round that little bend.'

The others were in awe of her suggestion and everyone gave their approval; all but Jimmy, who, annoyed at the way his idea was totally dismissed, stood defiant before facing up to Tillie. 'Yo think yer sa clever don't yer miss know it all? We won't have time to build a snowman <u>and</u> swing on the rope, silly.'

Rosalie looked on, angry that Jimmy had been made to look foolish. Tillie, however, oblivious of the embarrassment felt by Jimmy in front of his friends, continued to fuel his feelings of inadequacy. 'Jimmy Mitchell, it's no wonder yer get a beltin from yer dad sa often. Yer need brains to get yer aht of a sticky situation.'

Rosalie could see that Jimmy was blushing and looked really upset, so to make him feel more important, went up to him and snuggled under his arm. She looked up at him in admiration and stuck her tongue out at Tillie. 'Tillie might have more brains, but, without you looking after us, we wouldn't do anything exciting.'

The others nodded in agreement as Jimmy regained some credibility. 'Well let's not argue. It dun't really matter who had the idea, if we don't gerra move on, wi won't 'ave time to do oat.'

The little group gathered around Tillie to hear her plan. 'What wi do is, tell Mrs Merchant and Mrs Armstrong that wi go-an ta build a snowman. Then three on us build the snowman and the others play on the rope.'

Despite feeling sorry that she had tried to show Jimmy up, Tillie stood proudly, waiting for the group's approval. Even Jimmy was in awe of her plan and his face broke into a grin.

Tillie softened towards him and so that he wouldn't lose any more face with the group, allowed him to choose who would do what. 'Right Jimmy, who da yo think should start ta build the snowman first?'

Jimmy considered his options, pleased that Tillie had allowed him to regain control. 'Well, I think I should be first to try out the rope, as I am a boy and the strongest. Rosie and Nora can come with me and Tillie, as the oldest, you can help Alice and Annie start on the snowman.'

With everyone in agreement, they left Rosalie to put the idea to her mam and Mabel. Rosalie tugged at her mother's coat for attention. 'Mam, we've all been thinking that it would be a lot of fun if we could build a snowman. Tillie says that there's a patch of flat ground just round that bend, that'ull be grand for us to build a really big one. Can we do that mam?'

Lizzie looked at Rosalie and not wishing to go back on the promise she made earlier, agreed. 'Well Rosie, I don't see why not. Would you like Mrs Armstrong and me to help you.'

Rosalie had to think quickly. The last thing they wanted was for the grown ups to accompany them. 'Err no mam, not really. We thought we could build it in secret, then shout you when it is ready. Will that be all right?'

Lizzie wondered whether her initial promise had been a little hasty and sought Mabel's opinion. 'What do you think Mabel? I suppose the area in question is the other side of the tow path, so it is well away from the river.'

Mabel considered the circumstances. 'Well Hannah, Tillie is fourteen, so she—' Mabel stopped as she saw Jimmy Mitchell frown and dig his boot into the snow. She did not want to belittle him in front of all the girls, so she revised her thoughts. 'Tillie could help Jimmy supervise. I am sure they will be okay Hannah.'

Lizzie finally approved. 'All right you can go, but I want you to promise me that you will not go near the river and call us when you have finished. We will sit here on this bench and sort out the cones.'

The little group looked up at the two women and promised faithfully, with their fingers crossed behind their backs, that they would not go near the water. They quickly scampered off out of sight around the bend in the towpath.

Tillie, Alice and Annie started piling up snow to make the body of the snowman, while Jimmy, Nora and Rosalie scrambled down the little bank to where the Willow tree hung its branches over the narrow stretch of river.

Jimmy was the first to jump up and grab the rope, which hung three feet off the ground and pushed himself off the side of the bank. Above the swirling water, backwards and forwards he swung, laughing as the two girls threw snowballs.

It was Nora's turn next. Jimmy helped her up on to the rope. 'Now Nora, yo have to oad on tight and put yer legs around the rope. I will give yer a little push ta get yer go-an.'

Nora wasn't too sure she liked doing it and after a couple of swings she begged Jimmy to take her down to the safety of the bank.

Rosalie had been watching the pair with envy and now wanted a turn herself. She asked Jimmy to place her on the rope and stepped forward near the edge of the river. 'Right Jimmy, can yer lift me up to the rope?'

Jimmy felt a bit unsure, as Nora hadn't fared too well. He felt that both girls weren't really strong enough to hold on to the rope for any length of time. 'I'm not sure that yo will be able to oad on Rosie. Perhaps yer'd better not have a go. Yer mam 'ull kill me if yer fall in and she knows a 'elped yer ta swing on the rope.'

Rosalie felt Jimmy was letting her down. After all, he promised to let them have a go. She pleaded with her friend to help her get on to the rope. 'Aw Jimmy, come on, am not going to fall in dopey.'

Jimmy's concern grew as he looked at the swirling water, but Rosalie was desperate to have a go and was obviously disappointed, so he came up with a compromise. 'Look

Rosie, I can't let yer have a go on yer own, but a tell yer what, if yo put your arms round me neck, I can swing both on us.'

Rosie grinned as she climbed up on to Jimmy's back.

'Oad on tight Rosie and don't let go. Can yer gee us a push Nora, we need ta get the rope ta swing and a can't reach the bank and oad on ta Rosie.'

Nora did as she was asked and gently pushed Jimmy so that the rope started to swing. 'Harder Nora, push us harder, we're hardly moving,' pleaded Rosalie as the two swayed back and forth over the river. The branch bent under the weight of the two bodies and without warning it snapped with a sudden crack and Jimmy and Rosalie fell. Fortunately, Jimmy had the presence of mind to push Rosalie away from him towards the bank, but could not stop himself being carried away by the swirling water.

The screams from Rosalie and Nora carried along the bank to Lizzie and Mabel, who immediately rushed towards the sound. They passed the other three girls, who had been engrossed in building the snowman and shouted to them. 'Where's the others' Tillie? I thought you were all building the snowman.'

Tillie felt very frightened as she confessed where they had gone. 'They...they're dahn the bank by the Willow Tree Mrs Merchant.'

'Oh my God,' Lizzie cried as she scrambled frantically down the snow-covered bank, Mabel fast on her heels. The sight that met her eyes stunned her into silence. There on the river's edge stood her daughter, dripping wet and covered in mud. Then her eyes looked beyond Rosalie and focused on the moving body of the young boy as it was thrown about in the icy water. Staring blindly, as if in a trance, she watched Jimmy as his arms flailed about in the water. Horrified she called out to him - 'Robert, Robert, I'm coming, hold on, try and swim to the bank.'

Rosalie stared at her mother incomprehensibly, as Lizzie repeatedly shouted out the name Robert. She tugged worriedly at her cloak, as she witnessed her mother's crazed expression. 'Mam, mam why are you shouting Robert? It's Jimmy...Jimmy Mitchell.'

Lizzie came to her senses, as if she had been slapped, just as Jimmy managed to grab on to the branch of a large old tree that lay across the river. She called again to the boy, only this time she used his real name. 'Jimmy...Jimmy, hold on to the branch while I get some help.' But Jimmy was made of sterner stuff and managed to claw his own way back to the riverbank, although Lizzie pulled him the final few feet on to dry land.

The whole group stared at the bedraggled pair and considered the consequences of the lie, which had nearly resulted in a disaster.

By now, Lizzie was fully recovered from the strange sense of déjà vu that had enveloped her. Her powerful vision of herself and a boy, apparently named Robert, swinging precariously on a rope just like Rosalie and Jimmy, made her less angry with the sorry looking pair. They now stood before her, quite contrite, soaking wet and thoroughly miserable.

Jimmy was the first to speak. 'Am very sorry Mrs Merchant, it were all my fault, the others just went along wi it.'

Lizzie glowered at Jimmy and Rosalie, but knew it was natural for youngsters to want some adventure. She had probably been guilty of the same thing herself, if she could only remember. Her last thought helped temper the sharpness in her voice, but she still chastised the pair, pointing out the foolishness of such actions. 'Well Jimmy, no matter who the instigator was, it was a very silly thing to do. You could have both been swept away with the current, then what would your mother and father have thought of my ability to take care of you?'

Jimmy began to answer, emphasising the fact that his father couldn't have cared less, but was cut short by Lizzie. She ignored the damning indictment of his father's lack of parental concern, but did not want to dilute the point she was trying to make. 'I'll tell you what their thoughts would be. They would think I wasn't capable of keeping you safe...that's what they would think Jimmy.'

Jimmy hung his head and, although he disagreed with her sentiments as far as his father was concerned, he felt his best option was to keep on her good side and agree with everything she said. 'Yes, Mrs Merchant, a' know and am very, very sorry. I'll not do it ever agen.'

Lizzie felt sad that the day should end on such a miserable note and decided to forgive them all, but she knew it must come with a proviso: that they understand the seriousness of what they had done. A softer tone had crept into her voice as Lizzie addressed the group. 'Well now all of you. You need to listen carefully to what I am about to say.' Nodding heads and six pairs of eyes were riveted on Lizzie as she chastised them all. 'I want you to promise me that you will never, ever, play down by the river again. The consequences of what you did could have ended in tragedy and Rosie and Jimmy could have been swept away, lost to us forever. Do you understand?'

In unison the whole group responded. 'Yes Mrs Merchant.' This time there were no crossed fingers!

'Well now, as that awful consequence was some how avoided, I suggest we all go back to my house and get dried off.'

Again the sombre group replied as one voice. 'Yes Mrs Merchant.' There was a palpable silence as they made their way back to Lizzie's house, each one thinking their own gruesome thoughts about what might have happened.

The atmosphere quickly changed as they entered the kitchen of Marsden Court. The smell of freshly baked mince pies assailed their senses and their eyes widened as they saw the array of baked treats amid the Christmas decorations that covered the kitchen table.

Lizzie was anxious to remove the vision of the day's darker moment and suggested that, apart from Rosalie and Jimmy, the others' make a start on the paper chains, after everyone had tucked into a hot mince pie. The two very subdued culprits were stripped down, bathed and changed and their wet and soiled garments were washed and placed on a clotheshorse to dry in the living room.

Within half an hour, the parlour was filled with lively chatter and happy laughter as the children enjoyed their painting. Glue and murky water was being sloshed around in a frantic quest to paint leafs and cones and strips of paper were glued together to make colourful paper chains. Two plates of mince pies had vanished in an instant and by the end of the day, the rope incident had been largely forgotten. Jimmy and Rosalie's clothes eventually dried in front of a blazing fire and the children departed with arms filled with decorations to take home to their mothers'. Thankfully, only happy memories from the day's outing lingered. Rosalie, however, looked thoughtful as she pondered a question she intended to put to her mother, which had preyed on her mind all afternoon.

She was tucked up in bed with the blankets right up to her chin, when she looked to her mother for clarification of the strange event down at the river. 'Mam, why did you call Jimmy, Robert? Did you forget who he was?'

Lizzie didn't know how to respond to a question to which there wasn't an answer. She was unsure herself why she called out the name Robert, so consequently kept the answer simple, even though explanations were never simple where Rosalie was concerned. 'Well Rosie, I think I did just forget. I was so worried about Jimmy, that for a moment, I quite forgot his name.'

Rosalie grinned up at her mother. 'You told me that only grannies and grandpa's forget people's names because they are old. Are you old now mam?'

Lizzie smiled and cuddled Rosalie to her breast, amused at the perception of someone so young. 'No Rosie, I'm not old yet, but perhaps I just recalled someone from my past.'

Rosalie appeared satisfied with that and snuggled further down into the bed. 'Oh that's good mam, cause old people die, don't they?'

'Well Rosie, not everyone who dies is old. People sometimes die if they are very ill, but nobody we know is that ill, so we shouldn't think about that. Let's think about

Christmas and all the fun we will have. I have been given a large hamper filled with delicious food by Mrs Phillips, so it would be a nice idea to have all our special friends over for Christmas day supper. Would you like that?'

Rosalie's eyes were slowly closing, but she still managed a big smile as she gave her approval. 'I think that's lovely mam, especially if Jimmy can come. Can Jimmy come mam?' Before Lizzie could confirm her wish, Rosalie drifted into a happy and contented sleep.

※

St Mary's church bells peeled out on Christmas morning. Rosalie was up at five o'clock and looked to the end of her bed to see if Father Christmas had been - he had! She called to her mother in her excitement. 'He's been mam...he's been. He must have forgiven me for all the naughty things I did this year.'

Lizzie got out of bed and slipped into her dressing gown, almost as excited as Rosalie. She sat on her daughter's bed and watched her unwrap the presents that had come tumbling out of her stocking. 'Look mam, Nora has given me some sugared almonds. There's a pair of knitted mittens from all the Milligans' and a scarf from Annie. I wonder what this is from Jimmy.' Rosalie carefully opened a small parcel containing six coloured marbles, which bounced off the bed and on to the floor. 'That's the best thing ever mam. When I grow up I'm going to marry Jimmy Mitchell. He's my best ever friend.'

Lizzie laughed as Rosalie unwrapped her other gifts. There was one present from Lizzie, which she left for last. 'What's this mam? This is from you...look, it says, to Rosie with love from mam and three kisses. I'll collect them later.' Rosalie carefully opened the brightly coloured wrapping paper and inside was a book entitled 'The Snow Queen' by Hans Christian Anderson. On the front was an illustration of a snowy scene depicting a queen, a little girl and a fairytale castle. 'Oooh mam isn't she lovely, all white and icy. Is she real mam?'

Lizzie, didn't want to destroy the moment, so decided to bend the truth a little. 'Well Rosie, she lives far, far away in another land. It's called the land of dreams and one night when you go to sleep you might be lucky and see her.'

'Really mam? Do you think I'll be that lucky?'

'Yes Rosie, I do believe you will.'

'Will you read the story to me tonight when I'm in bed? Then when I go to sleep, if I am thinking about her, she might come and see me. What do you think mam?'

'Well, she might Rosie, but if she doesn't, you'll still hear all about her in the story.'

'Mmmm...yes I suppose. I've had a good idea mam. Next time me and Jimmy build a snowman, I'll make it into a snow queen instead. I can make a wand for her to hold, instead of a broomstick and put holly in her hair like a crown. Can I go and tell him right now?'

'Well, not right now Rosie, as I expect he is opening his presents. Perhaps you could tell him tonight at the party.'

Lizzie's house was bursting at the seams as friends from the Marsh arrived on Christmas evening. The large table had been moved into the centre of the living room and ten people squashed around it on several chairs that David had brought on the cart. The only people missing were the Leach family, who had been invited to spend Christmas with relatives in Cinderhill and Jimmy Mitchell's dad. Ida had given the excuse that he was unable to come, because he wasn't feeling too well. The truth was that he had spent all afternoon in the pub and was incapable of raising himself to his feet, let alone walking the distance to Lizzie's house. Not that he would be particularly missed and Jimmy would be happier that his bully of a father was not around.

The hamper provided by Mrs Phillips was a godsend. It contained a large goose, an iced cake, two boxes of fudge candy, two bottles of cordial, a cranberry pie and a box of pink sugar mice. Lizzie provided vegetables from the market and the Milligans' contributed fresh butter, cream, milk and a large slab of cheese.

Lizzie sat Arthur at the head of the table and he made a speech on how lucky they were to have been provided with such a feast. He also thanked God, a tradition he embraced every year since 1832, to keep them safe from cholera before they tucked in to Lizzie's mouth-watering offerings, which included a plum pudding.

The silver sixpence Lizzie had kept on the blue ribbon around her neck had been placed in the plum pudding, to bring luck to whomsoever found it. How lucky was she to have had so many good friends help her through the trauma suffered following her accident. In consideration of this acknowledgement, she also added three little trinkets given to her by Mrs Phillips. There was a small child's silver ring, a wishbone and a miniature horseshoe. The lighting of the plum pudding was the highlight of the meal and everyone was excited at the prospect of finding something in his or her share.

Ida Mitchell found the wishbone, David the horseshoe and little Nora the small silver ring. Much to her chagrin, Lizzie uncovered the silver sixpence herself, but Clara spotted her attempt to put it back into the remaining pudding. She laughed loudly as she admonished her. 'Hannah Merchant, yo fount the sixpence and yer cannot purrit back. I suggest yo keep it nah, as it looks like it's destined to be kept by yo.' Then Clara pretended to have an insight into the future and made a prediction. 'I think yo's in fer a surprise in 1846 Hannah and a big un at that!'

Everyone laughed, but Lizzie fervently hoped she was correct.

Significantly, the Christmas of 1845 would be remembered for more than one reason.

CHAPTER TEN

Rosalie and Jimmy

The summer of 1846 passed without any serious occurrences. In late September Lizzie sat at the kitchen table of number 4 Marsden Court contemplating. Today, Rosalie was having lunch with Annie Leach and wasn't due back until the middle of the afternoon, which gave Lizzie time to reflect.

She poured herself another cup of tea and pondered her decision to continue allowing Rosalie to spend Saturdays' with Jimmy. She knew there were many hazards and dangerous places around the Marsh but conceded that Rosalie was a 'tom boy' and could run fast if she was in trouble. Fortunately, Jimmy was always close by to protect her, proven by the latest incident at the quarry.

Lizzie recently purchased a brand new pair of shiny black boots, after Rosalie jumped a whole shoe size. Unfortunately, these boots now sported a small hole in the sole, which needed fixing at the cobblers on the High Street to restore them to their former glory.

Last Saturday, Rosalie accidentally slipped in the old quarry where she went with Jimmy and her boot became lodged between two boulders. She had been warned numerous times about playing in the quarry and promised her mother not to go there again. Lizzie suggested that Jimmy come to their house and play in the back garden, but an adventurous Rosalie intended to have more fun in the Marsh area, particularly the deserted caves and the quarry.

Temptation prevailed when Jimmy told her he had found some glassy marbles in a secret place by the water's edge and she jumped at the chance to accompany him. She was so excited, that she clean forgot the warning given by her mother the week before.

※

'Come on our Rosie, don't be a scaredy cat. Ya mam'ull never know, we'll be back before ya cun say 'Jack Robinson',' said Jimmy running towards the quarry.

Rosalie called after him. She was wavering between risking a telling off and finding some precious marbles to add to her collection. It was really a no contest, but she felt she should make a half-hearted stand, even though in a few moments she would be high-tailing it after Jimmy, as fast as her little legs could carry her. 'Oh you, our Jimmy,' she shouted. 'Yu'll get me inta trouble. I'm not supposed to go down there in me shiny new boots and me clothes will get all mucky.' Rosalie put her hands on her hips and stood defiant for a few seconds, but soon realised her protest had fallen on deaf ears, so quickly gathered up her skirt and scampered after him.

They scrambled down the rock face and had almost reached the water's edge when Rosalie's foot slipped between two boulders. She cried with the pain and Jimmy was quick to lift her up, but as he pulled her free, her left boot became wedged. 'Ooooo Jimmy me foot hurts us. Me mam'ull kill me if she knows we've bin down here. You'll have to pull the boot out, no matter what.'

Jimmy sized up the situation and realised that the boot was well and truly stuck. It would take all his strength to pull it free. 'Look Rosie, a can't gerrit aht wi'out damaging it. D'ya want me just ta pull it?'

'Oh Jimmy, sometimes you are just too daft fa words. Whatever happens I have ta 'ave it back, so just do it and 'urry up.'

Jimmy pulled hard on the boot, but it was stuck solid, having wedged itself further down, after he pulled her free.

'It's not coming. I'll 'ave ta find summat to lever it aht. Pass us that stick Rosie. That'ull da the trick.'

Rosalie reached over, picked up the strong stick and handed it to Jimmy, who stuck the end between the rock and the boot. After a few attempts at prising it out, the boot loosened suddenly and flew out of the hole, hitting him hard on his forehead and knocking him off balance. This made him feel dizzy, so he reluctantly sat down with Rosalie to recover.

'Oh Jimmy, I'm so sorry. I didn't want ya to get hurt. 'Ere teck me hanky and hold it ta ya head, it'll soon stop bleeding. Thanks fa getting me boot though.'

'S'aright Rosie, it in't much, justa scratch that's all. Ya boot's come off worse though, that rock stuck through the sole and made a hole. Yu'll be forrit when ya' mam sees it. A shunt'ave let ya cum wiv me. Might 'ave known yu'd da summat daft. Ya not clever on ya feet yet are ya?'

Rosalie folded her arms and looked challenging at Jimmy. 'Ya cheeky bogger, I can beat you at running any day Jimmy Mitchell, even with an 'ole in me boot.'

Confident that she had got the better of him, she tried standing, but immediately slumped back to the ground wincing in pain.

Jimmy went over to her, concern showing on his face. 'Are ya all right Rosie, can ya walk?'

Rosalie rolled her eyes in exasperation. 'Does it look like I'm all right? I've done summat to me ankle, it won't let me walk on it. 'Ere give me an hand to get up, I'll 'ave to lean on ya.'

Jimmy was happy to assist Rosalie on their journey home and gave her a 'piggy back' for the last few yards down the entry to his house in Foundry Yard. He pushed open the door and helped Rosalie to a chair in the scullery where Ida Mitchell looked immediately to her son for an explanation. 'Well, well, what's all this? What on earth's 'appened ta ya Rosie? Have ya both bin dahn that quarry agen?'

'No mam,' lied Jimmy, knowing he'd get a belt from his dad when he got in from the pub, if he found out.

'Don't lie to me our Jimmy, 'cos I can tell when ya do. It's written all ovver ya mucky face.'

'Aw mam, don't be mad at us. We weren't causin trouble. We just went ta look fer marbles. I fount some the other day and thought there might be some more dahn there.'

'Look, Jimmy, ya know Mrs Merchant don't want Rosie dahn the quarry. There's no need fo'rra to be playing in such places as she 'as a back garden to play in nah she lives in the Court. Ya must remember if ya want Rosie to come ta play, ya 'ave ta consider the fact that she don't live rahnd 'ere no more and Mrs Merchant only lets 'er come 'cos you've bin friends since they arrived. Why you two don't play in Rosie's garden, I've no idea. Ya are a daft bogger sometimes Jimmy, although ya 'eart's in the right place, but I'll never know where ya brains are. She's three years younger than yo and could easily fall ovver, which looks like 'as 'appened now. Let me teck a look at ya ankle me duck. Let's 'ope ya 'an't broken it, or they'll be all 'ell to pay.'

Rosalie lifted her foot for Ida Mitchell to inspect. Ida probed gently until she was satisfied that it was only a sprain and nothing broken. 'Aye well, ya lucky yu've just sprained it. I'll put some grease on ta fetch aht the bruise and wrap a rag round it, then ya can teck 'er 'omm ta Marsden Court our Jimmy, but only after she's had a cuppa tea. Lord knows wot her mam'ull say. She'll think I don't look after ya proper and probably won't let 'er come agen.'

They both looked aghast at that statement, each deciding that come what may, it would be the last time they would venture down to the quarry.

Jimmy knew he might have jeopardised the only day they were allowed to play together, so looked suitably contrite. 'Don't tell me dad mam, 'e'll gi me a belting. A din't mean no harm, it was just a bit a fun.'

Ida never had any intention of informing Bill Mitchell of Jimmy's misdemeanour, but she wanted to ensure he didn't risk going to the quarry in future. 'Well I won't tell on this occasion, but ya ta promise me it'ull be the last time ya ga dahn there. A mean it our Jimmy, the last time da ya 'ere me?'

'Yes mam. A sharn't go agen, a promise.'

'Right, put the keckle on and get some tea aht the caddy lad. I think there's just abaht enuff to meck a weak brew. There in't any milk left but just a bit a suga ta purrin Rosie's mug fa the shock.'

After an hour or so Rosalie felt much better and was able to hobble about the kitchen. 'Am all right now Mrs Mitchell, a can go 'omm to me mam. Thanks a lot fa fixing it fa me.' Rosalie hobbled towards the door then ably assisted by Jimmy, they walked the quarter mile to Rosalie's house.

Lizzie acknowledged the pair as they entered the parlour.

''ello Mrs Merchant, am afraid Rosie's 'ad a bit of an accident, but me mam's fixed it so she's all right now, aren't ya Rosie?' said Jimmy looking sheepishly.

Lizzie looked at Rosalie's skirt, which was torn and covered in dirt and then her eyes alighted on the once shiny boots, one of which sported a large scuff down one side and a hole in the sole. In a firm but concerned voice she demanded an explanation. 'What on earth have you been up to Rosie? I hope you haven't been down that quarry, after I forbade you to go there?'

Rosalie could tell by her tone that her mother wasn't pleased with her actions, but quickly realised the best way to elicit sympathy at a time like this was to turn on the water works. It always worked when she was about to be chastised. In addition, if she spoke nicely, without the Nottingham accent that she reverted to with her Marsh friends, she might not be banned from seeing Jimmy. She did her best and squeezed out some tears, looking sorry for herself, then appealed to her mother's better nature. 'Oh mam, my foot's really hurting me. It could be broken. I know I shouldn't have gone down the quarry, but we thought we heard Nora Armstrong crying out and we went to see if she was all right.'

Jimmy smiled to himself, full of admiration for the quick witted thinking summoned up by Rosalie. He wished he had that talent, as it would get him out of many a belting from his dad. Rosalie really was the best friend a boy could have. In fact, next time she came over, he promised himself to teach her how to whistle.

'What was Nora doing down there anyway as I know her mother has forbidden it? Someone will really hurt themselves one of these days, if it's not cordoned off.'

'Yes mam, I heard Mrs Armstrong saying that to Jimmy's mam the other day. I expect that's what will happen. What about my foot though, is it all right?' She knew she had hoodwinked her mother on this occasion, but still thought she would milk the sympathy for all it was worth.

Lizzie took a good look at Rosalie's foot and, satisfied that she would live, thanked Jimmy for helping her home. 'Thanks a lot Jimmy. You're a good boy. I am very grateful that you watch out for Rosie. Now you go straight home and don't get dawdling.'

Cheered by Lizzie's kind words, Jimmy said his goodbyes and went out the door whistling a tune, confident that his friendship with Rosalie was intact. He was just a bit disappointed that they hadn't found any more marbles.

PART THREE

Nottingham, England, October 1846

Return of Lizzie Cameron

CHAPTER ONE

Old Friends

It was exactly five years since Daisy and Archie Pickering last pitched their stall at the Nottingham Goose Fair. The surprise birth of their daughter in July 1842 had kept them at their base in London, but now that young Gracie was four years' old, they felt able to travel the country again. Gracie was being supervised by their friend's fifteen year old daughter, in Daisy's caravan. Her parents were also seasoned traders and travellers.

They rose early on Friday for the fair's opening at noon. It looked like becoming a bumper year, which would generate a good profit during the eight days. Archie was so successful that by Saturday he was already replenishing his display. 'Well that's the last of it Daisy, how about we have a cuppa 'rosie lea' and one of your home made scones?'

Whilst Archie was sorting out his bric-a-brac, his mind drifted back to October 1841. He wondered if Daisy also remembered the afternoon when they met the young girl who had been travelling to London with her daughter. He sat on an upturned barrel drinking his tea and spoke to Daisy about his thoughts. 'Daisy do you remember the young girl who was going to look in on your mother when she reached London during our last visit to Nottingham...wasn't her name Lizzie...Lizzie Lorimer...that was it I think.'

Daisy thought for a moment then pictured the pretty young girl with the dark brown curly hair and her very young baby. 'Aye, you're right Archie it was Lizzie and the baby's name was Rosie, or Rosaline, something like that. Funny, she never did look in on mam and she didn't seem the sort to break a promise. I often thought about her and wondered what happened. Do you remember giving her the little 'cart' Archie? We could have done with that as it turned out, although I doubt if our Gracie would have fitted in it.' Daisy smiled as she remembered when her own baby was that young and how she struggled carrying her around.

The previous evening in another part of Nottingham, Daniel Lorimer sat in the lounge bar of the 'King's Head' perusing the contract he had drawn up with Birkin's the lace manufacturers, who were using the most up-to-date machines to produce lace.

Finlay McEwan, Daniel's friend, had taken his advice about giving up farming to invest in the cotton industry and now had a thriving business of his own. He had returned the compliment and given Daniel information about the quality of Nottingham lace, which was considered the best available, hence Daniel's visit this weekend. He had arrived late on Thursday evening and spent a comfortable night, although this particular inn would not have been his first choice. Unfortunately, all the better inns were booked up. People were flocking from afar to enjoy the famous Goose Fair so he struggled to find decent accommodation. Not that the 'King's Head' was bottom of the pile, far from it, in fact, the inn was clean and the landlord a decent sort, but nowadays, he preferred to travel in style.

Since his father sold their farm with its fishing rights in 1842 and bought a small cotton mill, Daniel had taken a more important role in running the business. The move in 1845 down to Ardwick Green, a well to do, elegant leafy Manchester suburb, with an artificial lake, saw his business of supplying wholesalers with premium cotton, go from strength to strength. Now he was looking to diversify. His immediate goal was to supply finished lace trimmings, which were in great demand.

He intended to buy the lace in strips and employ workers to 'free' the lace, which meant drawing out the long threads.

He was aware that many women would be grateful for work to do at home as they needed to earn extra money to feed and clothe their families, especially those living in the back-to-back terraced houses in Beswick. Daniel could afford to pay them well and still make a profit on the finished article, after the lace was drawn, clipped and scalloped.

The importance of the contract meant that Daniel would remain in Nottingham over the weekend. He had already met with the factory manager earlier that morning and would meet with him again on Saturday, before travelling back to Manchester on Sunday morning.

The worse part of travelling away from home was that he missed his wife, Georgina and newborn baby daughter, Victoria. It would be too difficult for them to travel far at present, so he tried not to be away too long. Usually, he was only away for two days at the most. However, this particular trip was taking longer, because he needed to ensure the purchase price of the lace would produce a decent profit from a manager who drove a hard bargain. He needed time to plan a strategy to convince the manager that Manchester would be an excellent city in which to advertise his product. Daniel had been lead to believe that Birkin's were considering moving premises and a plan for expansion was on the cards. New outlets for the lace would boost profits and lead to new business. Consequently, Daniel had a bargaining tool in the negotiations, where he needed to pitch the price just right. The manager would be foolish to turn him down.

He came up with a price after working out his overheads that would suit both parties. Pleased with the figures, he finished his pint, put away the papers and decided on an early night.

He was up early Saturday morning and after three hours of offers and counter offers, the contract was duly signed to the satisfaction of both parties. After a bite of lunch and with time to spare, he took a walk into the town to wander around the famous Goose Fair, as suggested by the landlord. When he reached the centre, the fair was in full swing.

CHAPTER TWO

Reunited

On Saturday morning Rosalie sat at the kitchen table swinging her legs and making light of the boiled egg and soldiers that Lizzie cooked especially for her breakfast. Now she waited patiently for her mother to clear away the sewing, which lay strewn across the table, before asking the question she had been building up to for the last half an hour. 'Mam...can we really go to the Goose Fair this afternoon?'

'Yes Rosie, I said we could if you were a good girl and managed to stay out of trouble this week.'

'Well, mam, I have haven't I? I haven't been anywhere near the quarry and I've played with Annie in the garden liked you asked.'

Lizzie was pleased that Rosalie had made the effort to play with little Annie, even though she would rather have played with Jimmy. Would her daughter's friendship with Jimmy sustain the passage of time, she wondered?

Impatiently, Rosalie reminded her mother she was still awaiting an answer. 'So mam, are we going then?'

Lizzie smiled with amusement at her daughter's insistence, as she realised how excited she had become with the prospect of attending the fair. 'Yes, Rosie, we certainly will go. We will leave after an early lunch and stay until teatime. How does that suit?'

'Oh mam, I can't wait. There'll be lights and sweetie stalls and cakes and all sorts of lovely things...' Rosalie chatted on while Lizzie finished the chores that needed doing before preparing lunch.

SILENT TORMENT

For the second day running, the fair was very busy and the weather held good. There was a nip in the air, but the revellers were in good spirits. Daisy and Archie were rushed off their feet and hardly had time for a break, but during a small lull, Archie was able to leave his stall with his friend, before joining Daisy for a quick bite to eat. 'Well Daisy, how are you doing? Folks seem to have a bit more to spend this year and the sunshine is putting everyone in the mood to splash out.'

'You're right Archie, I've not stopped. We will be running out of items to sell at this rate, but while there is a lull, how about a cuppa and a scone. What do you say?'

She handed him a home-made scone and went round the back to brew the tea. She waited for the kettle to boil on the cast iron brazier, while observing the excited crowds bantering happily as they pushed and shoved their way around. Suddenly she noticed a woman with a young girl, whose face seemed familiar. She tried to remember where she had seen her before, then realised it must have been here at the fair. Recollection dawned. With a sharp intake of breath she confirmed her recognition. 'Lizzie...Lizzie Lorimer...I'm sure it is her...Five years ago now. That's how old the little girl would be who is hanging on to her skirt.'

Certain of her belief, she shouted the name out loud, cupping her hands to her mouth to carry the sound over the noise of the fair. 'Lizzie...Lizzie Lorimer, over here. It's me, Daisy...Lizzie, Lizzie.' Daisy was shouting for all she was worth and several curious revellers turned to look in her direction, including Lizzie who appeared to look straight at her. Daisy smiled and waved as she did so, but Lizzie, walked on oblivious to her calls and gesticulations. The young woman disappeared into the crowd and Daisy felt disappointed that her efforts to attract her attention had failed. Sadly, she went back to give Archie his cup of tea.

Archie was surprised at the length of time she had been gone and couldn't resist a bit of sarcasm. Unfortunately for him, it was not well received. 'Well my old China...that's where I thought you'd gone to brew that tea,' laughed Archie, but when he saw the crestfallen look on her face, added, 'it's very welcome all the same.'

Daisy was not amused. 'Shut up Archie and listen. You will never guess who I have just seen?'

In response and still in jovial mood, Archie made a suggestion. 'The Emperor himself?'

'No Archie...I'm being serious for a minute. I feel sure I saw Lizzie Lorimer. You know, we were only talking about her earlier. She had a toddler with her who looked about five. It's definitely her and she's hardly changed at all. The only thing is, that when I shouted out and waved, she just looked straight through me. It was if we had never met before and she just walked on, until she was lost in the crowd.'

Archie stroked his chin. 'Are you sure it was definitely her? It has been five years...people change and anyway, she might not have remembered you.'

Daisy placed her hands on her hips and raised her eyebrows. 'I'm not daft Archie, nor am I blind and I've a good memory for faces. It was definitely her, definitely.'

A young gentleman had witnessed Daisy trying to attract the woman's attention, but from his vantage point, her face was hidden from view. His curiosity had been immediately aroused when she shouted the name 'Lizzie' and even more so when it was followed up by his own name 'Lorimer.' He didn't wish to intrude, but was eager to find out if Lizzie Lorimer was who he thought she might be, so engaged Daisy in conversation. 'Hello there young lady, I would like tea and a piece of that delicious looking cake.'

Daisy was not one to resist flattery, especially from such a presentable young man. 'Yes sir, if you will wait two minutes for the kettle to boil again, you'll have the best cup of tea served here today.'

Daniel smiled at Daisy. 'I'm sure I will and served by such an attractive young lady.'

His compliment made her blush and he felt her warming towards him. Confident she would respond, he chanced his arm again and light heartedly broached the subject of Lizzie. 'I see you didn't have any luck attracting the attention of the young woman just now. Do you know her well?'

Daisy smiled. 'Ah, you mean Lizzie Lorimer. Actually, I only met her once. It was five years ago when she was down the fair. She was travelling with a small baby and on her way to be with her husband in London. She spoke to me for a few minutes and we did have something in common. She told me they would be living in Carlton House Terrace, near St James Park, which is not far from my mother's place of work. I hadn't seen my mother for a while and Lizzie promised to drop in and say hello when she was settled. However, for some reason she never did, so when I saw her today, I was curious to know why she was in Nottingham again, but when she looked at me, it was as if we had never met. I was surprised she didn't recognise me because we had quite a conversation before Archie gave her a cart in which to wheel the baby back to her lodgings. You'd surely remember that wouldn't you?'

Daniel agreed that it was something to be remembered. It seemed to him that she didn't ignore Daisy, but just failed to recognise her. He obviously needed to know more about her strange behaviour, but knew he had to tread carefully when eliciting information. It might be advantageous to suggest he and Lizzie Lorimer had been good friends but had lost touch. That was certainly not a lie. 'I used to know a Lizzie Lorimer about five years ago, but I don't suppose it is the same one, as she wasn't from these parts.' Daniel did not give her correct name on purpose, nor disclose the fact that Lizzie did not have a baby either.

Daisy wouldn't normally reveal details of her friends and acquaintances to strangers, especially males, but this man seemed genuine and anyway, the young woman had vanished again as quickly as she had appeared, so she didn't see the harm. 'Well, it could be the same woman as she originally came from Scotland...Glasgow I think and if I'm not mistaken, you have a Scottish accent, so I guess you also come from those parts?'

'As a matter of fact I do. The Lizzie I knew was about five foot four, very pretty with long dark brown curly hair and the sweetest smile.'

'Why yes, Lizzie did fit that description but the young baby had golden hair, unlike her mother. Probably took after her father we thought. Were you hoping to find her again?'

Daniel was cautious about his reply, but he felt pretty certain that this was Lizzie Cameron and, for whatever reason, she was living in Nottingham with a young daughter. It was certainly a mystery, as his Lizzie definitely wasn't pregnant when she left and it would have been impossible for her to be travelling with a young baby, at least not one of her own. Perhaps she was minding it for someone, although Daisy was adamant it was Lizzie's own child. It also seemed most unlikely that she was married as well. He summed up the evidence; the timing was right and the description was right. The fact that she was Scottish, possibly from Glasgow was right, but nothing else made any sense. Nevertheless, he was determined to seek out this 'Lizzie Lorimer', if only to rule out any possibility that it was indeed his Lizzie.

My God, he thought, after all this time, he may well have found her again. He couldn't quite believe that it was possible. Indeed, it might not be, but he had to know. 'Which way did she go Daisy?'

'Well she was over there by the hot peas stall, but she could be anywhere now, there are so many people at the fair it might be impossible to find her again. If you are lucky enough to come across her, remember me to her won't you?'

'Yes, yes Daisy I'll certainly do that.'

༺༻

Daniel Lorimer set out determinedly to find Lizzie. He knew it would be difficult locating her amongst the crowd, but he would call her name while walking along. This would draw attention to himself and she might turn to look if she heard him, but after half an hour of calling her name, he began to despair of ever finding her. Lots of people turned to look at him, but none resembled Lizzie or anyone like her.

He considered that she might only be here for one visit, but promised himself that he would return again tomorrow just in case. He was still making his way through the crowd and was about to leave, when he saw a woman with long dark curly hair, standing with her back to him. She was queuing up at a bric-a-brac stall displaying lots of children's wooden and cloth toys. The little girl was pointing to a wooden train and the woman was laughing and steering her towards some rag dolls, although the girl was insisting that she wanted the train.

Daniel's hopes rose as he walked up to the woman. He could see her face in full profile when he stood next to her and almost gasped out loud in recognition, but not wanting to alarm or shock her, he spoke softly to her. 'Hello Lizzie, how are you?'

Lizzie spun around to face the stranger addressing her, who obviously mistook her for someone he knew. Politely, she informed him of his error. 'I think you mistake me for someone else sir, my name is not Lizzie.'

He was shocked at the response, but remembered that when Lizzie left without a word, it was for a very good reason so understood her ambivalence to acknowledge him. However, Daniel could not leave without establishing the reason for her sudden departure. She owed him that at least. 'I do not wish to be rude and if you do not want to speak to me, I will not bother you further, but you are Lizzie Cameron and I am not mistaken.'

Now it was Lizzie's turn to be shocked. Unable to be totally certain this man was not telling the truth, she pondered the reason, other than mistaken identity, that a stranger would approach her by a name she did not recognise; especially such a well dressed, presentable stranger.

Suddenly Lizzie felt quite faint, what if he was telling the truth. For five years she had lived with the possibility that her husband or family might be looking for her and this man was adamant he recognised her. Could he be her husband, or brother or some other family member?

It was in that instant that Daniel realised Lizzie wasn't trying to deny him, rather that she genuinely believed he was mistaken. He was even more shocked now at the possibility that something terrible had happened to Lizzie and that she didn't know her true identity, so decided to tread carefully with his reply. 'I am sorry if I have shocked you. It certainly wasn't my intention, but I do know you and your friends and family have been searching for you for five years. I have also been searching for you and never thought I would ever see you again.'

Shocked at the realisation that this man could be right, she was immediately curious to hear what he had to say and what his relationship had been to her. 'I am known as Hannah Merchant, but supposing you are right and my real name is Lizzie Cameron, who is she to you?'

Daniel worded his reply carefully, as he did not wish to distress her so he bent the truth and played down their relationship. 'I am a very good friend of your brother and yourself.'

At the mention of a brother, Lizzie's ears pricked up as she remembered the incident down by the River Leen when Rosalie's friend Jimmy had fallen into the river and she shouted 'Robert'. That gave rise to the possibility of a Robert being connected to her past. Now she needed to ask the question. 'You say I have a brother. Is his name Robert?'

This time it was Daniel's turn to look surprised as he confirmed her thoughts. 'Yes, yes his name is indeed Robert. Do you remember him?'

Lizzie shook her head, but explained the reason behind her question.

Daniel was very hopeful that he could help her to remember, but it would need to be handled sensitively. Look, I can see this is all a bit of a shock and that you must have met with some kind of accident that has affected your memory. However, you don't have to take my word that I am telling the truth. If you come with me to the far side of the fair, there is someone there who also knows you and will be happy to confirm that what I say is true.'

Lizzie looked Daniel straight in the eye and decided that he was someone she could trust. Anyway, it would be foolish of her to just walk away from the person who might be able to piece together the life she had before she came here. 'All right, I will go with you, but I am not yet convinced I am who you say I am.'

Rosalie was getting impatient and hopping from one foot to the other in desperation. She wanted her mam to buy the wooden train so that Jimmy and herself could have fun playing with it. She made herself known by tugging at her mother's skirt and in a loud voice, reminded Lizzie that she was still there. 'Mam, can I have the wooden train now?'

Lizzie looked at Rosalie and realised that she had completely ignored her for the last five minutes or so, which was a long time for a child excited at the prospect of receiving a new toy to wait. She smiled and bent down to Rosalie's level. 'I'm sorry Rosie, I just needed to have a chat with this gentleman and for the moment, I forgot about buying the train.' She explained to Daniel. 'I told Rosie that she could spend a few pennies on a new toy today. I was rather hoping she would choose the prettily dressed rag doll, but, true to form, Rosie would rather have a wooden train.'

Daniel smiled and addressed Rosalie, who was looking expectantly at them both. 'Well now, why don't I buy you the wooden train and your mother can buy the rag doll. How would that be?'

Before Rosalie could reply, Lizzie, embarrassed by the situation, jumped in. 'That's very kind of you sir, but I hardly know you and I couldn't possibly accept your offer.'

Daniel moved closer to Lizzie and whispered to her so that Rosalie could not hear. 'I didn't mean to offend you, but I assure you I am not a stranger. I know you very well and we can't disappoint Rosie can we?'

Lizzie realised that it wouldn't be fair if they didn't buy the two items now and reluctantly allowed him to make the purchase.

Rosalie was jumping up and down, so excited at receiving two new toys, albeit one was a doll. 'Thank you very much sir. Jimmy will love the train, but he isn't bothered about dolls.'

Daniel realised that until then he hadn't officially introduced himself to either Lizzie or the little girl and even at five, she might wonder who he was. Treating her as a grown up, he introduced himself. 'You're very welcome. By the way, my name is Daniel Lorimer. I am an old friend of your mother's and I am very pleased to meet you.' Daniel took Rosalie's hand and as he shook it, she bobbed a curtsy.

'How do you do Mr Lorimer. You already know my name is Rosie, Rosie Merchant, but you don't know how old I am do you?' Before Daniel could reply, she put her hands on her hips and proudly announced her age. 'Well Mr Lorimer, I am five and I can run really fast. My best friend's name is Jimmy and he will be really jealous of the wooden train you've just bought me.'

Daniel grinned. 'Well that's a very pretty name for a very pretty girl. I am sure Jimmy will be really envious when he sees the train. I bet he hasn't got one like that?'

Rosalie looked smug as she turned to leave. 'No he hasn't, but we've got to go now, as I want to get home to try it out.'

Daniel looked from Lizzie to Rosalie and spoke persuasively. 'Well before you go home Rosie, I wonder whether you would mind accompanying your mother and me to meet a friend of mine who runs a stall that sells tea and cakes.'

Rosalie smiled at Daniel and gave her approval. 'I suppose it's all right, if me mam says so.' Then paused before asking persuasively. 'Can I have a cake as well?'

Daniel gave a broad grin. 'Tell you what Rosie, if your mother agrees, I will give you a piggyback over to the stall and you can choose the cake yourself.'

Rosalie's face lit up, as she had never had a piggyback from a grown up before, only from Jimmy and he usually dropped her when he ran fast. She couldn't imagine this tall man dropping her, as she had seen other children riding along on their father's shoulders without problems. To Rosalie it had looked great fun. 'Can we go then mam?'

Lizzie grinned. 'All right, but you mustn't fidget. You need to sit very still up there Rosie. Are you sure you can manage her Mr Lorimer?'

'Daniel, please. Remember I said we were very good friends a few years ago...Come on Rosie let me lift you up.' Daniel hauled Rosalie up on his shoulders and put his arm under Lizzie's, guiding her in the direction of Daisy's tea stall.

When they approached the stall Daisy's face lit up, satisfied that she had been right when she recognised Lizzie earlier. She put out her hand and greeted her warmly. 'Why Lizzie, I knew it was you the moment I saw you, but then when you didn't acknowledge me, I thought I must have been mistaken. How are you?'

Lizzie was dumbfounded, not able to respond to this woman who had clearly made her acquaintance on some previous occasion, but Daniel came to the rescue, stepping in with an explanation. 'Well Daisy...Lizzie, or rather Mrs Merchant, has suffered some kind of amnesia and she didn't recognise you. I am hoping that if you speak to her about your encounter with her five years ago, her memory may become more clear.'

Lizzie looked hard at Daisy, but without a flicker of recognition. However, she listened to what this woman had to say.

'Well, it was five years ago now and you stopped at my stall for some refreshment. We got talking and I noticed that you were speaking with a different accent to the locals and asked where you were from. You told me that you were from Glasgow and that you were travelling down with your daughter to meet up with your husband in London. Then you mentioned that you were to live in Carlton House Terrace, near St James' Park, which is close to St James Street where my mother worked. You said you would look her up when you arrived and had settled in. That's about it I think, but let me introduce you to my husband Archie, who also spoke to you.' She called over to Archie who had just finished wrapping up a small vase in some brown paper. 'Archie, Archie look who's here. It's Lizzie Lorimer. I told you I recognised her. Come and say hello.'

Archie ambled over and gave Lizzie a beaming smile. 'Why, you've hardly changed Lizzie. No wonder Daisy was sure it was you and this must be Rosalie. She's very bonny. Hello Rosalie and how are you?'

Rosalie looked up at this jolly man, but wasn't sure why he was calling her by another name, so she put him straight. 'I'm all right, but me name's Rosie, Rosie Merchant. Mr Lorimer said that when we got to this stall, I could choose a cake. Isn't that right Mr Lorimer?'

'Yes Rosie it certainly is. Which one would you like.'

She looked at the large plate of fairy cakes, some with white icing, topped with 'hundreds and thousands' and some with pink icing and little silver balls scattered on the top. Rosalie made her decision. 'If it's all right with you Mr Lorimer, I would like the one with the silver balls.'

While Rosalie was busy with the cake, taking off the silver balls and sucking them until they lost all their colour, Daniel addressed Lizzie anxiously. 'Hannah,' he paused. 'I am calling you that until you feel comfortable with your real name. Does any of this seem familiar?'

Lizzie looked again at the two stallholders, but nothing at all jogged her memory. 'No, I'm sorry to say that nothing seems at all familiar.'

Undaunted, Daniel asked again if there was anything else they remembered.

Archie chipped in with the fact that he had given Lizzie the cart to wheel Rosalie back to the inn where she was staying. Then he asked Daisy if she remembered the little note on which was written the address of her mother.

Daisy's eyes lit up. 'Why yes, I wrote my mother's name and address on a piece of paper, to remind Lizzie of her name when she arrived in London.'

'Well', Daniel considered. 'It might not be important, but what exactly did you put?'

Daisy thought for a moment. It had been a long while and she couldn't be sure. 'I would have put my mother's name, 'Hannah' and where she worked in the cotton merchant's shop at 64 St James Street.'

This profound statement, left Lizzie reeling and she put her hand on Daniel's arm to steady herself. She realised that Daisy must be telling the truth. Although there was nothing about the story that meant anything to her at all, she remembered what had been written on the piece of paper that had been found in her pocket by Clara when she had been ironing her dress and petticoat. The paper had been crumpled and the writing was barely visible, but it all made sense now. Clara had mistaken the name 'Hannah' for Lizzie's Christian name and the word merchant to be her surname, followed by the address. It seemed to be the answer to the mystery at the time and an easy mistake to make.

Daniel realised immediately how shocked Lizzie must be feeling and put a concerned arm around her shoulders. 'I think you are in need of a cup of tea, Hannah. We need to have a talk in private.'

The significance of her mother's name suddenly hit both Daisy and Archie when Daniel again referred to Lizzie as Hannah. They weren't sure why she was using Daisy's mother's name, but they realised it had also dawned on Lizzie that they were telling the truth.

Daniel turned to Daisy. 'Do you know of anywhere we could go for a while Daisy, so that I can talk to Hannah and she can recover from the shock.'

Daisy nodded. 'I'll tell you what Daniel. You can go and sit in our caravan for a while and make her a cup of tea. My daughter, Gracie is in there with her friend, so Rosie can play with them a while.'

Daniel thanked Daisy for coming up with a solution then approached Lizzie. 'Would you like me to take you to the caravan Hannah? We will be able to talk while Rosie is busy with her new toys.'

Rosalie suddenly found her voice again, after keeping quiet for the last fifteen minutes or so. 'Can we go to the caravan mam? I've never been in one?'

Lizzie still very shocked, agreed to the suggestion, as she felt quite unwell and welcomed the chance to sit down. 'All right Rosie, we will go, but only for a short while.'

They wended their way through the town, which was still crowded with people. It took fifteen minutes to arrive at Daisy's caravan, located amidst many others belonging to the fairground travellers, parked on scrubland, away from the town centre.

They were greeted at the door by Esther, the young girl tasked with looking after Gracie during her mother's absence at the fair.

Esther ushered them in after they explained why they were there. Rosalie immediately went to Gracie to show her the new toys she had been bought and Esther settled them down to play, then prepared a cup of tea for the guests in the little alcove. She took her own cup outside the van and sat on a stool in the sunshine, so that the two strangers could have some privacy. In truth, she was rather relieved to have a break from building houses of cards, only to have them knocked down for the umpteenth time.

Daniel looked at Lizzie and wondered just how much he should reveal to her. He decided it should only be quite basic information at this stage. 'I think we have already established the reason for your change of name, but if you wish, I will continue to call you Hannah.'

Lizzie was unsure now what she wished to be called, but felt she still wouldn't feel comfortable being called something that still sounded totally alien to her. 'Thank you Mr Lorimer, I think that will be best for the time being. I have some questions I would like to ask you though, as I am still very confused.'

'Go ahead Hannah. I will do my best to answer them for you.'

Lizzie felt rather embarrassed at the first question she wanted to ask and blushed as she faced Daniel to ask him for an explanation. 'Why do you think I gave my name as Lizzie Lorimer, when that is your name and, as I understand it, you are nothing more than a good friend to my brother and myself?' She felt strange as she heard herself admit to apparently having a brother. So many questions needed answering. Would this young man be able to help her?

Daniel smiled warmly. 'Well Hannah, it was a long while ago, but you and I were a bit more than just good friends and maybe you had a reason for not wanting to reveal your real name to a relative stranger. You probably used my name as one that popped into your head at the time.' He was happy that he had found an explanation that did not reveal everything about their relationship and he smiled at Lizzie, hoping she would not pursue this line of enquiry any further.

He need not have worried, as Lizzie was mortified that she now sat facing someone from her past with whom she had had a close relationship. She quickly changed the subject, asking about her roots instead. 'Mmm, you are probably right. What can you tell me about where I lived before and what of my family?'

'Well Hannah there is so much I can tell you, but I am worried that some things might upset you and maybe it would be better if we went somewhere else, after you have finished your tea. Do you have anyone you can leave Rosie with for a couple of hours? If so and you agree, you could accompany me back to my lodgings, where we can continue our conversation.'

Lizzie thought about whether she wanted to go with this man to his place of lodgings, but decided she didn't have anything to lose and everything to gain. She could learn more about her past life and the mystery of her presence in Nottingham. 'Yes all right Mr Lorimer,' said Lizzie before Daniel quickly interrupted. He was finding it very difficult being addressed as Mr Lorimer, when he actually knew her intimately.

'Hannah, do you think you could call me Daniel, after all

you must know now that I am telling you the truth and all my friends call me Daniel,' he paused, noticing her reticence. 'We are friends Hannah but it seems strange to be called Mr Lorimer, especially by you.'

Lizzie blushed furiously and quickly brushed over her agreement. 'All right, Daniel it is. I could leave Rosie with my neighbour, Gladys Leach. She has a daughter, Annie who is Rosie's friend.'

'Very well, but let's call on the Pickering's on the way and thank them for their hospitality.'

Daniel picked Rosalie up and hoisted her on to his shoulders before taking Lizzie's arm to return to the fair. They thanked Daisy and Archie and after another fifteen minutes reached Marsden Court. Daniel waited for Lizzie at the end of the road, while she settled Rosalie in with Mrs Leach. Lizzie explained to Gladys that she had to meet with someone and it would take a couple of hours. 'Would you mind giving Rosie a bit of tea if I am a little longer than that Gladys? I'd be ever so grateful. I wouldn't normally ask, but it is really important.'

'Don't you worry none Hannah. You're always helping me out, so it'll be my pleasure to return the favour. Off you go and I'll have a nice cuppa waiting for you when you get back. Tarrar me duck.'

Gladys was happy to help out a neighbour, especially Hannah. However, the unusual request had given her food for thought. Intrigued by the circumstances, she asked herself what on earth could be so important and just who was the mysterious stranger Lizzie was meeting.

CHAPTER THREE

Enlightenment

It was late afternoon when Lizzie and Daniel arrived at the 'King's Head'. The landlord's wife was serving afternoon tea for the few guests at the inn, as most of the clientele were still at the fair.

Daniel found a table in the corner of the room next to the unlit fire. The day had been quite warm for the time of year and the fire would not be required until later in the evening. He ordered some tea and Lizzie settled down to hear more facts about her life that Daniel said he could provide. Lizzie made herself comfortable in the chair as his mind recollected the day he went to Low Wood with the intention of asking her to become his wife. He remembered the feelings of deep despair, felt for such a long time after she disappeared without even a goodbye. The reason she left was open to conjecture, why had she left what he thought was a lasting relationship? What were her true feelings for him? We <u>were</u> in love. She had told so him only a few weeks before.

All that was in the past and he mustn't dwell on 'if only's'. He was married now with a young baby and everything that he and Lizzie shared then could not be resurrected, either now or in the future. He brought himself back to the present and began to tell Lizzie as much as he knew about her life. 'I'm not sure where to start Hannah. Maybe from when I first met you up at the big house, Low Wood Hall.'

Lizzie looked intently at Daniel and saw sadness in his eyes for perhaps what might have been. She could see that he obviously thought of her as more than a good friend, so maybe now was the time to revert to being called by her true name, Elizabeth, or Lizzie Cameron. She voiced this opinion to Daniel and felt that a huge weight had been lifted from her shoulders. 'Daniel, before you tell me what you know, I am happy now for you to call me Lizzie, after all, that appears to be my name. I must try and forget Hannah Merchant and the situation I found myself in, so that I can face the truth about my life. However, I feel that Rosalie should still be called Rosie, as she has never known any other name and is too young to accept being called something different.'

'Oh Lizzie, I am so pleased. It has been a real effort to call you Hannah, having known you as Lizzie since you were nineteen. It is also a step forward for you in understanding and accepting your past, which I assure you, despite much sadness, was also filled with happy times.'

They sat together for well over an hour with Daniel recounting the story of what he knew of her life from the time they met.

Lizzie listened and tried hard to remember any small incident that she could relate to, but sadly nothing at all seemed familiar. In fact it was as if he was telling a story about someone else; a stranger that she now knew quite a bit about, but the story didn't have any personal meaning for her at all.

When he had almost reached the end, he began to feel quite sad and Lizzie noticed that his voice had changed. He had become morose and his eyes betrayed the sadness he obviously felt in his heart.

Lizzie considered he may not want to continue and gave him the opportunity to end it there and then, but Daniel explained that reliving this episode of their lives had been cathartic for him, as well as for her. She did not want to disappoint him by telling him that the story had not helped her and that she still felt totally detached from everything about her past. 'Thank you so much Daniel, I am sure that what you have told me will really help me to move forward in the knowledge of my true identity. Even though there are still many unanswered questions, I feel at least that I have a point at which to begin my journey.'

Daniel was anxious now because he had decided to reveal something of their intimacy. It would lay his feelings bare, but there was no going back. 'I haven't quite finished yet Lizzie; there is another piece missing from the jigsaw that might jog your memory. It will be quite painful for me, but you have to know. It may help you to remember why you left so suddenly and why you came to be living in Nottingham.'

Lizzie smiled warmly. 'If you are sure Daniel. You have been so good to me that I don't want to upset you.'

'No...I will be all right, but it has to be said.' He took a deep breath and continued. 'The day you left Low Wood, I was going to ask you to become my wife, but, of course, I never got the opportunity, as you had already left. I think you had an idea of my feelings and maybe you left to spare me the embarrassment of turning me down.'

Lizzie listened intently, shocked, but fascinated by this latest revelation. At that moment, she was really confused and understood even less of the reason for her departure, but nevertheless Daniel continued with his story, despite his discomfort. 'I had been delayed that morning and didn't arrive at the Hall until late on Tuesday. Clara the cook ran out into the yard and asked if I had seen you. You had been due back at lunchtime but hadn't turned up, which, of course, was unusual and out of character. She told me that on Monday lunchtime you left to go into town. I saw your brother later in the week at the Feathers and he was shocked to learn of your absence, apparently having left without letting him know where you were going. I really hoped Lizzie that you would have given me an explanation for your sudden departure, in consideration of how close we were, even if it was, as I said, to spare my embarrassment. Now I understand that it wasn't as simple as that and there must have been good reason for you to—'

Lizzie could not hold back the question that for the last few minutes she had felt compelled to ask and interrupted

Daniel in mid sentence. She wanted to know who Rosalie's father was...was it Daniel himself, but if not, who?

She lowered her voice and looked pleadingly at Daniel. He was clearly struggling with what was a very difficult conversation, which had provided more questions than answers not only for Lizzie, but for himself. 'Daniel I know this is painful for you, but you must tell me if you are Rosie's father?'

With a deep sigh and wishing with all his heart that he was the father and that Lizzie was the mother, he delivered what he knew to be the truth. 'I am sorry Lizzie, I am not the father. One thing I know for certain is that when you left Low Wood, you were definitely not pregnant.'

Lizzie gasped and put her hand to her mouth. This particular truth shocked her to the core. Yes, she was unsure at first that Rosalie was her own baby, but over the years, she had grown to love her as her own, even to the point of being certain that she was her own. To have this certainty taken away from her was just too much to bear. Her eyes filled with tears at the thought of giving Rosalie up to her birth mother who, at this very moment, might be looking for her. 'Oh Daniel, this is too much, I couldn't bear to lose her now. I have cared for her and loved her since she was only a few weeks old. It wouldn't be fair to have to give her away to a stranger now. What am I to do?'

Daniel leaned over the table and took both her hands in his. He was shocked that the old feelings he thought had gone were now flooding back through his body, as if it were yesterday, despite his protestations a few moments ago that it was all in the past, never to be resurrected. He tried to remain calm, confirming to himself that he loved his wife and this was neither the time nor the place to think about what might have been. At this moment, however, Lizzie needed him and because he considered her to be a very dear friend, he wasn't going to let her down. 'Listen Lizzie, I know this is very hard for you, but you may yet be able to bring Rosie up as your own. After all, no-one has come looking for her as far as we know. Maybe she was given to you to look after by someone who couldn't cope. Unfortunately, I cannot help clear up that mystery at the moment, but we will get to the bottom of it Lizzie. When Daisy, the stallholder, told me you were travelling with a baby, only a few weeks old, I was totally shocked and mystified, more so when she said you were going down to London to meet up with your husband. I knew then that something was very wrong. Unfortunately, at this stage I do not know any more than you do, but I promise you this Lizzie, I will help you discover what happened to make you take off without a word to anyone.'

'Oh Daniel will you do that for me? I would be so grateful.'

'Yes, I will try and help you as much as I can, but we cannot do this here in Nottingham. The answers I feel will be found in Glasgow and I believe Rosie is the key to this mystery. Would you be willing to spend some time there? Can you put your life on hold here until we learn the truth Lizzie?'

Lizzie looked straight into Daniel's eyes. 'I have no choice Daniel, it is something I must do. My employer, Mrs Phillips will understand, although she will have to find someone to take my place while I am away.'

Lizzie looked down at the table and wondered if there could be something between them again. He must have loved her once, as he was going to ask her to become his wife. She was lost in these thoughts, when she realised that Daniel was speaking to her earnestly and when his words penetrated, her question was answered. 'There is something else you need to know Lizzie. I am married now with a young baby and they must come first. However, I know my wife, Georgina, will understand and will help us all she can. She is a wonderful person Lizzie, very kind and thoughtful. You would like her.'

Lizzie tried to hide the fact that she was hoping they would get to know each other again, but was really not sure what she felt for this man who had reappeared in her life.

Am I disappointed? she asked herself, or is it that I would jump at the chance for Rosie to have a father, even though

I am not her birth mother? The knowledge that Daniel was a married man, made her instantly put aside such thoughts, so with some effort, gave him a cooler friendly smile. 'I am sure I will like her Daniel, but I don't want to cause any difficulties between you. I probably wouldn't be so understanding of someone who had been in a close relationship with my husband turning up 'out of the blue' asking for help with her past.'

Daniel grinned. 'It will be okay Lizzie. Georgina knows I will always be faithful to her and would never do anything to hurt her. My family mean everything to me.'

'They are very lucky Daniel. I hope one day I will be as lucky.'

Daniel looked earnestly at Lizzie. 'I am the lucky one Lizzie. Georgina helped me through a very bad period in my life and for that I will always be very grateful.'

To Lizzie it seemed a very odd thing to say about one's marital position. The relationship, she thought, did not seem to be one based on passion, more one based on guilt and a desire to look after the woman who brought him out of the darkness into the light. However, it was not for her to judge and anyway Daniel seemed very happy with his choice of a wife. She hoped that if she ever got married, it would be based on love and passion; nothing less would do.

The time passed quickly and Lizzie had not realised they had been sitting for so long. She finished her tea and thanked Daniel again for everything he had done.

She stood up to say goodbye for the present, but at that moment, the landlord, who was collecting glasses and crockery, made an appearance. He stood at their table and looked quizzically at Lizzie. 'I hope you won't mind me asking Miss, but your face seems very familiar, have we met before?'

Someone else, Lizzie thought, who apparently knows me, but now she wasn't so quick to dismiss it. 'I don't think so, but maybe. Where do you think it was that we met?'

'Well now, I have been thinking about this ever since you walked through the door earlier. Did you stay here several years ago? The lady I am thinking of had a young baby with her and the reason it stuck in my mind was, she left a valise in the lobby near the entrance and never came back for it.'

Lizzie tried to stay calm, but felt quite excited by the prospect of obtaining a valise that just might give up some more answers, if indeed it belonged to her. 'Unfortunately, I have been suffering with amnesia and could not say whether I stayed here or not, but I was, apparently, travelling through Nottingham in October 1841. My name is Lizzie Cameron if that helps to confirm my stay here.'

'If you will just wait a moment, I will try and find the visitor's book for that period. It shouldn't be too difficult, as my wife is a stickler for keeping the visitor books in year order down in the vault.'

The landlord reappeared minutes later triumphantly waving the book in the air. 'I knew I could remember you and I was right. There is a signature written on Thursday 30th September, 1841. It clearly says Elizabeth Cameron and daughter.'

The landlord handed the book over to Lizzie, who immediately recognised her own writing. 'Oh Daniel, this could be a breakthrough. There might be some documents in the case.' She addressed the landlord and made a request. 'May I take a look at the valise?'

'Of course, I kept it in the side lobby located near the entrance.'

The landlord walked off in the direction of the lobby, when Daniel put his arm on Lizzie's to recommend a little caution. 'Lizzie, I don't think we should get our hopes up. Even if the valise belongs to you, there might not be anything inside that will help us piece together your journey.'

Lizzie smiled resignedly. 'Yes, I know Daniel. I am trying to keep my feet on the ground, but I know so much more about myself now, thanks to you, that it is very difficult to stop getting carried away with events.'

The landlord stopped at the entrance to the lobby and pointed to a large, barrel shaped, dark brown figured leather valise, an item of obvious quality. He dragged it out into the entrance, where they surveyed it, each having different thoughts. Daniel wondered how on earth Lizzie could have afforded to buy such an expensive piece. The landlord was fairly neutral, but pleased to be getting rid of it after such a long time. Lizzie's eyes were staring at it, disappointed that what she saw, although a lovely item, meant absolutely nothing to her at all. She hid her disappointment, but was anxious to see inside.

She bent down and made to open the lid. 'It would seem that there isn't a lock and it opens by pushing the two straps through the little leather holders. Would you open it for me Daniel, I am a little anxious and cannot steel myself to do it.'

Daniel bent down beside her, undid the two straps and lifted open the lid. Lizzie peered nervously inside and moved the clothes around that were neatly rolled up for travelling. 'Well it seems that there is only clothing inside and no documents, which is very disappointing.'

Daniel had a look himself and his hand rested on a moneybag at the bottom of the case. He also noticed a pocket on the side of the valise. 'Wait a minute Lizzie, there is a bag in here and I think there is an envelope inside this pocket.'

'Oh Daniel let me see.'

Daniel handed the brown envelope and the moneybag over to Lizzie, with the suggestion that she sit down somewhere first before opening them. 'Look Lizzie why don't we go up to my room where you will be comfortable and I will order some more tea.'

Lizzie replied. 'Yes you are right. Oh gosh Daniel, I'm so excited.'

The landlord suggested that they fasten the lid of the valise for now and push it to the back of the lobby, until they were ready to remove it. Then he went off to the kitchen to brew some tea.

Lizzie's heart began to beat faster as they climbed the stairs to Daniel's room. She was barely able to contain her excitement and her hands began to shake as they entered the room. Lizzie sat in a comfortable armchair close to the window, before she opened the envelope, which revealed the 'punched' first class passenger ship ticket from Glasgow to Liverpool. Disappointingly, there were no other documents, but the moneybag contained a surprisingly large amount of paper bills and gold sovereigns.

'Well Lizzie, at least we now know something of <u>how</u> you travelled here, but only as far as Liverpool. We will need to visit the city to see if we can find out what happened. Somehow you arrived in Nottingham, either via Liverpool or perhaps Manchester and booked into the King's Head. We could just accept that your journey may have taken a different path to the one intended and leave it at that of course, but I suspect you would like some closure. You may feel it is important to trace every step of your journey, in an effort to regain your memory.'

Lizzie hid her disappointment, unsure of exactly what she expected to find and whether there was any point in pursuing the route she took to arrive in Nottingham. However, she had agreed that retracing her steps might help in her quest to find the missing pieces to the jigsaw. 'Yes you are right Daniel I know now that I travelled under my own name, with Rosie accompanying me and the date and time plus the ship's name, 'The Royal George'.

Lizzie picked up the gold sovereigns and paper bills, which were in various denominations. She was clearly shocked by the value and looked to Daniel for an explanation. 'Why on earth do you think I would be carrying such a large amount of money? There must be around two hundred pounds here. I've never seen so much and I cannot imagine that it would belong to me.'

Daniel was surprised himself and wondered whether the large amount of money was also connected with Rosalie. 'I'm not sure at this stage Lizzie, but the fact that it is in your valise means that it is rightfully yours and you may need to put it to good use in your quest to find the truth.'

Lizzie realised that Daniel was right. She would require money for travel and accommodation. She began to feel quite tired because so much had happened in the space of a few hours. Fortunately, the landlord brought in some tea, which Lizzie drank eagerly and after sitting a while longer, recovered. Eventually, she asked Daniel if he would call a cab so that she might return to Marsden Court. 'Where do we go from here Daniel? I am not sure what my next step should be, although I want to meet my brother at some point, if that is possible?'

Daniel moved his hand over his chin and looked engagingly at Lizzie. 'I have a proposition for you Lizzie, which I hope you will consider. I leave Nottingham on Sunday to return home to Manchester and I would like to suggest that you and Rosie come with me. It would be my pleasure if you would agree to stay as guests of my wife and myself for a few weeks so that I can help you in your quest to seek out the truth.'

'Oh Daniel, I couldn't possibly impose on you like that. You have your wife and new baby to consider.'

'Nonsense, Lizzie, I have already told you that Georgina would understand. I am sure she would love the company. Perhaps you could go shopping together. I seriously think you should take the opportunity of a few weeks away from everything before you meet up with your brother. The meeting could be quite traumatic, especially under the circumstances. I think if I speak to him first and give him the news, it may come as less of a shock. We can then arrange a suitable date, time and venue for you to meet. He travels around a lot, as he no longer works a farm. When he saw the profits to be made in cotton, he followed me into the trade and now owns a mill in Littleborough, that's three miles from Rochdale in Lancashire. He too is married and has a daughter, Harriett, who is just over three years old.

'I think you need some time to reflect, you never know, something may connect in your mind and the past will be revealed. You definitely travelled to Liverpool and I would say the chances are that you went on to Manchester, before travelling down to Nottingham. A wander around those cities may spark off a memory.'

Lizzie became thoughtful and agreed. 'All right Daniel, if you are absolutely sure. It would be nice to have a change of scenery and it would be a holiday for Rosie. She has never travelled outside of our own small community before.'

'That's settled then. If it is all right with you, I will have a cab waiting at Marsden Court at 12 noon on Sunday. You can come over to the inn before we travel to Manchester on the Royal Mail coach.'

Daniel replaced the money in the moneybag, together with the tickets from the ship and handed them to Lizzie before escorting her to the entrance of the inn where a cab was waiting to take her back to the Court. The coachman put the valise at the rear of the coach and helped Lizzie aboard. 'Bye for now Lizzie, I look forward to seeing you and Rosie on Sunday lunchtime, packed and ready to indulge in a rewarding but restful vacation, although I doubt that Rosie will do much resting,' he said with a smile.

'Bye Daniel, you are right about Rosie, it's not often that I see her resting. I will meet you at noon on Sunday and thank you so much for all you have done.'

Lizzie arrived to see Gladys Leach taking the boiling kettle from the hob to make a welcoming cup of tea. 'Here we are then Hannah, you look like you could do with a cuppa. I hope you don't mind, but after the girls had tea, they were both so tired, I put them in Annie's bed. It was a bit of a squeeze, but Rosie thought it was a great adventure to stay over. I said that you would be round for her in the morning.'

'Why thanks a lot Gladys, it will give me time to think over the day's events in peace.'

Lizzie wondered how much she should divulge to Gladys, but it was only fair to inform her that she would be going away for a while. She decided to tell her that she had been invited to go to Manchester to stay with some long lost relatives she didn't know existed until today. She'd say she met an old friend at the fair and an aunt and uncle of hers had been with him.

When Lizzie moved into Marsden Court, the neighbours knew nothing of her past, but assumed that her husband had died leaving her to bring up their daughter alone. Lizzie could not enlighten them, as she did not know the truth herself, so her story to Gladys would seem believable. She gratefully drank the tea then asked her friend for another favour. 'I wonder if you would mind keeping Rosie until mid-morning, as I have someone I need to see in the Marsh and I need to pack a valise. It would be easier if Rosie were occupied until we are almost ready to go and then I will tell her my news.'

'Yes Hannah, that's fine. I won't mention anything to her.'

'Okay Gladys. I'll be off now and thanks for the tea and for looking after Rosie for me.'

Gladys smiled. 'She's no trouble Hannah and Annie loves to have her round to play. Now you run along and don't worry about Rosie, I am sure I can keep them occupied.'

Lizzie sat in the parlour thinking over the day's events. So much had changed in her life since her encounter with Daniel earlier that day, it was a lot to take in. She opened the moneybag again and carefully counted out fifty pounds in paper bills and sovereigns, which she placed into her handbag. Such a lot of money, she said to herself, and emptied the valise of its contents, putting the remainder of the money into the side pocket. It was now very late and Lizzie was too tired to do any packing that night so took herself off to bed. However, a thousand and one questions buzzed around her head, which kept her awake until the early hours. She was excited too, because she knew she was about to embark on a new chapter in her life.

Chapter Four

Goodbye Hannah Merchant

Despite a restless night, Lizzie awoke as dawn was breaking. She could hear the birds singing a joyful chorus, happy to be alive, which was how she felt herself. 'Yes,' she said out loud, 'I actually feel happy, happy and full of anticipation of what may lie ahead.'

She was out of bed and washed and dressed before 6 o'clock. She put the kettle on for a morning cup of tea and found herself singing as she stirred the porridge in the pot on the fire. After breakfast she donned her cloak, picked up her handbag and made her way to the Marsh.

She arrived at Clara's back door and knocked loudly, although a few moments passed before Clara answered. 'Why 'ello Hannah me duck, come on in. What brings ya to me door, so early on in the mornin. Evryfing is all right init?' she asked anxiously.

Lizzie stepped into the parlour and sat down next to the fire before responding. 'Well Clara everything is fine. In fact, I have some very exciting news and I couldn't wait for you to be the first one I share it with.'

'Well, bless you, I am flattered. Wait a mo' while I put the keckle on. We can probably do we a cuppa eh?'

'That will be lovely Clara. I hope everyone is well. Where are the girls?'

'The lazy bones are still in their beds. Still I won't wake 'em, now I've the chance to hear some gossip.'

Clara handed a cup of tea to Lizzie, who had difficulty stopping the smile on her face from breaking into a full-blown giggle. She wondered where to start. 'I don't quite know where to begin Clara. So much has happened in one day, I cannot quite believe it.'

Clara gave Lizzie a quizzical look, but smiled to herself in anticipation of Lizzie's exciting news. 'Look Hannah me duck, it's allus best to start at the beginin I find. So don't keep me in suspense any longer. Aht we it gel.'

'Clara you are going to be so surprised; you see, I have discovered that my name isn't Hannah at all...it's Lizzie...Lizzie Cameron and I'm from the Highlands of Scotland would you believe?'

Clara was clearly shocked. 'Well I'll ga ta the foot of ah stairs. 'Ows this cum abaht then? Ya wa Hannah last time a looked.'

Lizzie smiled to herself at Clara's strange vocabulary, which never failed to amuse her. 'It began yesterday Clara, down at the fair. I fortuitously bumped into someone from my past. I didn't recognise him, but he recognised me and, to cut a long story short, my former life has partially been revealed, although there are still some questions and riddles to solve.'

Lizzie regaled Clara for half an hour with the events of yesterday. The story was interspersed with many a comment from Clara. 'Ya don't say.' 'Well I never.' and 'Crikey me'; finishing with 'Am well chuffed fer yer. Noat berra than ya deserve.'

Lizzie's news was, however, momentarily overshadowed by another sadder conclusion, which cast a dampener on the proceedings. She took a deep breath and spoke quietly, lest any little ears might be listening. 'The only awful thing is that Rosie isn't mine and I am worried that her birth mother may turn up; although Daniel says that no one has apparently been looking for her, so far, anyway.'

Clara placed her hand over Lizzie's arm. 'Well then, he seems ta 'ave his 'ead screwed on the right way I'd say. Pity he in't the dad though, but no daht it'll all come aht in the wash me duck.'

'You're probably right Clara,' said Lizzie and bent down for her handbag to take out the money she had carefully placed in there.

Clara's eyes came out on stalks as she saw the bundle of

paper bills and gold coins spirited out of Lizzie's bag, just like a 'rabbit out of a hat'. 'Good God me duck, where'd ya get all o' that? Wot ya done, robbed a bank?'

Again Lizzie was amused by Clara's take on where the money might have come from. She laughed as she placed the money on the table in front of them. 'This money is rightfully mine Clara. It was secreted in the valise that I left at the 'King's Head' five years ago. The thing is, I would like you to have it as a thank you for saving my life.'

Clara appeared positively dumbstruck. 'Aw I couldn't teck it from ya Hannah, it in't right. It'ud be more than ah Tillie could earn in five years. No me duck, wot would a do we it all?'

Lizzie spoke positively. 'Listen Clara, you have earned every penny of that money. I wouldn't be here if it wasn't for you and your family. I insist you take it. I'll tell you what, we are celebrating my good news, so, while I'm making us another cup of tea, you go round to the beer-off and get a large jug of brown ale. That is what Arthur and David like isn't it? I've a mind that you are partial to it as well. Oh and on the way back, stop off at the bakers for a slab of Madeira cake and we'll spread some of your homemade butter on it nice and thick. No one's going to stop us pushing the boat out on this occasion!'

'Well me duck, I don't know what ta say. I've never seen sa much money in all me life. If ya sure abaht it, I'll accept it, not fa missen, but fa me gels; though Lord knows what Arthur 'ull say. 'E don't accept charity from no-one.'

Lizzie smiled and reaffirmed her reasons for giving Clara the money. 'Clara, it isn't charity. It is payment for everything you have done for Rosie and me. Now be off with you while I put the kettle on.'

Clara picked up her shopping bag on the way out and strode off purposefully to the beer-off. She collected the beer and continued on to the bakers. Mr Braithwaite was more than a little surprised when she produced a shiny golden sovereign in payment for the slab of cake. The family hardly ever came into his shop because as a general rule residents of the Marsh never had money to spare. He knew the Milligans' were a hard working family, but splashing out on cake was something new and he couldn't resist a jibe. 'Well now Mrs Milligan, have you come into some money? I guess you must have to be able to afford a whole slab of cake.'

Clara was affronted at Mr Braithwaite's insinuation, even though she knew he was right, that her sort couldn't afford the likes of bought cake, especially his best Madeira. Nevertheless, her windfall gave her some self-importance so she retorted, which was something she would not normally do, because she had a lot of respect for people in business. 'Yo cheeky bogga, 'appen we've 'ad a bit of a windfall and I don't have to teck that rudeness from yo. I'll be pleased if yu'd just wrap up the item and I'll be on me way, thank you.'

Mr Braithwaite looked suitably ashamed. 'I'm sorry Mrs Milligan, I didn't mean anything by it. Here pass me your shopping bag and I'll put the cake in for you.'

A little more contritely but not pulling her punches, she risked passing another comment. 'Aye well, manners cost noat ya know. I'll possibly be in tamorra fa some more. Now, I'll bid you good-day,' she said in her best Nottingham accent and swaggered off down the street.

Clara returned to Knotted Alley, just as her neighbour, Mrs Brown was scurrying along to the toilet carrying some torn up newspaper. A scarf covered the curlers in her hair and she still wore her dressing gown and slippers. She was surprised to see Clara, who was obviously returning from the shops, but didn't fail to notice the jug of beer she carried in one hand and the bag of something in the other. Mrs Brown wondered where Clara had found the money to buy such items and couldn't resist being nosey. 'Mornin Mrs Milligan, bin shopping? A bit early for that innit? What 'ave ya got in ya bag?'

'It's a slab of Madeira. Not that it's oat ta do we yo.'

Mrs Brown was what they termed a 'scrounger' and Clara usually tried to avoid meeting up with her at all costs, but as Mrs Brown never let an opportunity go begging, she still cajoled Clara for a share of the goodies. 'Well that's nice a must say. I'm just being neighbully. Cum inta some money 'ave ya. If yuv got any spare, ya know where ta bring it.' Tossing her head back and laughing loudly, she entered the toilet and shut the door whilst singing at the top of her voice to alert other prospective users that it was in fact 'in use'.

Clara tutted at Mrs Brown's cheek and muttered under her breath, before storming up the twitchell and back into her own kitchen.

Lizzie welcomed her as she made her entrance. 'Hello Clara, I've just poured the tea. Did you get the cake?'

Clara showed Lizzie the large slab of Madeira, before she cut two good-sized pieces, layered them with a thick wedge of butter and handed one to Lizzie. ''Ere ya are Hannah, or should a say Lizzie. This'ull fill a hole, thanks to yo.'

'Thank you Clara, but about my name, I think it is best if you stick to calling me Hannah for the time being, that is until everything is settled, when there won't be any harm in the information becoming known.'

'Yes, you're right Hannah. Folks round 'ere are quick ta judge and 'arf the Marsh would be buzzing with a story like that. Folks exaggerate and we'd certainly be robbed if they thought we'd come inta some money. Best keep it quiet.'

Lizzie nodded. 'Yes you're right Clara. Well I need to be off now, as I've a case to pack and need to get Rosie ready as well. Never fear, I will come back to see you on my return, so use the money wisely Clara. It isn't a fortune, but it should keep the wolf from the door for the foreseeable future.'

'Ya very kind Hannah and I'll not fergerit. Don't fergerus now and come back ta see us as soon as ya back. Teck care now and safe journey. Tarrar me duck.'

❦

Before going home, Lizzie called on Mrs Phillips to relate her good news and to explain that she would be absent from her post for a short while. Back at Marsden Court, she packed several warm autumn dresses, some thick stockings and several pairs of drawers for herself and Rosalie. Afterwards, she collected Rosalie from Gladys Leach's, as she needed to explain her plans to her daughter, prior to them joining Daniel for the journey to his home in Manchester.

She sat Rosalie down on the settle and began her explanation. 'Rosie, I have arranged for you and me to go on holiday. What do you think to that?'

Rosalie frowned, as she had never been on 'holiday' before and she was uncertain as to what it entailed. 'What mam, like going down the Goose Fair do you mean, or like Annie when she stays with her aunty in Cinderhill?'

Lizzie smiled. 'Not exactly Rosie. This holiday means we'll be travelling by coach to another town. We are to stay with Mr Lorimer and his family in Manchester. It will be really exciting journeying through the countryside. I believe he lives in a rather grand house with a big garden where you will be able run and play.'

Rosalie put her hand on her chin and with her head on one side, she posed a very important question. 'Is Jimmy coming with us mam?'

Lizzie felt that Rosalie might need a little persuasion to leave Jimmy behind so she handed her a cup of milk with a little honey in it as a treat, which would go a long way in appeasing her. 'Well no, Jimmy won't be able to come with us Rosie, but while we are away, we can choose a present for him and you can wrap it up yourself and give it to him when we come home.'

Rosalie looked pensive and unsure as to whether going on 'holiday' without Jimmy was something she could bear to do. 'How long we going for mam? Is it a day or two days?'

Lizzie realised this might be more difficult than she thought, so tried including an aspect of being away that would really excite Rosalie, that would be sufficient for her to tear herself away from Jimmy for a little longer than one or two days.

In a bright and hopeful voice, she appealed to Rosalie's

sense of adventure. 'Well, it is a little bit longer than two days, but there will be some very exciting things for you to do. Mr Lorimer has said that when we visit Liverpool, he will also take us to Southport, where there is lots of sand. You can build sandcastles and decorate them with shells then paddle in the sea afterwards.'

Rosalie had never seen the sea. The nearest water was the canal, the River Leen and the water at the bottom of the quarry where she and Jimmy had dipped their feet on occasion in the summer. She liked the idea of being able to walk on sand and paddle in the sea. 'Well that sounds good mam. Perhaps I could collect some shells and sand in a bottle and take it back to Jimmy. He's never been on holiday and neither have I, but if I explain it all to him when I get back, it will be like he's been as well, won't it?'

Lizzie was relieved that Rosalie was agreeable, but was anxious to keep up the momentum by suggesting other things she could do as well. 'Yes, that's a really good idea and perhaps I could help you to build a model of the beach with rock pools that have all kinds of little creatures in, like crabs.'

Rosalie's eyes were out on stalks as she imagined herself running along the beach and splashing in the sea. By now, she couldn't wait and was badgering her mother to hurry up and finish packing, so they could go immediately. 'When are we going mam...today? Now, in a minute or have I got to go to bed first?'

'It's today Rosie. In fact we should be leaving in about an hour, so run along and fetch a couple of toys. You can take your rag doll and we've room for the little wooden train...There is one more thing I need to tell you Rosie. I discovered from my friend Mr Lorimer, that I used to be called 'Lizzie' by the friends I had before we came to Nottingham, so they will probably continue to call me that, would that be all right with you?'

Rosalie looked thoughtful, before giving her answer.

'I don't mind what people call you, as long as I can call you mam...I can still call you that can't I...mam?'

Lizzie smiled and thought how accommodating and deliciously naive children were. 'Of course Rosie, you can always call me that.'

Rosalie, secure in the knowledge, responded positively. 'That's okay then. Can we go now...mam?'

Lizzie felt her own levels of enthusiasm rise at Rosalie's eagerness to depart and cheerfully packed the remaining items into a case.

Rosalie was very excited and climbed the stairs to her bedroom, singing to herself. 'We're going on holiday, we're going to the seaside'.

This spontaneous holiday would reveal much more about their past than they could ever imagine.

CHAPTER FIVE

Reflection and Regret?

Daniel waited anxiously for Lizzie and Rosalie to arrive. At five to twelve he ordered some sandwiches and tea to be served in his room, where he had spent a thoughtful couple of hours, mulling over the happy times he had spent with Lizzie at Low Wood. These reminiscences' inevitably included shared intimate moments, which lead him to question his feelings for Georgina. He had been very happy until Lizzie reappeared, so maybe he wasn't quite so happy with his lot as he thought. Lizzie's re-emergence had refuelled his passion and he was angry for allowing himself to question his own desires. 'Damn you...Damn you Lizzie Cameron, why did you have to go away? We could have been so happy.'

He immediately felt deeply ashamed of the thoughts that infiltrated his mind and tarnished his feelings for his wife, with a consequence he again promised himself there would not be any impropriety. In future he would devote himself entirely to his beautiful wife, Georgina and their daughter, Victoria. There would be no more dwelling on the past.

His musings were interrupted by a knock on the door. The landlord politely announced that Lizzie Cameron was waiting in the foyer, so Daniel requested she be shown up to his room. 'Thanks Richard. Would it be possible to bring the sandwiches and tea up at the same time?'

'Yes sir, I'll do that for you. Shall I bring a lemonade for the young girl?'

'Yes, thank you Richard. Please accept this sixpence for your trouble.'

The landlord acknowledged the tip, then brought Lizzie and Rosalie up to the room, along with a tray of sandwiches, tea and lemonade.

Daniel greeted them at the door and offered them two comfortable armchairs in an alcove near the window. 'It's lovely to see you again Lizzie. You too, young Rosie. I hope you like lemonade?'

Rosalie's face broke into a grin. 'I love lemonade Mr Lorimer, especially when the bubbles tickle my nose, but we don't have it very often, do we mam?'

Lizzie smiled at the forthright manner her daughter adopted when speaking to Daniel. 'No Rosie, we don't, but we could probably have some as a special treat while we are holiday.'

While Rosalie was busy drinking the lemonade, Daniel advised Lizzie on his plans for their stay. 'I may have already mentioned, that I think it would be wise to delay meeting up with Robert again for about a week, for you to get used to the idea. I realise that you are anxious to be re-united with him, so I intend to contact him when we arrive in Manchester but it might take a week to get something organised. Anyway, he will need to arrange to be away from his business for a few days.'

Lizzie smiled in agreement. 'That sounds a good idea Daniel. Of course I am very excited about seeing him, but accept that things take time to organise. Do you think we could go to Liverpool during the first week? I have promised Rosie a day in Southport, as you suggested and she is very excited about going on the beach.'

'Yes, I should be able to arrange that, but at this time of year it's often quite misty and the wind can get up. However, I am sure we can show her a good time despite the weather.'

They finished lunch and Daniel took his case and Lizzie's valise downstairs. He loaded them on the cab, which would take them to the Royal Mail Coach Park in Maypole Yard.

The journey to Ardwick Green on the outskirts of Manchester passed without incident, although the motion of the coach caused Rosalie to sleep most of the way.

Lizzie and Daniel chatted earnestly about solving the mystery surrounding Lizzie's stay in Nottingham, with Daniel speculating why she had undertaken such a journey in the first place. 'You were obviously en-route somewhere when you met with an accident in Nottingham. The most likely and probable destination would be London, which Daisy and Archie suggested, although I cannot think for the life of me why on earth you would be making such an epic journey Lizzie. You loved Scotland so much and it is where I thought you would stay forever. The circumstances must have been really dire to force you into leaving, but I doubt you have had much time to think about it since you discovered who you are?'

Daniel couldn't have been more wrong, Lizzie had done nothing but think about the life she may have had in Scotland, but that's all it had been - a thought. So far nothing significant or tangible had resurfaced from the dark recesses of her mind, so her answer was rather negative. 'No Daniel, unfortunately, I haven't been able to piece together any of my life, until I was taken in by the Milligans'. When I say your name, I'm sad that I cannot remember our relationship whatsoever, but I hope the visit to Manchester and Liverpool, will spark off a chain of memories and bring clarity to the missing years in my life.'

Daniel, still suffering from mixed emotions, nodded. It understandably angered him that she had left him without a word, but it also cheered him that as her friend, he could help piece her life together again.

They arrived in Ardwick Green around 8.30 p.m. and continued down the wide tree lined avenues, which bordered the canal. The coach stopped outside a pair of large iron gates, on which hung a sign announcing the name of the property as 'The Beeches'. The gates were opened by the driver and the coach and four cantered through, before stopping outside the entrance to a grand Regency Lodge.

Lizzie was surprised when the door was opened by a maid, who was very pleased to have her employer back. She greeted him with a wide smile and welcomed him into the hallway. The scene wasn't what Lizzie was expecting. Her employer in the grand house in Nottingham had insisted on complete professionalism from the maids and housekeeper and that certainly didn't include familiarity and friendly banter on the doorstep. 'Welcome back sir. You've been missed you know. I'll just announce your arrival to Mrs Lorimer. She is presently in the nursery and will be delighted to have you home again.'

Daniel returned the maid's welcome with equal friendliness whilst handing his hat and coat to her. 'Thank you Beatrice, that's very kind, but I will surprise her myself. Would you show Lizzie and Rosie to the sitting room and bring some supper? If I am not mistaken from the delicious smell wafting through, cook's already prepared the meal and it's waiting to be served.'

Beatrice did not wish to speculate on the identity of the young woman and her daughter, so discreetly made a comment about the supper instead, in the hope it would bring forth an introduction. 'You're right sir, we had been expecting you back some time this evening and I am sure supper will stretch to another two mouths.'

Smiling at the audacity of his favourite servant, he made the introductions. 'Oh do forgive me Beatrice, I must formally introduce you to my friends. This is Lizzie Cameron and her daughter Rosie. Lizzie is a very old friend of mine and they will be staying with us for a while. I thought they could occupy the green room on the first floor, as it has an interconnecting door, which I think Rosie will enjoy.'

Rosalie, who had been looking around at the splendour of the house, looked up at Daniel with a puzzled look on her face. 'What's an intacontin door Mr Lorimer. I've never heard of one of those?'

The commendable attempt at such a word coming out of the mouth of someone so young seemed quite comical and caused Beatrice to let out an audible giggle. However, this solicited a look of horror from Rosalie, who considered herself to be quite grown up and hated being laughed at.

Daniel, hid the urge to chuckle, but knew Rosalie considered herself to be an adult and expected to be treated as such, so he stooped down to her level and cupped her hands in his, before apologising diplomatically. 'Well Rosie, I think Beatrice giggled because she was surprised you could pronounce such a word. However, an interconnecting door joins your mam's room with yours, so that you can pop in and out whenever you want. She also has another door which opens on to the landing.'

Rosalie was pleased that she had impressed the maid and was happy with the explanation. 'That'll be fun mam. I want to go to the toilet now please. Is it in the back yard?'

Once again Beatrice was tempted to giggle, but fought back the urge and informed Rosalie of the whereabouts of the toilet. 'Come with me young Rosie, the bathroom is next to your bedroom up the stairs.'

Again Rosalie looked puzzled, as she didn't think she would be having a bath for another few days yet. 'Oh no, I don't need a bath just now. I had one last Wednesday, didn't I mam? I just need to do a wee thank you.'

This time all three adults were struggling to contain their mirth. Even Lizzie had to admit that Rosalie came out with some funny, but innocent remarks. It reminded her that she would have a lot of coaching and explaining to do to educate Rosalie on the lifestyle that existed beyond the streets of Narrow Marsh.

She was only a baby when Lizzie had taken Rosalie to the grand house where she worked in Nottingham. After they moved in with Mabel Armstrong, she had stayed at home and hadn't accompanied her mother to St James Street again. Thus her only experience of 'toilets' was the shared one at the bottom of the terrace, which consisted of a plank of wood with a central hole and a bucket underneath. The cut up newspaper hanging on a piece of string was as luxurious as it got. The toilet at Marsden Court was marginally superior, but was still located outside in the garden.

Beatrice began to understand that Rosalie was not used to having any kind of indoor washing facilities where she lived, but couldn't comprehend why Mr Lorimer would befriend someone from the lower classes. However, she quickly embraced the situation and put her prejudices aside, before taking Rosalie by the hand to mount the stairs. 'Well now Rosie, you will be pleased to know that the toilet is in the same room as the bath, so if you want to go in the night, you don't have to go outside.'

Rosalie looked at Beatrice and gave her a curious look. 'What if you or Mr Lorimer are in the bath when I want the toilet. Do we just all stay in there together?'

Beatrice stifled another giggle before thinking that this little girl and herself would get on famously, then kept a straight face as she explained. 'Well, not exactly, Rosie. I think you'll find that you can lock the door when you are in there, so you won't be disturbed. Unless, of course, you want me to help you when you are taking a bath?'

Rosalie was happy with the explanation and climbed the last few steps of the grand staircase two at a time, whistling as she followed Beatrice along the landing.

Whilst Lizzie relaxed in the sitting room, Daniel proceeded to the nursery to surprise his wife. He crept in through the door and glimpsed her as she sat in the nursing chair next to the window. She was holding Victoria to her breast.

Georgina saw Daniel immediately and after laying her daughter in the wooden cot, rushed over to put her arms around him. 'Oh Daniel I am so glad you are back home. We've really missed you. I get so lonely when you are away.'

Daniel kissed his wife softly on the lips and held her away from him to reappraise her beauty. She was a young, pretty, slightly built woman, who had perhaps put on a little weight while pregnant. She had not lost it as yet, but it definitely suited her and gave her a more womanly shape, which appealed to him sexually. Her long straight dark brown hair, was worn in a chignon, secured with a tortoiseshell slide and was immaculately coiffured as always. He looked into her hazel eyes and then at her full lips, which revealed a warm smile and straight white teeth. He pulled her to him again and slid his hands over her gently rounded hips, before slowly making his way back to her small firm breasts, which despite feeding Victoria remained pert and perfectly formed. He knew that to some men she was too petite to be thought of as sexually desirable, but for him it was this vulnerability that had first attracted him to her.

For a few moments his mind wandered back to the decision he had made earlier, that Lizzie was lost to him forever. In a determined effort to expunge everything she had ever meant to him, when she left that day in September 1841, he looked for someone totally opposite, someone exactly like Georgina. If only Georgina could discard her puritanical attitude to sex, it would benefit them both...if only he could arouse her sufficiently to abandon her obsession with covering her body. He blamed her mother for convincing his wife that sex was not meant to be enjoyed, only tolerated.

In contrast, Lizzie had never been prudish. She had been quite naïve like Georgina when they first met, but quickly blossomed into someone who was comfortable in her skin and eager to please him. Both of them had experimented sexually, after he had assured her that giving herself to him did not mean an end to their relationship, just a beginning. At times he was quite shocked at her abandonment but enjoyed their lovemaking immensely.

By complete contrast and probably due to her mother's guidance, Georgina had insisted on celibacy until after they were married, assuring him that 'things' would be different afterwards.

He reluctantly agreed to wait for the glorious moment when she would give herself willingly to him, but it wasn't until their wedding night that he discovered just how nervous and tentative she was about enduring the perceived abhorrent act that she was expected to perform, that of the consummation of their union, allowing Daniel to enter her most private parts.

To this day he had never seen his wife naked. She insisted on changing into her nightwear behind a screen in their bedroom and always, always, wore a long silk nightdress in bed.

Her mother had played a big part in Georgina's attitude to sex. She had projected her warped ideas on to her daughter and told her how she would have to subject herself to what was, in her mother's mind, a barbaric act; that of allowing her husband his conjugal rights. She had drummed home how distasteful it would be, but that if she could lay back and allow her husband to enter her once a week, it could be used as a weapon to gain what was rightfully hers and have the opportunity to wear beautiful clothes and live in sumptuous surroundings.

Georgina believed that her mother must be right, after all, she always wore expensive clothes and appeared content living with Gordon, her father. They very rarely argued, so it appeared to Georgina that their marriage was a happy one. Of course, she omitted to inform Georgina that her father enjoyed many sexual encounters with the young servants, to which she turned a blind eye. In fact, these infidelities were actively encouraged, as they kept her husband out of her own bed. She was, therefore, eternally grateful that she didn't have to perform these vile acts too often herself.

For his part, Daniel was disappointed that he was unable to feast his eyes on his wife's nakedness and rarely embrace the pleasurable feelings and sensuous closeness of being locked together, skin on skin.

Their lovemaking was always conducted in the dark and was never, ever, spontaneous. Nevertheless, Georgina loved him dearly and tried hard to please him in other ways; clearly not understanding how pleasurable it could be to freely enjoy uninhibited lovemaking. Unfortunately, Daniel was a man with needs and those needs so far lacked the full intensity a young man desired. Now as he looked at her, he wished with all his heart that she could somehow find the courage to let go and give herself completely to him.

The thought excited him as he swept his hands over her body and he momentarily forgot that Lizzie was waiting for them in the living room. He decided there and then that he would work on her, awakening desires so overwhelming in their intensity that she would not wish to hide herself from him.

He would begin right now and pulled her closer to him. He kissed her deeply, using his tongue to explore the softness of her mouth, but disappointingly for Daniel, it had the opposite effect. She immediately pulled away from him, shocked at his sudden impatience. He apparently wanted to take her right there and then in the nursery, in front of their baby daughter.

Blushing furiously and clearly shocked at his actions she moved away to pick their daughter up from her cot, as a defence to any further attempts to seduce her. She took charge of the situation by handing Victoria over to Daniel. 'Look darling, your daddy is back home. Haven't we missed him?'

Disappointed with his wife's reaction, but suddenly remembering that they had a guest waiting in the sitting room, he reluctantly went along with Georgina's wishes to control his feelings, at least until they were in bed together later that evening. Anxious to keep on her good side, he apologised for his lack of control. 'I'm sorry if I was over zealous Georgina, but I have really missed you.' Daniel placed his arms around his wife's shoulders and kissed the top of her head. 'Anyway darling there is someone I want you to meet downstairs. You remember that I told you about Elizabeth Cameron, who appeared to vanish off the face of the earth? Well I bumped into her again in Nottingham. She appears to have had an accident about five years ago which left her with amnesia. She has a little girl, Rosie, aged five and I have invited them to stay with us to see if she can regain her memory by visiting places she went to before the accident. She doesn't think the child is hers, but she hopes to find the birth parents while she is here. Do you mind darling?'

Georgina trusted her husband totally and didn't have any reason to doubt that what he said was true. Despite the fact that she was aware of their past relationship, she readily agreed to help Lizzie. 'Of course not Daniel. I'll be pleased to do anything I can to help her. She must be in a very lonely place right now. We are so lucky that we have each other and our lovely daughter. Let's go down and meet her.'

Daniel mused on his wife's never ending capacity to help others in distress. He felt very proud of her and took her by the hand as they descended the stairs.

Lizzie rose to greet Georgina as the couple entered the sitting room. She extended her hand in friendship and smiled warmly. 'Hello Georgina, I am very pleased to meet you and thank you for welcoming me into your home.'

Georgina returned the gesture and seated herself next to Lizzie on the sofa. 'I hope you had a pleasant journey Lizzie. May I call you that?'

'Of course, although I only discovered that was my real name a few days ago...I am still getting used to it.'

Just then the door opened and Rosalie ran in like a whirlwind. 'Mam you should see the toilet. It's got a bath in it and a sink and thick towels and my bed has a thick pink eiderdown on it. There's an armchair, a chest of drawers and a little table and—'

Lizzie stopped Rosalie in mid sentence, as she was getting overly excited and really needed to get to bed and have a good night's sleep. 'I'm sure I will love it Rosie, but I think after you have had something to eat, you should take the opportunity of trying the bed out, after you have a quick bath. If that's all right with you Georgina?'

'Of course Lizzie.' She then asked Rosalie, to join them on the sofa. 'So you must be Rosie. Come over here and say hello and we will see what goodies cook can come up with before you go to bed.'

Rosalie liked the look of Georgina and was happy to sit by her. 'You're pretty aren't you? Are you Mr Lorimer's wife?'

'Yes, that's right and you can call me Aunty Georgina if you like.'

'Okay...Aunty Georgina. I like you. Have you got any children?'

Lizzie was used to Rosalie's constant chatter, but was unsure whether others might find it aggravating, so she glanced Rosalie's way to suggest she sit quiet for a time, which, of course, went unheeded. Fortunately, Georgina, far from being annoyed, was happy to chat to her. 'I've got a baby girl Rosie. Her name is Victoria. She is asleep at the moment, but tomorrow when you get up, you can help me to give her a bottle if you would like that?'

Rosalie gave Georgina one of her biggest smiles. 'I think I'm going to like staying here.'

'Good. I do hope so and if your mummy has to go away for the day, I hope you will stay with me and Victoria until she gets back.'

'That'll be all right I think. Is that all right mam? I call her mam you know, not mummy.'

Everyone again concealed smiles, although it was evident that Rosalie knew exactly what she wanted and wasn't afraid to say so.

Georgina nodded sagely. 'Okay Rosie. I'll remember to call her that.'

After finishing her supper and tired from the long journey, Rosalie finally fell asleep in the middle of eating a fairy cake, made especially for her by cook. Daniel carried her up to bed, as the bath suggested by Lizzie was now totally out of the question. Shortly afterward, Lizzie confessed to Georgina. 'I hope you don't think I am being rude, but I am really tired myself and wonder whether you would mind if I went to my room to unpack before going to bed.'

Georgina flashed her a warm smile. 'Not at all Lizzie, I will ask cook to send some hot milk up to your room. You will find some clean towels in the bathroom if you've a mind to take a bath before you retire. We will see you at breakfast tomorrow, but don't worry about time, if you would like to lie in.'

'Thank you Georgina, but I would like to be up and about fairly early, as I intend to start on my quest to discover my past as soon as possible,' said Lizzie bidding them goodnight.

Georgina and Daniel retired shortly after. Daniel was anxious that his wife wasn't over tired, as the idea of a night of passion had been at the forefront of his mind, ever since her rebuff earlier in the evening.

He felt that this was their chance to take their love making to another level, if he could persuade her to shake off her inhibitions. Victoria was six months old now and the doctor had given them the all clear a while ago to resume sexual relations, providing they were both ready.

It was three years since they had married and Georgina had come to question some of the ideas her mother had passed on to her regarding such matters. She had found, over time, that she enjoyed the closeness a loving relationship brought. She felt safe in Daniel's arms and actually wanted him to make love to her, providing it was on her terms - in the dark and never naked.

Later, Daniel stood behind her in their room. He kissed her neck and stroked her back in an attempt at arousal, so that he could slip her dress off before she disappeared behind the screen.

Georgina was enjoying the feelings that her husband so expertly aroused in her, but when she felt his hands on the buttons of her dress, she froze, and placed her hand over his, which prevented him from undoing the garment any further. 'No Daniel, please don't do that. I am not ready for this. I would prefer to change into my nightdress as usual, but would like us to continue to make love in our bed.'

His planned attempt to seduce her, somewhere other than the bed had failed. The rigmarole of her escaping behind the screen to change into a nightdress, irritated him slightly, but he told himself to be patient. It might be a while before he would be able to persuade her that being naked was nothing to be ashamed of and that most couples made love without clothes on! However, he hadn't given up entirely so he moved his hands to encircle her waist whilst whispering tenderly into her neck. He hoped she would accept a compromise. 'Darling, why don't I switch off the light, it would be so much better if we could just make love without the need for you to change into a nightdress. You have a beautiful body and there is nothing shameful about me seeing you naked.'

Fleetingly, she almost agreed, but the moment passed and she decided she was just too embarrassed, even if they made love in total darkness. 'I'm sorry Daniel, I really cannot bring myself to do that. Please don't make it a big issue. I do love you and one day I promise I will try to do what you want.'

Disappointed, but resigned, Daniel climbed into bed and waited for his wife to join him. The excitement he had felt earlier diminished. The longer he had to wait for her to change into her nightdress and climb in to bed beside him, the more his passion subsided. Eventually, they lay together in each other's arms, but with lovemaking now completely forgotten.

For a long time sleep eluded Daniel and he wondered whether they would ever be completely compatible. He couldn't help but compare her to Lizzie and so was once again angry with himself for allowing his past to dominate his thoughts. Was he still in love with her, despite the betrayal when she left him without a word? Had she meant to contact him later, when she had reached her destination? Had the accident prevented her from doing so? Had she deliberately walked out of his life for ever? Had he ever truly loved his wife or did he seek her out just to mend his broken heart? Would he ever really love anyone as much as he had loved Lizzie? or was he destined to accept that the wild excitement and sexual promise he had experienced with her could only happen once in a lifetime? If only he could wipe the past from his memory. Perhaps he should not have brought her here - perhaps he should not have pursued her that day at the fair. Perhaps, perhaps - It was no good, he couldn't change anything and in his heart of hearts, did he really want to?

CHAPTER SIX

A Visit to Manchester

Lizzie rose at 8.30 a.m., after experiencing her best ever sleep. Rosalie was conveniently still in the land of nod, only her golden curls peeped out from under the bedclothes. Lizzie took the opportunity to wash and dress and go down for breakfast. The aromas emanating from the morning room of bacon, kippers, smoked salmon, mushrooms, black pudding and a variety of eggs were deliciously inviting, although the atmosphere did not reflect the ambience.

Georgina was seated at the table opposite Daniel, but a definite coolness existed between them as they engaged in a perfunctory conversation. Georgina was adamant that whatever problems they had could be sorted out in private. It had nothing to do with their guests and she was determined that Lizzie and Rosalie's stay would not be spoiled. She rose from the table and greeted Lizzie warmly. 'Good morning Lizzie, I hope you and Rosie slept well.'

'Yes, thank you Georgina, I feel well rested and ready to tackle anything,' smiled Lizzie then addressing Daniel sought approval for her plans. 'I wonder Daniel whether we might take a cab into Manchester this morning, if that is all right with you both?'

Daniel smiled at his wife graciously and felt grateful that she had made a special effort to welcome Lizzie, despite their own disagreement. 'Yes, I am happy to do that. We were talking about the arrangements before you arrived and Georgina has offered to look after Rosie so that we can concentrate on the task ahead.'

'That's really kind of you Georgina, but are you sure you will be able to manage, Rosie can be quite a handful at times?' Lizzie smiled.

'Don't worry Lizzie, I will find plenty to occupy her mind and she will be company for me while you are gone.'

Daniel again conveyed a smile of gratitude to his wife, as he still felt guilty about escorting Lizzie, albeit formally. 'That's settled then. Thank you Georgina, I will call in on cook on the way out and ask her to prepare a special meal for all of us tonight. Her speciality, fresh lobster is exceedingly delicious. I'll request it for the main course, as I know it's your favourite darling.'

Daniel resumed his breakfast and began chatting more amicably with his wife now that his mood had lifted. 'I'll have James bring the trap around at 9 o'clock Lizzie, so that we can be away as soon as you are ready. I recommend a good breakfast before we depart, as there may be a fair amount of walking to do in Manchester. Smoked salmon topped with a lightly poached egg is something cook makes exceedingly well and the porridge has been made with fresh thick double cream and honey, delicious.'

Lizzie took Daniel's advice and plumped for the porridge followed by cook's speciality salmon, which certainly lived up to expectations. The breakfast would have been a most enjoyable affair, except for one thing. Despite their friendly banter, the atmosphere between Georgina and Daniel was definitely cooler and in complete contrast to yesterday. She hoped that it wasn't her presence that had been the cause, as this would greatly concern her. Perhaps they had changed their mind about her staying, so, she decided to broach the subject later with Daniel, if the opportunity arose.

***

They reached Manchester mid morning and James dropped them off in the centre, amidst a conglomeration of cotton factories, a few hotels and shops. Daniel had been very chatty on the journey, which allayed Lizzie's fears, with a consequence that the atmosphere at breakfast was forgotten.

Daniel had already formulated a plan, which he hoped would bring some results. He was eager to share it with Lizzie and suggested they take mid-morning coffee in the Cobden Coffee House on Port Street.

Daniel ordered coffee and they sat at a table for two, underneath a large reproduction painting of 'The Great Western Railway' by Turner.

He took a sip of his coffee and smiled briefly at Lizzie across the table. She returned his smile and although he tried to keep his emotions in check, a great sense of wellbeing flowed through his body. He took a deep breath, determined to keep their relationship on a 'good friends only' basis, but not wanting to alienate himself either, addressed her as he would any good friend. 'Well Lizzie, I never thought I would be sitting here with you five years on from when I last saw you. However, time has moved on and I know you are anxious to fill in the missing gaps of your life. I have been thinking what we should do with our day in Manchester and I had the idea that if you did come here, you might have stayed in an hotel overnight. I assume you would have stayed somewhere like the York on King Street, so I suggest we make that our first port of call'

'That's an excellent idea Daniel, but I am not sure I would have stayed at the York, as I understand that it is one of the more expensive hotels.'

Daniel remembered Lizzie's financial status was sound at the time. He recollected that she sailed first class aboard the Royal George and proof of that journey was the 'punched' tickets found in her valise. He put this idea to her and felt distinctly positive about what they might achieve today. 'When I last saw you Lizzie, you wouldn't have had a great deal of money and certainly not enough to purchase first class tickets on the Royal George; but the fact remains that you did travel on that ship. Consequently, someone must have paid for your passage and also given you a considerable amount of money, not least for your ongoing journey and presumably for some overnight stays in quality hotels.'

'You are right Daniel. I suppose I could have stayed at the York, it does make sense.'

'Mmm, we need to find out if they have retained their visitor's book for 1841, it's worth a shot.'

༺༻

Their investigations at the York proved negative, but they lunched there anyway and Lizzie came up with another idea. 'Supposing I arrived in Manchester and intended to continue on that day by coach, without stopping over. If, as you believe, I was making my way down to London, then it would make sense for me to go by Royal Mail coach.'

'You could have a point there Lizzie. We'll take a Hackney Carriage to the Royal Mail Coach station which, incidentally, isn't far from Liverpool station where you would have disembarked.'

The Royal Mail Coaches were parked in preparation for their journey to London, via the Midlands. All coaches were due to depart at 4 p.m. sharp, so there was plenty of time for Lizzie and Daniel to mingle and question the coach drivers. Although five years had passed, they both hoped that if Lizzie had made this journey, one of the drivers might just remember her. After all, it was quite unusual for a young woman to travel alone with a small baby.

Unfortunately, no one remembered her, but one driver suggested that, if she arrived late and missed the Royal Mail coaches, she might have used an independent coach. 'Sorry I can't help you Mrs Cameron, but you should try questioning the independent drivers who are parked up the street near the warehouses. They do not follow a time table and only depart as required.'

'Well, thanks very much, we'll do that.'

Three independent drivers were parked up in the little side street. Their passenger compartments were not as elaborate or as comfortable as the Royal Mail coaches, but most were functional and reliable.

Daniel approached the first driver, a well-built man of around thirty years. 'Good afternoon sir. Are you a regular on the Manchester to London route?'

'Indeed, I am. Been working this route for the last six years. You wanting to travel down to London today sir?'

'Well no, actually, but I wonder if you have a good memory. This young woman, Elizabeth Cameron, may have travelled by coach from this station five years ago. Do you recall seeing her? She was travelling with a young baby, which is quite an unusual occurrence.'

The coach driver peered at Lizzie, but didn't appear to recognise her. 'I'm very sorry, but you don't seem familiar. I feel I would have remembered you both, maybe you could ask Bill or Jacob, they are the only other drivers operating now.'

Daniel's ears pricked up, was the driver inferring that there may have been other drivers' travelling the route that were no longer operating. 'You say 'now', does that mean that there were more drivers around a few years ago?'

'Why yes, but only one. He had an accident on his way to London on the Dunstable road. The story goes that his horses careered into a tree lying across the highway. They found his body and some unidentified luggage, scattered down the hillside, which I understand was never claimed. A Royal Mail driver reported his death and apparently, there weren't any passengers, so it remains a bit of a mystery. One of the horses was missing and the other three died in the accident. His name was Jack Garrett and a bit of a rogue, one for the women if you know what I mean. He once told me he would take the road to Nottingham, instead of the usual Derby route, so that he could see a woman there, but that is all I know I'm afraid.'

Daniel dropped him a tip and thanked him for the information, then he sought Lizzie's opinion on the story, before speaking to the other drivers. 'What do you make of that Lizzie? Does the name Jack Garrett mean anything to you?'

Lizzie was pensive, as she tried to search her mind for some recognition of the name, but nothing surfaced. 'I can't say the name is familiar Daniel, but we shouldn't give up. Maybe one of the other drivers might recognise me or be able to provide more details.'

Unfortunately, neither of the other two drivers could provide any information and they didn't remember Lizzie as one of their passengers.

Daniel was still optimistic about the man called Jack Garrett. He wondered if they could find out more about him from some other source and explained his reasoning to Lizzie. 'If you took a coach from here Lizzie, Jack Garrett seems a good bet. It's strange that there was luggage on the ill-fated coach but no passengers, or at least none that have come forward to claim the luggage. He was found on the Dunstable road, so obviously on his way to London.' Daniel became deep in thought. 'We should elicit more positive information when visiting Liverpool on Wednesday. For example, were the trains running on time that day and did you catch the Royal Mail Coach, or travel with an independent. What do you think?'

Lizzie's mind was whirling but her excitement was increasing. 'Hopefully we will Daniel. I am really looking forward to our day in Liverpool as it just might hold the key to how I came to be in Nottingham. The fact that Jack Garrett stopped there en-route is extremely significant, because the Royal Mail and the independents' stage at Derby and not Nottingham. The point about the lack of passengers is also significant; because if I was his sole passenger and I failed to turn up for the onward leg, the luggage could be mine and it would explain why no passengers were found.'

'Why Lizzie, you're turning into a real little detective. I don't know if it's because we are desperate to know how you came to be in Nottingham, or if we have actually stumbled on a possible answer. There must be evidence in Liverpool, but we have exhausted our enquiries today, so how about we browse around the Drapers' Bazaar on Brown Street and look for some fabric for a new dress for Rosie? It's Georgina's favourite shop when she comes into town. Perhaps you could also help me choose a hat for her at Mountcastle's the hatters on Market Street, as she hasn't been able to come to town since Victoria was born and I would like to buy her a gift to cheer her up.'

Lizzie smiled. 'That's a lovely idea Daniel. I would be happy to help you choose a hat and I would also like to buy some fabric. I agree Rosie and myself need new dresses, so I will use some of the money from the valise. Of course, I need to keep an amount for expenses and travel, but there will certainly be enough for a few yards of fabric.'

They laughed together as they took a Hansom cab across the main thoroughfare to the Bazaar.

The shop had some lovely fabrics and Lizzie picked out some warm brushed cotton in a cobalt blue for Rosalie and a length of lighter blue cotton chambray for herself. She went to pay for the items, just as Daniel appeared at her shoulder carrying lengths of heavy navy blue and red wool worsted fabrics, ideal for winter coats. The assistant began to wrap the two lengths of blue fabric, when Daniel requested that she include enough blue worsted to make a coat for a lady and some bright red thick woollen worsted for a child's coat.

Lizzie turned and spoke in hushed tones to Daniel. 'Daniel, this is rather embarrassing, but at the moment I cannot buy fabric for a coat for Rosie, so if you just want to buy the blue worsted for Georgina, I will put the red back on the shelf.'

'No Lizzie, the blue worsted is not for Georgina, as she has more than enough coats to see her through several winters. The fabrics are for you and Rosie and I will be paying for them. I don't want any arguments and any way it wouldn't be seemly to raise our voices in this establishment.'

'But Daniel, I can't possibly accept it, you have your own family to provide for.'

Daniel laughed heartily; as it was obvious Lizzie hadn't any idea of his financial position. It was only a few pounds he was spending and nothing in comparison to the money spent by his wife every week. Georgina had a whole dressing room full to the brim with clothes, some of which had never been worn.

Daniel lowered his voice. 'Georgina would want me to buy you and Rosie this fabric Lizzie, as you cannot manage with the few clothes you have brought with you. Please don't be offended. It is my pleasure to buy you this small gift.'

Lizzie shrugged her shoulders. 'Very well Daniel, but I am not in the habit of accepting charity. However, it is most kind of you and because I don't want to make a fuss, I will accept your offer to pay for the items, if given as a loan, rather than a gift.'

Daniel gave an eloquent smile. 'Oh Lizzie, there's really no need to pay me back. I can easily afford them. Why shouldn't I be allowed to buy an old friend a gift in recognition of our good fortune at meeting up again? Please allow me this little indulgence.'

She realised she had no choice in the matter, so Daniel went ahead with the purchases. 'I believe my wife makes purchases here from time to time under the name of Lorimer, so I should be grateful if you would arrange delivery to our address in Ardwick Green which will be annotated in your ledger.'

The assistant beamed at Daniel. 'Certainly, sir. Will that be all?'

Daniel turned to Lizzie. 'Is there anything else you would like Lizzie?'

Lizzie declined, quite anxious now to leave the shop and emotionally disturbed by the familiarity of the scene, which sparked another memory. She failed to recollect the circumstances, as she believed she had never set foot in the shop before. Nevertheless, there was definitely something familiar about the conversation, but shaking it off as 'de ja vu', she thanked the assistant and preceded Daniel onto the street.

'Now Lizzie, I suggest we have another coffee while we are in the area and then onwards to Mountcastle's for that hat.'

They sat in Day's coffee house and chatted about the recent events. Lizzie opened the conversation with a question, because the incident in the Bazaar still puzzled her. 'Do you think it possible that I could have been in the Bazaar before? It was vaguely familiar, but I can't think why. Perhaps the conversation with the assistant had some relevance.'

'I'm not sure Lizzie. I doubt you would have had time for shopping if you were only passing through Manchester on your way to London. Sometimes one gets a feeling about a place. It might seem familiar, but it is often that we have been somewhere very similar, so maybe that was what you experienced.'

'Yes, maybe you are right. I have really enjoyed today. In Nottingham I would never have been able to sit and have coffee with anyone, nor buy fabric such as we bought today. It was a real treat and I am really looking forward to Wednesday. Rosie will love the seaside and being able to play in the sand, so I just hope it doesn't rain. At present the weather is much warmer than it usually is at this time of year.'

Daniel felt uplifted and looked forward to another excursion with Lizzie. 'I am so glad you enjoyed today Lizzie. I enjoyed myself too. I don't very often have the chance to come into town with Georgina. She prefers to shop for clothes with her friend, Miriam, who is very modern and has a big influence on Georgina's purchases. To be truthful, I am not sure I would want to be dragged all around Manchester 'window shopping' with two women.'

That comment reminded Lizzie of the awkward atmosphere that prevailed over breakfast earlier that morning and she took the opportunity to ask if everything was all right, in particular, that Georgina was still happy for them to stay. 'Can I ask you something Daniel? I don't want to upset anyone, but something has been preying on my mind since breakfast.'

'Anything Lizzie, you can always ask me anything, whatever the situation, so go ahead, I won't be upset. Unless, of course, you are intending to cut your visit short...then I won't be happy.'

'Well actually it does have something to do with that. Georgina was so welcoming yesterday evening and we got on very well, but this morning you were both a little subdued and I wondered if you were having second thoughts about accommodating us? After all, Rosie can be quite boisterous and with a baby in the house as well, it could be quite chaotic. I will understand if you have changed your mind and would be happy to find hotel accommodation while we are here.'

Daniel frowned and his cheerful face darkened. He knew that what Lizzie had witnessed this morning must have made her feel uncomfortable, despite his wife's best efforts. However, he was powerless to put on a show of wedded bliss, especially as neither Georgina nor himself appeared to be enjoying married life, specifically with respect to their intimate relationship. An ashamed Daniel sought to reassure her. 'Oh Lizzie, you couldn't be further from the truth. Georgina and I are happy to have you both for as long as you want to stay. We were rather subdued this morning because we had an argument last night after you retired.' He hesitated, undecided whether it was a good idea or not to seek another woman's opinion on the matter. 'It was my fault and I need to try harder to make Georgina happy. I do love her, but sometimes I wish she would be more loving towards me.'

Lizzie was unsure where this was leading, but the more she had got to know Daniel, the more comfortable she felt in his presence. She was confident that she would not feel embarrassed if the subject became personal. 'What's the matter Daniel, Georgina seems devoted to you and you to her.' Lizzie deduced that Daniel desperately wanted a woman's perspective on a very personal subject, so she braced herself for what he might say.

Daniel was unused to having discussions of such an intimate nature with a woman, but if understanding more about the female mind could save his marriage, then he couldn't think of anyone better than Lizzie with which to hold a conversation.

Lowering his voice, he plunged in. 'I discovered recently that Georgina had a very authoritarian upbringing, with sex being a taboo subject. I suspect her mother put some silly ideas into her head which has spoilt her trust in men somewhat...' Daniel blushed as he realised he had revealed a very private side to his marriage. It wasn't going to be as easy as he thought, so he quickly apologised. 'Gosh, I cannot believe I have just discussed such a delicate matter with you Lizzie. Do forgive me, and accept my apology, but we were very close once and I could always talk to you about anything. I guess old habits die hard.'

Lizzie grinned and excused Daniel his embarrassed outburst. 'Don't worry Daniel, I am not offended, but I can understand Georgina's attitude, especially if her mother primed her to believe that sex was something women just had to put up with.' Then it was her turn to feel awkward. 'Personally, I have not had any kind of a relationship with a man since I started my new life as Hannah Merchant living in Nottingham. I knew nothing of my past, so I was unsure whether I was a married woman. I believed Rosie was my baby, so assumed she was the result of a respectable union. I considered that it would just be a matter of time until a husband came back into my life again. Consequently, I could not allow myself to become intimate with anyone. This may have an effect on how I behave once I do become involved with another man. I haven't any recollection of previous encounters, so I would be entering into a relationship with some trepidation. With respect to Georgina, I expect she needs some time to adjust after the birth of Victoria. I suspect that having a baby must be a traumatic experience.'

Daniel agreed and realised it would be disloyal to reveal anything more, although he was sorely tempted to reassure her on the complexities of an intimate relationship. Instead, he stuck to reassurance of a different kind. 'Yes, of course, I can see that some women might take longer to recover from the experience of a birth and I just need to be more patient, but let me assure you Lizzie, that Rosie and yourself are very, very welcome at the Beeches. Georgina was only saying this morning that she thought you would become good friends.'

Lizzie agreed. 'Yes, I think we will Daniel. Georgina is kind hearted and very accommodating and you are lucky to have her as your wife.'

Daniel was left to reflect on that observation with a certain foreboding.

Dinner was altogether a more convivial affair, with lots of chatter from Rosalie and a definite thawing of the earlier awkwardness between Daniel and Georgina.

Lizzie complimented her hosts on the quality of the meal. 'This lobster is absolutely delicious Georgina and it was clever of cook to combine Rosie's portion with some creamy mashed potato. I doubt she was quite ready to tackle it directly out of its shell.'

Georgina smiled and leaned over to Rosalie. 'Did you enjoy that Rosie?'

'Oh yes, I did, it was delicious and I'm full now thank you.'

'Not got room for dessert then? I know cook has prepared a pavlova, or you could have some freshly made strawberry ice-cream.'

Rosalie's eyes lit up. 'Oh yes please, I am only full with dinner, but I can manage some pudding if that is what desset means. Could I have some ice-cream please?'

'You certainly can. I'll ask cook to bring you two scoops if you've got room.'

After dinner, Lizzie took Rosalie up for a bath and put her to bed. She snuggled down into the cosy blankets, heated by a warming pan and smiled contentedly at her mother. 'Mam, I do like it here. I'd like to live here forever, but I would miss Jimmy. If we stay here, can Jimmy come and live with us?'

Lizzie stroked her daughter's hair and tucked her in, before explaining a bit more about the reason for their stay. 'Rosie, you know how I said we have come here for a holiday, well, there is another reason as well. When you were small I had a little accident and banged my head. It meant that I couldn't remember anything that had happened to me in my life before that time. I knew I had a beautiful baby girl, but I wasn't sure whether your daddy knew where we were, so the time has come to try and find him. This means that if we do, we may be able to go and live with him. If he has another family of his own now, we may possibly go back to Nottingham and live there until you are older. Either way, we cannot stay here forever, just for a little while. Do you understand?'

Rosalie nodded. 'I think so mam, but I think I would rather live in Nottingham, because if we live with my dad, I won't be able to see Jimmy and I wouldn't like that at all. Why do we need to find him anyway? I like it just being you and me and Jimmy.'

Lizzie remained pensive recognising the difficulties that might lie ahead, but spoke reassuringly. 'Well Rosie, your daddy needs to know that we are all right. I think he got lost when I had the accident and he has probably been trying to find us all this time. However, I promise you that if you don't want to live with him, it will just be you and me,' she paused, 'and Jimmy of course.'

Satisfied with the answer, Rosalie closed her eyes and drifted off to sleep.

Lizzie crept silently out of the room and closed the door, then returned to the dining room to join Daniel and Georgina.

Georgina poured Lizzie a cup of coffee. 'Is Rosie all right? I must say she seems to have settled in very well. You have done a good job of bringing her up on your own Lizzie. It cannot have been easy for you.'

Lizzie reflected on her recent past. 'No, it wasn't easy, but I was surrounded by good friends and neighbours, so that made life more palatable than if I had been totally alone.'

'I can understand that,' Georgina agreed, as she looked pensively at her husband. 'Having good friends and neighbours is invaluable when bringing up children. Sometimes when Daniel is away, I wish I had more friends to pass the day with and to discuss parenting. I do have a good friend in Miriam, but she is a free spirit and not really interested in settling down and having a family. Anyway, enough of that, I am dying to hear what happened today. Have you discovered anything that might bring a resolution?'

Lizzie was cautious with her reply. 'Well, I don't want to sound too optimistic, in case it turns out to be a red herring, but we did uncover some fascinating information that needs following up when we visit Liverpool.'

Georgina listened intently to what Lizzie and Daniel had discovered and shared their excitement at the prospect of being one step closer to solving the mystery.

Everyone, with the exception of Daniel enjoyed the sunshine the following day. Rosalie played with a ball and the two women discussed the joys and pitfalls of motherhood, outside on the patio.

Daniel took the opportunity to travel into Manchester again, this time with the specific aim of sending a telegram to Robert Cameron. He would inform him that Lizzie had been found and, in addition, send a letter containing all the relevant information, with a proposed date and time for them to meet. Let's hope, he thought to himself, that this meeting will provide Lizzie with the answers she needs and an insight into her early years in Strathy.

Chapter Seven

A Visit to the Seaside

The happy band of travellers made an early start on Wednesday morning to ensure catching the 8.15 a.m. train from Manchester station to Liverpool. Rosalie was so excited and clutched her own wooden train in one hand and her rag doll in the other. You could tell immediately that this was her first time on a train as her eyes never left the view from the window. She almost became dizzy, as the countryside careered by so fast.

They arrived at Liverpool at 9.35 a.m. and decided to take a coach directly to Southport, to make the most of the unexpected good weather. They booked into the Adelphi Hotel, the best in Liverpool, prior to leaving. At Southport an ecstatic Lizzie and Rosalie stepped on to the beach and breathed in the fresh salty sea air.

Rosalie immediately slipped off her shoes and ran to the sea with Lizzie close behind, whilst Daniel lay down a woollen blanket for Georgina and stuck a large parasol into the sand, to protect Victoria from the wind.

Rosalie and Lizzie allowed the waves to lap over their feet, whilst they gazed at the horizon. Then Rosalie had many questions needing answers. 'Mam, look out there, is that the end of the world?'

'No Rosie, it's called the horizon and that means it's as far as the eye can see.'

'What if you had really, really good eyes, could you see further than that?'

'No Rosie, that's it, you cannot see over that, even when there is land beyond.'

'What land is that mam, is it Nottingham?'

Lizzie, used to Rosalie asking constant questions, was always patient and informative with her reply, although Rosalie did not always understand. Lizzie's experience as a tutor had enabled her to fence all sorts of strange and wonderful questions, especially from five year olds. 'No Rosie, it's not Nottingham, it is a place called Ireland. It is part of England, the country where we live, but it is separated from the mainland by this stretch of water called the Irish Sea.'

'Why isn't it called the English sea, if it is part of England?'

'Well, that's because when I said it was part of England, I meant it was part of the United Kingdom which also includes Wales and Scotland. I was born in Scotland and, possibly, that's where you were born too. Our Queen, Queen Victoria, is Queen of all those lands, but I am not sure who named it the Irish Sea.'

'Should be called Victoria Sea then if she's in charge of it all. She's not the Snow Queen is she mam with a crown and a wand? Is she Queen of Nottingham as well?'

'She's not the Snow Queen, Rosie, but she does have a crown and she is Queen of Nottingham as well.'

'Does the Queen have lots of money?'

'Well, yes I suppose she does.'

Rosalie thought for a moment and decided that was what she wanted to be. 'When I grow up I think I want to be Queen of Nottingham so that I can buy everyone, espeshly Jimmy, a beautiful house to live in an' we can all eat lobster and strawbry ice-cream. Can I be Queen of Nottingham mam?'

'Well Rosie, not just anyone can become the Queen. If your mam had been the Queen, then there would be the possibility that you could be a Queen some day, but as I am not the Queen, it isn't very likely.'

Rosalie for once was lost for words and the conversation ended abruptly. 'Oh,' she said whilst dejectedly wriggling her toes into the sand.

Lizzie felt sorry for Rosalie, who was very disappointed that she couldn't be Queen, so tried to lighten her mood. 'Tell you what Rosie, why don't you and I have a race up the beach to Georgina and Daniel, who I can see waving to us. It looks like Daniel is holding a bag of sweeties for you Rosie.'

Rosalie scampered away quickly gaining a head start before she shouted teasingly. 'Okay mam, last one there's a moose!'

Daniel and Georgina observed all and laughed at Rosalie's antics as she powered her way up the beach. Lizzie, trailing behind, lifted up her skirts to gain more speed, but failed to catch the little girl. Rosalie arrived first, ahead of an out of breath Lizzie.

'Okay you two, how about we have a look what cook packed for us in the basket,' said Daniel, opening up the hamper.

Rosalie's eyes grew wide as she eyed the delicious food being placed on plates on the rug. There was home made lemonade, little sandwiches cut into triangles, sausage rolls, pork pie and lots of Rosalie's favourite fairy cakes. Some had silver balls, some had 'hundreds and thousands' and some had a sugared almond sat on top. Rosalie asked if she could save some for Jimmy, as she was anxious he should try them. 'Mam, can I put one of these in my pocket for Jimmy. He loves these silver balls. We had some once at Annie's birthday party.'

Georgina smiled and suggested a better idea. 'Tell you what Rosie, you eat these and I will make sure that before you go back to Nottingham, cook bakes some especially for Jimmy.'

'Thank you Aunty Georgina, can I have one now?'

Lizzie didn't normally allow Rosalie to eat cake before she had eaten her main course, but as they hardly ever had cake, she made an exception. 'All right Rosie you can have one before you have some of the savoury food, then if you have room, you can have another one afterwards.'

Lunch was a success and enjoyed by everyone, but before they left, Rosalie, Lizzie and Daniel went back down to the sea for one more paddle. All too soon, it was time to leave, which left Rosalie hugely disappointed.

※

The exhausted group caught the train for the return journey, at the same time as a young couple and their son boarded the end carriage, after a short family holiday in Southport.

Amy Brandreth's curiosity had been aroused as she watched the young woman, hand in hand with a small girl, board the front of the train. She gestured to her husband. 'Do you know Charles, I feel sure the young woman we travelled with on the Royal George five years ago, just climbed aboard this train. She has a young girl with her who would be about the right age...Lizzie Cameron...Do you remember her Charles?'

Charles Brandreth replied absently as he carefully placed their cases on the overhead rack. 'Oh yes, Amy, I do remember, but it's hardly likely is it? She was travelling to London if you remember. Probably someone who resembles her.'

Amy Brandreth shrugged. Perhaps she had been mistaken. 'Yes...yes, you are probably right.'

Both parties settled down in their seats, as the Manchester bound train pulled slowly out of the station.

Chapter Eight

The Adelphi Hotel Liverpool

The two exhausted children were settled before the party congregated at the entrance of the Adelphi Hotel's restaurant. Lizzie felt immediately that she'd been here before. The hotel and particularly the restaurant with its elegant surroundings seemed overwhelmingly familiar; especially the pure white linen cloths, silver cutlery and the vases of fresh freesias, which adorned every table. A shiver went down her spine making her grip Daniel's arm tightly.

Georgina and Daniel turned as one displaying identical quizzical looks. Lizzie appeared to be in a world of her own, as her eyes took in the ambience and familiarity of her surroundings. 'Are you all right Lizzie?' Daniel spoke with concern. 'You look a little pale. I think you should sit down.'

They guided Lizzie to a lounge area adjacent to the entrance and sat down on a settee. Daniel was really concerned now, as Lizzie was oblivious of the fact that he was speaking to her. 'Lizzie, are you all right? Can I get you some water?'

Lizzie was surprised that Daniel was beside her but recovered sufficiently to reply. 'Oh...Daniel, yes, I am all right. I would like a glass of water thank you, as I do feel rather faint.'

Daniel immediately requested the maitre de bring a jug of water. When it arrived, he poured a glass and handed it to Lizzie, steadying her hand with his own.

'Thank you Daniel, I feel better now, but I did feel strange when I remembered something from the past. I could see myself entering this restaurant to meet somebody. Of course, that's very unlikely, but I do believe I have been here before.'

Daniel recalled that this was the second time she had had such a feeling: In the Bazaar in Manchester and now at the Adelphi. He hoped that her memory might be returning, as that in itself was cause for celebration. He spoke encouragingly. 'Oh Lizzie, that's really good news. Can you remember anything else about it? Who were you supposed to meet? Do you think you stayed here?'

'I think I did, but I don't know who I was supposed to be meeting, the figure was blurred and I could not make out their face.'

This made Daniel even more determined to find out if she had indeed stayed at the Adelphi five years ago. 'Was it a man or a woman Lizzie?'

Lizzie tried hard to bring the vision back into focus, but it had vanished. 'I'm not sure, but hopefully it will come back to me again. However, I am certain that I have stayed here. Do you think we can find out Daniel?'

'Yes Lizzie, I believe we can...leave it to me.' Daniel left the two women seated in the lounge and went to the reception desk to ask about the hotel records.

Daniel addressed the receptionist in almost a whisper. 'Excuse me, would you know if the hotel keeps past records of clientele?'

The receptionist gazed at Daniel who was giving one of his most disarming smiles. 'Why yes, I believe we do. Why do you ask?'

He leaned forward, anxious to have the receptionist on his side. It was probable that the information wouldn't be disclosed. After all, this wasn't the King's Head, it was the Adelphi Hotel, with, he imagined, high principles. He hoped fervently that a diplomatic approach might bring about a result. 'Well you see, my wife seems to remember that she stayed in this hotel five years ago, on her way down to London to meet me. Would you be able to check for me please?'

The receptionist wasn't sure where the books would be kept so asked the manager for assistance. 'Mr Johnson, this gentleman wishes to inspect the visitors' book from 1841. Do we keep records going back that far?'

Mr Johnson turned to speak to Daniel. 'Good evening sir. I am not sure we can be of assistance? Are you staying at the hotel as a guest?'

Daniel groaned inwardly at having to deal with 'Mr Johnson', but continued doggedly. 'Yes, that's right. My name is Daniel Lorimer and I am here with my wife and a friend of ours. I asked the receptionist if you keep records of past clients. My wife stayed here five years ago, in September 1841. Unfortunately, I was unable to accompany her so she and our baby daughter were travelling alone to London. I thought it would be nice if we could occupy the same room, which my wife described as exceedingly pleasant, if it is available?'

'Oh, I see. One moment sir, I should be able to assist you with both requests.'

The manager returned after ten long minutes with a rather dusty red visitors' book, which he placed on the reception desk. 'What name would she have booked under sir?'

Daniel instantly realised that he would have to concoct a reason for Lizzie using a name other than his own, so quickly came up with a little white lie which he thought sounded feasible. 'Well this might sound a little odd, but it could have been Elizabeth Cameron. You see, although we have been married for some time, she occasionally signs documents in her maiden name in error. On the other hand she may have signed in under the name of Lorimer.'

The manager ignored the urge to laugh at the somewhat absurd position of his guest. He assumed that Mr Lorimer was checking whether his wife had stayed here with someone other than himself. Nonetheless, his absolute professionalism dictated his response. 'Why yes, of course, sir, an easy mistake to make.' He ran his finger down the list of clients booked in for the month of September 1841 and was surprised to see the entry of a single guest, Elizabeth

Cameron, followed by a limited address of London, England. The manager was clearly disappointed that his deduction had been incorrect, but he graciously pointed it out to Daniel. 'Anyway, sir, looks like this could be the one. The lady obviously forgot her married name as you thought, as she is booked under Cameron. There isn't an entry under the name of Lorimer for that month and it was just for the one night.'

Daniel was hardly able to contain his excitement, but gratefully thanked the manager, before walking purposefully towards the lounge. However, Mr Johnson called after him and in a low voice reminded him of the reason he wished to check the entry. 'Excuse me sir, your wife occupied Room 32, which is a double room on the first floor. I will ascertain if it is available, if it is still of interest.'

Daniel realised his error and turned to face the manager. 'Why yes, of course, how silly of me. Is it available?'

The manager checked the bookings and smiled at Daniel. 'Actually sir, you are in luck. Would you like me to have your baggage transferred for you?' The manager smugly continued without waiting for Daniel's reply. 'Would it be convenient for you to move after dinner this evening?'

'Yes, thank you that will be splendid.' He felt foolish that in his excitement he had forgotten the reason for his request and consequently scuttled swiftly away to the lounge area.

Lizzie eyed Daniel expectantly. 'Were you successful?'

Daniel grinned. 'Yes Lizzie, you did stay here. Your name was in the visitors' book. I managed to persuade the manager to allow me to see the entry, on the pretext that, if possible, we would like to have the same room. It transpires the room is vacant, so I said we would take it. We won't disturb Rosie, so Georgina and I will take the room. You could come up and have a look around. Is that okay with you Georgina?'

'Fine Daniel, that's no problem at all, we could go after dinner, as I expect they will want to check that it is ready to be occupied before our bags are moved.'

When dinner finished, the three went to find the room on

the first floor. Lizzie lead the way, stopping at the large double height window at the end of the corridor. She gazed out transfixed at the stars which were just beginning to appear. Georgina and Daniel, observed her, anxiously aware that another episode might occur. Lizzie felt their presence as they approached and turned to them. 'Oh sorry you two, I was looking up at the stars. Don't they look beautiful? For a fleeting moment I was back in the past standing at this window with someone. It was brief and passed as quickly as it came, but don't worry I feel all right now. I guess I might well have stood at the window if the room I occupied was just along the corridor. Come on, let's take a look inside Room 32.'

Lizzie entered the room first, which immediately seemed familiar. 'Why yes, I do think there is a connection. The bed's in the centre, as I imagined and the small table and chair are by the window which I think looks out over the front of the hotel.'

Daniel felt it might help if she spent an hour or so in the room alone. Then a better idea began to formulate in his mind, but first he must ask Georgina. 'Would you mind awfully Georgina if we shared a room with Rosie on the floor below, so that Lizzie can sleep here? I think the more time she spends in the room, the greater the chance of her remembering something. It is sometimes an insignificant event which sparks off a memory.'

'I don't mind if Lizzie doesn't mind, so long as you think Rosie won't be upset if you aren't there when she wakes. What do you say Lizzie?'

'Well yes, I am sure Rosie will be fine. She has stayed overnight with friends in Nottingham many times. So long as she knows who she's with, it wouldn't be a problem—' Lizzie was interrupted as the porter deposited the cases.

Daniel grinned and the porter departed, unaware of the change of plan. 'Don't worry, I will take the cases back to your room Lizzie and bring your case up here. It's been quite a night, but I am hopeful that we can sort this out soon.'

'I hope so too Daniel. Goodnight Georgina and thank you.'

'Goodnight Lizzie, I do hope you can remember something that will help you. We'll see you at breakfast and don't worry about Rosie, I can see to her and Victoria.'

After Daniel dropped off Lizzie's suitcase and bade her goodnight, Lizzie sat at the table watching the guests arrive at the hotel. Their cheerful conversations and laughter could be heard, spiralling up into her open window. She sat there until around midnight when the last coaches, carrying the late night revellers pulled up outside the entrance. The occupant of one particular cab caught her eye. A tall, single, well-dressed gentleman in a top hat and dark suit, instantly recalled a scene familiar to her. He alighted from the coach and looked up as he strode towards the entrance, aware that someone was leaning out of the window above. He smiled at what he perceived to be a very attractive woman looking at him. He tipped his hat to Lizzie, who was obviously unaware that she had been leaning out to get a better look, until he disappeared into the foyer. She withdrew swiftly behind the dark red velvet curtains, embarrassed at such a foolish and stupid action. She blushed to think what he imagined she was doing.

Lizzie lay awake for some time, while she ruminated on the day's events and the several curious episodes that had occurred. The vague, but sometimes disturbing visions, gave her hope that her memory was at last returning, but how she wished that they were clearer. There was the somewhat ethereal presence of another person, indicated by the three episodes at the hotel. The strong vibe at the restaurant entrance, someone on the landing near the window and now, the tall gentleman alighting from his cab. Had she arranged to meet someone in this hotel? Was there a connection with Rosalie? Suddenly, a startling thought came to her, could it have been Rosalie's father? So many questions required an answer but eventually, totally drained and exhausted, she drifted into a deep sleep.

The early morning hustle and bustle from the street below permeated up to the open window of Room 32. Lizzie Cameron still fast asleep, awoke suddenly. For a few seconds she was back in 1841 and chastised herself out loud for having overslept. 'My goodness, what is the time? Lizzie Cameron you lazy bones.' She looked at her bedside clock, and clambered out of bed, dressing hastily. 'Oh nooooo, it's half past eight. I have to be somewhere.' Her panic was interrupted by a knock at the door. Someone was whispering her name.

'Lizzie, Lizzie, are you awake, it's Daniel. We've all slept in. Georgina has dressed Rosie and organised Victoria's sitter. When you are ready, come down to the restaurant. I will order some coffee and fruit juice...Lizzie can you hear me?'

Lizzie was momentarily totally bemused and detachedly repeated the names she had heard through the closed door - 'Daniel, Georgina, Victoria and Rosie.' Then she remembered and collected herself before responding. 'Oh yes Daniel, I am almost ready. I will see you there.'

'Okay, Lizzie, see you shortly.'

Lizzie rushed round and quickly applied some rouge to her face before brushing her hair. There wasn't time to contemplate this latest recollection: that of rising late, after hearing people chattering in the street below. The moment had been so fleeting and misty that she almost dismissed it out of hand. Her only thought now was to hasten down to breakfast and join the others.

They were seated at a table for four near the entrance. Rosalie waved to her mother. 'Hello mam, it's lovely here, lots of toast and jam and eggs and bacon. Are you going to sit next to me?'

Lizzie greeted them and seated herself near Rosalie.

Daniel informed Lizzie. 'Our breakfast has only just arrived Lizzie, so I took the liberty of ordering you salmon with a lightly poached egg because I know you enjoyed that the other morning and some fruit. The waitress will bring fresh coffee.'

'Thanks Daniel, sorry I overslept.'

'Don't worry Lizzie we overslept as well. Rosie was up with the larks and woke us, but Victoria slept right through the night for the first time, so we can't complain.'

The salmon and fresh coffee was served and silence rained while everyone enjoyed their breakfast. Rosalie re-started the conversation as she wanted to know what they would be doing that day. 'Mam, are we going to the seaside agen?'

'I'm afraid not Rosie, not today, but we will go before we return to Nottingham,' said Lizzie positively.

'When are we going back to Nottingham?' queried Rosalie.

Lizzie was surprised that Rosalie had asked that particular question, because she believed her daughter was enjoying their holiday. 'Not yet Rosie, we will be staying a while longer. Is that all right with you?'

'Oh, yes mam, I really like it here. I miss Jimmy, of course, but we are doing some really exciting things and I will be able to tell him about it when I get back.'

'Good Rosie, I am pleased,' Lizzie smiled and addressed Daniel. 'What ideas have you for today Daniel? Are we going back to Manchester or do you have something else in mind?'

Daniel took a sip of coffee before replying. 'I do have an idea Lizzie. I thought we should go to the station to ascertain if records exist of train times to Manchester in 1841 and...and this is a long shot, see if the ticket officer can remember you. Georgina, Rosie and Victoria can ride an open top carriage around Liverpool and take in St John's Gardens. Would that be something you would like to do Georgina, while Lizzie and I visit the station?'

'That's fine with me Daniel and I am sure Rosie would enjoy riding along in an open coach. You will feel like royalty Rosie, just like a queen.'

Rosalie's eyes opened wide at the mention of the word 'queen'. 'Do you mean I will be the queen today? Me mam told me I could never become a queen because she wasn't one.'

All three adults hid a smile before Georgina attempted an explanation. 'Well Rosie, you probably won't become <u>the</u>

queen, but I meant you would feel like a queen riding along in a carriage. It's what she does on special occasions. So you will feel really special.'

'Will I, well that sounds very nice. Should I wear my best frock and cape mam?'

'That would be a good idea Rosie.'

⁂

Lizzie and Daniel arrived at the train station booking office to find a youngish gentleman issuing tickets and giving out information. They queued for several minutes, before their turn finally came. 'Do you have a time table for the trains to Manchester and how often are they delayed?'

The man bent his head forward and surveyed Daniel over his half rimmed glasses. 'Here we are, this is the daily timetable for trains to Manchester. They run fairly frequently from Monday to Saturday, with a reduced service on a Sunday. When do you want to travel?'

'Well, we aren't sure yet. In fact, we aren't travelling back to Manchester until later this evening.'

The ticket officer raised his eyebrows and tutted under his breath. 'Look sir, why not come back when you know. It helps to have an idea of the time you wish to travel. In answer to your second question, we don't have too many breakdowns these days. The trains are fairly reliable sir. Will that be all? I don't wish to be disrespectful, but the queue is building up and passengers don't have much patience, especially if they are running late for their train.'

Daniel cast an exasperated look at Lizzie. He considered that the officer wasn't too helpful, but he wasn't about to give up. 'I wondered if you might be able to help us with a problem we have, although we don't want to keep people waiting.'

The man's eyebrows rose again as he responded. 'Look sir, is it a problem with the trains, your ticket, departure and arrival times, or something else?'

Daniel felt desperate, but realised he needed to get this man on his side, so made a suggestion which would allow the officer to give them more of his time. 'Look I can see that you are really busy at the moment, would it be in order for us to return later when you don't have a queue? We really do need your help.'

The officer began shaking his head in a negative manner, when Lizzie intervened, thinking that a woman's touch might be needed. 'You see sir, I travelled from this station several years ago and I was hoping you might remember me. I was travelling alone with my baby daughter?'

The officer was now rapidly losing patience and anxious to reduce the queue building up behind them. 'I'm sorry madam, but I have only been in this job for three years, so if it was before that time, then no, I wouldn't remember you. Hundreds of passengers pass through this station every year, so, begging your pardon, but it really isn't likely that I would remember one person amongst all those is it?'

Lizzie felt dejected. 'No, I suppose not, but can we come back later anyway, in case there is anything else we might need to ask you?'

'Yes madam, please do that. I finish my shift at noon today, after that Will Barker takes over. He's been doing this job for thirty years, so you may have more luck with him. I am sorry I cannot help you further.' With this dismissive comment, he looked beyond Lizzie to the person standing immediately behind...'Next please.'

Lizzie and Daniel moved down the platform, before commenting on the man's attitude. 'He wasn't very helpful was he Lizzie? I suppose it's a thankless task, answering numerous questions on departures, arrivals and problems with tickets. Do you think it is worth coming back later to see Will...what was his name?'

Lizzie smiled weakly. 'Will Barker. I think we should Daniel, I don't hold out much hope, but we cannot leave any stone unturned.'

'All right Lizzie. Let's find somewhere to buy a drink before we return at twelve.'

༺༻

The queues had diminished when they returned to the booking office. This time the ticket officer was a much older man with white hair and a ruddy complexion. Daniel posed the same question he asked his colleague earlier and this time received a much friendlier response. 'Well now let me see. I never forget a pretty face, so come closer missy and let me have a good look at you.'

Lizzie moved forward and removed her hat; her dark brown curls tumbled down around her shoulders.

The man looked intently at her face and stroked his chin meditatively. 'September five years ago you say? That would make it 1841?'

Lizzie nodded and looked so anxious that Will Barker felt he should do all he could to help her. He adjusted his glasses and peered closer. 'You do look a bit familiar. I'll tell you what, the ledger clerk, Samuel Booker, is a friend of mine. I could ask him to look back on the pre-bookings ledger and see what we can come up with. Now you say your name is Elizabeth Cameron? I'll just write that down. Sam drops by around 1 p.m. so I could have a word with him then, although I doubt he would be able to get back to me before 5.30 p.m. after his shift. Can you come back?'

'Can we Daniel, would that fit in with your plans?'

'Yes Lizzie, of course, there is a train that departs for Manchester at 6.30 p.m., so that will give us plenty of time.'

Lizzie smiled disarmingly at Will as they walked away from the office.

He had a feeling as he watched her go that he had indeed met with this young woman before and her smile was intriguing. He was hopeful that Sam would be able to provide some good news. Somewhat significantly, he remembered that it wasn't the first time someone had enquired after the young woman.

They returned to the station at 5.40 p.m. Georgina, Victoria and Rosalie seated themselves in the waiting room café and Lizzie and Daniel proceeded to the booking office where a gentleman and a young couple waited for tickets. It wasn't long before they faced Will Barker at the ticket office window. He was all smiles as he welcomed Lizzie. 'I said I never forgot a pretty face. I was a little unsure, but after I inspected the ledger, I realised I was on duty in the first class booking hall on the day your name appears. See here.' Will turned the ledger around for Lizzie and Daniel to view the entry. 'Look, here we are...*Name: Elizabeth Cameron. Date of travel: Thursday 30th September 1841. Booking date: Friday, 17 September 1841.* I knew I recognised you. It all came back to me when I saw the alteration to the train time in my own handwriting. It's something we're not supposed to do you know, re-issue pre-booked tickets. If a passenger misses a train or doesn't want to travel on the pre-booked date, then they have to purchase a new ticket. However, because it was only a re-issue for the same day, I made an exception. The train you travelled on would have left the station at 3 p.m. I know that because, 'a' I always come on duty at noon, so you couldn't have travelled in the morning and, 'b' there is a brief underlined note down the margin here - *2 p.m. train delayed until 3 p.m. due to a points failure*. Is this information any use to you?'

Lizzie excitedly expressed her gratitude. 'Why yes, yes it is. Thank you so much for all your trouble.'

Daniel leaned forward. 'Just one more thing. Was the name of the person who made the booking listed anywhere?'

Will made a grimace. 'I'm afraid not sir, only the passenger's name is recorded. I have, however, been giving this a lot of thought since you enquired earlier and I do recall that someone else visited the booking office about a fortnight later and asked if I had seen a young woman with a baby. It is embedded in my memory for several reasons. He was a most insistent gentleman and offered me a reward for the information. He told me he was a friend of a relative of hers and that they were anxious to trace her movements. I confirmed that she, or you, Mrs Cameron, had indeed travelled from this station. Unfortunately, I don't remember anything about him, only that he gave me five pounds for my trouble, which was an awful lot of money for such a meagre amount of information and the reason it stuck in my memory,' Will chuckled. 'Me and the wife were able to holiday in Blackpool for a week and still have change.'

'Well, thanks a lot Will. You have been very helpful. Now we will be able to piece together the journey that Mrs Cameron made on that day, which is very important. Cheerio and thanks again.' Daniel tipped his hat to Will and gave him another generous tip for his trouble.

Lizzie echoed Daniel's appreciation. 'Yes Will, thank you so much,'

'Anytime Mrs Cameron, anytime,' said Will, watching with satisfaction as they walked away.

Daniel beamed at Lizzie, pleased with the information they had elicited. 'Well Lizzie, it seems you definitely travelled to Manchester on the 3 p.m. train. That fits in with missing the Royal Mail coach and maybe why you travelled with the mysterious Jack Garrett. What is also very interesting is the fact that another concerned person enquired whether you did indeed make that journey. So intensely interested that they were prepared to pay a King's ransom to have that fact confirmed. I really feel we are getting somewhere Lizzie don't you?'

Lizzie smiled enthusiastically. 'Yes definitely, it all seems to be fitting together. I stayed at the Adelphi and then, for whatever reason, I missed the earlier train and did not travel until 3 p.m. that afternoon. Oh Daniel this really is a breakthrough. What do you think we should do next?'

Daniel moved his hand over his brow, as he thought of the best way forward. 'Well, the logical thing is to go back to

Nottingham and ask around about this Jack Garrett, but you might want to wait until after you have met with Robert. I should receive his reply to my letter in a few days.'

Lizzie agreed. 'Yes I am anxious to meet Robert and it would be better to seize the opportunity while I am staying here. He may be able to shed some light on the days leading up to my disappearance.'

Daniel decided that Lizzie was probably ready to learn more about her life in Glasgow. He didn't want to bombard her with too much too soon, but he felt, the time was right. 'Tonight after supper Lizzie, when Rosie is settled in bed, I will tell you more of what I know about your life at Low Wood Hall where you were senior maid and also our close relationship, but it's up to you how much you want to hear.'

Lizzie wanted to hear all about the important incidents of her past life, including their story. She could cope with the truth. 'I would like that Daniel, but when the time comes to return to Nottingham to seek out information on Jack Garrett, would you would accompany me, or is that asking too much?'

'Well, I'll have to speak to Georgina and make arrangements for my business to be attended to while I am away, but from my perspective, it is something I would like to do. We have started on this journey together and it would seem only right that we finish it together.'

Lizzie seemed pensive. 'I don't want to cause any friction between you and Georgina. That is not my intention at all. However, I do wonder if she will object to you going away again, especially with someone who was, apparently, very close to you in the past.'

Daniel pondered a while, knowing he must be true to himself. 'Remember what I said to you when we started this venture, Georgina trusts me implicitly and, whatever existed between us in the past, we both know that's where it must stay...in the past. If you can cope with that, then so can I.'

'I agree entirely Daniel,' she smiled hesitantly and paused before continuing. 'I have no intention of whisking you away to Nottingham to seduce you. I know that you will be faithful to Georgina and I would not expect any less of you.'

'Okay, now we have got that out of the way, it is agreed, provided there aren't any objections from Georgina.'

After supper, Georgina, Daniel and Lizzie retired to the sitting room where coffee and biscuits were served from a low table in the centre of the room. Georgina was interested to know more of what they had discovered during the day's venture and both were keen to update her with the latest news. When they ended their story, Georgina gave her opinion. 'That's great news Lizzie, you must go back to Nottingham to see if you can discover more about the driver, Jack Garrett,' she paused. 'I hope you have already offered to escort Lizzie in this latest quest Daniel, because a lone woman would not be able to move in the right circles to elicit information on the circumstances surrounding the fate of this unfortunate man. I imagine enquiries may have to be made in some less than salubrious establishments for that kind of information.'

Daniel raised his eyebrows and thought how lucky he was to have such an understanding wife. 'Thank you Georgina, I had considered accompanying Lizzie, but not without gaining your approval first.'

Georgina looked surprised. 'Daniel, I cannot think of any reason why I should object, except that I will miss you. It is an honourable mission that you will be undertaking and it might be pivotal in solving the mystery of Lizzie's disappearance.'

Lizzie was somewhat surprised at Georgina's unconditional support of her husband, but eternally grateful that she would be given the opportunity to discover what could turn out to be the ultimate clue to her disappearance. Hopefully, it would reveal the name of Rosalie's father.

Georgina quietly listened to Daniel relate the story of Lizzie's role at Low Wood Hall, but it didn't reveal any clue to her disappearance. She felt the dialogue was between Lizzie and Daniel, although both had been at pains to include her in the discussion. Understandably, Georgina was quite tired, due to the lateness of the hour and the fact that she knew she would be woken around 4 o'clock when Victoria usually required a feed. Regrettably, she made her excuses and retired, slightly unsure as to her real motives. Did she want Daniel to join her? or, was she genuinely tired and just needed to sleep? It didn't matter either way, because Daniel intended to complete the story of Lizzie's life in Glasgow.

'I'll just prepare a fresh pot of coffee to keep us awake Lizzie.' Daniel announced.

Lizzie wasn't sure she could drink any more coffee, as her senses were already heightened by the day's events and fascinating history of her time with Daniel. 'Not for me Daniel, but I wouldn't mind a cup of cocoa, as I think I need to wind down.'

'Actually, that's a good idea, I'll join you,' he nodded in agreement.

Daniel disappeared to make the cocoa and returned shortly afterwards with two large mugs and another plate of biscuits. 'Just in case you feel peckish,' he smiled as he placed the drinks and biscuits on the table.

Lizzie took a sip from the mug and relaxed in the comfortable chair. She felt very happy with the progress made so far.

He resumed his theme where he had left off about the different people at Low Wood and her relationship with them.

Lizzie queried his assessment of the family for whom she worked as a maid. 'So David didn't like me for some reason, but Kate and I were quite close?'

Daniel explained his reasoning. 'Well from what you told me, he didn't really have an opinion either way. I would say, rather than dislike, he was indifferent. Kate, however, was a completely different kettle of fish. I would say you were very close to her. You used to go into town together and meet up with a group of young men from the farming fraternity, which included me. We would sit and have a drink outside the Exchange. It wasn't seemly for young women to be seen anywhere near a drinking place, but that didn't stop Kate, she flouted the rules wherever she went and had no time for the 'class' thing.'

Lizzie smiled. 'She sounds a lot of fun and did I go along with all this?'

Daniel grinned. 'Not exactly Lizzie, she always wanted you to take a few risks and let your hair down, but I think you struggled with that concept. She was a bit flirty and all the lads fancied her, except me of course.' He smiled across at Lizzie with a look that spoke volumes. 'I only had eyes for you.'

Slightly embarrassed by this revelation, she purposely kept the conversation light. 'Flatterer! No seriously, surely, if we had been seen together, the daughter of my employer and his servant cavorting with a group of farmers, my position would have become untenable and I would have been dismissed?'

Daniel shook his head. 'No, no, Kate wouldn't have allowed that. She was very protective. You told me that if ever the situation arose, she would say she had forced you to accompany her. Kate had all eventualities covered. Any arrangement that might be frowned upon was always planned meticulously; no one would get one over Kate, she had a habit of coming up roses no matter what.'

Lizzie reflected on her relationship with her employers. 'Did Georgina and Howard like me, or don't you know anything of my relationship with them?'

'Everybody liked you Lizzie; you were warm, friendly and hard working. You could keep a secret and you were very loyal to your employers, working colleagues and, most of all, to your friends.'

Lizzie pondered on the last exposition. If it were true, why had she left without word to anyone, it didn't make any sense. 'So here I am, this warm, friendly, loyal person, who ups and leaves without a word. Why on earth would I do that?'

'Well you've hit the nail on the head Lizzie, you wouldn't. There has to be more to your disappearance. Perhaps you intended to contact us when you arrived at your destination. Perhaps you were protecting someone by acting in the manner you did. One thing is for sure, you would not have left without a word to anyone. It must have been to help someone else, but why? That's the intriguing question.'

Lizzie remained pensive while she drank the last of her cocoa. 'What happened to the Hemmingways'? Are they still at Low Wood? If they are, perhaps I should pay them a visit.'

Daniel shrugged. 'Mmmm, I thought of that, but, shortly after you disappeared, the family moved somewhere down south. Apparently, there was a scandal of sorts that was quickly papered over. They moved lock, stock and barrel, before any of it was made public. In fact, the house wasn't sold until last year, it remained boarded up until the new owners moved in.'

Lizzie tutted, she was disappointed not to have the opportunity of speaking to them. 'That's a shame, because they might know the reason why I left in such mysterious circumstances. What were their immediate thoughts?'

Daniel reflected. 'Well, on the day you failed to turn up for your duties, I came over to see you and cook asked me if I knew where you were. She said that Mrs Hemingway asked her, but the last time cook saw you was on Monday before your half day off. None of the other servants had seen or heard anything from you either.'

Lizzie frowned. 'What about Kate Hemmingway, did you speak to her?'

'No actually, she hadn't been at Low Wood for a few months prior to your disappearance; apparently holidaying with an aunt, so she wouldn't have known your whereabouts or even that you had left. In fact, I hadn't spoken to her since before she went on holiday. She never returned to Low Wood as far as I am aware; then, as I said, shortly after that, the whole family moved away.'

Lizzie shrugged. 'Then I doubt whether I would get much information from a visit to Low Wood?'

'No Lizzie, I don't think so, especially as there are new owners.'

'Oh well Daniel, I don't feel downhearted. In fact, I am very happy with what we have achieved. I think I will retire now, as it has been a very busy day for us both.'

'Good idea Lizzie. I'll see you at breakfast tomorrow. Goodnight, sleep well.'

'Goodnight Daniel.'

Daniel quietly entered his bedroom, but the lights were off and Georgina was fast asleep. He had mixed feelings as he climbed into bed beside his wife. What would the future hold for Lizzie and would this impact on his own life?

Lizzie also lay awake, reflecting once more on what might have been.

CHAPTER NINE

Revelations

A week later a letter arrived addressed to Daniel. He knew at once who had sent it and in excited anticipation rushed to the breakfast room to find Lizzie. She was helping herself to some fresh fruit from a dish on the buffet table and her eyes lit up immediately as she saw the letter. 'Is it from Robert?' she asked expectantly.

'I think so Lizzie, go on, open it.'

'It's addressed to you Daniel, so I think you should have the honour.'

Daniel sliced through the envelope with a silver letter opener and extracted the carefully folded, single paper sheet. He read the contents out loud.

Dear Daniel, Georgina, Lizzie, Victoria and Rosie

I was so pleased to receive your telegraph and letter Daniel, informing me that you had found Lizzie and that we have another addition to the family. I was very surprised, but relieved to know Lizzie is alive and well. I cannot wait to be reunited with her again, but unfortunately, I have a business trip arranged that I am unable to cancel. Amy and I will travel to Glasgow on Saturday 23rd October. She and our daughter Harriett are staying with her parents until 21st December when they return for Christmas. I return a week earlier on Tuesday 14th December, so if it is convenient, I would love to come down to Ardwick on Friday the 17th. I should arrive around 10 a.m., but I have to leave early on Sunday morning. I would love you all to come to us for Christmas for a real family get together. Please let me know as soon as you are able; a short telegraph confirmation would be fine, as our coach leaves at 3 p.m. this Saturday.

Please give all my love to Lizzie and young Rosie. Tell her I'm ecstatic about seeing her again and meeting my niece.

With kindest regards,

Robert Cameron

Lizzie's smile became broader as the contents of the letter sunk in. In just a few weeks, she would be reunited with her brother. 'Oh Daniel, that's really good news. I am disappointed that I will have to wait several weeks, but it does give me an opportunity to go down to Nottingham in late November. I will ask Rosie if she would like to stay with Gladys Leach and Annie for a few days, so that she can see Jimmy and her other friends before Christmas.'

'Well, I will discuss it with Georgina, although I cannot find a reason not to go. I must resume my factory duties next week, but will be able to take a week off from the last Sunday in November...the 28th. We could travel that morning and stay in Nottingham for a few days and return on Wednesday 1st December. That would give us Monday, Tuesday and a good part of Wednesday to investigate Jack Garrett.'

Lizzie responded eagerly. 'I'd like that very much Daniel and thank you for helping me see this mission through.'

On the morning of their departure, Daniel packed a small suitcase with enough clothes to last the few days he would be spending in Nottingham, when Georgina entered the bedroom. 'Can I help you with that Daniel? There are four freshly laundered collars and several clean shirts hanging up in the tallboy and a couple of jumpers in the chest of drawers by the bed. It looks as if the weather might remain dry for the next week, so you won't need to pack any rainwear.'

'Thanks Georgina. We'll have to leave at mid-day to catch the Royal Mail Coach from Manchester at 4 p.m., so we'll grab a bite to eat at the York hotel.'

Georgina moved across the room and placed her hand on Daniel's arm, giving it a gentle squeeze. 'Please don't take any unnecessary risks Daniel. I know you might have to go into some undesirable places in your quest for information on this Jack Garrett, so please take care.'

'Don't worry Georgina, I can look after myself and won't be seeking trouble. We'll be back before you know it.'

After kissing her tenderly on the mouth, he held her at arm's length so that he could keep her image in his mind. 'Georgina, I'll really miss you and Victoria,' he said with sincerity.

'We'll really miss you too. Have a good journey and come back safe to me.'

'I'll definitely do that my love. Is Lizzie ready to go?'

'Nearly Daniel, she is tending to Rosie's needs. I know her own case is packed, so she will be ready to go quite soon. I asked cook to bake some fairy cakes with the silver balls for Rosie to give to her friend Jimmy. They are in a separate container on the hall table, so don't forget to take them.'

Daniel placed his hands on his wife's waist and kissed her lightly on the cheek. 'Really Georgina, you never forget anything. I am so lucky to have you as my wife. I'll just finish packing and then ask James to bring the trap round to the front.'

They arrived in Manchester just after 1.30 p.m. and lunched at the York before boarding the Royal Mail Coach to Nottingham. The coach reached its destination on time at 9 p.m. Daniel and Lizzie dropped Rosalie off at Gladys Leach's, before taking a cab to The George Hotel on George Street. Lizzie considered that she would stay in an hotel, rather than her own home in the Court. Rosalie and Gladys would distract her and she really needed a clear head to concentrate on the task in hand.

Daniel was anxious for Lizzie to approve his choice of accommodation. 'Do you like the hotel Lizzie? I have booked two single rooms with a bathroom on the same floor. The hotel is fairly central, so I can easily make my way around the local inns.'

The rooms of the hotel were comfortable and the facilities excellent. Lizzie was really pleased with her room, which was right next door to the bathroom.

They met later in the coffee lounge to discuss their movements over the next few days. Daniel had devised a plan, which he outlined to Lizzie. 'I thought I would visit several establishments across the town and gain as much information on Jack Garrett as I can. Would you like me to escort you to the Marsh, so that you can visit your friends Lizzie? or would you rather browse around the shops?'

Lizzie realised she couldn't return to Nottingham without visiting Clara and Mabel, so told Daniel she would take a cab. 'I will visit Clara and Mabel then walk back into the town centre. I assume you will not allow me to accompany you when you visit the inns?'

Daniel was resolute. He alone should enquire about the fate of Jack Garrett. 'No Lizzie, it would be better if I went by myself. We can meet up later at that cosy tearoom in the Market place.'

The following morning Daniel hailed a cab, which dropped Lizzie off in Narrow Marsh. She walked the short distance to Clara Milligan's house in Knotted Alley and knocked lightly on her door. Clara was singing as she went about her chores, but put down her scrubbing brush when she heard the knock. She heaved herself up from the kneeling position adopted to scrub the kitchen floor and shouted to the visitor. 'Oad on me duck, am coming. Just gi me a minit while a git me oad body to its upright position.'

She achieved her goal and opened the door, astonished to find Lizzie standing on the doorstep. She stepped to one side and welcomed her in to the warm kitchen. 'Well now, this is a supprise, a want expectin yer back just yet. Come on in me duck.'

Lizzie kissed Clara lightly on the cheek and went through to the kitchen. 'I hope I am not disturbing you Clara, but I couldn't come back to Nottingham without looking you up for a cup of tea and a natter.'

'Ooer, yer not disturbin me, me duck. Sit yersen dahn at the table and I'll meck us a brew.'

'That will be very welcome Clara. You've been busy scrubbing the floor I see and now I have just walked right across it.'

Clara shook her head. 'Don't worry me duck, but if it ud bin our Arthur or our David we tha muddy boots, there'd 'ave bin 'ell to pay. Nah then Lizzie wot yer bin up ta?'

'Well Clara, so much has happened which has been very exciting. Daniel Lorimer brought me down here for a few days to try and clear up part of the mystery surrounding my amnesia, although I've learnt quite a bit about my journey already.'

Clara was waiting impatiently for the kettle to boil, but could hardly contain herself in anticipation of a good story. 'Come on then me duck, don't keep me in suspense. Yer not related to royalty or summat like that are yer?'

Lizzie smiled to herself as she recollected Rosalie's wish to be the Queen of England and answered brightly. 'Nothing as grand as that Clara, but quite interesting all the same.'

Lizzie retold her story as it had unfolded so far, except for the details of her intimate relationship with Daniel. '...So you see Clara, I only came to Nottingham because I missed the Royal Mail Coach in Manchester. Daniel is combing the local inns this morning to see what he can discover about Jack Garrett.'

'Well, me duck, I can't believe it. Wahrra piece of luck yer 'ad finding aht abaht the poor unfortunate fella. Let's 'ope there's more information ta follow.'

'Well Clara, I am quite hopeful and so is Daniel.'

Clara placed two mugs of tea on the table and fetched some home made biscuits from the cupboard. ''ere ya are me duck, get that dahn yer. It's proppa coad aht there today. I'll put another shovelful of coal on the fire, the draught don't 'arf blow through that door, straight up me skirt. Good job 'ave got me warm drawers on. Most of 'em rahnd 'ere 'ave to meck the coal stretch aht a lot longer these days, after...yer know, what 'appened ta Sam Armstrong. Mind, thanks ta yersen, we've got plenty o' coal ta last the whole winta and this Christmas 'ull be a good en. 'Ave bought the family some treats wi some of the money, but, like yer said, kept some saved fer a rainy day. There's a little package fer yo and Rosie on the dresser. It's not much, but it comes wi all our love me duck. There's still a lot of folks ull be 'ard pushed to scrape up a decent Christmas, but if yer've the love of yer family, it don't matter as much does it?'

Lizzie reflected on her rise out of the poorer parts of the Marsh to Marsden Court and realised just how hard the residents here struggled to make ends meet. 'You shouldn't have bought me anything Clara, but whatever it is, you can be sure I will treasure it. You are right of course, if you have the love of your family, it's worth a million Christmas presents. I'll always be grateful to you, as well as Arthur and David and Mabel and Sam. Everyone wrapped Rosie and me up with so much love that our time spent here was richer for it. I was sad to leave you, but I knew it would be better all round when I moved in with Mabel. I know Mabel and Sam were disappointed when I left them too, but I had to think of Rosie's upbringing Clara and it was right for me to leave. They needed time together to reclaim their relationship and I intend visiting them later to see how they are.'

'Eye me duck, they'd be pleased as punch to see yer. An' a understood abaht yer moving to Marsden Court an' so did Mabel and Sam. We wuz all well pleased fa ya.'

'Anyway Clara, how is everyone?' asked Lizzie with interest.

Clara was happy to report that all the family were well and thriving. 'We can't complain me duck. As a said, the money yer gen us 'as really bin a real 'elp. Av bin able to stock up the cupboards fa the winter and, like a said, there's a cellar full o' coal,' Clara looked sheepish as she continued...'which a 'ave the receipt fer! ta see us through. As ya know, our David gorra job in a lace facktreh, but he still guz dahn the Mechanics to improve 'is mind. Sez he won't be stuck in a dead end job. Ya know 'e started as an apprentice, well, last week 'e got promoshun ta being a supervisor or summat like that. Anyrode, he oversees the gels on the machines. In fact it's where he met his gel friend, Beryl Turton. She seems keen as mustard on him; round here every verse end she is. Yer know Lizzie, a thought at one time he wah sweet on yo, but then turns aht 'e thought on yer as a sister, just like Tillie and Alice. Our Tillie's at wock and Alice is ovver at Nora's. Arthur's on his shift dahn at the canal today, so 'e won't be back 'til tanight. They'll all be disappointed ta 'ave missed yer me duck.'

'Well Clara, I am disappointed too. Please give them all my love and tell David I am really pleased he has a nice girl, he deserves someone special.'

Lizzie kept Clara company for an hour or so, then made to leave for Mabel Armstrong's house in Foundry Yard. 'I'll get off now Clara, so that I can spend some time with Mabel, before meeting Daniel for lunch in the Market Place.' She hugged Clara as she said goodbye. 'Cheerio Clara and take care of yourself. Don't forget to give my love to everyone and hopefully I will see you again before Christmas, which should be a good one all round.'

'I yer could be right me duck. Tarrar fer now. Yo teck care yersen and come back and see us soon.'

Lizzie was left with mixed emotions as she walked the short distance to Foundry Yard.

Daniel strode purposefully into the Golden Fleece on Drury Hill, which solicited several inquisitive stares from the locals as he approached the bar. The landlord absently took a pint jar from the shelf, but immediately changed his mind. He decided from the look of this customer that he was unmistakably middle class, so replaced the beer glass with a whisky glass instead. He readied himself to pour a double measure of whisky then looked at Daniel to confirm the order. 'Double scotch is it sir?'

Shaking his head, Daniel surprisingly interrupted with a request for a half pint. His 'modus operandi' allowed for visits to several of these establishments, consequently he knew he would be distinctly worse for wear after several double scotches. 'No thanks landlord, I'll just have a half pint.'

Somewhat annoyed with himself that his assumption was incorrect, the landlord placed the half pint of beer on the bar, while the locals continued to stare at the stranger in their midst. They wondered why this well-to-do gentleman would visit their lowly tavern. The landlord, curious, struck up a conversation. 'Stranger in these parts are ya?'

Daniel, eager to get the landlord on his side, answered in a friendly voice. 'Yes, I am actually. Just down for the weekend on business from Manchester. Thought I'd check out some of the local inns. I've been told the beer is excellent in the Golden Fleece.'

Pleased that Daniel had been complimentary about his beer, Arthur Pendleton continued proudly. 'I well, ya not wrong there, is he Sid?' Arthur grinned as he addressed a middle-aged man playing dominoes at a table in the corner.

Sid looked up from his game and nodded in agreement. 'Best pint in town wi'out a daht.'

Daniel surveyed the clientele surreptitiously and considered that this would be the type of place Jack Garrett would stay on his journey through Nottingham. He then broached his intended subject tentatively with the landlord, but ensured that the regulars picked up on his question. 'I wondered if you know someone by the name of Jack Garrett?' Then guardedly, so that he didn't give too much away. 'I understand he runs a coach through Nottingham on his way to London.'

The landlord stroked his chin as he repeated the name. 'Jack Garrett you say? Can't say as a do. Not many of the coach drivers stay 'ere. Most like to stay closer ta the centre. In't that right Sid?'

Again Sid looked up from his game. 'Aye that's abaht right Arthur. Never 'eard of 'im.'

Daniel looked around to confirm that no one else had heard of him either, all nodded in negative agreement.

Daniel thanked the landlord as he finished his half pint and also tipped him generously, even if the information offered wasn't helpful.

The next inn was the Elephant and Castle on Hounds Gate, where he received a similar reception. However, the barman at The Salutation Inn, situated at the other end of the road had some advice. 'The best place you could ga ta find oat aht about a coach driver is the Loggerheads, top end o' the Marsh. Most of the drivers stop off at Derby, but one or two of 'em kip dahn there fa the night. Run by a woman who don't stand fa no funny business. Runs a tight ship so ta speak...' The landlord laughed and the regulars joined in as he proceeded to explain the joke. '...Funny that! 'cause 'er 'usband's a sailor. In fact he's back 'omm from the sea at the moment and 'e's a right tough nut. Yer don't mess wi 'im, so keep on his good side.'

Daniel thanked the barman and walked the short distance to the Marsh, where the Loggerheads Inn was situated. It looked pleasant enough from the outside, the windows were sparkling clean and the step had been red bricked, but as he entered the bar, the atmosphere changed. The landlord, whom he assumed was the seaman, loomed large and threatening and Daniel wasn't relishing any kind of a conversation with him. He approached him in the friendliest manner possible and gave him a broad smile before addressing him as respectfully as possible. 'Good day sir. I'll have a pint of your best bitter please.' Daniel ordered a pint, as he didn't think someone ordering a half would overly impress this man.

Bill Brown looked Daniel up and down before pouring a pint of best ale into a jar. Bill was thinking that the customer seemed a right toff and that they didn't get many like him round here. He's probably after something, he thought. "Ere ya are then. You'll not gerra a berra pint anywhere in Nottingham.'

Daniel thanked him and wondered how he should approach the subject of Jack Garrett. He was pondering the method of attack, when Bill Brown asked him something himself. 'What brings yo dahn 'ere then? Obvious ya in't from these parts.'

'No, no, I'm not, you're right, but I had some business in this part of the town and was told you pulled a good pint,' Daniel explained, but wished he could just high tail it out of the door.

Bill shrugged. 'Aye well, as a said, yu'll not find better. So is there oat else ya after?'

It was now or never Daniel thought, to spit out what he was really there for, so, clearing his throat, he plucked up the courage to ask the question. 'I was wondering,' he began and cleared his throat again before continuing, 'if you might have heard of Jack Garrett, a coach driver, who I understood might stop off at this inn on his way to London?'

In an instant, the room went inexplicably quiet and you could hear a pin drop. Men stopped their games of dominoes and put their pints down on the tables. Others' gasped as they heard the name Jack Garrett. An atmosphere of sheer disbelief reigned throughout the inn, but no one spoke a word, until Bill, with a thunderous and a considerably raised voice replied. 'Jack Garrett, yes I've heard of him. Who's asking?'

Daniel was feeling very uncomfortable, as it became obvious that everyone in the bar knew Jack Garrett, very well indeed and Bill's menacing tone, indicated that Jack wasn't a friend of his.

The silence of the patrons persisted and all looked expectantly at Daniel, waiting for his reply. He needed to make it clear that Jack Garrett wasn't a friend of his either, so replied. 'I'm Daniel Lorimer and Jack Garrett isn't a friend of mine, but does anyone know anything about the last journey he made from here to Dunstable and if he had a passenger.'

William's face darkened as he shouted to his wife. 'Molly, you there? Some punter is asking about lover boy. Why don't yer come through and tell him what 'appened to the infamous Jack Garrett?'

Faces were agog in the bar as they waited for Molly Brown to appear. When she didn't come through immediately, Bill shouted to her again. Molly was petrified and had instantly frozen at the mention of Jack's name. The worst day of her life came flooding back; at least she thought it was the worst day. She had arrived back in Nottingham to be greeted by Bill, who had unexpectedly returned from his ship. Albert Green and Michael Drake had fallen over themselves to inform the landlady's husband of her shenanigans whilst he had been at sea, although both received a thick lip for their trouble.

Molly had been beaten black and blue by Bill and was within an inch of her life, when the local constabulary interrupted them. They were called by a passer by who had heard screaming coming from behind the top window of the inn. Now, after five years, she had been reminded of it again. Terrified he would start on her later; she stayed where she was and pretended not to hear his calls. Bill, however, was having none of it and once more bellowed loudly, cupping his hands to his mouth so that the sound carried through to the kitchen loud and clear. 'Molly Brown, get yersen in 'ere, afore a come and fetch ya.'

Bill had eventually, but reluctantly forgiven his wife for her misdemeanour and no mention had ever been made of Jack Garrett since that day. Now though, the same vehement anger coursed through his veins, which stood out on his temples and gave him the look of a bull ready to charge.

Molly feared that if she didn't move herself quickly, she would face the wrath of her husband ten fold, so moved like someone possessed into the bar area. She chose her words carefully to minimise the damage and tried to keep her voice calm. 'Why ya mentioning that man's name agen in this house. I thought we'd got past that years' ago. I'm always telling ya, yer the only man fa me Bill Brown and yer knows it.'

Placated somewhat by Molly's clever tactics, Bill Brown calmed himself; it would do him no good creating a scene, especially in front of a stranger who might report him to the police. More to the point, Molly would cut off his rights in the bedroom if he chastised her too much. No, he thought, best go along with helping the stranger and let her answer his questions.

'Yer all right Molly, I'm not mad at yer. This gentleman here is wanting some information about him that's all. 'appen, he'll pay well if ya can tell 'im oat?'

'Right Bill me duck, shall a teck him round the back? We don't want them lot noseying our business do we?'

Bill Brown thought for a moment and considered that there was nothing his wife would tell the man that he hadn't heard already, so grudgingly he agreed. 'All right Molly, but don't teck long abaht it, we'll be getting busy round lunch time.'

Molly opened up the hatch in the bar and guided Daniel to the back of the inn. 'Come through. We've not bin intraduced, but me name's Molly Brown. I expect yu've cottoned on ta that from Bill.'

Daniel wasn't comfortable moving to the other side of the bar, but knew he must try and find out what he could from Molly.

Molly beckoned him to sit at a table where she had been preparing vegetables for the lunchtime stew, popular with her regulars.

She fetched Daniel's beer and closed the door between the kitchen and the bar, before asking him how she could help. Daniel requested that she tell him all she could about Jack Garrett.

Her eyes saddened a little as she began. 'Thiz not much ta tell, but as yu've gathered from Bill, a knew Jack Garrett very well. Despite what yer might hear, he wah a good sort. Treated me really well,' then in a lowered tone, 'berra than that thug through there. But 'ave made me bed and I'll have ta lie in it.'

Daniel sympathised with her position. 'I'm sorry to hear that. Will my being here cause you trouble later?' asked Daniel, who was concerned about her welfare.

'No, no. I cun 'andle 'im mostly. Anyrode, 'e knows where 'is bread's best buttered. Cun't manage this place wi'out me. A look after the whole shebang when he's away at sea.' Again she lowered her voice. 'Ta be 'onest, a sometimes wish he'd drown and never come back.'

Daniel ignored the last statement and pressed on with the vital question. 'Do you know whether Jack Garrett brought a passenger down from Manchester by the name of Elizabeth Cameron?'

Molly went silent for a moment as she thought about how much she should disclose to Daniel. She had looked at that name every morning for nearly four years, engraved on the front of a box, which stood on her dressing table up until earlier this year, when she pawned it. Every time she looked at it she was reminded of Jack, her Jack, but she had to move her life forward and rid herself of all reminders of that fateful day. In an instant, she made up her mind not to tell Daniel about the box, as she did not want him to think badly of her, taking something that wasn't hers. She would, however, tell him everything else she knew. 'Yeh, a believe that wah the name of the passenger Jack brought dahn from Manchester. I remember him telling me that he wah waiting fer a passenger by that name who wah continuing on ta London. A believe she also had a baby with her.'

Daniel disguised his excitement and wanting to know

more, encouraged Molly to continue. 'Do you know why she didn't turn up for the onward journey?'

Molly was hesitant. If the green cloak belonged to this Elizabeth and she had died right there on the towpath, how would she break the news to this man? She spoke guardedly. 'Can a ask why yer want ta know? Are yer a relative of this Elizabeth Cameron?'

Daniel shook his head. 'No, I am not a relative, but I am a good friend. You see we met up again after losing touch with one another five years ago and she is, at this moment, in Nottingham. Let me explain, when she travelled here, probably with Jack Garrett, she suffered some kind of accident that caused her to lose her memory. Right now, she is trying to piece together her journey, so she can make sense of it all.'

Molly inwardly breathed a sigh of relief because Elizabeth apparently wasn't dead, which enabled her to be more forthcoming with her reply. 'A see. Well, a think a might be able ta 'elp piece some on it together. Jack wer waiting in the bar of the Loggerheads fer Mrs Cameron who wer supposed ta meet him at 8 p.m., but she din't turn up. Later, Jack got inta a bit of a disagreement wi two drunks who wah trying ta sell me a cloak they said they fount on the towpath. They said the woman it belonged ta 'ad no further need forrit. Jack thought that woman might be Elizabeth Cameron and he suspected they might 'ave murdered her, although he cun't prove oat. Either way, there wah nothing he could do. He waited until arahnd 9.30 p.m. before deciding that Mrs Cameron wun't be joining him fer the rest on the journey, then he asked me ta ga we him dahn ta London and I agreed.' Molly's face crumpled and she became close to tears as she related the story. 'It wah on the road from Dunstable and the weather wah really bad when we met wi an accident. The horses crashed inta a fallen tree, the coach ovverturned and Jack died in the accident. A wah lucky, a survived. A fount some clothing that had spilled aht from Mrs Cameron's trunk and, as luck would 'ave it, a managed ta gerra lift on a

Royal Mail coach ta Derby. That's it, I don't know oat else.' Dabbing her eyes she reached out and touched Daniel's arm. 'I hope that 'ave bin some help ta ya and am right pleased that Mrs Cameron survived.'

Daniel gave a sigh of relief now that he knew the whole story, apart from the unanswered questions surrounding young Rosalie. He thanked Molly and gave her five pounds for her trouble.

Molly felt guilty about pawning the box and this prevented her accepting the money, which she pushed back into Daniel's hand. 'A can't accept yer money sir, 'ave done noat ta deserve it.'

However, Daniel insisted and readily absolved Molly of any guilt. 'You must have it Molly. You had no choice but to take the clothes for your survival on that bitterly cold night, so don't feel upset. You supplied many answers which will help Lizzie discover why she came to Nottingham.'

Molly was now in two minds whether to reveal the information about the box, but decided it would complicate things, so let the matter lie. 'Well thanks alot sir. A hope you and Mrs Cameron find the answers yer need. Goodbye, it wah a pleasure meeting yer.'

Daniel took Molly's hand. 'Likewise Molly. Goodbye and thank you again.'

Daniel left the Loggerheads, but overheard Bill Brown quizzing his wife on how much money she had been given for the information. He smiled to himself as he heard her reply. 'He offered me money, but a refused ta accept it. It's all in the past nah Bill, so let's move on.'

Oh yes, Daniel thought, she had his measure all right.

He was pleased with the information he had elicited from Molly and walked purposefully into the Market Place to his prearranged meeting with Lizzie. The door of the tearoom was slightly ajar when he arrived and he saw Lizzie sitting at a table in an alcove by the stairs. He was barely able to contain his excitement as he approached her. She looked up expectantly. 'Well, how did you get on? I was getting worried about you as you are quite late.'

Daniel apologized, but was unable to conceal his excitement. 'Yes, sorry Lizzie, I was delayed, but you are not going to believe what I've learnt. I feel that the jigsaw puzzle is only waiting for its final piece.'

Lizzie's face lit up. 'Oh gosh, Daniel. Shall we skip lunch and go back to the hotel, where you can relate all the details?'

Daniel agreed and they hurried the short distance to the George Hotel. Over coffee and sandwiches, Daniel brought Lizzie up to date with everything Molly had told him.

'Gosh Daniel, fancy you striking it lucky going into the Loggerheads like that and actually meeting Jack Garrett's mistress.'

Daniel grinned. 'I wouldn't exactly say lucky in one respect. Bill Brown is a man to be reckoned with, although Molly, bless her, can handle him. However, I am excited, as we've only been here one day and it looks as if we've everything sewn up, so, as we are booked in until Wednesday, we may as well stay for the remainder of our visit and we could do some Christmas shopping tomorrow. There are several antique shops around the Market Place, which I noticed on my way from Drury Lane to Houndsgate and a couple of toy shops on the High Street where we might find something for Rosie. Now Lizzie, tell me about your day?'

The following morning, Lizzie picked up several bargains on their way around the shops. In fact she almost managed to complete her Christmas shopping in one go: A warm woollen scarf for Clara, woollen mittens for Mabel, Gladys and Ida, bottles of fine whisky for Arthur, David and Sam, rag dolls for Tillie, Alice, Nora, and Annie, teddy bears for Victoria, Harriett and Laura, trinket boxes for Isobel and Olivia and a second hand buck knife for Jimmy. She still needed presents for Daniel, Georgina, Robert, Amy and of course, Rosalie. Significantly, there was one more present she intended to buy, but it needed to be very special. She was, of course by this time, struggling with her parcels. 'Give all those parcels to me Lizzie. It looks like you have bought everyone in Nottingham a Christmas gift.'

'Not really, only for those people who are my friends. I couldn't have survived without their help,' smiled Lizzie.

'No that's probably true,' said Daniel, 'I noticed a pawn shop further up the road, which sells bric-a-brac and some antiques as well. I fancy having a look in there to see if I can find something unusual for Georgina.'

'Good idea, I'll browse around with you. I wanted to buy Georgina and Amy something, perhaps a small enamel brooch for Georgina to complement her lovely blue coat and maybe a brush and comb for Amy. Oh yes, Daniel, I also want something extra special for a friend, a small music box perhaps.'

They approached a shop displaying three balls in a triangular formation, the sign of a pawnbroker. A bell located above the door tinkled loudly as they entered, alerting the owner of their presence. They browsed around, fascinated at the vast array of items, until a small enamelled music box, with an engraving of an angel floating on a cloud caught Lizzie's eye. 'Daniel, this box would be perfect for my friend, Tommy Bradley. He is one of life's unfortunates who now resides at the Asylum. I knew him very well when I lived in the Marsh. I'd like to take a small detour on our way back to Manchester, so that I can pay him a visit.'

Daniel smiled warmly, same old Lizzie, always thinking of others. 'Of course Lizzie, what a lovely idea. Oh look at the fine detail on the lid...'

Lizzie admired the box, which she passed to Daniel. 'Lift up the lid Daniel, I want to know what tune it plays.'

Daniel lifted the engraved top and the wonderfully sublime notes of Robert Schumann's 'Dreaming' filled the little shop with its haunting melody. A fitting gift indeed for an old friend.

'Oh Daniel, Tommy will love it.'

Daniel agreed and picked up the small, but delightful box. 'I'll ask them to wrap it for you.'

Further browsing uncovered a beautiful mother of pearl jewellery box, which Daniel bought for Georgina.

They were leaving the shop, after paying the proprietor for the items, when Lizzie's heart skipped a beat. Partially hidden among the sparkling jewellery boxes, napkin rings and trinkets sat a plain oak box, which was unremarkable, except for the hand carved lettering across the top, bearing Lizzie Cameron's full name.

'Oh my goodness Daniel, look here. It's a box with my name engraved on the top. I don't suppose...you don't think...' Lizzie was shaking inside. She hardly dared hope that the box belonged to her, but lifted it up to show Daniel. 'I don't recognise it Daniel, do you think there are many Elizabeth Cameron's out there?'

Daniel scrutinised the box. 'Why don't we ask the proprietor if there is a key for it Lizzie?'

Lizzie took the box over to the pawnbroker standing behind the counter. 'Excuse me, do you have the key for this box please? It doesn't appear to have one.'

The man looked over his glasses and then at Lizzie. 'Well now, the keeper box is it? I am very sorry, but that particular box doesn't have a key. The woman who pawned it said she had owned it for some time but didn't want to break the lock, as it would spoil the box. She maintained it was empty and only kept it for show, but as she seemed desperate to want rid of it, I took a chance. I imagine a buyer would remove the existing lock and replace it with a new one; otherwise, it would be a waste of a good box. Are you interested in buying it?'

Lizzie nodded. 'I am yes, how much do you want for it?'

The pawnbroker looked again at the box. 'Well it's not worth much in its present state.' Then he laughed as he pointed to the engraving. 'And if your name's not Elizabeth Cameron, I can't see why you would want to buy it.'

Lizzie did not disclose her name, but agreed that after the lock was sorted out it would make an admirable present. They settled on a price and the man wrapped the box in some tissue paper, before handing it over to Lizzie, who by now was trembling inwardly. 'Thank you, thank you very much, that's lovely.'

Outside the shop Lizzie was bursting with curiosity and anticipation. 'Daniel, if this box is mine, then it's possible this little key around my neck might just open it.' She could hardly wait but refrained from opening the box in public.

Back at the hotel, Lizzie invited Daniel up to her room to ascertain if the key did indeed fit the lock.

She removed the key from around her neck and her hand shook as she inserted it into the lock. An anti-clockwise turn and the lid opened immediately. The keeper box was empty! Lizzie gasped in disappointment, as she stared into the empty box. 'Oh Daniel, this is my box...it's definitely my box. I can't believe it. It's so exciting, even though it is empty. I bet Robert will know who gave it to me. I can't wait to ask him.'

Later in the evening, they celebrated their success with a meal at the hotel and then, exhausted, retired to their rooms. Lizzie sat on her bed holding the box. She ran her fingers over the engraving, before opening it again to examine it more closely. She noticed it was very shallow inside, despite the fact that the outer dimension of the box was deeper by about three inches, much more than was suggested by the inside space. Still unable to understand the discrepancy, but too exhausted to think, she placed the box on the bedside table and climbed into bed.

Just as she was drifting off to sleep, she had a vision of herself standing with an older man whose face was unclear, holding the box and showing it to her. He turned the key in the lock and the lid popped open, then he turned it again. She could see herself looking in wonderment as the bottom of the box, with its tiny concealed hinges, opened up. The man looked pleased, then threw his head back laughing, as he handed it to her. Then the vision disappeared as Lizzie drifted off into a deep sleep.

※

Unfortunately, the previous night's dream was not remembered and Lizzie spent the following morning wrapping and distributing the presents to her friends in the Marsh. Daniel accompanied her, as he was interested to see where she had been living these past five years. On the way to the Milligans' they encountered Aggie Fisher, who was busy stuffing a pasty into her mouth. She looked up as Daniel drew level and admired what she saw, a well presented young gentleman. 'Well now and who 'ave we 'ere. My God 'Annah, he's not 'yer run o' the mill bloke is he?'

Lizzie laughed. 'No Aggie, he isn't.'

Daniel tipped his hat to Aggie who had the temerity to blow him a kiss.

Lizzie felt obliged to introduce Daniel to Aggie, who bobbed a curtsy, as if she was being introduced to royalty. 'Charmed, I'm sure, Mr Daniel,' said Aggie.

Daniel took hold of her less than clean hand and kissed the back of it. She nearly fainted from the sheer pleasure, but turned to Lizzie to give her approval. 'Well 'Annah, you've a good 'en there me duck. Yer should keep 'im on a tight rein fer sure.'

Before Lizzie could reply, Daniel jumped in with an opinion of his own. 'Thank you Aggie, but if I had been the lucky one to capture this lady, it would be me tightening the reins.'

Lizzie blushed and smiled, unsure of what to make of Daniel's bold statement, as he continued. 'I hope I am not offending you Aggie, but can I offer you a crown to buy yourself a good meal?'

Aggie's eyes were out on stalks, as she gave a surprisingly, less than truthful, but cheeky reply. 'Well now thank yer, sir, I don't uselly accept charety, but a can see yer wun't accept no fer an answer, so 'ad be pleased to accept it and a'l meck sure a git a good meal we it.'

Daniel placed the silver crown in her hand and they both watched, grinning, as she staggered away, no doubt heading straight for the nearest inn.

'Well Daniel, she won't come across anyone as generous as you for a good while. It's just a pity she won't consider buying herself a few good meals.'

Daniel was sanguine. 'No, she won't Lizzie, but I expected her to behave in that way. She seems a harmless soul and by the looks of her, she has had a raw deal along the way. I doubt giving her a crown will change her habits, poor soul.'

Lizzie agreed. 'You are probably right Daniel and yes, I heard she did have a tough time of it.'

They arrived at the Milligans' and Lizzie knocked lightly on their newly painted front door. Clara opened it and was really pleased to see Lizzie for the second time that week. She glanced past her and was even more pleased to make the acquaintance of such a good-looking gentleman. She blushed uncertainly and, just like Aggie, bobbed a curtsy, before inviting them into the kitchen. 'Aye well Lizzie, it's not very often we are honoured wi the likes of yer friend 'ere. Am pleased ter meck yer acquaintance sir.'

Daniel put Clara at ease at once, by not standing on ceremony. He planted a kiss on her cheek and smiled disarmingly. 'Well I'm very pleased to meet you too Clara, very pleased indeed and I'm very grateful for everything you have done for Lizzie. Please call me Daniel, all my friends do and I'd like to think you would consider me as a friend Clara.'

Clara beamed and acknowledged his friendship. 'Aye well me duck I'll da that.' She turned to Lizzie eager to offer Daniel her hospitality. 'Show Daniel through ta the living room Lizzie and I'll get the keckle on. Would yer like a piece of Madeira cake Daniel? It'ull be spread wi some fresh butta that 'ave churned missen.'

'That would be lovely. I feel very at home here. You've made it very cosy Clara.'

She didn't wish to take all the credit for the soft furnishings that Lizzie had made, so put Daniel straight on the matter. 'Thanks me duck, but we've Lizzie 'ere to thank fer the curtains, the antimacassars and the chair coverings. She's a dab 'and wi a needle.'

Lizzie smiled and sat next to Daniel on the small settle.

The conversation flowed easily and after an interesting couple of hours, Lizzie and Daniel made their way to Mabel and Sam and Ida Mitchell's homes. They received the same warm welcome at both homes and later saw Rachael Phillips, who was surprised and delighted at Lizzie's change of fortune, despite her disappointment at losing such a capable tutor who would be greatly missed by all the family.

An early start was scheduled on Wednesday morning. True to his word, Daniel escorted Lizzie to the Asylum and waited half an hour while she visited Tommy Bradley.

Lizzie entered the building for only the third time and enquired if she could see Tommy. There weren't any problems and she was shown to his room on the first floor, overlooking the gardens. Tommy flew out of the chair he was sitting in and embraced Lizzie, obviously delighted at her visit.

'How are you Tommy?' Lizzie asked. She was concerned that he was being well looked after and that he was happy with his new home.

'Aw me duck, am that pleased yer've come. Sit dahn 'ere Hannah and teck the weight off yer feet.' A big smile spread from ear to ear as he sat gawping at his friend. Excitedly he told Lizzie of the visit he had had from David and about how he had settled in.

'David's bin yer know. I din't expect 'im ta, but 'e kept 'is word. 'E sez he will come and see me agen before Christmas. Nah yo Hannah. Am glad yer've not fergorren us. It's nice 'ere Hannah, 'cept when a 'ave ter 'ave things on me 'ead. Doctor sez they'll 'elp me ter get berra, so a suppose a 'ave ter 'ave it done. Matron lets me walk in the gardens. A like doing that best. A sit on the bench aht the back fer 'ours, dreaming about all sorts of things...Oh dear, am fergerrin me manuz Hannah. 'Ow are yer?'

Lizzie could barely get a word in during the course of the half an hour or so that she was there, but was pleased to listen to Tommy's account of his new life. He seemed fairly settled and she felt that she had made the right decision.

She took out the music box, which was wrapped in white tissue paper and tied with a blue bow and she handed it to Tommy. 'I've bought you this Tommy. I hope you like it. You can open it now if you like or save it for Christmas day.'

Tommy took the gift and smiled gratefully at Lizzie. 'Aw Hannah, me duck, yer shun't ave bought me oat. Am afraid a 'ant got noat fer yo though. Can a really open it nah?'

'Yes, yes of course you can Tommy.'

Tommy unwrapped the parcel and as he looked down at the box, tears filled his eyes.

'Lift up the lid Tommy and you will have a nice surprise.'

Tommy lifted the lid and the haunting sounds of 'Dreaming' floated in the air. He shook his head from side to side as he looked in wonder at the box and then at Lizzie. 'Aw, me duck. No one's ever bought me oat as nice as this. Can a really keep it?'

Lizzie smiled gently at Tommy, touched by the humility shown by this simple and somewhat misunderstood young man. 'Of course, you can keep it Tommy. Every time you listen to the music, you can dream about the things that make you happy.' Lizzie reluctantly got up to leave. 'I have to go now Tommy, but I will come and visit you again.'

Tommy rose from his chair and went to shake Lizzie's hand, but Lizzie gave him a big hug and kissed him on the cheek instead.

Just like before, Tommy placed his hand on the spot and smiling, wished her a happy Christmas, before watching her disappear down the corridor.

CHAPTER TEN

The Reunion

Robert Cameron arrived at The Beeches, anticipating a joyful and meaningful reunion with his sister. Lizzie was waiting excitedly for him in the entrance hall and rushed out to give him a big hug.

The physical contrast was striking, Robert, blonde with violet blue eyes like his mother and Lizzie with her dark hair and green eyes like her father, but they bonded straight away, as if they had never been apart and finished each other's sentences with a shared sense of humour.

Georgina and Daniel understood their need to talk and were totally excluded for the first two hours of their meeting. Robert was meticulous in his vivid description of her childhood, filling in all the missing pieces of her life as far as he was able, until they reluctantly surrendered to their need to sleep. It was a case of retire to their beds or fall asleep in their chairs. Georgina and Daniel had long given up the contest and taken to their own bed much earlier.

Their last evening together wasn't any different, because everyone was late to bed, despite the fact that Robert would be making a very early start the following morning.

Lizzie was the last to go up to her room, her mind still buzzing with excitement as she flopped down on the bed. Her eyes rested on the keeper box, which she had shown to Robert earlier in the evening. She couldn't resist removing the key from around her neck again to experience the thrill of turning it in the lock. She knew, of course, that the box would still be empty, but she didn't care, although she was still puzzled by its overall size and the fact that the box was quite solid even when she depressed the inner liner of the box.

She sat by the window deep in thought and placed the box on her lap. The rear garden was infused with the light of the full moon and the stars twinkled in the heavens.

Her resurrected childhood memories entered her mind. Robert's recollections of their formative years with Martha and Donald had helped Lizzie tremendously. He told her how she gave up school at thirteen to help her father with the household chores, whilst maintaining contact with him, although he had never ventured back to the croft.

When Lizzie showed Robert the keeper box that evening, he vaguely recalled that their father had made it for her one Christmas, but that was the extent of his knowledge.

Lizzie continued gazing out of the window, totally mesmerised by the flickering shapes and shadows, cast by the moon, which darted over the lawn and onto the shrubbery. The longer she sat there, the sleepier she became in this theatre of tranquillity. Her eyes were barely open, when the vision of a man she assumed to be her father came into focus, but this time with clarity. He was holding the box and turned the key twice to reveal a secret compartment.

Lizzie awoke with a start. The box had slipped out of her grasp and landed with a thud on the rug. She quickly picked it up, all fingers and thumbs as she excitedly turned the key once, then twice in the lock. In an instant the catch released and the false bottom opened up to reveal some official looking papers, three pennies wrapped up in a handkerchief with her name embroidered in one corner and three envelopes. She lifted them carefully and placed them on the bed. Then she held the three coins in her hand, wondering what significance they and the handkerchief had held for her. She reluctantly placed them back in the box, but hoped that at some time in the future, she would discover their importance. The first document she examined was a beautifully hand inscribed certificate which gave details of her own birth. She smiled and placed it on the dressing table, before turning her attention to the three envelopes. Across the front of the first one were the words, 'Only to be opened in an emergency - birth certificate of Rosalie'. She was totally taken aback, but tried to remain calm, as she carefully opened it. The information she had sought for five years was about to be revealed.

She unfolded the single sheet of parchment and stared down at the official document. There, clearly written, were the names and addresses of the parents of Rosalie. Her eyes were transfixed on the entry under the heading 'father'. Her hand gripped the bed rail to steady herself...It can't be true...He obviously doesn't know. Then, the enormity of the revelation sank in. If she revealed this earth shattering information, what ramifications would there be and what consequences. She needed time to think! She closed her eyes before coming to a decision. She would tell him! He had a right to know...but not yet. It needed to be handled carefully. She would pick her time.

Lizzie was aghast and shocked to learn that Rosalie's mother was Katherine Hemingway and even more shocked at the identity of the father, but why had she, Lizzie Cameron, taken Rosalie on the long journey to London. Astonishingly, that too was answered. The other document was an official signed affidavit giving guardianship of Rosalie to Elizabeth Cameron, 'until such time as Miss Hemingway was able to join them in London.' Full custody would then revert to Katherine. She pieced the facts together and realised that the birth had been deliberately kept from the father. He was totally unaware of the part he had played in Rosalie's conception and right up to the present day, was clearly painfully ignorant.

Apprehensively, she looked at the two other envelopes. She was surprised to see one addressed to her brother and the other addressed to Daniel Lorimer...in her own handwriting. She tore open the one to her brother and discovered that she had written to him about her sudden disappearance, although the exact reason wasn't stated. She was also pleased, as this was proof enough that at least she hadn't gone away without attempting to give him an explanation.

The second letter was more disturbing. It contained a declaration of her love for Daniel and her disappointment that they wouldn't marry. No wonder she still felt very close to him. By the tone of the letter, they had been very much in love. How strange that fate had wiped out her memory and intense feelings for Daniel, but over the last few weeks she knew why she had fallen for him. He was everything she admired in a man, but sadly, that was in the past and she must look to the future. Her mind whirred wildly as she folded the two letters with trembling hands and absently replaced them in the envelopes. She promised herself that she would give Robert the letter she had written to him, but the letter to Daniel would remain her secret.

How on earth would she be able to sleep, now that so many thoughts were going around in her head? Predictably, she lay awake until dawn, conscious of the repercussions of her startling discoveries.

In what seemed an instant, Georgina was calling through the door. 'Lizzie, are you awake? I think you may have overslept with all the excitement of last night. You must have been really late to bed. Robert and Daniel went riding just after dawn broke and now Robert is packed and waiting for the coach to arrive. Would you like some breakfast?'

Lizzie answered in a muffled voice. 'Thank you, yes Georgina, I will be down shortly.'

Lizzie sat down to breakfast eager to discuss Christmas, but silent about her discovery. Should she seek advice on the matter? She looked anxiously across at Daniel and then at her brother. Was there enough time to talk to either one of them about it? Before she could make a decision, Beatrice announced the arrival of Robert's coach. Hurried goodbyes were made and all too soon Robert was gone.

The reunion with her brother had been a huge success and the precious time would not be forgotten by Lizzie, even if the chance to move forward with her life had been seriously compromised. Her newfound knowledge about Rosalie's parentage blighted her otherwise joyous mood. Several questions required an answer. Would the father lay claim to his daughter? Would Kate Hemingway, if she could be found, wish to be reunited with her child? Where would she, Lizzie Cameron, fit into all of this? More time was needed to fully digest what this meant for Rosalie and herself. At some point, she knew she must reveal all to the people concerned...but not yet...not yet. It was too soon to let go. Yes, she thought, it would be better all round after the festivities. No point in spoiling Christmas. She convinced herself that she would feel rejuvenated and better able to deal with the consequences in the New Year.

CHAPTER ELEVEN

The Reveal

It was Christmas Eve and Lizzie, Georgina, Daniel and the two girls were due to arrive at any moment. Amy, Robert, Harriett and Amy's parents, George and Mary were in the sitting room admiring the large Spruce tree, which everyone had helped to decorate. Sprigs of mistletoe hung from the chandeliers and holly, with bright red berries adorned the mantelpiece, where a roaring fire burned in the grate. Excitement was in the air as Harriett danced from one foot to the other and twirled around to show off her new red velvet dress.

The doorbell chimed, as if on cue and the maid hurried along the hallway to open the door. 'Good evening everyone,' she said smiling. 'You must be Rosie. My you are a pretty little girl. I trust you had a good journey, sir? Come through to the sitting room, the family are awaiting your arrival.'

Daniel smiled and returned her greeting.

The maid took their hats and coats and was just about to announce their arrival when Rosalie released herself from her mother's hand and ran over to Harriett.

The room went silent and everyone stared in disbelief, aghast at the unfolding scene.

Robert turned pale. He couldn't take his eyes off the two girls standing side by side by the Christmas tree. Georgina and Daniel exchanged glances their minds working overtime in an effort to make sense of what they were witnessing. Amy, clearly alarmed by Robert's utter astonishment, felt faint. Her parents, equally concerned, were, nevertheless,

SILENT TORMENT

totally non-plussed as they failed to comprehend the implications of the scene.

Lizzie Cameron was the most shocked.

The one thing she hadn't bargained for was the striking resemblance of the half-sisters. Should she have said something sooner? She chastised herself, but immediately thought there had been precious opportunity. The time hadn't been right and Robert had left very early that morning. She really hadn't thought that the half-sisters would look so alike. The decision to reveal all was now paramount, but she was unable to utter a word and looked wildly around the room. Only two people were oblivious, 'Rosalie and Harriett'. They were totally unaware of the 'grown ups' confusion and just seemed intent on examining the presents piled up under the tree.

Harriett spoke excitedly. 'Look Rosie, see all these presents. Yours are piled up there next to mine and mother says there will be more tomorrow morning when Father Christmas brings them in his sack. We've got to be really good though, otherwise he will pass us by.'

At three and a half years of age, Harriett wasn't as au fait with Father Christmas as Rosalie, but realised the great occasion was looming when they trimmed the tree. Father Christmas always came then and left lots of wonderful presents for her and the family were always together. This year would be extra special because her older 'cousin', Rosie would be sharing the celebrations.

Harriett continued. 'I've written to him and asked for a dolly and my mother says that when he comes down the chimney, he will put the dolly in my stocking that hangs above the fireplace.' She pointed to the fireplace where two large red stockings hung on either end of the mantle. She couldn't read yet, but guessed her name would be on one of them.

The silence in the room remained charged, apart from the children's excited chatter. Not one person had moved since the visitors first entered the room, except the maid who was intent on serving drinks and even she was a trifle non-plussed at the silence. Drinks were usually requested when guests arrived, but, as yet, no one had requested them, so she decided to suggest it herself and approached Robert. 'Would you like me to serve the drinks sir? I'm sure the girls would like some freshly made lemonade, oh and the red wine you requested is ready to be poured.'

Robert, wanting to avoid further embarrassment, readily agreed. 'Yes...err...thank you that would be most welcome.' He cleared his throat and forced himself to speak. 'Welcome everyone. I think it would be a good idea if we were all seated. Harriett, why don't you take Rosie up to the nursery and show her your toys?'

Rosalie and Harriett skipped out of the room, laughing and holding hands.

Lizzie broke the silence when they had gone. She looked directly at her brother and enunciated a carefully worded request. 'Robert, it would be prudent if we have a private word.'

'Err...why yes of course. I'll ask Hettie to bring our drinks through to the library,' agreed a relieved Robert, anxious to remove himself from the situation.

Lizzie followed a distressed Robert, who somehow managed to squeeze his wife's hand reassuringly, as he passed her on his way out of the room. They entered the library, while the rest of the party were left in the unenviable position of making small talk. Each and every one, apart from Amy's parents, seemed confused and embarrassed. They almost certainly wished they could be somewhere else at that moment.

They sat on the small settee and Lizzie placed her hand on his. She looked into his eyes and began. 'Robert, what I am about to tell you might come as a shock, although you must already have your suspicions, judging by your reaction just now.'

'How long have you known Lizzie?...She's mine isn't she? I am Rosie's father.' He looked searchingly into her eyes.

Lizzie bit her lip and guiltily confirmed his paternity. 'It wasn't supposed to happen like this. I honestly had no idea until our last night in December at Daniel's, just before you returned home.'

Robert interrupted. 'How...how did you know Lizzie?'

Lizzie dropped her eyes and explained. 'I discovered the truth after I retired on the Saturday night. You remember the keeper box I showed you that father gave to me? I accidentally stumbled upon a secret compartment. It contained official documents and one was Rosie's birth certificate. I was really shocked Robert that you were named as the father, but I couldn't tell you that night. The following morning I considered that there wasn't enough time to impart such astounding news, so I promised myself to tell you after Christmas. It needed careful handling, as I knew it would come as a big shock. Unfortunately, I didn't bargain on the fact that the two girls, being half-sisters, would look like two peas in a pod.'

A bemused Robert muttered. 'Why is she with you and not with...not with...Kate Hemingway? She is the mother isn't she? It couldn't be anyone else.'

'Yes Robert, Kate's Rosalie's mother.' She paused for a moment, to consider the situation of the other guests waiting in the sitting room. She was anxious that their sudden departure wouldn't cause more embarrassment, but the longer they were away, the more awkward it would become. 'Listen Robert, do you think you could collect yourself together, at least for a few hours, then we could meet again later when everything has calmed down?'

Robert knew that he had been kept in the dark, but it wasn't Lizzie's fault, she was only the messenger. He swallowed hard and clenched and unclenched his fists in an effort to get rid of the anger he felt inside. He knew he couldn't spoil Christmas for his wife and her parents: that would be unforgivable. The three were still totally oblivious to the fact and would hopefully remain so, for the present.

He glanced at the worried face of his sister and realised that she felt totally responsible for the events that had taken place. He took her hands and looked into her eyes. 'Oh Lizzie, I don't blame you. It isn't your fault. I am obviously totally shocked, but I must recover my senses and bluff my way through the next few hours. It is neither the time nor the place for an open discussion, so we need to join the others as soon as possible, before the whole thing blows up in our faces. I suggest we make a plausible excuse as to why we needed to have this conversation in private. Can you think of anything sensible that we could say?'

Lizzie thought for a while as she sipped the red wine Robert had poured out for them and came up with an idea. 'Well...I am not sure how believable it might sound, but if we said that seeing the two girls together brought back sad memories of the Christmases we spent apart and it was so very moving to see them so happy.'

Robert pondered a moment and began to feel less stressed. 'Mmmm, we could say that we needed a moment alone together, as we didn't want our own feelings to detract from the happy atmosphere created by the two girls'.'

They became quiet, each with their own thoughts, but neither entirely convinced. However, it was the best excuse they could come up with and they believed that the others would accept them reminiscing, given the circumstances.

'Okay Lizzie, let's sit a few more minutes, before returning to the sitting room.'

Their arrival was less than spectacular. The others were behaving as though there wasn't anything out of the ordinary about their hurried exit and, consequently, eager to support them.

It was Mary who spoke first. 'Ah, there you are Robert, we were wondering if you were all right?'

Robert was composed enough to flash her a smile. 'Yes, yes we are now. We needed a minute or two alone. It was seeing the two girls, obviously so happy, standing under the tree. It reminded us both how many Christmases we had spent apart. We are all right now though aren't we Lizzie?'

Lizzie was proud of her brother and backed him up with their agreed story. 'Yes, we are fine. It was just one of those moments that affected us equally. Silly really, but we have just been reunited and I guess there will be many such moments when we reflect on childhoods spent, mostly apart.'

Amy went up to Robert and touched his arm. She smiled at her husband and spoke reassuringly. 'I can understand that Robert, it must have been really difficult for you both, but we are all together now and have much to look forward to.'

Amy Cameron knew in her heart that the real reason behind their private conversation was not the one being offered, but chose to support her husband anyway. She knew he would explain the true reason in his own good time, because she trusted him implicitly and wasn't about to challenge his motives now.

Georgina and Daniel were all smiles as they engaged in conversation with Mary and George, who accepted the explanation given by their son-in-law. Georgina and Daniel were not convinced, but it wasn't their place to question their two friends on their sudden need for privacy so when supper arrived, the party atmosphere had revived and conversation flowed easily. Coffee was served later and everyone seemed more relaxed. Robert eventually managed to get Lizzie alone and they slipped away to the library. She quietly recounted her discoveries so far. 'I am afraid I don't know everything yet Robert. What I do know is that, for whatever reason, I was given temporary guardianship of Rosie. Her given name is actually Rosalie by the way. I've known that for quite a while, but felt it was less confusing for her to continue to be known as Rosie. Our destination was London and we travelled as far as Nottingham where I had the accident and we've lived there ever since. For my part, I still cannot remember anything before my arrival in Nottingham, but my flashbacks are becoming clearer and more regular. Perhaps I will eventually remember why Kate did not tell you about her pregnancy, but at the moment it's inconceivable to me why she didn't.'

Robert speculated. 'Well Lizzie, the last time I saw Kate was before she went away on holiday. She didn't give me any explanation why she was going away and everything was still good between us.' He thought for a moment before continuing, 'not that good it would seem. She must have been terrified when she found herself pregnant. I cannot imagine what her mother said and I wouldn't have been surprised if she had shown her the door. I believe the reason you had guardianship of Rosie was something to do with the future Kate had planned for her. Maybe she didn't tell her mother at all...Oh dear, there are so many unanswered questions, that I am not sure where to begin. However, I don't think it is a good idea to inform everyone just yet. Might I suggest we celebrate Christmas first, before discussing any actions, along with the implications.'

Lizzie was relieved that Robert hadn't demanded he keep Rosalie with him and felt easier that he was happy to discuss the situation at a later date. 'I agree that would be the best strategy Robert. The situation needs to be handled very carefully and you will want to tell Amy when you are alone. More importantly, do we tell Rosie separately or together? I would favour that we do it together,' said Lizzie hopefully.

Robert reassured her. 'Don't worry Lizzie, I have no intention of taking Rosie away from you. I am sure we will be able to find a solution to keep us all happy, but for the moment, let's be thankful that we are back together again.'

A grateful Lizzie kissed Robert on the cheek and hugged him. 'Thank you Robert, I do love her very much and we are very happy. There is so much to discuss, but not now. Let's join the others and enjoy the rest of the festivities. I hope you will be pleased with my special present to you.'

Robert smiled at his sister, 'Whatever it is, Lizzie, I will love it.'

It was a week later when Lizzie and Robert huddled in the alcove near the fire at The Olde Boar's Head, in Middleton. A few moments elapsed before Lizzie gave the letter to Robert that she had written to him five years' ago.

'I want you to have this Robert. It explains my feelings with respect to our relationship at the time of my sudden departure. It doesn't totally clarify my reason for leaving, but it does indicate that my intention was to contact you after settling in London. Unfortunately, I relied on Kate, but apparently, her circumstances changed and she left Low Wood before letting you know my address.'

Robert quickly scanned the letter. He was more than horrified by its implications and embarrassed for Lizzie. He placed the letter back in the envelope and pretended that he hadn't digested all of its content. His intention was to keep it very much to himself, but he was dismayed that Kate had asked Lizzie such a big favour, particularly if she had known what a wrench it would be. 'Lizzie, I think you mixed my letter up with one for Daniel, although I only really scanned the content.'

Lizzie blushed to her roots when she realised what she had done. She hoped Robert hadn't had time to read the more intimate details and placed the letter hurriedly into her handbag, before lightly dismissing her mistake.

'Oh, I'm sorry Robert, I did write to Daniel as well, as I wished to inform him why I was leaving. I will give you your letter next time we meet. Anyway, to continue, how close do you think I was to Kate?'

Robert realised Lizzie was embarrassed by her mistake so didn't want to pursue it. From the letter's content, he now knew that Lizzie had been very much in love with Daniel and must have been devastated to leave without an explanation to those she loved most. He had huge admiration for her willpower in making an overwhelming sacrifice to help her friend. It also confirmed Kate acted in absolute desperation and under the direst of circumstances. Kate and Lizzie were even closer than he thought. 'I'd say you had a very close relationship,' said Robert. 'Especially after you and Kate started going to town once a week, which was really quite daring for two young women.'

'Yes,' said Lizzie, 'Daniel mentioned that. Was it on one of our outings that you and Kate got together?'

Robert smiled as he remembered those halcyon days, only a few short years ago. 'Yes Lizzie, you and Kate were in the café. Daniel saw you both first, sat in the window. I was drawn to her from the first moment I saw her. I had no idea who she was, but I soon found out.

'We realised there was chemistry between us as the weeks went by, but I didn't want the others to know. We agreed not to tell you or Daniel, as we weren't sure where it was leading, but I have to admit, I was totally in love with her. I would have married her in an instant, even before we became lovers, but the class thing would have made it impossible. Her family would never have allowed us to marry, but we couldn't stop ourselves from seeing each other and we met regularly at the old cottage on Lorimer's land.

'They were idyllic times and we were very much in love, until one day she just didn't turn up. I was frantic and couldn't determine the reason why. There had been nothing to suggest she didn't want to continue our liaison, even though we knew there was seemingly no future in it. I waited for hours before eventually admitting that she wasn't coming. I was distraught but still went on several other occasions, in case she was ill or something. Then you told me that she had gone away on holiday and I was really shocked because she hadn't mentioned it to me.' He fell silent, recollecting the feelings of utter rejection when he realised she had gone without a goodbye.

Lizzie felt sad at the desperation he must have felt at the apparent ultimate betrayal of Kate's sudden departure. She saw the sadness in his eyes and lightly squeezed his arm. 'I don't understand why she didn't tell you she was having your baby. I would have thought she owed you that much.'

Robert shrugged, he was at a loss for an answer to that question himself. 'I'm not sure 'why' Lizzie, but I believe it must have been a huge shock and she knew we could never be together. Maybe she thought it was kinder to just go away. At the time, I thought she had fallen out of love with me...but now I don't think that was actually the case. Maybe she didn't have any choice.'

Lizzie agreed. 'I think you could be right. We need to consider what may have happened when she left. The holiday was probably a ploy so that no one would realise she was pregnant. It would make sense, because if her family discovered her plight, they would have acted swiftly to avoid the scandal...Talking of scandal, Daniel told me that the family moved shortly after I left to avoid...to avoid a scandal,' Lizzie paused, 'except that doesn't answer the question of why Kate was the one to give Rosalie to me, suggesting her parents didn't know.'

'Mmm...maybe.' Robert fell silent as he tried to conjure up a possible explanation. 'Perhaps they did know initially Lizzie. They would have been enraged, especially if they knew the identity of the father. She may have been sent to a home for unmarried mothers'...A private one, of course. I've heard that girls are sent away as soon as possible to have their babies before an adoption is arranged straight after the birth. When they return home no one is any the wiser.'

Lizzie's mind was working overtime as she listened to Robert's suppositions, which didn't quite add up. 'But Kate wouldn't have given the baby to me, if her parents had arranged an adoption.'

Robert considered another option. 'What if Kate hadn't wanted the baby adopted, what if she somehow managed to give Rosalie to you before the adoption went ahead?'

Lizzie looked pensive. 'Mmm...I suppose that could have happened. Maybe they discovered what Kate had done after I left.'

Robert agreed. 'I think you could be right Lizzie. We will have to dig deeper if we are to find the truth.'

After further discussion, they agreed to put the search for the truth to one side and concentrate on Rosalie.

'In the meantime, what do you suggest we do about our immediate dilemma?' Lizzie asked anxiously. 'You will obviously want to play a part in Rosie's life.'

Robert answered positively. 'Yes, you are right, I would like that. I have a proposition for you, but if there is any aspect you don't like, you must say and we will think of something else.'

Lizzie became thoughtful; Robert would undoubtedly keep his word and not separate her from Rosalie, but she was anxious to know his plan. 'That seems very fair Robert, so what idea do you have?'

Robert was taciturn as he tried to find the right words. 'Well, the first objective may be quite a major undertaking and I am not sure how you will react to such a suggestion, but here goes. How do you feel about moving up to Lancashire?'

Lizzie was silent for a moment, but she suspected he might have wanted her to leave Nottingham. It was obvious Robert could not relocate his business, so she knew a move for her was on the cards, if they were both to have a hand in Rosalie's upbringing. 'I knew that you might suggest that but I am not sure how I feel about it. Rosie has made many friends in Nottingham and I would have to ask her if she wants to move. For myself, I love the job of tutoring Mrs Phillips two girls and I would, therefore, need to secure a position, which fulfilled my ambition to teach full time. Are there such opportunities in a small place like Littleborough?'

Robert had already pre-empted this possibility and enquired about a position of interest. 'I asked a friend of mine last week and he informed me that the local Hollingworth Endowed School might be looking to replace a part-time teacher of first year pupils in the spring. The present teacher is apparently moving down to London to take up a post teaching older children. I couldn't guarantee that you would get the job of course, but you have as good a chance as anyone, especially if Mrs Phillips provides a reference. Meanwhile, you and Rosie would stay with Amy,

Harriett and me. I am sure Rosie would love to have a sister to play with. They got on really well at Christmas, despite the difference in age. What do you think?'

'Well Robert, you seem to have thought it through and, yes, I promise to consider it, although I must satisfy myself that Rosie would want to leave Nottingham. I might have a hard time convincing her, but I believe it is the right thing for both of us.' Lizzie paused, then looked quizzically at Robert. 'Have you told Amy and Harriett anything yet?'

Robert gave a wry smile. 'I haven't yet, I thought we should tie up all the loose ends between us first, but I know that Amy will understand and, of course, Harriett will be delighted.'

Lizzie nodded her agreement. 'Yes, that's best. No good informing everyone before we are sure about the details ourselves.'

When they left the Olde Boar's Head, Robert placed his arms around his sister's shoulders and pulled her towards him, the pleasure he felt added a resonance to his voice. 'Well Elizabeth Cameron, welcome home.'

Lizzie turned towards him and with equal pleasure responded. 'Thank you Robert, I am very pleased to return.'

Chapter Twelve

Moving North

Lizzie and Rosalie had been back home for three weeks when Lizzie decided to broach the subject of leaving Nottingham.

A thick covering of snow appeared overnight, which gave Rosalie the opportunity to build a 'snow-queen' in the garden. She laughed as she placed a very large carrot, hardly befitting a snow-queen, into the snowball that formed the head. This sat disproportionately on the small, oddly shaped body, where two twigs formed arms and pieces of coal created buttons down the front. A garland of holly became her crown and finally, a long twig served as a magic wand. Satisfied, Rosalie stood back, folded her arms and surveyed her handiwork, with obvious pleasure.

Lizzie observed the scene while placing some hot freshly baked scones on to a cooling tray and mixing cocoa powder with warm milk to make a hot drink for Rosalie. This small treat might lessen the impact of the difficult subject she was about to broach with her daughter, that of leaving Nottingham.

Lizzie called to her from the kitchen window. Rosalie turned and smiled, then tugged off her frozen gloves using her teeth. She gestured to her mother to admire her handiwork and waited for a compliment on such a splendid creation.

Lizzie duly obliged and clapped her hands, nodding her head in approval. Rosalie bounded into the kitchen, her face and hands quite blue with the cold. 'Sit down with me near the fire Rosie and warm your feet. How you can play out there for hours in these freezing temperatures is beyond me.'

The unmistakable twang of the local dialect coloured Rosalie's response. 'Aw mam, me feet didn't feel cold 'til I took off me boots, but now they feel freezing.'

Lizzie retrieved her daughter's slippers from the small oven in the large black range, where a roaring fire had been going all morning to compensate for the icy conditions outside. 'There you are Rosie, put these on and you will soon thaw out.'

Rosalie felt deliciously warm and totally contented as she snuggled into her slippers, before drinking her hot cocoa. The blazing fire quickly brought the colour back into her cheeks.

Lizzie observed her daughter and wondered how she would react to the news. Since meeting at the inn, she and Robert had carefully considered their strategy for telling Rosalie. Tell her together in Manchester? or speak to her at home, where she wouldn't feel pressured?

A decision was made and now the time had come. Lizzie took a deep breath. 'Rosie, you know how you said you might like to live in Lancashire when we were on holiday. How do you feel about that now we are back in Nottingham?'

Rosalie frowned, as she was not sure quite how she felt about it. 'I don't know mam. I really had a good time up there, but now I am back, I like it here as well.'

Lizzie continued, 'Yes, yes I can see that Rosie. I expect you missed your friends while we were away?'

Rosalie thought for a moment, seemingly preoccupied, while eating her second scone and drinking her cocoa. The dark liquid formed a brown circle around her lips, until she unconsciously wiped her hands across her mouth. 'Well, I did miss them, but when we came back here, I missed all of those we left behind, especially Harriett. Will we see them again mam?'

'Well Rosie, it is actually up to you whether we see them again,' Lizzie smiled.

Rosalie raised a quizzical eyebrow because her mother usually decided where they went and what they did. She couldn't quite understand why it would be up to her. 'Why's that mam? Why is it up to me?'

Lizzie smiled benevolently and explained. 'When we left Nottingham, you remember I told you that we hoped to find your father, so that we could be a family again?'

Rosalie's face brightened. 'Yes, but we didn't did we, we found Uncle Daniel and Uncle Robert instead. I liked them both and it were better than finding me dad.' A thoughtful look came over her face as she reminisced. 'We did have fun up there didn't we mam?'

Lizzie laughed. If only adults could see everything in its simplest form. 'Yes we did,' she paused, it was going to be much harder to tell Rosalie the truth about her father than she at first thought, so she tried a different tack. 'If you could have Robert or Daniel as a father, who would you choose?'

Rosalie sat swinging her legs, which were all mottled from sitting close to the fire. She thought hard before replying. 'Mmmm...that's quite hard mam. I like Uncle Daniel because he is nice to me and I like his house with the intacontin door and I like Aunty Georgina and Victoria, but I like Uncle Robert because he is like you mam and also Harriett can play with me and Aunty Amy is very kind.' She put her fingers to her lips to consider her final choice. 'I suppose if I really, really had to choose, I would choose Uncle Robert. Is that the right answer mam?'

Lizzie was amused by Rosalie's anxiousness to please her, but sought to assure her that there wasn't a right or wrong answer. 'Nobody can tell you what the answer should be Rosie. It is how you feel in your heart. Whichever choice you made would have been right.'

Rosalie seemed pleased and continued munching her scone.

Lizzie expected the next step to be very difficult. 'If I told you that Uncle Robert was actually your father, what would you say?'

Rosalie swallowed the last piece of scone. That was perplexing! Would there be a right or wrong answer to this new question. 'I think,' she said carefully, 'that it would be quite nice to have Robert as my father, but he's my uncle so he can't be can he?'

Oh, this is so complicated thought Lizzie, but undaunted she made another attempt to explain the situation. 'Actually Rosie, Uncle Robert and I discovered while we were in Manchester, that he is your father. He wants to help me look after you, but that would mean we would have to go and live with him, Amy and Harriett in Lancashire.'

Rosalie looked perplexed. 'If he's my real father, then Harriett must be my sister. Is she mam? Is Harriett my real sister?'

'Yes Rosie, she is your real sister and if we lived with them, you could grow up together, play together and go to school together.'

A perplexed Rosalie considered that if Harriett was her real sister and Uncle Robert was her real father, then Aunty Amy must be her real mother! This bothered her greatly, although she liked Amy, she wanted more than anything for Lizzie to remain her real mother. She looked down at her feet and prayed that this was the case. She hardly dared ask her mother for fear of the answer, so whispered in a low voice. 'Are you my real mother mam?...or is it Aunt Amy?'

Lizzie was taken aback. She had not intended to mention Rosalie's birth mother, as the truth was too painful to contemplate. In addition, she considered it too much for Rosalie to take in, so reverted to a white lie in order to reassure her. 'I will always be your real mother Rosie. Don't you worry about that.'

Rosalie was satisfied with the answer, but immediately wanted to know if some of her friends could go with her. 'Could Jimmy and Annie come with us to Lancshire mam?'

Would this be a stumbling block Lizzie wondered? She replied cautiously, adding a note of optimism. 'No Rosie, I'm afraid not. You see Jimmy and Annie have to stay with their own families, but I am sure, we could visit them, especially in the school holidays. How would that be?'

Rosalie fell silent as she considered her reply. 'Mmm. Could Jimmy come and stay with me some time?' she asked with enthusiasm.

Lizzie smiled. 'Well Rosie, I don't see why not, if his mam agrees.'

Satisfied with the answer she slid off the chair to put her boots back on and in a voice of contented resignation, she replied. 'Okay. We'll go then. Should I tell Mrs Mitchell and Jimmy now?'

Lizzie was taken aback at the simplicity of Rosalie's response and breathed a sigh of relief. 'Well, not just yet. We can go and see them on Friday to tell them. At the moment it will be our little secret.'

'Okay mam, I'm off back out now. See you later…bye.'

Lizzie watched as Rosalie wandered out into the cold afternoon air, then sat back in her chair with another cup of tea exhausted by the effort. It's funny, she said to herself, how quickly children adapt, but she wondered if Rosalie would have a change of heart when the time came to leave Nottingham.

※

Ida Mitchell was yet again chastising her son, Jimmy, after he came home with something unmentionable on the bottom of his boot. 'I swear, our Jimmy that yu've a magnet on them boots o' yorn. If there's any muck within a mile o' yer, you'll manage ta find it.'

Jimmy was standing at the door lifting his leg up to reveal the clogged up mess firmly stuck to the bottom of his boot. Shrugging his shoulders, he made to step inside on to the kitchen floor. Immediately Ida stuck out her hand in protest and raised her voice an octave. 'Wot yer on wiv, yer daft oaf. Teck 'em off aht side, before yer step one foot on me clean kitchen floor. I can't even say yer brains are in yer boots, 'cos if they wah, yu'd still 'ave stepped in it.'

Jimmy didn't wish to incur any more ear bashing, so placed the heel of his boot against the wall to ease his foot out. The boot flew off and landed in the wet gutter, just as Lizzie and Rosalie were arriving. Rosalie giggled as she surveyed the scene, until Lizzie jabbed her firmly in the back. 'Shush Rosie, it isn't funny. It will make Ida a lot of extra work, especially as he seems to have some on his sock as well.' It was obvious, that the offending mess had transferred itself to Jimmy's sock as he had been running home.

Ida greeted the pair, but not before throwing a final word of warning to her son. 'Teck yer sock off as well before yer come inside. I'm a good mind ta meck yer clean it up yersen.' But changed her mind immediately as he would be more of a hindrance than a help. 'Come on in yo two. I'll put the keckle on 'cause I'll be needing a brew after that and so will yo.'

'Thanks, Ida. It's really cold out there,' smiled Lizzie as she took a seat close to the fire.

A couple of minutes later, Jimmy came tramping in, minus his boots and socks, his dirty wet feet making puddles on Ida's newly washed floor. Lizzie barely concealed another smile and saw Rosalie stifle a laugh at the state of her friend.

Ida's resigned voice boomed out again. 'Yer oad boots are in the cellar, fetch 'em up and gerra couple o' pairs of clean socks on before yer go off aht agen. Yu'll need to stuff some newspaper in the soles to keep the water aht and try and stay aht 'o trouble.'

Ida poured Lizzie a mug of tea and sat down to join her by the fire. 'Well 'ow yer bin Hannah...or should a say Lizzie? Wiv not seen much on yer since yer've bin back. Our Jimmy don't 'arf miss your Rosie.'

Lizzie smiled. 'We are well Ida. Rosie has been pestering me daily to come round to see Jimmy, but I have been very busy and the weather has been too bad to venture further than our own back yard. However, I've some news about Rosie and me.'

Lizzie would tell only three of her friends in the Marsh about Rosalie's birth: Ida Mitchell, Mabel Armstrong and Clara Milligan. She made Ida her first port of call, so that

Rosalie could spend some time with Jimmy, while she visited the other two households. Ida digested the news in polite astonishment and then Lizzie asked a favour of her friend. 'Could Rosie stay here while I go round to Mabel Armstrong and Clara Milligan's to let them know my plans?'

Ida agreed. 'Why yes, that'ull be fine. Leave it till yer get back ta tell Jimmy. 'E won't be too 'appy, but I'm glad fer yer. It's good yer've fount 'er father. A kid needs a mam and a dad I allus say, although in ah Jimmy's case, am not sa sure.'

Mabel Armstrong's front door was ajar so Lizzie gently knocked and peaked her head through the gap. 'Hello, Mabel, are you there?'

Mabel was sitting in a chair toasting her feet by the fire when she nodded off, but when she heard someone calling, got up immediately to answer the door. 'Oh it's yo Lizzie, come on in. I must 'ave nodded off wi the 'eat o' the fire. By it's coad aht there innit?'

Lizzie followed Mabel through to the small sitting room, which hadn't changed very much at all since she lived there. The blue curtains she had made were still hanging at the windows and the old comfy but threadbare chair, in a matching blue fabric, still took pride of place by the fire. Mabel Armstrong was very house proud. Everything in the room was cared for and highly polished, especially since her Sam had come out of gaol. Samuel Armstrong was given a job by a mate of his down on the canal, loading cargo on to the barges. It paid less than mining, but he was glad to be bringing in a wage at all and felt lucky that he had secured a job so soon after his release. He was down the canal at this moment, so Mabel and Lizzie had the house to themselves.

Lizzie would be living in relative luxury in Lancashire, but would miss the Marsh and its residents, who all pulled together in a crisis. Of course, there were the odd one or two troublemakers, but generally speaking they were a benevolent group of people.

Mabel was sad Lizzie would be leaving Nottingham, but she shared the same view as Ida Mitchell, that it was no more than she deserved. Lizzie had helped Mabel pull through some rough times but in turn Mabel helped Lizzie and looked after Rosalie while Lizzie worked for Mrs Phillips. Lizzie thanked Mabel for everything and, unseen by her, placed ten pounds under a plate on the kitchen table. As she left after closing the door Lizzie walked over to Knotted Alley to say goodbye to the Milligans'.

Clara and Arthur were at home, but David was still at work. She was baking and Arthur was snoozing by the fire, while the two girls played with other youngsters in the street. Lizzie gave them a wave as she walked up to their front door.

Clara answered the knock. She had flour in her hair and was up to her armpits in the stuff, but still wore her unique mobcap, 'Why Lizzie girl, come on in,' she paused to warn Arthur of Lizzie's presence. 'Arthur, it's Lizzie, get yersen aht o' that chair and put the keckle on.'

Arthur was not long back from his shift, but was happy to make tea for the two women. Clara made herself comfortable, pleased to have Lizzie's company. 'Nah then me duck, wi ent seen much o' yo lately. Where yer bin 'iding yersen?'

'The weather's been really awful Clara and I've been very busy with an awkward task, which is why I came to see you today.' Lizzie took a deep breath before continuing. 'When I was in Manchester, I discovered the identity of Rosie's father and, well, we will be moving up to Lancashire very soon.' She told Clara about her discovery and expressed sadness at leaving her friends behind in Nottingham. '...So you see Clara, it is something I have to do in fairness to Rosie. She will have a better quality of life and will grow up with her family around her, including Harriett who is Rosie's half sister.'

Clara was extremely sad that Lizzie would be leaving Nottingham and seemingly this time for good. She wondered whether they would ever see her again. 'Well me duck, yer know 'ow pleased I am that you fount 'er father, but we'll be sad ta see ya leave, meck no mistake abaht it. Yer know a love yer both, we all do. Yer made our lives better fer knowing yer Lizzie. Yer've bin a ray of sunshine round 'ere and young Rosie's bright as a button. She's got many friends who'll miss 'er no end, but needs must a suppose,' she paused before taking hold of Lizzie's hand. 'Will we ever see yer agen Lizzie? Am filling up 'ere me duck and I'll not try ta hide it.'

Lizzie stood up, put her arms around Clara's shoulders and pulled her to her, then smiled as she outlined her plan. 'Why Clara, how could you think I would cut you out of my life. The very people who saved me and why I am alive today, live here in Nottingham. I have so much to thank you for, so it is my intention that you should all come and visit, when we are settled.'

'Aw, me duck, wi could never afford ta da that. Thiz five on us yer know. We'll not shame yer by visitin. Wid 'ave noat decent ta wear. Mind what we 'ave is clean and paid for, no daht abaht that, but folks up there ud think yer'd invited a right motley crew.'

Lizzie smiled at Clara's self deprecation. 'Listen Clara, I will pay for you all to come and I'll make sure you are not embarrassed by your clothes. I'll never be able to repay you for saving my life, so paying for a coach journey and buying a few new clothes doesn't come anywhere near what I owe you. I won't take no for an answer, so promise me you will come.'

Clara was still unconvinced. 'A don't know me duck. True yer can put us in new clothes, but yer can't gi us ellacusion lessons and yer folks ud not understand a word we sez.'

Lizzie spoke confidently. 'My folks, as you call them, are really kind and understanding, just like you Clara. I promise you that you will not feel embarrassed or inferior. Now what do you say?'

Clara pinched her mouth inwards and looked around for the absent Arthur to give his approval. He had returned to the living room, so she made her own cautious decision. 'On one condition Lizzie, that you come dahn 'ere and travel up there wi us. Can yer do that?'

'Of course, Clara, it will be my pleasure,' said Lizzie, pleased that she had been able to persuade her friend.

'A'right me duck, yer've convinced me, but I'll 'ave a job on convincing Arthur. The farthest we've ever bin is the meadow, down by the river Trent fer a picnic last summer.'

※

Lizzie walked up the road to Ida Mitchell's house and spied Rosalie and Jimmy on the walkway playing marbles. She realised how close the two youngsters were and how much they would miss each other when they moved North.

Rosalie waved cheerily as she approached. 'Hello mam, me and Jimmy are playing marbles and he's given me his very best 'two-er'. Do you want to see it? It's got special swirly patterns inside in blue. Look mam in't it lovely?' Rosalie proudly held the marble up for her mother to inspect.

Lizzie admired the glorious item. 'Why, Rosie it's really pretty; something for you to put inside your keeper box.'

Rosalie took the marble back and dropped it into the marble bag her mother had made. 'Oh I will mam. I've told Jimmy I will treasure it forever and never play it,' she paused, 'erm mam, don't be cross, but 'ave told Jimmy we will be leaving Nottingham. I wanted to tell 'im missen...yer not cross are ya?'

Lizzie grinned. 'No Rosie, of course I'm not cross. You will see each other again, I promise. But for now Rosie, you two need to say your goodbyes, while I nip in to speak to your mam, Jimmy.'

'All right Mrs Merchant.' Jimmy frowned and glanced anxiously at Lizzie. 'Are ya sure I'll see Rosie agen?'

'Why yes, Jimmy, I will make sure that you do,' Lizzie smiled encouragingly as she disappeared into Ida Mitchell's kitchen.

Rosalie and Jimmy stood together on the road and Rosalie suddenly felt very sad. 'I'll miss yer Jimmy. I wish yer could come with us.'

Jimmy gave a half grin as he too felt sad at losing his best friend. 'I'll miss you too young Rosie. Come here and let me whisper something in yer ear.'

Intrigued, Rosalie lent her ear to Jimmy who quietly whispered his secret. 'One day Rosie Merchant, I'm goan ta marry yer and that's a fact.'

Blushing furiously, Rosalie whispered back to Jimmy. 'I know yer are Jimmy. I knew yer would marry me that day in the quarry when me shoe got stuck between the boulders. I told messen then, when I grow up, I'm going to marry Jimmy Mitchell.'

Jimmy grinned from ear to ear. 'That's settled then...Yer mam's waiting fer yer Rosie, yer'd berra be off.' Swiftly, he kissed her on the cheek. 'Tarrar Rosie, I'll be seeing yer.'

'Tarrar Jimmy, not if I see you first.' She laughed as she followed her mother out of the gate. Jimmy Mitchell swallowed hard and watched as the pair disappeared out of sight.

Chapter Thirteen

The Dream

'Here, let me help you with your cases Lizzie.' Robert Cameron could hardly contain his excitement as he helped Lizzie and an elated Rosalie down from the coach, who was so excited being in her new surroundings. Lizzie was due to attend an interview at Hollingworth Endowed School, where she hoped to secure a part-time job teaching the elementary children reading, writing and arithmetic. This was the start of a new life for all of them and they were so looking forward to the future.

Rosalie was shown her room, which was right next door to Harriett's, who followed Rosalie inside and sat down on the bed. Harriett was in awe of Rosalie and smiled at her newly found sister in anticipation that she liked her new room. If she didn't, she surmised, Rosalie would probably leave and she would be alone again.

'Do you like your room Rosie? I helped mamma pick the colours. I remembered you told me that blue was your favourite colour. Mine's pink and you can hardly see my bed for dolls and teddy bears.'

Rosalie looked around the newly decorated room. The curtains were blue, the bedspread blue and the carpet, blue. She therefore declared it perfect. 'Well, yes, I do like blue and it is <u>very</u> blue, but I like it,' said a delighted Rosalie as she pulled out her only doll, the one her mother had bought at the Goose Fair and placed it on a pillow.

Harriett waited for more to follow, but that was it. Why did Rosalie have only one doll? Harriett was perplexed. 'Haven't you any more dolls Rosie? I've six myself.'

Rosalie ignored her for the moment and ferreted around the bottom of her case triumphantly producing her wooden train. She would proudly display it on the chest of drawers opposite her bed. 'I like boys' toys Harriett,' explained Rosalie. 'My best friend is a boy, Jimmy Mitchell. He couldn't come with me, because me mam sez he has ta stay in Nottingham, but she's promised he can come and visit me.'

'Oh, oh I see.' Harriett was disappointed that Rosalie didn't consider herself to be her best friend.

This didn't go unnoticed by Rosalie, so not wishing to upset her sister, quickly qualified her statement. 'You can be my best friend too, because we will be going to school together when you are old enough.'

Harriett was surprised at Rosalie's supposition, given that she had been told otherwise. 'I don't think I will be going to a school. My mummy told me someone would come to the house to teach me my lessons. She called them a tutor.'

Rosalie decided to go along with this information but knew her mother thought differently. 'Oh well yes, perhaps you're right. I dunno. Anyway, before we go ta school or get a tutor, mam sez we can go to the seaside in the summer. I went once with Aunty Georgina, Uncle Daniel and baby Victoria. We paddled and made sandcastles. It was great fun. Have you been to the seaside?'

Harriett was amazed that her sister had only been once. She was used to going most weekends throughout the summer. 'I go a lot in the summer, but when I start my lessons, I suppose I won't be able to go every week.'

Rosalie shrugged. She felt jealous that Harriett had been so often, but not to be outdone, she enthralled Harriett with tales of the riverside and of the fun times in the quarry. Overall, she was satisfied with the embellishments of such escapades and was quietly triumphant with Harriett's obvious astonishment and amazement.

'Tell me some more Rosie. It sounds a lot of fun,' Harriett said eagerly.

Rosie smiled, 'Well, I can't just now, but I'll tell you some more tomorrow. I've got to get ready for bed now Harriett, so I'll see you tomorrow. Night, night.' She would like it here, she decided and happily pulled on her pyjamas.

Rosalie snuggled down under the new blue counterpane and Lizzie came in to retell her favourite story of the 'Snow Queen'. When she finished she asked Rosalie a question. 'Do you think you will like living here Rosie?'

Rosalie remembered what she had left behind, but also considered what fun there might be in the future, here in the village. 'I do and I don't mam. I am sad that I have left my friends behind, but we will have fun here. We will be able to go to the seaside and I will have a sister to play with every day and a dad that will give me piggybacks.'

'Yes, that's right Rosie and very soon, you will be going to school, where you will meet new friends and they will come round to play with both of you,' grinned Lizzie, with satisfaction.

Rosalie's eyes kept closing as she listened to her mother's soothing words, while she painted a mental picture of their future together. 'I knew a would be going to school mam. Harriett thinks we will be having a tutor, but I don't think I want one. I would rather be at a school with lots of friends. I don't have to have a tutor do I mam?'

Rosalie drifted slowly off to sleep as her mother responded. 'No Rosie, you don't have to have a tutor, not if you don't want one and I promise Jimmy can come here in the school holidays and stay for a whole week. Would you like that Rosie?'

'Mmm mam, I would like that very much...'

The pair settled in very well and by the early spring of 1847, Rosalie had adapted amazingly to the new, but very different life in Littleborough, which was quite astounding for a little girl of only five and a half. She made many new friends at the school overlooking the lake, where Lizzie now taught the nine to ten year olds.

The school was due to reopen at the end of February, following the half term break. Late one evening in the library Lizzie was formulating an exercise for a literature lesson. She was using the book 'A Christmas Carol' as a platform on which to base a fundamental exercise question: 'Is it better to give, rather than to receive?' The idea was to convince her young pupils that the answer to that would be 'yes'. She hoped to educate them in the art of giving, as Christmas was usually the time when most children were thinking about receiving. However, after three hours, tiredness was taking its toll, so she decided to take a break and make a cup of coffee, in the kitchen in an effort to stay awake.

She was pouring the hot milk into the cup when she felt someone's presence, it was Robert. He too had been studying, reading up on spinning and weaving methods to investigate the possibility of installing new Lancashire power looms in his factory.

Lizzie smiled. 'Would you like to join me in a cup of coffee Robert. You look as if you could do with a stimulant.'

'Thanks, Lizzie, I'd love one, my brain's become a trifle fuddled, being stuck in on a beautiful night. Come over to the window and take a look at the stars and the moon. It's in its last phase now and there won't be a full moon this February so it's as big as it will get.'

Lizzie bowed to her brother's astronomical knowledge wondering where he had learnt such things. 'Robert, what do you know about the moon and the stars?'

'Probably more than you know Lizzie,' Robert said, teasing. 'Back in Strathy, Father Murdoch had a great interest and told me a lot about astronomy. He knew mither and faither very well which helped me understand more about them. He also helped me come to terms with mither's death,' he paused, saddened by his recollections, 'a burden I carried around for years. She would have lived if I had not been born and many times I wished I hadn't.

'I gained comfort from the stars, especially the little group called the 'Seven Sisters'. They are in the Constellation of

Taurus and our mither's birth sign was Taurus. One of the brightest ones is called Miai, which means mither. The most comforting thing is that the star cluster's name, 'Pleiades', means 'coping with sorrow'. I thought a lot about 'coping' when I was in Strathy. I had you, of course and Martha and Donald, who treated me as their own. You would have thought I couldn't have wished for more, but I did Lizzie. The thing I wanted most was my father's forgiveness and that was a long time coming. After you left, I gravitated to Father Murdoch and he helped me to come to terms with my lot. Consequently, I spent many a night gazing skywards, contemplating what life was all about. Being alone with plenty of time on your hands, especially at night, strengthens your character and sharpens your mind. I came to the conclusion that you have to be true to yourself which is the most you can hope for in life.'

They stood silently, each lost in their own thoughts as they gazed at the thousands of scintillating stars in the ink blue night sky.

The stars in the constellations formed recognizable shapes of mythical legends and every one of them told a story. This prompted Lizzie to remember another memorable night when she sat with her father, after Barney their horse had been put down. She turned to Robert excitedly. Once again she had recalled part of her precious past. 'Do you know, Robert, I believe faither told me about some stars on our journey down to Glasgow. Recently, familiar scenes have played themselves out in my head and that scene is one I remember. Faither and I were sat in the wagon and he was comforting me by explaining the meaning and giving substance to the stars. It was Father Murdoch who enlightened him to such wonders, so, in his own way, he was trying to reunite you by giving you a shared experience of looking into the night sky at the same group of stars at the same time. It would help understand why things happen the way they do.'

Another star cluster drew Lizzie's attention and she asked Robert their name. 'What is that group above the 'Seven Sisters'? Over there to the right.'

Robert grinned, pleased he had some minor knowledge to give to his intellectually minded sister. 'Oh, that's 'Perseus'. Haven't you heard of the Legend of 'Perseus' and 'Andromeda'? They were married and led a long, happy life together.'

Lizzie was enthralled, 'How romantic Robert. You'll have to tell me more about it some time, but right now it's time for bed. I need to be up early tomorrow morning to finish off my lesson, as it's much too late to complete it tonight.'

'Quite right Lizzie, it is very late. I will take to my bed as well. See you tomorrow, goodnight.'

'Goodnight Robert.'

※

Lizzie experienced disturbing dreams that night. She was floating in the heavens and passing through the constellations, as faces from her past appeared briefly in front of her, before disappearing again into the darkness. She recognised Martha and Donald and her mother and father. She tried to hold on to her latest vision by reaching out, but hand in hand they floated away.

Then she was in another time...a time more recent. There was a huge ship coming towards her and she could see people waving from the deck. A small boy smiled and waved his hand, but she had no idea who he was. Then someone joined her and floated with her across the sky. He was pointing out the constellations and interpreting their meaning, only it wasn't her brother, Robert, it was someone else...someone familiar, whom she could not quite recognise. His face was kind and he took her strongly in his arms. She felt safe and comforted as they went on their journey. He spoke her name and pulled her closer to him.

Lizzie sat bolt upright in bed, astonished. She was sweating and her heart was beating faster. For a moment she failed to recognise her surroundings, then realised she had been dreaming. It took her several minutes before she felt calm again, but remembered her dream in vivid detail. She felt happy to have seen her parents, who were together and at peace, but knew instinctively that the other person who had appeared to her was not dead. He was very much alive and she needed desperately to find him - this could be the final piece in the jigsaw. Tomorrow, she would return to the place where she was sure they had met, The Adelphi Hotel in Liverpool. Robert would look after Rosalie for her and she would go there. Of course, in all probability, he would not be there now, but spending time at the Adelphi might confirm her euphoria and excitement, that they shared a special moment in time together. That special time had been taken away from her - and now she knew the reason why.

CHAPTER FOURTEEN

'And I Will Come Again My Love...'

On the 1st March 1847, Marcus Van Der Duim sat forlornly at the window table, in the Adelphi's restaurant, just as he had done for the last five years.

Another year had passed without news of Elizabeth. The well-read book of poems lay open on the table with its pure white linen cloth and vase of fresh freesias. The pages fluttered as the gentle breeze caught the flimsy parchment, but Marcus hardly noticed, his eyes were transfixed on the entrance. He had pictured the scene so many times in his mind: Elizabeth would be wearing the same blue silk dress, which revealed a hint of her delicate breasts. Her heart would beat faster as she waved to him across the room. He would rush to her, embrace her and feel the full softness of her lips on his own...but, of course, she wasn't there and the harsh reality of his ambitious daydream once again hit him hard! He came out of his reverie and inspected his watch. It was 11.55 a.m. - only five more minutes to the time they had initially agreed to meet. He glanced thoughtfully out of the window and remembered the previous five years.

He had been full of optimism and anticipated a bright future on that fateful day in 1842. Now he waited patiently, hoping beyond hope that another year would not pass sadly by.

He arrived early that first time and was seated in the restaurant by 11 a.m. - a full hour before she was expected. He was overwhelmed with excitement but still felt strangely nervous, despite his absolute belief that she would be there.

An awful feeling of emptiness engulfed him, as realisation dawned two hours later, she would not be coming. Stunned and saddened he made his way back to his room and stayed there for the next three days, in the hope that she had been unavoidably delayed. He convinced himself that she would arrive eventually, all smiles and apologies with a story to tell of how she was unable to get a message to him and could he possibly forgive her. Forgive her? He would forgive her if she was a year late, two years even...Now it was five years without a word of solace. There had been nothing, no reports of anyone of her description being involved in an accident or incident of any kind, nothing! It was as if she had vanished off the face of the earth. He would not believe that she had decided not to meet him again...he was unshakeable in his belief that they were meant for each other and knew in his heart that something serious had prevented her from meeting him that day. He believed fervently that one day, even years from now, they would meet again...and he was prepared to keep returning every year until that time came...but sadly, he thought...not this year, not now.

Lizzie arrived at the Adelphi early Saturday evening and booked into room 32; the room she originally occupied in October 1841. She unpacked the few items of clothing from her valise. They included the blue silk dress, which Robert suggested was appropriate for such a grand place. Apprehensively, she sat by the window and wondered what the future might hold.

She was visiting the hotel on the strength of a dream and buried deep in her mind was the key to unlocking that dream. The answers and the reason for her presence were right here. Until she could unravel the mystery, she would remain incomplete, her destiny unfulfilled.

Brief flashes of past events had been triggered on her last visit with Daniel. The familiarity of the restaurant when she waited to meet someone, but that moment had been fleeting and had quickly passed. The strange feeling of someone standing close to her as she gazed at the stars through the large window on the landing. In addition, the feeling of unreality when Daniel called her name through the door, when they all over-slept.

She smiled ruefully as she remembered the gentleman alighting from the coach and his purposeful stride, before he looked up in curiosity, as he entered the foyer. He had tipped his hat in acknowledgement, seemingly amused that he had caught her eye, although this action caused her to hide in embarrassment behind the long, heavy drapes that framed the window.

It was dark now and the streets were almost deserted. Lizzie washed and changed into her night attire before climbing into bed quite sleepy. Absently, she flicked through Robbie Burns' book of poems, briefly allowing herself the luxury of escaping into the delicious world of poetry. She recalled how delighted she was to receive the book as a present from Robert this Christmas. Significantly, Martha had given her a similar book as a leaving gift on the very day Robert and she had fallen into the river. Sadly, that particular book was no longer in her possession, but Robert hoped that during a quiet moment, Robbie Burns' poems might trigger memories of her time in Scotland.

His idea paid off spectacularly. A few days after she read the poem, 'A Red, Red, Rose', Lizzie had a vision of reading the text in the home of Josiah Monks, the local priest in Glasgow. The meaningful words excited her as she recalled her beloved Highlands, but as she read the lines again, she knew there was something else, more significant. Sadly this memory remained locked away, although she tried hard to focus on its meaning.

She awoke bright and early the following morning and after breakfast, took a walk around the city, before returning to the hotel for a late lunch. When she sat at the table for two by the window she was instantly transported back to 1841. Magical feelings surged through her body and urged her to remember that eventful time, but, despite the intense experience, her mind refused to co-operate.

She decided not to dine in the restaurant that evening, but took dinner in her room instead, where she could see the guests entering and leaving the hotel. Then, a familiar figure caught her eye as he stepped down from a coach. He stood for a few moments looking up at the windows fronting the street.

Lizzie did not wish to embarrass herself a second time so quickly hid from view and instead observed the gentleman from a half hidden position. He appeared to be looking for something specific, so she could see his upturned face fleetingly, but quite distinctly. He looked like the man in her dream, but she couldn't be certain and in a flash, he disappeared from view. She chided herself for having such a vivid imagination and moved away from the window.

Much later, she lay on the bed staring at the ceiling and tried to bring his face into focus, but her eyes began to close, as she entered the half-awake, half-asleep state. Instantaneously, a powerful vision of a tall, good-looking stranger came into focus. Lizzie sat up and gasped. The vision had been crystal clear and unmistakeable.

She was completely convinced now that she had met this man before at the Adelphi. Who was he anyway? Was it a pre-arranged meeting? She had no idea; the only certainty she felt was that there had been some kind of relationship. She felt elated and excited but at the same time, strangely nervous.

Lizzie was wide-awake now so decided to take a walk to clear her head. She slipped on her robe before entering the corridor and paused for a moment at the end near the big window, where stars were shining brightly in the peaceful stillness of a cloudless night.

It's so tranquil, she thought, gazing up into the night sky. She indulged herself, remembering the night when her father pointed to the cluster of the 'Seven Sisters'. She felt very close to him at that moment, as she traced the line of the stars with her finger on the windowpane. Almost immediately her eyes were drawn to the group of stars, directly above the 'Seven Sisters' - 'Perseus'. Robert had recounted the romantic legend of 'Perseus' the night they reminisced about their young days and good times in Strathy.

Spectacularly, the veil of mystery lifted. Just as the double turn of the key in the keeper box revealed its secret compartment, everything jolted into place. All her memories were transfixed in vibrant colour, like a play being re-enacted in front of her eyes.

She was giddy with excitement and rushed back to her room to locate a notebook. She scribbled hastily and wrote down everything she remembered, easily interpreting the pictures that clearly told her story: Her childhood in Strathy; her time at Low Wood; her journey with Rosalie from Glasgow right to this hotel...and Marcus...Marcus Van Der Duim! She repeated the name out loud while a smile played around her lips as she vividly recalled their meeting and promises to each other.

So...it wasn't pre-arranged, it was purely chance! Their good fortune was that they had stumbled across one another, each with a story to tell.

She stopped writing, intoxicated by the deliciously heady feelings that surged through her body at the thought of his touch; his soft kiss and the smooth velvety tones of his voice. She allowed herself a moment of pure nostalgia, as she took herself on her journey through that day in 1841. Riding in the coach through the city and having dinner at the table by the window; the sudden realisation that, despite their brief encounter, they had fallen in love. She remembered the silver sixpence given to her, which she still kept around her neck and Burns book of poems she gave to him in return. It was Marcus who had stood close to her by the window looking out at the stars. Then there was that promise, to meet again on March 1st 1842 at 12 noon in the restaurant at their table...It couldn't be possible could it? that tomorrow was the 1st March, but she knew, even before she checked the date in her diary.

Only it wasn't 1842, it was 1847, five years after their proposed meeting. The time had passed and she had been unable to meet him. Dejectedly, she climbed into bed at 3 a.m. completely exhausted, but sleep eluded her. What should her next step be? Was it possible that she could find him again? What did she know about him? Not much more than his name and the town in which he lived. Would he even remember her?

It was if only a moment had passed, when she opened her eyes to find daylight streaming in through her window and the sound of voices rising from the street below. Good heavens, she thought, what time is it? I seem to make a habit of oversleeping in this room. She jumped enthusiastically out of bed, donned a robe and moved to the window. The clock in the centre chimed eleven, so obviously, she had missed breakfast and if she didn't get a move on, she would miss lunch as well.

She glanced again at the entrance and, miraculously, he was there, yesterday's stranger moving quickly through the throng of people into the lobby. Only he wasn't a stranger...he was Marcus, he *was* here at the hotel and she was hardly able to believe her eyes. She stood transfixed, long after he had disappeared from view. Was it possible he had come here on this day in the hope of meeting her again? Surely he couldn't imagine that five years later, she would some how be here?...But she was, perhaps unintentionally and she had been given a second chance.

She washed frantically and changed into the blue silk dress. She was overdressed for lunchtime, but didn't care and after sweeping her hair into a chignon, she was ready...ready to resume the life she was meant to share with Marcus. Nervously, Lizzie made her way to the restaurant. At five minutes to twelve she stood behind the lavish drapes, framing the entrance. She glanced anxiously towards the table in the window and saw Marcus exactly as she remembered, the sad beautiful eyes and the thick dark hair, which fell slightly over his forehead. Impatient as she was, she determined to wait, until the clock struck noon, only then would she make her entrance. She watched in growing trepidation as he gazed out of the window. Burns' book of poems lay open near the vase of freesias with their heavenly scent. Her heart beat faster as the designated time approached for her to meet him again, five years late, five long years in the wilderness, but now the moment was upon them...

The clock in the foyer struck noon and, as in previous years, Marcus thought there wasn't any point in waiting any longer. He stared at his untouched coffee and unfinished sandwich and moved sadly to gather up the book of poems.

He glanced momentarily towards the entrance for one last look and suddenly as if in a dream, a smiling Lizzie stood before him, silently mouthing the words from their poem...

Marcus was captivated by Lizzie's perfection. A sensuous smile played around her lips and her eternal love shone deep in her eyes. Once more he was able to bathe in her beauty and the disappointment of the last five years melted away. Joyfully and instantaneously they touched hands, just as he had imagined.

'My darling, you have come...where...why didn't...?'

A myriad questions were left unanswered as she silenced him by kissing him softly on the lips. He held her passionately and both were helplessly lost in a wondrous embrace...Time stood still as their love became plain for all to see...The final piece of Lizzie's jigsaw had fallen dramatically into place.

> '...And I will come again, my luve,
>   Though it were ten thousand mile...'
>
> *"My Love is Like a Red, Red Rose" (1794)*
> *Robert Burns (1759-1796)*

Read extracts from Tarn Young's second novel in the trilogy, ***Elusive Shadows*** *(Projected publishing date: Summer 2012 - see website for further details, tarnyoung.com)*

The year is 1855 - Lizzie Cameron is now thirty-five and Rosalie, thirteen. Lizzie shares the guardianship of Rosalie with her brother, Robert, Rosalie's father. He is seeking Kate Hemingway, Rosalie's birth mother.

Lizzie and Marcus Van Der Duim have not been blessed with children, which Lizzie accepts, but looks on Rosalie as her own child.

Marcus's wife, Belle and son Jack, are missing, presumed dead, when their ship sank off Newfoundland. Belle and her lover, Andries Dubois, Marcus's best friend, were attempting to start a new life in Philadelphia, prior to the shipwreck.

Lizzie has mixed emotions regarding the search for Rosalie's birth mother. Her conscience requires that she reunites Rosalie with Kate, but conversely, this could damage her own relationship with her 'daughter'.

The saga continues, with Lizzie's role pivotal to the unfolding plot.

CHAPTER ONE

Anxious Times

By 1855 most passenger ships on the New York run had been commandeered for the Crimean war effort, with only a few still available for overseas travel across the Atlantic.

On a cold crisp morning in February 1855, one such ship the 'New World' sailing from New York, docked in the port of

Liverpool. Three seemingly unremarkable passengers disembarked for their onward journey on the Glasgow bound paddle steamer, the 'Princess Royal'. Another passenger stood patiently on the quayside waiting to embark. They passed, almost touching, but oblivious to each other's existence, like elusive shadows in the night.

Two of these people would meet untimely deaths, but the re-aquaintance of the other two would bring untold joy...

Extract from a later chapter:

Chapter Five

Destinies

...She allowed the lantern to swing back and forth unaware of the danger. Moments passed before she spied the small fishing smack heading towards her through the gloom. It came closer and she could see a familiar figure in the stern. She hoisted the lamp high and swung it more robustly to guide the boat straight towards the beach. She waved excitedly...I knew he would come...I knew he would come for me.

Too late, he realised he was on the wrong side of the cove, where the currents were strongest.

What on earth was she doing there, when she should be on the other side, close to the inlet? He was struggling to bring his craft under control, when a strong gust of wind caught the boat broadside, throwing him into the icy cold water. He called out frantically to the figure on the shoreline, believing it to be his wife. I love you my darling, but I'm not going to make it...Please take care of our child for me. Please...'

She watched horrified as the man slipped under the waves, then resurfaced one more time, before vanishing into the murky waters. In her panic, she dropped the lantern and ran along the water's edge, peering into the blackness of the night. For a fleeting second, she imagined the dark figure resurface again, but she was mistaken. It must have been a trick of the light and in an instant her chance of a new life had tragically ended.

Terrified, she picked up her skirts and stumbled over boulders wet with spray from the waves buffeting the shore. Her boot came off as she negotiated the jagged rocks. Instantaneously, an intense pain seared through her ankle as the sharp edges jabbed at her flesh. She groaned in agony, lying there, as the waves washed over her. Her cries went unheeded, as no one knew she was there and only seconds passed before she was washed out to sea. The strong currents finished the job, pulling her down into the cold blackness of the unforgiving Atlantic. Her lungs filled, as she lost consciousness and sank deep beneath the waves.

It was eerily quiet on the shore, apart from the crashing of the waves, as the sea claimed its victim. The tide rushed in, covering the sandy beach with foam and seaweed, obliterating any sign that she had once stood there. It would be several hours later before her body would be found, lying on the beach near the secluded cave where a few short weeks earlier, her actions had determined her fate...

Lightning Source UK Ltd.
Milton Keynes UK
UKHW031014030919
349107UK00001B/4/P